IT

Blue Angel Knight

Nick Sambrook

Book 2 of 3

CHAPTER 1 - THE FOOL ON THE HILL

Sam was lying on his back in the spring sunshine.

Just for once he was all by himself, sprawled out on the short sheep-mown grass of the hillside, overlooking a very typically English, green idyllic, wide and flat country valley.

It was one of those rare moments of silent peace; warm isolated tranquillity, totally away from the rambler's paths, high up in the air, with a soft breeze drifting up from the rural countryside far below.

The landscape was comforting on the eye, with its green woods, hedge-lined fields, lanes, a river snaking its way along the valley below, and soft grey hazy hills in the distance.

He took another deep breath, and looked up into the soft blue cloudless sky, and then he closed his eyes. It was that purity of thought, that indescribable clarity of mind that only comes when the conditions are perfect.

Lying on your back, with your eyes closed, in the fresh clean open air. Thoughts that were totally free from worry, demands, pressures, and distractions. That easy flow of clear oxygenated air, breathed deep into your lungs, with the air around you still and quiet, and feeling neither too hot nor too cold; the still, fresh coolness of mid-morning held within it, and permeated with the rich intense aromatic scent of flowers, grass, and trees, purging your mind and body.

To get that depth of thinking and mindfulness your body also had to be free of toxins; no numbing after effects of alcohol, no caffeine, drugs or food additives.

Your body and brain had to be working in harmony, balanced, delivering optimum efficiency and focus, to give the maximum amount of energy for your mind to work, within you, and be combined with a good night's sleep, and somewhere comfortable to lay it all out on.

The gentle hillside breeze was so full of oxygen out here in the open air; wafting up the slopes from the fields in the valley below.

Nature was just there, all around. Birds singing in the trees, distant noises of life and people far away, all just somewhere else, out of your space and not requiring your attention or concern.

There were just sounds around that *should* be there, rather than those that should not; nothing distracting or irritating, just distant background sounds of life, nature going about its business.

It was that pure rush of oxygen into the mind that did it, and which opened it up into limitless space in the reddish darkness behind closed eyes, and expanded into depths beyond imagining, into the real.

Every lungful of air took you deeper into expanding, limitless depths, just allowing your mind to wander around, exploring ideas that flowed in and around with unparalleled clarity and complexity; pulling in knowledge, and forming undirected unstructured thoughts from the luminous iridescent blackness.

Yet with Sam though, these experiences were different to others. He didn't have visions, revelations, translated data coming up from the unconscious and discoursed into vivid dreams or expressionism. No, for him knowledge and thoughts and concepts came into his mind directly - a sort of hard-wired gnosis.

The real problem Sam had was how to express the complex concepts that came in, and how to choose which words or model or analogy to use to describe them.

Information was being generated and presented to him all the time and he was processing it, interpreting it, rationalising and converting it into thought forms.

But these ideas - were they his thoughts or were they from others in the past or present, or were they collectively generated, a sort of consensus, correlated view on a sort of human or cultural operating system level? Or was there really any difference - was it all just one mind, one macro information system of which we all had our fractal points of reference within, and our own perception, and interpretation of? The key was to understand it all from everyone's point of view, and on every level.

The important thing though was not to get drawn in by it.

He knew from his initial extreme experience many years ago, that although there was that overwhelming feeling of 'knowing everything', a feeling of 'being inside ultimate knowledge', or being suddenly aware of everything, that just because you had that gnosis, and all that visionary information coming in, and an overpowering sensation of enlightenment, it didn't necessarily mean that it was actually 'right', rational, scientifically correct, true, or even logical.

He knew there were misconceptions, errors, in the collective human mind, in the unconscious information system, and also a lack of perception or correlation within it of the physical. Along with quite a number of things that it didn't seem to know or understand yet, or have the answers to. IT just knew everything that we knew, and like any biological system it was trying to discover, learn, adapt, and work things out with perception.

By being able to understand that, to see beyond that beguiling effect, and rationalise it - and at the same time observe the process too - meant that you were then able to do something about it. You could make sense of it by combining scientific knowledge and logic and common sense, rather than just being hypnotised into another exploratory rabbit hole of belief or outlandish idea of what was going on over on the 'other side', naive spiritualism, and then trying to figure out who or what was to blame.

Wild random thoughts surged through his mind, one after the other, but they always had some linkage, some flowing story to them like a river; a journey, a linked sequence, just in the way dreams were constructed and flowed. The same way stories were put together and shaped into meaning.

It was as if somehow he was constantly being fed the information to make sense of it, and to physically process it into something new; a new intuitive logical perspective in some state machine which was then relayed back for him to then evolve it in some way, to make sense of it in relation to the physical world of science, logic, world-view of humanity, and current events.

To change things.

Was this how prophesies worked? Were they really just ideas that formed in people's minds, fed by collective unconscious data, which were then written down, and them amplified and reinforced through belief structures, fulfilling some need or desire for some visionary concept? Whatever the case it was important to be careful what you wished for, or thought about, or dreamed of.

Giving IT ideas and concepts at that level was potentially

disastrous. Clearly many people in the past had been jumping to the wrong conclusions of what IT was, at the same time as being hypnotised by IT, due to their psychology or cultural beliefs, and in so doing had subsequently aided in the religious reinforcing feedback process of what it was, this 'all knowing all seeing' mind.

Sam's mind opened up to the world in his mind, expanding its scope, drawing in information. It was a beautiful feeling, uncluttered, pure mental depth in the absolute darkness. Bliss.

An indescribably complex combination of sensations, thoughts, journeys, ideas, and concepts all going on at once in the pure darkness of his mind. The energy from the sun flowing through his skin, through his eyelids, and into his core. All as he lay on the grassy hillside, with his fingers tucked under his armpits, and a smile on his face.

The other advantage being up here of course was that there were none of the usual 'female distractions'; no talking, needless interruptions, constant demands, or confusing irrational emotions; no chaos or meaningless repetitive conversations and questions.

A sort of gentleman's club for one man and his dog, but without the stuffy library atmosphere full of public schoolboys who, understandably, were unable to cope with their women and their irrational hormonal, female, chaotic energy. The cowards.

He was now totally oblivious of how he must have looked to anyone who happened to be wandering by, just sprawled out on the grassy slope, eyes closed and smiling.

His dog was lying out a few yards away, tied up by his long lead to a small rocky crag. But Sam didn't really care how he looked, or what anyone else thought - besides the dog was providing a good defence against anyone that may mistake him for some mad loony, or an undiscovered abandoned corpse.

More thoughts flowed in and out like waves- clear and precise - in exquisite detail and clarity, and with limitless resolution.

He focused his mind, concentrating on an area a few feet in front of him. He felt sensations on his forehead, the area of his so-called 'third eye'. Images in the darkness started to form in complex form and shape, yet they were relaxed, unstructured, free, not seeking or trying - just flowing, unforced. He didn't try to deliberately create anything, he just let whatever came into his mind form there, and he then visualised it consciously in the dark space in front of him into whatever structure it decided to take, without applying any preconceived interpretation to it.

Images phasing in and out, with and without form, shapes and action, movement or edges - allowing it to use its own ability to form coherence and interpretation. It was therapeutic, calming, intriguing and enlightening, almost like reading a story that was unfolding in front of him.

There was that feeling there too though, that 'in the zone' sensation, an energy; a sense of being in the state of 'now' as a focal point. Being in the present and mindful of it.

How could you describe it though, this 'in the now' feeling?

There were no words, feelings or sensations that it was 'like', or anything to compare it to, or with. One minute you were 'normal', the next minute you could sense it, like a vibrational tension in your mind and in your head, 'working' on something, doing something.

You could feel your brain spinning away, buzzing, processing, making it hard to concentrate on everyday thoughts, processing and forming thoughts that were 'different', new and 'big', correlating it all with what knowledge you had, what you understood, and combined with your experience and skills, to process it into a new structure, ideas, thought forms, meaning, interpretation, and conscious knowledge.

His face had that 'fresh cold feeling' now too, the centre of his head ached in the middle of his brain. He could also feel his neck stiffening as the energy flowing through it tensed the muscles, and the top of his skull ached and felt numb and bruised. Thoughts and information and concepts were coming in and out all the time now with increased speed and intensity, but in parallel, trying to be interpreted into physical reality context, translated, interpolated, rationalised into sense, and into a meaningful logical interpreted story.

It was as if information was being processed through a transceiver, to and from a vast parallel biological operating system, a virtual information field state environment, to a serial program hologram perception of logical world physical reality.

The information though had focus, energy, urgency, as if

relating to some global situation, some newsworthy problem, some unconscious collective irrational worry, fear, or concern. Something that needed to be resolved, from some 'top down' macro perspective, as if something was going on, and it was trying to get him to work out what it physically related to, what it meant, what it really was, a sort of mind's eye interpretation.

Indeed, if you knew what was *really* going on, you would realise that everything was like a virtual reality simulation, a perception, based on knowledge and information. The more you understood how that was really the case, the less real it all became.

You become detached from it, disassociated from it, unconnected to the physical, drawn into the 'spiritual' software that was generating our physical virtuality game that we projected into the screens on the inside of our virtual devices. Devices at which at the same time you had to feed, look after, rest, take to the supermarket, and safely cross the *SimCity* roads, avoiding the lorries, that naively had no idea they were just projections in a hologram, uncaringly waiting to run you over.

If only it were all that simple.

It was a tough balance. One side was a virtual information system, the other a perceived real physical projection created from within it. The problem was that, as you were 'in the system', you were also stuck in everyone else's collective virtual game or operating system; tied to their shared perception of true reality, along with what *they* knew and how *they* had evolved to perceive it - and interpreted or believed it to be - and also what IT unconsciously thought it was.

Like being stuck in one mind, and only seeing your perspective part of it.

The structure of the information field - how it projected physical reality at many levels, its capabilities, nature and form — was all now described in some detail by physics, quantum mechanics, psychology, biology, philosophy, mathematics and so on.

It was also articulated and discoursed on the 'other side' by religion, literature, art, music, spirituality, even films. Working out what it was all about, going on within it, and describing it all in many new ways was one thing -but to actually *do* something about it all, and fix the situation we were in, and sort out the mess that has been unconsciously created by ourselves, is something else entirely.

Especially when IT has become so very clever at deluding and controlling us as a hyper complex hive-type unconscious mind. But then how could you even describe the whole thing that made sense to people? Even by using analogies, producing evidence and giving rational explanations it was still all too vast and complex, and everyone had their own perspective within it.

How could it ever be possible to sort all of this out? Without external influence or direction?

The image of a virtual *Titanic* came into Sam's mind once again.

He shook his head dispersing the thought. This was *his* time, *his* space to think about things *he* wanted. If indeed that were ever possible these days, rather than going wandering off in his mind and doing all of the processing for everyone else.

Why was it so hard nowadays to be able to do just this? Why was it so hard to find peace and quiet? Why was there so much noise everywhere?

Why was there so much pollution, why so many toxins, distractions, interruptions, stresses, machines, technology, busyness and dull, mindless thinking? Why, when we all wanted it, this wonderful thing called peace, was it so hard to find, or do, or achieve?

It was very irritating; anyone would think that there was some sort of conspiracy going on - something stopping us from thinking for ourselves.

Why were we not being allowed to do this anymore, why?

"Why Mr Anderson, why, why, why…?" he mumbled.

The thoughts rattled around in his head.

Sam knew that the thing in his neck, the small space down the middle of his spinal cord, and the pressure on it causing pain, was what was causing this effect to happen. Along with the interactions of Brina – this 'space' created a sort of bio-mechanical 'feature', that was generating, or simulating, the same natural connecting 'opening' or reopening of something that had been closed at birth.

This 'feature' created a transmitting and receiving effect to and from the field of collective consciousness – connecting to the REAL, it was achieved naturally with kundalini or meditation or certain activating frequency vibration, or sexually. It was a natural biological process that was there to be used in the right way when needed, or to collectively recognise success or failure.

So whereas some people could not control the process - or who had artificially forced it with visions, revelations and so on, or in corrupting ways as say using LSD, or those with certain psychological issues - Sam could more or less switch it on and off, or at least attune it to some extent like a throttle or a valve, control it consciously by sane rational choice.

It was in essence gnosis - but without the delusional and hypnosis effect - leaving his mind and brain intact, hopefully. But equally it was dangerous, exhausting and stressful, especially during certain phases of collective stress or global unrest events, or when he was tired and the levels and volume of the information coming in became too intense to process.

Sam didn't think of himself as someone special. He didn't want adoration, fans, followers or disciples. He was no Saviour, Messiah, 'chosen one', or prophet. He was, as far as he knew, just a 'bloke'.

Sam smiled as the image of Monty Python's *The Life of Brian* scene where Brian was being told off by his mother. The scene came into his head - "He's not the Messiah – he's a very naughty boy", and then he couldn't remember the rest of the scene.

Sam knew that it was just something that he could do, and he just wanted to understand it all and to make a difference, if everything was right he wouldn't need or have to, but it was just a responsibility thing.

He wanted to use the skills and knowledge that he had, take that feeling of responsibility, and change something that was, frankly, crap – a matrix-style operating system that although several thousand years ago was doing well then, now looked like it had been biologically programmed by monkeys on drugs.

He knew there was no benefit or gain for himself - indeed quite the opposite applied- it was just the right thing to do, the responsible thing to try. You just do what you can with what you have got – and you do it to the best of your abilities. That was life.

He breathed heavily, and then out again slowly.

There was so much birdsong all around him here - different songs, different meanings, different voices. It all sounded like happiness. Freedom.

Lying on a hill was a good thing for Sam to do sometimes. It meant, for a start, that he was 'away from the house', and away from things that had to be done, away from distractions.

There just didn't seem to be any time for yourself these days- which was very odd when you thought about the fact that we now live in a world where everything is designed to make our lives simpler, to be more efficient, time saving, and convenient.

In a world of computers and technology designed to give you more leisure time, why was everyone sat in front of them all day and night, illuminating their faces with artificial light and viewing sanitised lives of artificial people, and absorbing artificial information - 99% of which they wouldn't ever actually need?

This particular hill had a large amount of gravity associated with it as it was formed from hard dense granite rock with unusual crystalline properties. The very first so called 'ley line' ran along this hill and, coincidentally, straight through his new house, which had been partly built into the hillside.

Gravity was a key to consciousness and the mind. It was a field which contained and described it, with the interaction of others. The gravity of the hill competed with the gravity of the earth and yet was contained within it, and so on, fields within field intensities, one pulling you out of the influence and domain of the other.

Astronauts on and around the moon experienced the same cosmic consciousness experiences, being then outside of the influence of our Gaian bubble, our sphere of planetary fields.

It was all part of a system that projected the planets, within solar systems, within galaxies, within the universal field system; all there to compete, and be programmed with, life - to set rules, of which we were only seeing a tiny, but important, manifested 'non-dark' part.

There was something fundamental in that process; something key, something that had intentionally set it to be that way, for some non-random reason.

Hills and mountains always seemed to have formed a focal element for humanity throughout history, and not just from the obvious defensive properties.

Like say at Jerusalem, or with volcanoes, pyramids - all

providing a centre, not just physically, but also symbolically in the mind as well. Cultures had followed the same principles too.

He slowly moved his fingers in the grass beside him; felt the texture, the coolness, the shape of each blade.

We had learnt so much, but forgotten so much. Was there anything more important than this though, this feeling and interaction with nature? Can we so easily forget what life is about to us as individuals, and lose all of this, this being, to a virtual collective unconscious one?

But then you could think of it all in a different way, the system; a hologram, a matrix, a virtual perceived representation of the conscious mind, created to make sense of something that doesn't. You could, in theory, apparently create any perception you wanted, even your own universe - the idea of which though somehow seemed wrong, illogical.

Yet in any case, what would be the point of that? How boring would it be after a while? And even being in someone else's created universe wouldn't make any sense; there were plenty of people off in their own worlds already as it was.

He preferred to be in this one though. It felt as if it was everyone else's too - well at least a reasonable majority anyway- and rather than giving up on it, and trying to find or create a new one, it seemed to be better to try and make the most of this one, to make it better somehow, and save it where you were able to.

Sam had been doing a lot of reading lately, and his mind drifted to the one of the books he had recently finished.

It was one about Carl Jung and Gustav Pauli, some heavy duty post graduate level synthesis of the physics, psychology, and modern philosophical interpretations of what the two of them had been trying to resolve in the last century. The 'Pauli-Jung conjecture'.

It was not easy information to track down - not so much what they were saying, but more about what they had experienced, and had tried to make sense of, interpret and explain.

There still didn't seem to be much progress in the field of study, most of which ended up with that annoying large 'elephant in the room' problems that always seemed to be there. Trying to desperately make sense of something that didn't, something that had no logical or rational explanation or pathway. Indeed the more you knew and the further down you dug into the quantum levels and behaviour, the larger the elephants got.

Equally there were now hundreds of possible ideas, concepts, theories, all thought out as far out as it was possible to go, but still nothing that made any logical sense.

Which would always be the case if you were in fact trying to describe reality from the wrong direction, and not using the larger part and context or paradigm, from which it was all projected from within or by.

It seemed that Jung and Pauli had been in similar situations to Sam in the last century, and that they had also tried to get the two sides - physical and spiritual - to meet up, but had failed, losing again the game of chess, with most of the 'game records' being conveniently lost.

But in Sam's case he had a more first-hand experience of the REAL, rather than it being translated into words and imagery and story through his psyche, he also had more in-depth knowing, more recent scientific data and a greater understanding of information and management.

Worldwide information and knowledge was also more accessible these days using the internet and online books, and the nature of the information much more obvious now, so a lot of the gaps and dead ends that Jung and Pauli and friends had encountered were now easy to see past and work around - it was now a lot easier to create a picture from the pieces that worked, way beyond anything that science could do.

We had even unconsciously and naturally created our information systems, technology, internet, computer systems and infrastructure to simulate the natural biological inner workings of the collective unconscious system itself, technology as an AI simulation of the REAL.

Which meant that as such technology terminology, concepts, structures, and evolvement was probably the best way of creating an analogy with which to describe IT, or parts of IT, and its biological informational nature - especially as IT too was evolving.

Yet people were still being blinded, beguiled, and controlled by our collective mind, and the evolving cultural minds within it, and we were no further forward today in working out the 'two sides' - which was really one thing - than they were then.

It was still the same ongoing game, with both sides of the mirror self-evolving, when it couldn't see that it was all just one.

We were still left with the problem of the scientific 'elephant in the room'- the room itself also obviously being just a sort of hologram translation of it - but if you were able to see it from the other direction - whilst still having expert knowledge of both ends - you could work it out, gradually, in journey form, describing what we had here but from the other direction, from what was generating it, and conversely being programmed by it.

The real from the REAL, the all from within the ALL, as it were. Just with the ability to see it as that, and understand what it all meant.

CHAPTER 2 - MURMURINGS

Sam folded his hands under his armpits and breathed in again as he shuffled his back against the grass to get more comfortable in the sun.

These days there was always so much to be done, so little time, so many things to be sorted out, constant distractions that somehow you just aren't able to avoid. Life was just a constant 'To Do' list - even your own home was constantly demanding you to 'do things' for it - companies supplying it with energy needing your attention every year to stop them ripping you off, decorating it, fixing it, sorting it, tidying it, and filling it, even sorting the rubbish that was posted through your letter box every day.

It was all just crazy.

Sitting out and sunbathing in the garden of the house wasn't as relaxing as being up here, above and away from everything. There were no phones, no callers, no TV, no radio, no mail. Even Brina couldn't sit still for very long in the garden, she would get agitated, want to get up and 'do something', tick something off her list, and eventually would be unable to leave him to rest, getting up from her chair and finding things to do - which inevitably involved him, or at the very least, his opinion.

If it was sunny at home, then there was usually something she had found in the garden to prune, something untidy and unsuspecting. She liked to trim things - even things that were just doing what they did naturally - or weed a flower bed that looked untidy.

The house was treated in the same way - carpets vacuumed, kitchen cleaned and tidied, clothes washed and ironed, toilets and bathrooms immaculate. There was always something to do, something that needed 'doing'.

It was very important to her that it was all tidy, clean, organised and presentable, just in case someone visited or called round – just in case they might catch her out, and be horrified that it wasn't perfect.

It was a sort of 'nest building' thing, and almost all of it was subconscious. It was a type of defensive mechanism, protecting them from 'outside', 'others', anything that could 'get you', 'criticise' or 'say something bad about her', something that she wasn't doing, or heaven forbid, something that she might be doing wrong.

Sam had also noticed that when Brina didn't know where to put something, she simply shoved it away in selected cupboards or drawers out of sight. Things that didn't have an obvious 'home', function, or somewhere to be immediately organised into, were just lumped together out of sight and mind, into something.

That was really odd.

It was a sort of program function, the – 'I need to tidy, but I don't know where this goes, pick it up, and wander round with it , then put it in the cupboard or drawer to worry about and tidy later, as I am too busy' - thing.

It wasn't the same as hoarding, or laziness, it was an impasse of being confronted with something while doing something else that you couldn't deal with there and then, so you put it away somewhere so you didn't have to deal with it at that moment, as she was short of time, which of course was always the case.

Which was fine until the drawer or cupboard became full, and then everything tumbled out on you when you opened it. This had unfortunately happened to him a few days earlier.

This was and 'interesting' and also 'helpful' event, as now he knew where two or three things that he was missing had been relocated.

The only disappointing thing was that there wasn't enough space in there for him to put his things in there anymore, the very things that were supposed to be in there in the first place, i.e. 'his things'.

Not that he had many things in the first place that were personal to him anyway.

But then she was happy, and if she was happy, then so was he.

The other advantage of knowing this of course, was that rather than spending half an hour wandering around the house looking for something, he now just went to the 'home for lost and untidy items cupboard and drawers' to find them; just open the door and a moment later it would land on your foot or head.

It was a kind of magic.

He had thought about employing a cleaner and a gardener, but Brina said she just wouldn't be happy with other people being around, in her home, it was 'her space'. Which was curiously very much the opposite of her mother's attitude, who, in Roman times would have been the sort that would have been happily carried through the streets by slave pole bearers, whilst eating hand fed grapes, and dragging everyone in to her house for a party.

It was also a way of Brina trying to exert some form of protective control over him; shaping his house around what she wanted, converting it into her nest, changing and manipulating it, and 'looking after him'.

It wasn't done in a conscious way, it was a subliminal force, a drive or need, that was pushing her to effect things, and this was her way of expressing it, and how she translated it into something physical.

It seemed to be part of her role, what she had to do, part of her 'job' - which was all fine by Sam.

In a virtual game world she would probably be behaving differently, but this was reality, and she was taking care of him in a physical way that was her interpretation of a virtual or spiritual drive or role; keeping their home germ free, immune, inoculated, protected, not open to attack, and most importantly, keeping him safe. She was making sure that it didn't all turn into some jungle, a mess, or a cleaner's nightmare, and one which would undoubtedly go viral on YouTube for her mother to tell her friends about.

Sam had wondered if it was all to do with her losing the baby the year before, some complex psychological subconscious thing, but he knew it wasn't; she had coped with all of those emotions at the time in her own way, and this had all come on since they had moved to the new house.

The house, and where it was situated, and them being there together was having an effect on both of them.

He did all the things she asked him to do – he mowed the lawn, did the heavy jobs and carried out the set routines, her lists.

He didn't mind at all - but there was more going on than just loving partnership, or a negotiated communication process of domination, status, or control between two individual people - there was also information flowing back and forth all the time, and at much 'higher' levels too.

So he allowed it to carry on. Whatever was going on it was important, and not something you could describe in words or express in feelings, there was information and expression in it.

It was a way of her saying 'I am doing all this to show you something that I can't describe'. She was 'telling' him something, over and over again, 'showing' him something by what she was doing that he needed to understand, and he was accepting that, and he was learning - fast.

They both 'knew' it was going on, but neither of them had to actually say anything, there was a discourse of information in her actions, and he got it, he got the messages.

They both knew that whatever it was that was going on all revolved around him. It was something that he was, or needed to be, or something that he needed to do. It was an odd thing to realise this - to step back from yourself – to see your life like a story, a process of journeyed demonstration and events, and to recognise it in yourself. It was like seeing yourself as a function or a cog in the mechanism, in a play, as well as being a person, going through some sort of game or story scenario.

The concept also in itself had a detachment to it, which was also odd; a sort of accepting conscious realisation, but which seemed fine somehow; this sort of strange thing was going on, but somehow it was OK.

It wasn't an ego thing or a status thing, it just was. They both were who they were, and they were both also doing something else that needed to be done, something vastly important, a process and a function, and a role.

He just wasn't quite sure though exactly what it was, where it was going or what it all meant yet.

However, there was no point in fighting it, or resisting it - that would just delay or complicate it, and it would also potentially just upset the balance and make it harder.

You just had to go with it and do the best you could, with whatever it was, 'they' were doing. It was if they were two adults acting out roles in some childlike fairy tale story game. Playing some mythical stereotypical roles in a play, but one that was being manifested into a physical reality and events and people and situations around them - the realisation of which was truly immense.

Brina's 'role' or the character that she was playing wasn't something you could mess about with either. She was working hard at doing whatever it was that she was doing, and it was not a good idea to treat it lightly.

One day he had thought about leaving a stapler out on the sideboard, something out of place, untidy. Then supergluing it to the surface to see what her reaction would be, see if she thought it was funny, but he didn't, he knew it was too important to start making jokes like that.

Besides that was childish and would only damage the wood, and she may get upset or angry about being confronted with the situation and of what she was doing, making fun of or highlighting a subconscious process.

Anyway, he had no idea where the superglue was, he hadn't seen it for weeks, it was probably at the very back of the cupboard underneath fifty other untidy things, and she had put it there knowing unconsciously what he would eventually try and do.

God she was good.

Making unconscious processes become conscious was a very dangerous thing, especially if you didn't know where they originated from, and if you weren't sure exactly what you were in effect waking up. It was fine though, they were happy, and it all seemed to work well.

But up here on the hill there was no garden to tidy, no cupboards, no things to put away. It was all where it should be, all in harmony, balanced, in symmetry.

Well apart that is from the insects eating all the plants, and each other, and the small furry animals being butchered alive in the bushes.

But that was 'OK' - that was just nature, and its harmonising gentle balance at work, the circle of life.

In the darkness the thought of balance, processes, harmony, synchronicity and change started to form in his thoughts - the nature of the world, and how it evolved within this information field, projecting itself and programming the physical, and evolving biological life forms.

All as a representation of what was going on within it, in its own right with its competing life cultures inside it, forming it, defining it, yet with nothing external forcing it to evolve, just surviving on its own. With our own human biological operating system collective mind contained within that eco bubble, running rampant, unchecked, unconscious, trying to over code everything else, competing with itself, and busily toxifying itself and infecting its home, like an ever expanding mould over the surface.

He started to work it through in his imagination.

Then, just as that thought passed through his mind - there was a loud mechanical noise a few hundred yards away in the woods, further down the hill. It sounded like someone kick-starting a motorcycle, but after a few more 'kicks' it spluttered into life as a chainsaw. Then it started revving up, ready to slice through the heart of some tree.

Rage welled up inside him, disproportional anger and frustration at the lost and broken pattern of thought.

For Christ's sake, why the hell does this keep happening to me? He thought. *I have JUST stopped to relax for one bloody minute, why is there always something to stop me? Why can't it just leave me alone, give me a bit of peace, just for five minutes to think on my own, what's so bloody difficult about that?*

The chainsaw was in full flow now, and the sound got louder as the wind direction changed, it sounded now more like some mechanical dragon or giant demon monster hidden somewhere within the trees.

"There's always bloody something" Sam muttered under his breath. He opened his eyes and looked up into the blue sky - the brightness of the light now caused him to blink and squint.

All the thoughts and depth of mind were now gone, and now his brain was focused to where he was and what was going on around him.

He breathed in deeply, sighed, and sat up and looked around, his mind shattered by the sudden change in state, and with the adrenaline pumping through his body.

Sam sat up and wrapped his arms around his knees and

looked down the hill. He couldn't see anyone in the woods, they must have been somewhere on the other side about a quarter of a mile away, but the sound carried a long way when it was so quiet and still.

He appreciated that some trees needed chopping down, but why now on such a beautiful day, and why here?

It made him wonder how these woods survived before humans arrived to keep them in order.

Thank God we arrived eh? He thought sarcastically *They were probably on their last set of evolutionary trunks. All those trees falling over on their own without anyone noticing. All that lack of watching and listening to them crashing down, or caring if they did or didn't. It must have been soul destroying living in a jungle like that with nobody conscious to perceive you, or make you real.*

The sound had also disturbed all the wildlife around, and had startled a giant flock of starlings into the air. They had been lodged in the high branches of the trees in the wood a few hundred yards down the hill.

There were literally tens of thousands of them, flowing high into the sky, grouping together protectively, swirling and merging in patterns of varying density. Repeating the same patterns, circles, habitual spirals, structures and forms, over and over again, but never exactly the same, they were always different in some way, some variation, which meant you had to keep watching hypnotically, to see what happened next, it was mesmerising.

It looked like the same effect that you got when you moved a magnet under a piece of paper with iron filings on it - only in 3D - swirling, spinning, reacting, all moving instantaneously with no time gap between the reactions, and all collectively in response to some invisible force that shaped it, formed it and organised it unconsciously, and yet they all knew what to do at the same time.

It was fascinating, and hypnotic.

They all changed direction instantaneously, their wings reflecting the sunlight in flashes, like a single shoal of fish in the sea evading a predator.

But it was also the sound they made as all of their wings changed direction at the same time, a very loud rustling sound that increased in volume and frequency up and down, almost like music, but unpredictable, random, which in itself made it attractive, as if somehow it were in tune with something earthly.

He knew animals could even do this in pitch darkness - so it had nothing to do with vision - it was field related and used the instant information transfer within some field information structure.

Migrating birds used the same ability to stay en masse and in chevrons for efficiency, which they too could carry out in darkness and in some common, defined, unspoken collectively remembered and programmed direction.

Was 'flock' the right word?

There were so many names for collective groups; colony, hive, murder – no - that was for crows - and just another word thought up by some academic group of pretentious 'holier than thou' Victorian ornithologists, probably for their own amusement.

The formation and effect he knew was called a murmuration, but that was more a name for the continuous structure, the pattern - like a religion - coming together to follow an unconscious program pattern, rather than the collective name.

Sam watched them and thought how easy it must have been for people in the ancient past to have tried to interpret meaning to the forms and happenings as a sign, an augury of an event, some divination.

Days earlier he had seen the whole sky filled with thousands of swifts - or maybe they were swallows - he never had learnt the difference - all congregating at once. They were everywhere you looked, as if this place, this hill, was some sort of meeting point for them - a focus or rallying point.

But as the whole sky was full of them, you couldn't call them a flock. There was no start or end, no grouping, no container, they were all just everywhere up there, and with no close dynamic structure other than just all being there at the same time.

Yet, somehow they all knew to be there at that moment in time, at that place, and were all ready to go on with their journey together. Unlike these starlings that were shaped in a different form, but none the less seemed to be having a lot of fun.

He looked closely - which these days is something people rarely do with anything other than at LED screens. They didn't behave or act like bees; bees swarmed and flew together in the air, and didn't act as the starlings were. Bees flew with and around the queen, like a cloud, surrounding one focal moving bee, an omega point, one single point in a field of bees.

The chainsaw sound stopped abruptly, the brief job, or dirty deed having been done. The silence took several moments to nervously and cautiously return, as if everything around that had been disturbed that was also now making noises could return back to harmony again, which also included his brain.

Sam remembered that he had read about how you could take a queen out of a beehive and keep it alive, and that the hive would carry on as normal, gathering food and so on; but if you killed the queen, even if it was well away from the hive, the hive would stop.

Somehow the bees knew - even from a distance, somehow even without scent or sound of sight, they knew…

That was probably the failing of insects compared to birds and mammals, that evolutionary intellectual cul-de-sac of single point of collective control that they had gone down. All successful to a point, but unable to move forward - but then it depended on how you measured success - numbers, intelligence, happiness?

Success for the group or just the individual? Anyway, they were alive and happy in their evolutionary niche, what more could anything or anyone want?

He remembered back to when he had been about twelve years of age. It had been a long, late-summer's day, and he remembered lying on his back in a field watching a pair of swallows feeding a line of five baby swallows along a telephone wire, high up in the air above him.

The parents would come in several minutes apart with some form of food offering, and the babies would all start reacting to the parents' arrivals with open beaks and flapping wings, even if they had just been fed by the other bird. Yet the parents always fed them exactly in order, one after the other in a line, over and over again for hours.

How did they know which bird was next, how did they know which one had been fed by the other parent? It was just like a program - but unless you stopped and watched, unless you 'looked' and saw what was going on and thought about it, took notice, you would never understand what was really happening everywhere around you.

It was lovely just being able to let your mind wander and think; think thoughts through into knowledge and understanding.

The starlings seemed hypnotised in some self-perpetuating trance, an unconscious holding pattern, locked into a single flock machine, becoming all as one, losing their individual identities and selves for the time as they did so - the needs and priorities of the many outweighing the needs of the one.

They had switched from being nomadic individual birds to a collective single form in both thought and shape. They had unconsciously evolved to have within them, both physically and mentally, the capability to become both levels, forms, and to adapt to the environmental situation and circumstances that favoured either.

When on its own, each individual bird was quieter, a sedate hunter-gatherer - just as we humans had been in our ancient nomadic history; wandering unprotected into the wilds of nature, being in the world and yet part of it; in balance and in harmony with it.

Only since the last ice age had humans come together in larger static groups, built civilisations, cultures, cities, states, countries - spheres and walls. Protecting and immunising from one another, from the world, and setting themselves against it.

All to survive, grow, gather, defend, build, learn, and fight, and just make things easier.

Which had also created an explosion of knowledge, invention, civilisation, art, music, culture, entertainment, and the production of tools.

Yet they were fixed, static, tied to physical structure and walls - unlike the starlings who were free to flow, move and adapt - theirs was no 'city in the sky', they were free to be part of it or not, attracted to its benefits, or remain nomadic, it made no difference for it would all be gone by morning, as would the hawk which had followed the path of the 'lone wolf'.

So what was right, and what was wrong? Who was to say?

We are, after all, where we are - here by some fashion or by some means.

The problem now is that there is nothing outside of it all to force us to evolve, nothing forcing us humans collectively to adapt and change or to take direction or responsibility.

There's also no one at the helm - not really; all the politicians, governments, leaders were all puppets placating the masses, and there are no external predators for us to evolve by, and compete against, other than those we had created for ourselves.

There was no way back either, back to how things were before we started forming collectives and cities. No way back to that happy nomadic tribal, cold, dangerous, hungry, hard, short, disease ridden existence.

What was needed was a Plan; a blueprint for the future, a future in which we were happy- happy together and also as individuals, a sort of joint benefit programme; doing the right things both for ourselves individually and collectively, and in harmony with the rest of the planet - yet one that was not lazy or corrupt, but workable and sustainable.

Like cells working in a body that itself was eco-friendly. It all sounded so easy when he thought it through like that, you just had to get everyone to see, understand, realise what was going on, write it down in a book and show it to everyone, and then it would all be sorted, so no, not tricky at all, it was all so simple.

However, he didn't bother to get up at that point.

"Yeah, like that is going to work" he murmured.

The starlings continued to swirl around in vast numbers. Then high in the air and from further down the hillside, something as yet unseen and unheard was drawing in other smaller groups of starlings from further afield to join them all together, as one.

The birds would break away from their original small groups which had settled in trees, and individually flow along lines of flight to the bigger, more stimulating, exciting, energetic, and a more powerful gathering. The mass grew larger, denser, and more intense new patterns formed, and the sound of the birds became louder. With all the birds now instantly synchronous, performing the same function, the same instantaneous operations, and programming as one.

Then a hawk appeared from way off, drifting in the air currents from over and behind the hill.

It was a Sparrowhawk and it paused for a moment, hovering motionlessly, and then it darted fast overhead, then in and out of the mass of starlings. A gap formed, a hole shaped itself in the formation around the hawk, making a doughnut formation as it passed through, before it seamlessly closed up behind it again.

Everything happened instantaneously, like a reverse pole magnet placed in the middle of the field of a bigger one, moving the iron filings out of the way within it.

How were they able to recognise it, perceive it as a threat and respond to it collectively, instantly, in thoughtless coordination?

Electromagnetic fields, Sam thought, just one type among many. Nature would use anything that it could find to send or receive information. It would use and gather whatever it could to survive.

It was clear to see that there must have been some organising force at work that the individual birds were subject to and part of; something that was instant and instinctive that governed and yet protected them all. Without any of them being aware as individuals of what they were doing, or how it was being coordinated, a collective decision process to look after them all in the face of adversity had kicked in, the whole and the one acting on behalf and for themselves and individually to survive.

Parts of the one contained in parts of the many.

That was the same with us, and we had become blind to it - if you were in it, and part of it, you just reacted and responded to it without even thinking, and in most cases you probably would not even have been able to think.

Powerful reinforced subconscious urges and instincts kicking in to preserve you, and those around you, and at the same time making it hard to see what you were in and part of. Which would be fine if it was actually working *for* us and not *against* us.

It was fine if everyone was happy, and you only had to look at cities these days to see how happy people were.

For some reason cities didn't seem to be the lively, exciting, energetic and stimulating places that they had used to be.

The hawk darted back and forth, round and around, forcing the starlings into tighter swirls and denser torsional shaped spirals, and doughnuts.

Yet the mass behaved very differently to that of an individual starling. The mass was just reacting to the hawk, it was not frightened by it – it was just like some emotionless program or stimulated operating system, and it moulded itself around the hawk - using it to react to, learning from it, while unconsciously forming patterns that confused it.

It was indifferent; naturally and automatically recognising it by its form and behaviour, and then as one adapting to the threat and rendering it powerless from the overall group's perspective.

To an individual starling on its own, the hawk would have been a terrifying demonic symbol, with its talons, its hooked beak, pointed wings and that fearsome way it had of moving.

It would have appeared a giant to it, a focus, and a nightmare to haunt its dreams - but in a group, the reactions were very different, almost unfeeling, and it was more of an exciting plaything that it didn't need to fly away from.

Then, suddenly, the hawk grabbed a lone starling; its victim was too slow, having become disconnected from the rest, not able to keep up with the flow due to some failing or weakness, or perhaps something that had been out of sync with the collective thought formation.

It was all over in an instant, a sacrificial filtering mechanism. The nomadic 'hunter gatherer' hawk and its prey fell to earth, and the hole vanished and the uncaring mass of iron filings continued to swirl away, bonded within its flowing field, oblivious and uncaring of the evolutionary casualty of nature.

When you were outside of it you could see it working, see it for what it was, that was the difference.

When you were in it, and subject to it, and being controlled, you were unaware of what was happening. When you were awake, conscious, observing it from the outside, and knew what was going on, you could see things very differently.

However being on the outside, out of the system, also made you vulnerable to attack - a hermit starling, out of step with the collective group - potentially not playing the game, not keeping shape, rebelling against it, and a threat to it if you did the wrong thing.

That could be a dangerous situation to put yourself into.

It was rewarding being part of the unconscious flock, forming the greater mass. On the outside you were open to attack, you were 'them' and not one of 'us', consequently gigantified to help highlight you as a potential threat, and were even given an energy signature to be attacked, isolated, immunised - but then that was evolution, that was nature, that was life – or death.

But if there were no hawks, no predators, what would the group become? How would it evolve, refine? Would it weed out the weak, the slow, the overweight, the sick? If there was nothing forcing it to change other than itself and the constraints of its domain, it would never evolve - there wouldn't be anything to drive a change.

We, humanity, were becoming more like Dodos rather than starlings. We as humanity had become exactly what the fashion industry culture had evolved into – a self-shaping, de-masculinised, irresponsible, nepotistic, hierarchical, religious mass. Corrupting and poisoning our children and our children's minds.

It was immunising itself and its 'intermediary customers' from its original, now forgotten, purpose and Freudian drives.

This group of birds, this starling macro-organism, was mentally far more basic in its evolutionary maturity than the starlings as individuals.

It was more primal, feral, and did not have the intelligence or wisdom of the individual bird - but then it didn't need to, and it also had a different form, nature, and purpose.

The starlings unconsciously just reacted and behaved differently depending on what state they happened to be in, and in the collective state this by necessity overrode their own individual conscious decision making capability.

The human collective consciousness and the cultural mind groups within it were the same, but it was all vastly more sophisticated and evolved in comparison - as was the macro-organism and information system data that generated it.

It was far more advanced compared to the starlings and other animal collectives.

Yet it was still immature in its awareness, thinking and experience compared to an individual human mind, well most of them anyway, and it was also still unconscious and had a lot of unrefined unresolved legacy issues to cope with.

To see it all you had to get past all the evolved layers of individual psyche, the individual egos, archetypes, habits, beliefs, cultural influences, all placed there to hide it from you, to disguise its presence and its nature.

It was also evolving with us on a macro level, but not for our individual benefit, and it was getting worse. It was controlling, governing, manipulating, hiding in ever adapting and more vastly sophisticated ways, but underneath it was still obvious that it was a hive-type mind, you just had to look around the physical world, and open your eyes, and you would see that it was painfully obvious.

Unless of course you were blind, or couldn't be bothered.

The big problem was that the only threat collectively these days, was not from 'them' but from ourselves.

On the ground the hawk started pulling the starling apart before it was even dead. Its feathers were plucked into the air and meat was ripped and stretched out of the bird and gulped straight down. It had no care or feeling for its prey, it was just doing what it did to survive; a simple program and functional sequence.

It carried on for a few more minutes and then decided to abandon its feast, having probably already eaten that day, or maybe it had just been getting in some practise. It sprang into the air and hovered above the trees for a moment causing the ball of starlings to billow away further along the hillside; they were clearly aware of it but did not want it to prick their bubble again.

It was such a rare sight these days these murmurations, he had seen so many more of them here when he had been a small boy.

He remembered having seen a recent news item on the television that had said that the starling population had shrunk by two thirds over the last forty years. But then in either form, bird or flock, they wouldn't be able understand or see what was happening to them, or even comprehend why.

Sam was still watching when he saw two crows fly out of the trees and spiral around the hawk; harrying it, bombing it, trying to drive it away from the general location of their nest.

In response the hawk looked around to see if it could spot the nest but was unable to, clearly distracted by being dive-bombed by the crows. It then appeared to decide that it was too much bother, besides it wasn't that hungry.

It gradually glided away effortlessly down the valley away from the trees. The two crows carried on harrying it for several minutes, oblivious in their state of awareness and perspective of how far they had strayed away from their own, now vulnerable, nest - their defensive 'fight off predator' program locked in to their systems.

Moments later the hawk swerved, and took off at speed. Nature was such a simple and overused word for something so vast and complex, and hidden from our plain sight.

It was all so obvious, seeing it all like this; fields, waveforms, physicality. Why couldn't people see what he could see, why couldn't they see what was going on everywhere? What was stopping them from understanding?

It was happening everywhere, every day, so many characteristics of everyday life played out unconsciously in this form -but most were oblivious to it. They just couldn't see it, or were being dissuaded from seeing, all these underlying unconscious programs, all far more advanced than he was viewing here with the starlings. The human ones were very controlling and powerful, and we were blind to them all, but it all affected most of our everyday habits, beliefs, feelings and thoughts.

There was nobody directing though, in and of itself, nobody to wake it up, and nobody at the wheel, nothing giving it direction.

Watching all of this going on right in front of him made Sam feel as if he was being shown it all to 'see' - to make sense of it all with what was coming into his mind – to understand the symbolism and the analogy.

He couldn't help feeling that he would have been better off just lying there with his eyes closed.

But no such luck - the chainsaw had seen to that.

CHAPTER 3 - FIELD OF DREAMS

Sam's dog had been lying down peacefully a few feet away from him.

The dog suddenly stood up out of the blue, seemingly already knowing reactively that Sam was about to do the same.

Sam got up and brushed himself off, and began walking along the hill. After several minutes he joined the winding path down the sunny wooded slopes towards home.

The dog walked several feet in front of him, occasionally looking back at him in some 'working' symbiotic relationship.

Sam's dog always seemed to know what Sam was thinking, but it wasn't something you could show people, or even try to explain.

People who owned dogs and cats knew that these things happened, and those that didn't weren't that interested, or didn't care, so there wasn't much point in talking about it.

You either had them - and lived with them, and saw these things happen - or you didn't.

Sam knew that his working relationship with his dog was complicated, there was a lot of involved communication going on that was subliminal, and it worked both ways.

He also knew that more measurable, and more complex instances of strange animal behaviour had been studied to try and identify what was going on, to find out how and where this information was transferred and where it came from.

From his studies, Sam knew of one such effect that was commonly known as the 'Hundredth Monkey Effect'. This had been studied and reported about the Macaque monkeys that lived on Japanese islands on the beaches.

It had been observed and noted that the Macaque had originally ignored sand covered fruit – but that one day, a young female monkey seemed to 'know' that the fruit needed to be washed, and could then be safely eaten – so she took the fruit and washed it and then ate it.

It was not long before all the other monkeys on the island also started to wash the fruit before eating it- until it became a habit with all the Macaque – but not only on the first island, but also on all the other isolated surrounding islands- all at the same time. It was also something that had been learnt many generations ago in the past and then forgotten.

Bizarrely, these monkey colonies on different islands were not in contact with one another. Somehow this 'program' had been reactivated from long ago, and then when successful behaviour was resonated across islands, it became a successful program, and it had helped them all.

You could see the same effect with the start of civilisation cultures 12,000 years ago; skills, tools, techniques of building, ideas and thoughts, structures, shapes, concepts, rippling through the system; inspirational ideas that somehow ignored geographical boundaries. Somehow this 'program' and associated information had been stored somewhere and then accessed and copied, then permeated through the system, over distance.

These days, Sam thought, you could see similar effects with people with 'genius minds' who lived in different countries and continents but who had stumbled on the same ideas at the same time.

You could also see it with common expressions of artistic discourse from cultures in the form of films, music, technology and fashion; simultaneous genius discoveries occurring somehow spontaneously - just happening – and then everyone just taking it all for granted that this is way it should be, and not investigating.

All this influence and collective knowledge from the collective unconscious, gnosis, visions, combined with the need to express what was coming in through various forms.

All the other genius scientists then used this to formulate their ideas; to see and map this collective data into new thought forms and integrated concepts as it evolved, and so on.

There were so many indications of this going on everywhere. It was just so obvious really, but no so obvious that it could be seen.

Even the animal world had their own collective 'operating systems' which coexisted with ours. Theirs were attuned to this same field system structure, all on the same server mechanism, all competing and integrating within the field system and evolving within its laws, parameters, and blueprints, with DNA becoming utilised in ever increasing levels of sophistication, bootstrapping and data transfer.

Some dogs for example, just as Sam's did, knew when their owners were about to come home, and 'knew' what they were thinking without the need for words - and there were various other inexplicable behaviour traits; dogs bonded with their owners through a natural selection process that had evolved for them to be the best, and it was really quite common.

This collective knowledge and information system was fairly easy to see, test and measure, and yet people didn't seem to be able to 'get it' – they appeared unable to 'see' what was going on even though it was fairly obvious, and happening all around them.

They just seemed to snap back into the day-to-day process of life's treadmill, and to get reabsorbed into the internet or soap opera TV or continue with their blinkered, hypnotic beliefs and lifestyles, and uncaring oblivious attitudes.

Sam looked at his slightly overweight dog walking a few yards in front of him. He didn't need to worry about washing sand off his food, or fighting for it, or coming up with new ideas as to how to get it.

Not when there was some gullible monkey who would do all that for him, hit a few keyboard buttons and have it all delivered.

The dog looked back at him at that moment as if he had picked up the thought, and looked at Sam questioningly.

The human race seemed to have 'forgotten' how, or had become more unable to, integrate with the natural global biological system, and was being almost beguiled away from even seeing it or coexisting with it. Replacing the natural tools that were there with electronic versions of them.

We were all behaving ever more now like various flocks of overfed, poisoned, zombie sheep.

The process of which was in turn being blamed on some 'secret Illuminati', some secret hidden elite that 'controlled' everything – or an invisible virtual alien 'them' - which was keeping everyone blind to everything around them and keeping the human masses in servitude and under mindless control.

Which was of course wrong. No group could do all that - it was purely the system itself, lazy *'us'*, our macro-organism, our global consciousness field-based biological evolving hive-like mind of humanity. Along with all the various sub-cultures within it; all of which were competing and growing consciousness structures - but only within itself and within the influences of the laws, boundaries, limits and influences - of itself, not by itself.

Yes, these 'super-elite' people may exist, but they are just as much slaves as everyone else to the unconscious collective system; all just trying to use the collective unconscious mind to manipulate others within certain areas, and in certain cultures for their own benefit as well as the system - to keep the ants in order – and yet in the end they are being just as controlled and bribed by IT as much as everyone else, and were equally as unhappy.

Sam had experienced that effect first hand on many occasions - a natural, unconscious, manipulative controlling force. No group of individuals could do that. They had, he was sure, much more interesting things to do like spending all of their money, or worrying about losing all of their fortunes, attending the devil worshipping parties, and living in fear and wondering what the hell was really going on at the top of this demonic force - just like everyone else.

But then unless you had had some form of experiential exposure to it, and some involvement in part of IT outside of your safe bubble or sphere of consciousness, then it was both difficult to see or to understand, and put into context.

Also explaining concepts like these, to those that hadn't any experience was impossible, because not only could they not appreciate it, they we deliberately prevented from seeing it by protective insulating and immunising programs within their own mind bubble; which was correct just as long as the whole thing was working properly.

As long as something was managing it, and directing it all, it should all be fine - but of course it wasn't.

The main reason being that there was no real 'hawk' for humanity, just plenty of imagined virtual ones, so it had all become a very complex situation, with no overall management in place to deal with it all, just drifting around in the space available.

Yet with so many good and open historical records available

online now, it was easy to see that all of this stuff was progressing over time - changing, evolving.

If you looked carefully you could see how this vastly complex system of belief structures and cultural control mechanisms of information knowledge and biological evolution as a whole could be misunderstood and interpreted as something else.

In the past, if you hadn't known what it was, understood the science, the reasons, the nature, it would have been very easy to create some mental religious rabbit hole - with its mental hypnotic, refined, beguiling traps to safely fall into - or indeed to just jump into someone else's reinforced created rabbit hole for safety, one that seemed to conveniently answer all the riddles.

It didn't matter if it was illogical, irrational, and looked very much the same as a lot of others - aside maybe from a few cosmetic differences – what mattered was that it was safe and warm and cosy; something to believe in that made the big complicated frightening thing go away, and at the same time was hypnotically fascinating. With a tick in the box next to the answer of 'It will be all OK and someone else is looking after it all'.

Better to believe in something, be part of a gang, than be out in the dark, cold, stark REAL all by yourself – scary stuff!

And of course there were even more and more imaginative ideas about 'what was really going on' these post-war days - all the elaborate ever adapting, colourful, collectively-constructed alien and cosmic spiritual theories - fabricated, reinforced, internet driven, photo-shopped, video engineered, into the collective imagination, ready to be tuned in on the next channel; then brought into a new technological evolving religious structure, presumably out of secret meetings. And when all the inconsistencies and contradictions had been ironed out; a new networked church where truth, science, and the painful and uncomfortable reality were too boring to get a look in.

If you could just step back from it you would be able to see an underlying collective hypnotic trend of control still there, using and expressing itself - its nature and shape - into technology, the internet and information systems, and the organisation of compartmentalised academic science disciplines.

And if anyone who really knew what was going on popped up,

spoke out, they were hammered down, immunised and stuffed into some *Hobbit* hole somewhere, or in some cases - worse.

It was also interesting to see the flip side of all those views too - those that knew to some extent there was something going on - were aware that there was a collective consciousness field, for want of a better term - yet because they couldn't get their heads around the vastly complex science, and the psychology and philosophy of the whole thing - they had progressively got together with others and filled the remaining gaps with collectively engineered and imagined concepts. Then insisted that 'that's who were ultimately controlling it all', which they then reinforced as a concept to be 'told' to everyone, so that someone could '*do something about it*'.

The word 'preached' being very carefully avoided, these days.

But it was always a 'they', a 'them' - never an 'us'.

That was not to say that these aliens were not actually there from our perspective – 'they', in the virtual sense, *had* been imagined, thought-formed into elaborate, yet contradictory, virtual role playing game-like world scenarios and armies within our collective minds' imagination. So real – in a sense.

Springing into existence in our hierarchical spiritual landscape of naive virtual perception, translated from older, now less believable, demonic archaic forms.

People then convinced that that was what was really there, that was what was *really* going on. All arguing with each other about the story, characters and gameplay and rubbishing each other's interpretations, without stopping to wonder why all of them saw it all in various different ways, had different interpretations, or that there was no real logic or consistency to the whole thing.

Over recent decades these virtual gamescapes had been hastily refined and expanded using interpretations driven by fear and phobias, and all the alien conspiracy programmers had been busy writing their code and data, into the collective mind, in ever increasing dimensionality and complexity, and added sci-fi.

They had also wasted a lot of time arguing between themselves about what actually were the correct shapes, sizes, origins, nature, colours, species and histories; new and advanced versions of what had once been *Demons and Devils Version 2.1* - but which were now far more technical, complex and sophisticated hierarchies of Greys,

Draco Lizard men, Anunnaki and other 'ancient' alien races in conjunction with its associated *Dungeons and Dragons* internet-based evolving *Monster Manual*, or *Top Trumps*-style hierarchy, dimensions, and attributes from size, shape, abilities, alignment, psionic abilities, and enhanced childish artwork - which was in itself a bit of a giveaway to where it was all actually coming from.

All with a somewhat obvious traceability and shape to it all if you had studied psychological types, sci-fi comics, science fiction films, phobias and fears of certain government and military organisations, cultures and religions.

You could easily go back over the last 60 years to work out who 'they' and 'them' really were and where they had originated from.

Concepts of secret aliens from the local Pleiades star cluster had been circulated for decades now, and are still being refined all the time into a more and more elaborate concepts, adding in layers of complexity with keys, symbols, links to archaeological shapes and geometry.

It's all been combined and joined with other similar ideas, clinging on, despite lack of proof and logic, only to disappear as soon as it was shown that there was no possibility of any habitable planets to have ever existed in that group of blue stars which were only two hundred million years old. Not enough time for planets to form – which was as far as the collective story went was a big logical hurdle to get over, but one which was easily achieved by simply ignoring it and pretending it wasn't there.

All of this was being envisaged and mapped out and generated on multi-dimensional, virtual, out-of-body terrains that uncannily looked more and more like something put together in 'Minecraft', with a somewhat hollow unperceived underground - the entrance to which had a sign next to it with the words

Abandon hope all ye who enter here

which was now covered with a newer sign stating that it was actually now... **Unda construcktion.**

Several weeks would go by before their software updates went live, and were subsequently tested out on the ever growing masses of hypnotised 'believers' - all of whom were similar psychological types, with access to the internet discussion and exchange groups.

But the problem was, thought Sam, that in effect, these things then *became* real - with real effect, real information - a negative feedback loop of thought into the one system.

These new devil-code or dragon programs would find their way into biological devices, and even start working together - taking on a demonic organised nature - and possibly ending up in the server somewhere lodged in walls, buildings and cities. Demons now *becoming* aliens in the structures of ever adapting control systems.

You *really* had to be careful what you thought about, especially if it was going into the collective imagination of a child.

But hey give it a few more decades, and it would all be into something else, but hey kids these days – what can you do ?

Sam gave a slight laugh but the dog ignored him.

So in effect these things *were* real, they existed as information, thought forms, but collaborative and evolved biological symbolic interpretations of something else in the system, a 'them' - some part of it that wasn't you or part of your group, culture, compartment - something that you were afraid of.

So most likely the 'little men in grey coats', certain ancient religious groups, other cultures, or 'Them there Ruskies' - many of whom were, on an individual basis, surprisingly nice and friendly - just like you in fact, once you got to know them. Which of course he hadn't.

It was just the same with good old-fashioned religions that had been developed in the past, which had then been replaced when blind logic, proof, and some stepping back and looking at the bigger picture processes revealed some fairly obvious glowing gaps in the initial logic.

They all still included lots of colourful and outlandish mythical stories, with no scientific or physical evidence or proof to back them up, but that still didn't stop people falling into the same traps, and the same hypnotic processes - and that in fact was what imaginative dreaming was all about, and all part of growing up from a collective or cultural perspective.

So as far as Sam was concerned there were no real aliens, there was no ancient alien conspiracy, no - it was all far worse than that, it was all just *us*.

It all made Sam hope that there would be something else – and then he would be very happy to be proved wrong. And if it was something else, real aliens, it would be a lot more interesting and exciting than the truth.

He stroked the long hillside grass with his hand reassuringly.

Sam realised that now he had actually thought about it - the Pleiades thing - the logical impasse in the dream would probably be realised **now**, and this realising thought, would now be out there. In the system, he wondered how long it would take to percolate.

But these legacy concepts and ideas were very difficult to shift, very hard to move on from; they existed in the collective mind as a string of concepts - thought forms in the mind of a child like an irrational phobia or a set of stories or fanciful imaginative dreams.

In effect these were things that it had to grow out of. But that took time, by which time it would have come up with a load more sophisticated ones to worry about.

The early dinosaurs would have laughed themselves into extinction at the idea that our DNA had come from the Pleiades as they watched the Seven Sister's blue stars being formed at night, under the light of our uncommonly large moon – 'Theia' as it used to be - which had that big, responsible, 'stirring things up', 'guilty look' about it.

But hang around for a few more years... he thought *and a quick rethink in the collective nursery virtual chalk board for some other 'ah yes but wait ...' more outlandish explanation to 'buy into' to explain it all away again, the details of which have somehow never been mentioned before in various 'channellings' over the last 30 years or so.*

Sam knew that the structure of DNA had come from elsewhere, outside of the planet, either via an asteroid or as a blueprint resonated into the field biosphere, but it was probably something structurally inherent in the universe - one of its structural core seed data parameters - and any planet would pick it up as soon as it was capable of supporting that brand of life. But he didn't know for sure.

He wasn't absolutely totally certain about that one at the moment.

But then IT was very good at doing just that sort of hypnotic dream thing with us - and it was getting better at it all the time. It had had thousands of years of practice, and was able to use whatever means it had at its disposal.

IT was a survivor after all. It was just that there wasn't much for it to survive against, other than itself and its own vivid childish unconscious imagination.

Which, right now, wasn't actually good for its nature, and so it was starting to mutate and vegetate, overconsume, and becoming self-destructive, stagnant and ill.

IT was even lying to itself about the toxins it was creating within itself; the drugs, chemicals, heavy metals, pollution, system technology and media - a side effect of unconscious control.

A spinning coin with two sides - light and dark, good and evil, left and right, male and female - that was running out of energy and time in what was a cold, hard, indifferent distant and remote universe of feral change that it was in, on a spinning globe server that it was growing on, and existing in.

It was all about spheres of influence, fields of torsional energy, all spinning and evolving, building up more and more complex structures of programs within programs.

Adapting, developing, refining. But this planetary sphere in which it existed was alone and far away from any other that could easily affect its field of influence even if it chose to listen.

An isolated spinning dot of dust, in the apparent silence of space, confining itself and its field of evolved selfish organ-like programs and knowledge.

Spinning around, and living off, the energy of its solar parent.

The collective human mind was very good at hiding itself from its own human components though — from its cells that are contained inside its macrocosmic bubble.

It constructs beliefs, mental hypnotic patterns, blocking, and in some instances eradicates errant cells - immunising itself against what it thinks it doesn't need, and just as within ant colonies, it could also defend itself if you stepped out of line.

Sam now knew that the key was to take the middle neutral line. Not to become trapped into the corrupt 'evil', 'dark' side of control and suppression or become beguiled by the fluffy colourful 'good'. the 'it will all be fine as long as we all love each other and ride off into the sunset of ascension on our magical coloured *My Little Pony* unicorns into tree hugging fairy wonderland' - side.

Good and bad were simply perceptions from where you were in

the system, based on your objective views and values that you have been hypnotised to have, and for which you would adamantly argue for, and blindly reinforce.

You had to apply a neutral viewpoint, to understand and experience everything from all sides, and then make objective decisions - in the same way that a parent may act.

But, of course – just in the same way as parenting - it wasn't quite a simple as that.

You had to stand back from it all and work out what needed to happen, and then somehow tell IT what to do. But because nothing else is giving IT any direction or advice, and because IT is unconscious, this is somewhat tricky - like walking on razor sharp eggshells of responsibility.

Especially these days.

But that was nature, biology - the hypnotic effect and systems that have evolved.

There were some advantages to it - and over time that made all the difference and direction to what shape it was in, and what we knew now - but for the last hundred years it didn't seem to be going very well.

There was a distinct lack of balance, harmony, logic, ethics, or management, and there was no direction other than that set by the underlying system constraints, rules and functions.

You could see it going wrong everywhere, and no one seems to be happy.

Sam thought about the city of London - the ebb and the flow and the closeness of everyone moving around and forming an identity, watching the channelling of people from high above. Then he thought of New York, and then of the hawk, the Twin Towers, the reaction. Were we predators, or prey, or perhaps a combination of both, or neither, or had we just lost sight of what we were and what it was all about, and whose fault it actually all was? That lack of a real 'them' to blame and fight, rather than looking more towards 'us' or 'me' as the culprit.

It had all worked well to a point - but when the whole was one; one world, humanity all interconnected, itself, with nothing to fight, compete, evolve against - a Catch 22 situation arises, which forces it to change and evolve.

His mind kept going down that path, and troublingly, it kept ending up at *his* doorstep. The main problem though, as far as Sam could make out, was that it was a very big path, with a lot of people on it - and a very small doorstep.

The whole thing was so vast and complicated that the power and complexity would make a billion quantum supercomputers look like an abacus, and even the most advanced concepts of Artificial Intelligence in science fiction look amateurish.

Yet the whole thing was still based on fundamentals, simple laws and patterns and rules, just as they were in the *Matrix* films, which only in themselves covered a small part of the picture.

This collective mind was the thing that all the religions were based on, and interpreted from, at any given time.

Experiences from it and within it were discoursed and interpreted as it evolved, grew, learned and adapted in each of its cultural areas. It was vast, complex, powerful, controlling - and yet regressive, lagging behind us as individuals in maturity and awareness in its level of mentality and 'humanity' and 'conscience'.

It was contained by the planetary field and was integrated with other biological systems, and it evolved in parallel with us. But to say there was nothing else, no higher force, no 'greater' thing would be naive - just because he had no exposure or contact with anything 'out there' didn't mean there wasn't anything there at all.

In fact, knowing what he now knew about the laws, the probabilities, the dynamics, the maths and the rules in place - along with the ever more suspicious structure of DNA - it seemed to Sam that the universe had been very much 'created'; just not by 'God' or anything that logically fitted into any of the religions he had studied over the last few years - not by a long, long way – and not before any questions of divine accountability and responsibility had come into play.

So he was happy to admit that there was a creator of the universe or the universal field structure, but in terms of its involvement with us and the planet, it was - from his perspective - missing and having little influence. The cosmic egg concept.

However, the god or gods described by prophets and transcribed into belief structures, and then adapted into religious control structures by all the different religions, and archetypes, had the fingerprints of our collective human and cultural mind all over them - they were all the same thing - IT - they were just seen and interpreted in different ways and at different stages of its evolution within the global field structure that supported it.

Maybe IT would eventually be capable of integrating into something 'larger', be part of a bigger universal or competing galactic consciousness - but at the moment it all felt very 'lonely' and isolated - as did he.

What was needed was something to make it obvious, to make it change, evolve, become what it was supposed to be, present itself, show itself, with measurable evidential actions and synchronised events that were visible - physical evidence, cause and effect - so that IT, and we, could see itself in the physical as manifested thoughts and conscious actions and events.

Not just more elaborate 'visions' and 'channellings' and 'experiences' - picked up on by individual minds, and then discoursed in the same recurring forms and dialogues as always – but with ever more updated and imaginative interpretations.

But what could *he* do?

Sam looked up into the sky as he walked and sighed.

It was no good.

He continued his way back down the hill following the path to his home, his dog walking steadily several feet ahead, just so that he could be the first to deal with any potentially interesting thing, like alien squirrels, or demonic cats.

Sam just couldn't understand why people were being kept so stupid, so naive, so blind. No one could see what he saw, understand what he knew, they all seemed unable to see through the hypnotic fog, and understand what was *really* going on.

Everyone was just so blinded by belief structures, academic stove-piping, institutionalisation and all the mental control systems that were in place everywhere in our society - and all of it was our own collective making, and instead of saving us, it would all be our undoing.

It was just staggering to watch it happen; not just individuals, but groups of people too - organisations, countries, cultures.

He felt like waving his hand in front of their faces to try to 'wake them up', but it was just futile – it was a never ending process that they couldn't ever change.

The only way to do something about it would be to confront the root of the problem head on - a top-down approach - and change things for the better in a balanced way.

He had even tried using analogies or allegories to try and explain things to people, to try and convey some shared perspective, some common understanding of what was really happening.

Analogies were great in that you could relate to people from two sides, build up a shared perspective understanding of a situation, an environment, a context, and interpretation - it was a story and a position within it, a page, a line, that meant you were both there in the same place at the same time, but somewhere not here and not now.

Using these analogies was really the only way he could get people to see things from his perspective, as well as their own.

For them to gain an understanding, a feeling that was so completely different from anything they may have ever experienced before, it was essential to build up that analogy picture to gain a common ground, especially if you were both in the same place mentally but couldn't describe it - but even then it didn't work very well, and people would just snap back into their own bubble of perception and mental position after a while.

Until you had that depth and breadth of understanding, that clear depth and expanse of knowledge, that freedom from any hypnotising pre-established belief structure you had associate with, and an experiential point of reference and connection outside it all, it was very hard to define and describe, to get to that out-of-the box thinking and perspective of it all.

So why was he bothering to carry on, even after knowing what was going on? Why bother?

Well, perhaps there *was* something else, something that IT cannot stop, that *will* change things. Maybe there was some other way, some other thing that will happen from the outside that will change things.

But if there was - it had to be down to us to stimulate it, bring it to life, get it to do something, create a reaction. Bring this collective emotional consciousness to the fore and give it the power to open the cage before it was too late.

Failing that, the only hope we could hang on to would be that some real physical alien race gets the call, and comes and rescues us from ourselves - and hope that they don't just end up eating us, or stealing all our women instead.

It was all just a game, one vast complex game, being played on so many levels, adapting, learning, evolving. All created by us, learning against us, and *for* us at the same time. All set within a framework of rules, structure, layers and limits. But one that wasn't working or even that much fun to play anymore.

You could not escape it though, not now - well not without a rocket ship anyway - you couldn't avoid playing either, no matter how nomadic you became, and how remotely you placed yourself - not even with a lead lined bucket on your head whilst sitting on an island.

Also if you just stood back and watched you just got left behind, you ended up not moving forward or achieving anything.

It was a game that set itself in a self-resolving macrocosm of virtualscapes, with no external evolutionary direction to compete against or even receive guidance from.

It was time for everything human to stop being selfish, which is what ironically everyone seemed to be saying, but were just not aware or understanding of why it wasn't happening.

What IT needed to do was to start listening to itself – to have that little Jiminy Cricket mature calming voice of conscience and responsibility - a guide to right and wrong coming from within itself, methodically and gradually, and also objectively from outside of its unconscious, wooden, little, childlike, but slowly reacting, bubble.

IT needed something to calm its worries, to guide it and to sort the problems out before it was too late. But it all had to be done in a balanced way, with benefits from all perspectives.

As he walked back to his house along the lower shaded woodland paths on the hillside, Sam thought about all the crazy things that had happened over the last year or so.

Yet somehow it no longer mattered, he seemed settled now here, sort of 'where he needed to be', at least for the moment.

He looked up to the sky and thought of the hawk and the starlings again - nature was so simple and yet so complicated.

The sun shone down into patches of bright light through the trees along the lush green grass-lined path as he walked.

Here and there were strong scented carpets of bluebells, which seem to shine out a radiant deep vibrant colour in contrast to the browns or light and dark greens of the wood.

They bloomed only for a short time each year, but they were beautiful, intense, and a perfectly formed radiant display.

Around the next corner he came across a field covered in them; a massive intense carpet of deep blue glowing in the sunshine. Their aroma filled his nostrils, the scent lifted his emotions, and the whole sensual explosion gave him energy - it was just breath-taking. He stopped just to look at it, to stare and to take it all in.

His dog stopped and looked back at him questioningly.

There must be a way of fixing all this he thought, *after all nature is an amazing thing.*

There must be **something** *that can be done about us ...*

CHAPTER 4 - THE CASTLE ON A CLOUD

The last few years had been a roller coaster ride of emotions and had brought about big changes for both of them.

It had all started when Sam had decided to sell his own home following a whole series of bizarre events. Everything about his house and the surrounding area had just turned a bit 'weird' – they'd encountered issues with new neighbours, been badly let down by builders and decorators and they perceived a general unrest in the village which had been caused by a group of gypsies setting up camp in one of the local fields.

There had also been a couple of instances of violence in the village - including the local Post Office being robbed at gunpoint – and talks of new train lines and bypasses being planned around the village and ultimately everything had added up to a slightly uncomfortable feeling, and in complete contrast to how it had all been up until then.

It had felt as if some oppressive multipronged force had 'come to town' and knocked at their front door. Gone was the quiet peaceful little English country hamlet with friendly locals, and in its place had moved an oppressive darkness, disquiet, an unsettling sense that it didn't want him there - or more to the point perhaps - that *he* didn't want to be around anymore. It wasn't just him that felt that way, lots of locals had commented on it and it had appeared to have no apparent real reason behind it. All around them people had started to behave oddly, and Brina was the most sensitive to it of anyone, and it had made her very uneasy.

Brina had lost the baby a few months before, and the house now held a lot of bad memories and associations for her as a result of it. She had lost a lot of her energy and, combined with what had gone on months before, things had taken a toll on her - there were a few wrinkles appearing here and there and she had developed a slightly more defensive hard-edged persona.

The olde-worlde friendliness of the village had gone too, and it had been replaced with distrust, fear, and new faces that didn't go with the old community ethos. It was as if something was trying to get them to move, be somewhere else, and it channelled negativity like a dark cloud around them, over-coding the village in every aspect.

He had decided it was time for them to go.

The decision was quickly followed 'coincidentally' with him unexpectedly winning a new government department contract job. It had been offered to him by a colleague he had worked with years before but it had been located a few hundred miles south from where they lived. It would have been just a bit too far to drive or commute every day, and 'coincidentally' fitted in with the option for Brina to make a fresh start and work where she had been happy before, in the City of Bath in Somerset. He really wouldn't have been comfortable leaving Brina for days on end, and the thought of staying in some unwelcoming bed and breakfast or hotel on his own had seemed utterly pointless and so the decision to sell the house and move on had been made easy for them.

Remarkably, everything had been straightforward after that and within two weeks the house had been sold for its full asking price, with no complications, and without any troublesome property chain. Everything had been packed up and put into storage, with no bother or any fuss.

They had rented a holiday home out in the middle of nowhere down south in the countryside while they looked around for a new permanent home from which they could both commute to and from their new jobs. When they had explored the property market in the area online it had looked as if there would be lots of suitable properties for them to either buy or rent – and as they weren't in any particular rush to make a decision – they felt that it would all be remarkably easy and that they would just take their time and choose exactly the right place.

After settling into his new job for a few days, Sam had been keen to spend their first weekend getting out and about to explore some of the local ancient archaeological sites that he remembered having visited as a child; Stonehenge, Glastonbury, Aylesbury, and the many Roman settlements - and of course, the Roman Bathhouse and sights in Bath itself - all called to him.

It had all felt quite exciting at the time, something new, a change, and getting out together, from somewhere and something that had gone wrong to somewhere new and interesting. Because when they were together everything was fine - they could leave everything behind and start again, have a new 'adventure', a new life.

He hadn't felt any sense of nostalgia or sadness at leaving his old home, it had just seemed right to move on, to leave the past behind, and detach himself and Brina from whatever it was that had happened to them.

His new contract was relatively easy and straightforward and everything seemed to be right and at the end of the first week Sam had felt relaxed and happy for the first time in a very long time.

On the Saturday of the second weekend, Sam, Brina and the dog had driven to an impressive, but remote, old Iron Age hilltop fort at a place called South Cadbury, which, like Glastonbury, was alleged to be one of the possible locations of King Arthur's Camelot, or perhaps where he had been buried with his knights. If he, or they ever existed that is, other than just in myth and legend. The area was also surrounded with stories and legends of King Alfred and numerous other ancient events, most of which had been lost over time.

Sam had actually been more interested in the walk and the views of the valleys than anything else. It had been a fine, bright, fresh day, and they had parked the car at the bottom of the hill and had started up the steep climb up through the woods, winding along the leafy tree-lined layers of grassy earthwork rings, and up and out onto the breezy plateau at the top.

Sam looked carefully at the structure of the land and knew that it had all been built long ago as defensive layers of enclosures to protect many stone and wooden Iron Age and pre Anglo-Saxon buildings, and by the looks of them, he figured that he was standing on the remains of what had once been a large hall. However, all that you could see now was a lot of grass, mounds of grass, and dozens of hardy weatherworn sheep.

The hill fort was very similar to the one on the hills where Sam had been born; undulating short grassy mounds and layered rings around a central grassy flattened hill mound. These forts had been built out of necessity by ancient peoples who had evolved the designs over time to respond to increasing external threats from raiding parties and wandering foreign armies.

In this area these ancient villages and hamlets had resorted to grouping together defensively, just in the same way that later cities had evolved - successfully deterring predatory roaming aggressors in an immunising protective womb-like bubble. These places had also provided future protection against other tribes from other hilltop settlements, with their smaller roaming opportunist armies who knew how much effort would be required to penetrate the opposing bubble, a deterrent, establishing a sort of symbiotic stalemate, one in which everyone was happy again.

Unless of course the army was driven by some angry and dissatisfied hero, who had hypnotised his army of ant people into some exodus to a new land, inspired by divine powers and words, creating some new myth, new legend. Then of course all the common sense logic went out the window, and then you'd have been in trouble. There was nothing worse than a stupid crowd being driven by an excitable idiot. If that had happened you would have had to get busy adding more levels and layers and taller wooden walls.

Eventually as always, came the bubble-busting, more advanced Roman style foreign armies appearing from abroad, to smash, conquer, and then assimilate and integrate the once nervous population into a more refined peaceful civilised structured existence.

Well those that survived anyway.

This had all got Sam's imagination going though, and as he continued to walk, he had tried to visualise what it must have been like living there in those times and what life may have entailed before, and after, the Romans had arrived. The people, the battles, the storms and the cold they must have endured. All reflected into the faces and bodies and hardiness of the peoples, what they knew, what they believed in, dreamed of, and what their thoughts may have been of what was going on around them.

Sam and Brina had reached the top of the hill. The view was amazing and they could see Glastonbury and its tower miles off to the north, and many other hills and sites in the panoramic distance. It was just like one of those scenes from *The Lord of the Rings*.

That was when he had a very strange déjà-vu feeling, as if he *really had* seen this scene before, more of a 'déjà-<u>view</u>' feeling. He definitely couldn't remember having visited here as a child, or at any time in fact, and yet there was that feeling somehow of knowing he *had* been there, had seen this situation, this place. There was a sense, that 'in-the-now' feeling of having already looked in that specific direction from this very place. But with it also came anger, frustration, and a strong feeling of loss.

Brina had huddled up to him as they stood there. The wind had blown around them on top of the hill, and she seemed very content. Sam's brow furrowed. He wasn't.

As they had walked around the upper ring of the earthworks circumnavigating the hill, stronger emotions had welled up in him. They became even more pronounced when he stood by the remains of the foundations of the gatehouse - one that would originally have barred entry to the hilltop. He had sensations of events having happened there - motion, attacks, fear, and he could almost hear the echoes of desperation.

It was as if something was trying to show him something, feed him information, but at the same time convey feelings, emotions, of doing, or being something. It was progressive as if a child was showing you a set of flash cards; a child that was trying to get you to figure something out in a game, and that it wasn't allowed to communicate to you in any other way. They had continued to walk along tracks that became surrounded by woods of fir and oak and sycamore trees and around undulating slopes until they were at the northern part of the hill. It was there that Sam spotted a small lake down at the foot of the hill. Energy had surged through him and all sorts of confusing concepts and thoughts had gone through his head.

He had experienced a similar feeling when he had gone around the Roman thermal complex in Bath the weekend before. He remembered that he had stopped at one point and had stood looking at the main large hot spring pool spring which fed the whole complex.

Sam knew what déjà-vu was, that information flow, and how you could pick up echoes from within the collective mind of information, like picking up error data from an operating system, residual memory stored in the system from links to places, memories. It was the same concept as a computer server which had data left on a disk linked to locations that could be picked up by programs when the odd glitch happened.

But this feeling had been slightly odd. It was a *series* of déjà-vu moments all pulled together trying to link back to a myth – to something that had never actually happened in reality. It was trying to shoehorn things in its imagination to get him to work out of it was actually true, real, physical.

Myths were, in effect, reinforced dreams within the collective mind, like imagined thought forms; habits on a macro scale, which tried to reoccur unconsciously in individuals - like echoes - over and over again, and which, over time, were updated with new characters and situations until they were accepted, or fitted in. Sam also knew that the process itself had probably derived from natural biological evolutionary processes.

And then he got it. He understood what IT was 'saying'. He knew what IT was trying to get him to do, unconsciously.

He stopped. "You are bloody kidding me" he whispered under his breath. He shook his head. "You have got to be bloody kidding me." Sam had instantly worked out what it was all about, why he was there and what was actually going on. He stood there for several moments thinking it through, trying to form the pictures, the story, the connections, the mythology.

The 'sword in the lake', King Arthur, Camelot - *that* was what this had all been about. IT had been leading him on, tagging him as a 'hero', getting him to 'play the game', get the message, live the myth, re-enact the role, take up the sword, and, probably along with several other unsuspecting individuals, IT had made him follow the imaginary story.

Sam closed his eyes and visualised a card with a picture of a sword on it. There was a surge of energy, which sort of confirmed what he had thought. He had opened his eyes again and breathed in. "Not heard of rust then?" Sam whispered under his breath. He closed his eyes and created visual thoughts of a rusty crumbling sword in his mind together with childish nursery images of such legends and, just for fun, added in an inner sort of smirk type emotion.

In hindsight it had been a damned stupid thing to do. It was one thing to work out what IT was unconsciously trying to communicate to him, what was being 'said', and what game it was playing. But by immediately reacting to it - and in that particular way - had not been Sam's best idea. Just because he 'got it', and had consciously understood what was going on unconsciously in a system, didn't mean that he should have responded to it in such a rude way. To have reacted like that was like ridiculing a child or baby for being naive and immature and for clinging to fairy-tales. Not so smart when you were part of it and when your fate is tied to it.

The energy had drained from his body in an instant. He had felt bone cold, and his head started spinning, a cold tingling sensation filled his muscles, bones and organs, accompanied by a feeling of dread and abandonment and bleak exposure. He had braced himself against a tree to stop himself from falling over in the mud and found himself fighting for his breath.

It was as if something had pulled away and he felt immediately faint, detached and vulnerable.

'Not playing the game' was not a sensible thing to do when you were dealing with something with that kind of power, especially when it had an immature subconscious raw nature at its heart. It was a bloody stupid and careless thing to do, and Sam was quickly angry at himself for making such a silly casual mistake. He knew that he should have just played along, seen where the game led, used the process to learn, experiment and observe objectively.

What a stupid error to make - and what was worse was that he now didn't know where he stood in the scheme of things.

Brina had been oblivious to this episode taking place but had felt the change in his body language and saw that something was really wrong with Sam. He hadn't the energy to speak, but eventually, after juggling with both the dog and supporting Sam down the hill, she managed to get him to the car and drove them back to the holiday home. It had taken a few hours for the colour to return to his face and for him to even be able to communicate other than to assure her he was OK and that he would recover.

He had obviously upset something by 'not playing the game', and it had reacted in some form of child-like unconscious sulk. It may have been that IT was annoyed that he had 'worked out' what was really going on, and that IT had felt that Sam had spoiled it all - but Sam didn't think that IT was that grown up - this was a very immature and unconscious reaction, a kind of instinctive response.

Sam had felt awful, and from his perspective, also very angry that they were both being manipulated and played around with like toys in some sort of fairy-tale dream-like game. He wasn't some stereotype hero, action man, no Jedi with a flashing sword. Nor was Brina the lovely 'Princess Brinavere' doll with detachable fairy wings. If anything she was more of a dynamically professional, yet lowly ex-barmaid, girl-come-good action figure. In any case, Sam thought - it had to do better than that. IT had to start playing some new games.

He had read enough about the nature and the structure of the collective mind, its stereotypes, legacy forms and myths, archetypal imagery and symbols, roles and cultural frameworks. He also knew the way its information was organised and how the processes within it worked.

In essence he was meant to be fulfilling the Brave Idiot Hero-with-the-sword role 'function', the champion Paladin, the Saviour carrying the Christ-consciousness-organising-saviour program - blindly going on to form a newly evolved belief structure or religion, which would have then just turned into yet another control structure.

Unfortunately, Sam had already known all of that, and as a result he had gone one step ahead of the 'game', sussed it out and recognised the pattern of programming as it was actually happening. So if IT still wanted to play it had to come up with something new now.

Sam knew that Brina was not just some sort of a smart blonde bimbo with wings, or some scantily clad buxom Amazon clinging to the leg of a Barbarian on the front cover of some 1970's rock vinyl record. She was smart and intelligent - she had tracked him down for starters - probably drawn to his magnetic personality, his beacon of light, venturing forth into the world to find her Knight in Shining Armour, and bestow on him her favour.

Obviously the female half of the myth had evolved quite a lot while nobody was actually looking.

He had been sure it that it was meant to be the other way around though - him seeking her out, winning her hand, finding her in her tower, and on a quest to rescue her from the dragon, and carrying her off on his noble 4x4 steed to live happily ever after. Times had clearly changed, and it was obviously getting a bit tough out there on the mythical front, and things were getting a little desperate. Such that these days any male that gave off the wrong divine mythical hero signature, could face being taken down like some unsuspecting wildebeest, and eaten alive by an overfriendly lioness.

Fortunately in both their cases it wasn't like that, and Brina could see straight through everything and would never be fooled by any fake celluloid celebrity hero - and somehow her destiny didn't have a footballer-trophy-wife direction to it either. She was already there and knew it all and she was just waiting for him to work it out for himself.

Sam had the distinct impression now that the ball was firmly in his court, and being aware of this situation, this outsmarting position, or whatever was going on - had moved things into new territory. Already knowing what IT thought he was supposed to be, what was 'meant to happen, and what he was supposed to do, put him outside of that unconscious mythical role playing game. He was now in a subjective position where probably no one had been before.

He saw that he had to get some high end expert advice. He knew he would need to get a lot more reading done on philosophy, metaphysics, religious and mythical history, and in-depth psychology. Clearly ignoring it wasn't going to do any good. IT had been pushing him, moving him, getting him to be somewhere and then to start a mythical game process or function. So if IT was going off to have an unconscious rethink, then he had better try and get ahead of it.

Brina had seemed to know what was going on - but then she always seemed to know somehow, she always knew what had to be done, what she was meant to do, what had happened, and what was really going on - but without talking or knowing any of the technical stuff or understanding the science, or philosophy of it all. It was if subconsciously she knew it all, and was waiting for him to 'get there', work it out for himself, understand, and then do what he was supposed to do.

She hadn't seemed to want to know the specifics either, the science, the technical stuff, she never read any of the things that he did, none of the books, and yet she always seemed to be 'there' waiting for him to arrive and to have worked it all through in his own mind.

She had her own encompassing multi-faceted ways of working out what was going on, and knowing what she was supposed to do, sort of in parallel, unconsciously, she just *knew*, but not in the way he knew, sort of in a complimentary way. It was frankly amazing, perplexing, unnerving and also bloody frustrating. Especially as she would convey information to him in subtle ways that he was then meant to understand and translate from her perspective or view.

The following week, while they were still in the holiday home, and after he had recovered, they had started looking for a permanent home. It was only then that they discovered that every property they had seen online – and liked - either to rent or buy – had disappeared from the market either having been sold or let out in the last week. All of a sudden there was no room at the metaphysical inn. It wasn't even subtle.

This had continued for weeks until, out of desperation, they had ended up renting a house in a cul-de-sac on an estate in Chipping Sodbury some sixty miles North of where they had originally been looking. The houses and streets all looked exactly like something out of a *Harry Potter* film set.

Oddly enough, after they had moved into the house, Sam had felt more and more like Harry Potter every day that passed. Like a hermit in a box made of brick cladding, wood, fibreglass insulation, tiles, and plastic, in his house-sized cupboard under the stairs. But then Little Whinging or Chipping Sodbury wasn't somewhere that Sam had ever previously thought of living.

It had been, however, all just a little too weird, too surreal - as if they were being forced to exist in some virtual reality film-scape, full of sheep-le actors; androids acting out the same routines in some fictitious *Westworld*-like scenario. The only thing that had been missing was the owls.

But in the house that they were living in now, on the hill ringed by woods, he was surrounded by owls hooting all night, like they were waiting for him expectantly - but he didn't mind that.

Sam though hadn't fitted into Chipping Sodbury at all. It just hadn't been his type of place, they weren't his sort of people, he hadn't liked the surroundings or anything about that area or that house at all, and neither had it felt right for Brina. It had just felt very uncomfortable for them, as though it was where they shouldn't be and they had just simply been unable to rest and settle.

It was obvious to Sam that he was being processed, taken on some mythical journey. It was a process, a series of learning events for some 'hero role', either evolved from the ancient times or a newer media age character that he was meant to be fulfilling. Only in his case he was intelligent and awake enough to recognise this. You just had to step back see what was going on, and then use the system and learn from the examples of others who had gone through it in the past.

The 'enlightening theosophical experience' that he had encountered in New Zealand years before had been followed by his 'time in the desert'. Now he was being put through another part of the gnosis 'journey' process – but this time on an industrial scale.

But Sam had decided that he wasn't going to be some unconscious puppet, treated like some mythical hero toy just replaying all the same roles, same act, same story. He had made his mind up but was also aware that it would be dangerous to fight IT and so he knew that he had to carry on with the show for now - pretend to play the act, be his part in the childlike fairy-tale game, a Luke Skywalker in this cartoon-like film, or be the fabled Gilgamesh in the play.

He knew that until he had a much better understanding of what it was that was 'doing' the playing, he had to go along with the charade. He had seen far too much, was aware of its energy, and knew way too much to be deluded by IT or to be hypnotised by what was going on.

The question was though – that if he knew that, and if he knew what was happening, would that simple fact by itself change things? Would it change the game? And if so - where would that leave things then, and what would IT have to do to step up, to outsmart him? What would all that lead to?

Or was it up to him to define that direction now? Should he step outside of himself, and the game he was in, and be one step ahead of the director for the moment? It was a conscious direction of outsmarting, like Donkey and Shrek on the broken bridge that led to the castle with the dragon.

He had held that thought in his mind.

It was as if both he and Brina were both being expected to be roleplaying characters in some giant virtual game. It was an ever repeating game over history, based and formed on existing legend patterns, myths, and stories, ones that were biologically 'successful', fun, popular and were well 'followed'.

But in their case they were all combined together at once. A sort of 'combo set' of epics rolled into one, enacted and played as they had always been. The same symbols, signifiers, scenarios, journey landmarks, rules, battles. Yet added to, refined, adapted, evolved each time it was played out in each 'cycle', with ever more modern settings and scenery and language and technical understanding.

But now it was him as Luke Skywalker, King Arthur, Frodo, Gilgamesh, Hermes, Thoth, Neo, and several other unsuspecting 'sword bearing' fairy-tale hero characters and all being amalgamated into an all-in-one version, new, but still the same program journey.

Brina was also being cast as Princess Leia, Trinity, Scully, Valkyrie, Athena, the various Muses, and several other characters that he probably hadn't even met or even heard of yet. It was all a very childish, naive scenario, but one being played out and supported in the real physical world, where people and events occurred to support it, enact it, live and evolve it.

It had all been translated now though and hidden into modern day speak, language, situations and nuances and events; a modern stage for an ancient, yet evolving, story. Something was mapping what was going on in the virtual/spiritual-world-gameplay scenario, into physicality, through a narrowband modem connection, to attempt to bring the one side in line with the other.

This process probably happened every 19 years or so for every 'generation', but more recently several 'missing' generations of players were lost in the field of battle since the mid 1980's when they had their brains blown apart with the growing scale of it all before they had even been able to realise what was really going on, or never even being able to make it to the child director's film set or stage.

This was a different process though from the geniuses in their compartmentalised areas of understanding, who secretly were 'gifted' their gnosis knowledge from the collective mind database, or Akashic records, with inspirations, insights, visions, illuminations, and revelations.

They then processed them into new meanings, ideas, concepts and creative thoughts in combination with current scientific understanding and physical perception. All imagining new ideas, organising the flow of data together with what they had studied and learnt, into new thought forms, within the physical and conscious world.

These insights and illuminations were usually driven by what IT needed or wanted to understand unconsciously, the collective energy and interest being focused like a child's imagination in the direction of what it didn't know and what it wanted to understand.

In very recent years most of the geniuses, and their rewards systems, were based around technology systems and software, quantum mechanics and DNA. This was driven by the unconscious, with desires to know about itself, driven by its feelings and needs, energy direction, flows of cultural desires and expansion and natural simulation, and also as a means of control.

The main problem now though was that the control, and also the direction IT was leading everyone in, was coming from the collective unconscious - the drives, the rewards, the hive or ant-like mentality, gathering and using resources, was hiding itself from us, keeping people blind and zombie-like with the lack of external influence and evolutionary direction.

It all had to change. IT couldn't go on like that - it had no direction of its own.

But Sam knew that this had been realised before. He knew from his studies that the psychologist Carl Jung had been through a similar process in the first decade of the 20th Century. Jung had lived through, and experienced, the reality of a myth structure, which was where all his work and ideas and thoughts had come from.

The gnosis, extreme visions, vivid dreams, channellings, illuminations were something that Jung had also studied in others. When Jung had realised what was going on though, he had stepped back from himself and from what he had experienced - what the Kundalini twin snakes 'thing' was generating within him - and had documented it in his journals and 'fessed up to it in his *Red Book* – but his book was only released by his estate in 2009 – 48 years after Jung's death. *The Red Book* came as a total shock to his academic 'followers' who had him down as a genius, like Einstein or Wolfgang Pauli, Newton, and so on.

It was also no surprise to Sam that Jung had been surrounded by many powerful and highly intelligent women, who unconsciously all knew what was going on, and were trying to control and manage him.

And yet surely Jung had just been another normal sane person, yet gifted with cleverness? Surely he was one of those amazingly smart people that just thought a lot harder than everyone else but without realising that all of them had all got this 'genius' knowledge from the same place? Newton's 'apple landing on the head' hint was clearly being a little too subtle and all the 'mad', behind closed doors stuff being hidden away, guiltily protected behind walls of embarrassment, which in itself was equally convenient for hiding what was really going on, preventing people from seeing the 'bigger picture'.

Sam had figured out that if a list of people that had been through this process were made, had everyone known, and had they all admitted to it, would have at least several hundred names on it.

For goodness sake, there were even academic groups that study these phenomena - Theosophy and Philosophy are all about this subject! And yet all these scientists seem to come across as a bunch of grey absorbing librarians, who turned up to listen, nodded a lot, and 'politely', but slightly condescendingly, said "Gosh that's very interesting", drank the tea and ate the cakes, formed their own opinions on the subject and then went back to where they had come from not having actually achieved anything, and just simply serving to waste the time of people who were 'in the game'. They were like some sort of holding mechanism - controlling, limiting, and beguiling - a compartmentalising condescending function - as is the case with so many academic institutions.

The whole process was like going to talk to a load of scientists, explaining what was going on and why, and then realising that they were not able to understand it at all and that they had made you into an exhibit in a modern day Jacob Boehme zoo so that they could study you and understand you better - only to eventually end up as just another book, another bunch of study papers and another set of journals on a dusty shelf in basement library and yet still NOTHING CHANGING.

But whereas Jung had been exposed to the rigours of the collective unconscious over several years in visions and gnosis, and had been exposed to one progressive 'story' - what Sam was being subjected to was several combined mythical stories all at once, and he was also having to physically live through and see it all in just a few months. Things were speeding up, and getting 'larger' and a lot more intense, and it was all happening in rapid processes.

Sam knew that he wasn't up to Jung's level of understanding of psychological concepts, or even knowledgeable about more modern academic developments in that area yet, but he seemed to be being driven along those lines - to know, to understand, to work it all out. But Sam wasn't required to simply learn and understand just psychology - he would need to master everything; philosophy, religions, science, and a whole range of other areas and academic stovepiped compartments. A plethora of disciplines that he was expected to 'know', have tenure of, understand the lingo and the meanings, and make sense of and integrate it with everything else. Sections with large gaps in the logic would need to be filled with solutions and understandings from others. Equally he had to try and piece together what was going on the other side of the mirror - in the 'spiritual' field.

The other concern for Sam was that Jung also had a higher self, and daemons, spiritual guides, to give him suggestions and inform him, sort of gentle advisors.

Sam had nothing like that. All he had was just raw collective knowledge being piped in directly, every day. It felt as though even if his 'higher' self were there, he, or she, was being very quiet, probably hiding in a *Hobbit* hole somewhere, or adopting the 'frankly mate this is all a bit too extreme for me, and I am really a bit out of my depth here, and you are on your own pal, but I am happy to hold your coat for you' attitude. That was the problem. IT had all become so complex, so vast, so much more intelligent and sophisticated over the last hundred years and it all seemed to have grown exponentially in its inventiveness.

The problem for him seemed to be that he was being expected to pull all these departments and compartments - or pieces - of the unconscious together, to integrate them, rationalise them, join up the dots, resolve the elephants in the room. He was seemingly being required to plug the large missing gaps, cast illumination on the dark voids of logic that couldn't be answered or filled by themselves.

Only by drawing on and integrating parts from other pieces could a lot of them now be resolved. Many had reached points of impasse in the logic of what we were able to understand, perceive and think logically of, mainly as we were looking and trying to understand everything from the wrong perspective or direction.

What was really needed was a sort of synthesising process, something to integrate areas together – like, say, quantum physics and individual spirituality - the two sides of the mirror. You could then relay this back into the system itself, forming a macro-holistic consciousness structure, like some sort of management device which had to, or was supposed to be, an expert in everything, a sort of synthesising or macro level genius of everything. Which of course was impossible. Not to mention physically dangerous. There had to be another way, and it had to be a team effort, he didn't have the capacity or bandwidth to cope with it all by himself.

Sam's mind started pulling in various hero characters and situations from different movies all at once; Neo from the *Matrix* appeared before the interactive computer screen that was fed by the Precogs from the *Minority Report*, with him trying to correlate the knowledge coming in from the screens into the real physical world, and too much was happening much too quickly. It all became too cluttered, incoherent, and full of legacy scenes, using more and more energy and creating so much frustration that the screen just exploded.

What had gone wrong? If they were being expected to fulfil these roles all at once, had the 'others' fallen by the wayside, taken the wrong decision in the choice of A, B or C in the third paragraph on Page 3 of the evolving gamebook?

Had it all got too much? Was there too much knowledge, and the scale of it all too vast, for them to take in or cope with? Had they all either ended up in asylums, gone mad, or opted to hide from it by immunising themselves through drugs, alcohol, and chemicals, or, ultimately suicide?

Sam had figured out the only way to manage it was to just keep stepping back from it, to keep playing along with the game, but be aware of himself within it - being the character in the child's play without letting his character dash off ill-advised and unprepared to slay the dragon with sword in hand and ring on finger.

He could not rush in blindly to the obsessive mission that only he, 'The One', could solve. He had to wait until had had first dealt with the real world things he needed to do like checking if he was getting the best deal from his home energy supplier company, and getting the car serviced, before going to the supermarket, and only then ensuring that everything else that he was standing on was securely in place.

That was the key - balance, doing what you could with what you had and knew, but not going blindly full steam ahead in one direction that just took everything from you for the 'play', leaving no obvious benefits to you, yourself.

That was one of the skills he had learnt in business management; 'Their' crisis didn't constitute his emergency, and a lack of planning on 'ITs' part didn't constitute an urgency on his. If IT wanted him to 'save the world' he wasn't going to become just another self-adjusting 'also ran' statistic.

Sam changed the scene running through his mind.

What he was envisaging now was Neo driving off at the end of the new *Blade Runner* film, with Rachel, having both escaped with a boot full of lottery cash, along with Pris - who was still played by Daryl Hannah in Sam's version - in the back seat of the car. But he knew it would never end like that, it was more likely to end with him being blown to pieces at the end of the *Matrix* with Trinity pierced by several spiralled bits of metal, and dead in a crashed ship, again. Unless he changed the pattern.

Yet equally he wasn't just going to turn his back on it all either, that would be irresponsible, not to mention dangerous, and he had the distinct impression that whatever was shoving him into this from the 'outside' wasn't going to just let him give up either. IT had to learn, grow up and evolve against him, one way or another, for everyone's sake.

In which case he had to do a lot of 'reading up' first, all the departmental guides, manuals, cheat sheets, Dungeon Master's rule book, along with a few 'lessons learned' reports from previous leading edge 'participants', who had 'skin in the game'.

Hindsight was a useful tool. He just had to try and add a new 'level' to it all, and being conscious that you were in an unconscious collective role playing game was part of that, as well as seeing where everyone else had gone wrong. Objectively seeing the naivety, where the lack of knowledge had got them at the time, the misconceptions, and applying current knowledge, intelligence and understanding to the problem. All that before wading in with the sword and failing again.

But hey at least it was a direction, and at least you got to see it and learn something, as it came out of its cave, with its new stealth coated Kevlar scales.

At the same time he could see Brina going through her own battles trying to maintain balance and manage the flow of data coming into her fields. She was keeping parity too, her Jungian archetypal psychology female personality types, whilst still being the modern professional strong woman, in a world of post modernity.

She was trying to juggle and satisfy the demands of the Medial, the Amazon, the Mother and Hetaira woman, keeping the four sides in balance. The roles of the oracle-medium, independent woman, caring-nurturer, and supporting-sex goddess, whilst at the same time 'being the Anima' and the Avatar of the Zeitgeist, while also finding time to fit in the ironing, cooking, freaking out at traffic cameras, and avoiding unconsciously starting any world wars.

To add to the mix, Brina was also having a personal physical struggle against what she now understood to be first-hand experience in post WWII collective alchemy, and the use of heavy metals, and the negative application thereof into the environment and body, especially in her case, mercury, which was still residual in her body.

She, like everyone, had her shadow to deal with too, her daemons, her supressed unconscious elements to manage. She was probably even trying to deal with group and cultural shadow programs too.

Yet even though it was likely that she was being actioned by the global system, the Gaia bubble server-system-thing, as it were; something causing her to effect change in the collective human mind, an angel on an 'outside' mission - she wasn't in herself supposed to, or be able to, instigate those changes - she had to action it all through someone else, someone who was capable of not only doing it, but knowing what he was doing and understood it all in totality.

She was an enabler, an empowering instigator, an agent provocateur, with a direction and power and message and mission or agenda that she, more than likely, wasn't even aware of consciously.

An angel in search of a knight with a phallic-like sword who could summon and direct the collective energy, with the power and rigorousness to effect that change, directing that powerful female energy to influence, not just at the cultural or country level and the group minds and cultural psyche shadows, but at the overall collective human consciousness level, both the mind and thinking of 'humanity' and its shadow,

Memories, archetypes and structures that were evolving within the planetary global field - the child and the dragon in the server. To bring order and meaning to the chaos. Or to chop the logs and fetch the water, all depending what had highest priority on her subconscious list.

There was certainly an awful lot of chaos around that needed 'fixing' these days, it was a mystery as to what had caused it all, yet it was a good job he knew a lot about information programming and operating systems, and the people that had put them together.

CHAPTER 5 - THE MAN IN THE HIGH CASTLE

Sam and Brina had tolerated the Harry Potter house for six months, along with all the corresponding film by film related symbolisms being brought to life in their day to day lives. But in the end they both agreed that Chipping Sodbury was not the place they needed or wanted to be. Sam's contract had finished and the lease on the house was up for renewal and so they agreed to start looking for a permanent home in the area where Sam had been raised – a place where he felt safe and where they could be closer to his family.

The property search hadn't taken very long and they soon discovered a house for sale on the hills just a few minutes from where Sam had been born. The house was in a poor state of repair and terribly neglected after having been left empty for nearly a year, but was a large, spacious house that had been built high up on the hill facing east over the river valley – and most importantly – it was set back in the woods and was surrounded only by trees, birds and squirrels and was very, very quiet.

The purchase of the house had gone through very smoothly and Sam and Brina had moved in by early Spring.

The house was very odd. Sam had negotiated on the price and managed to secure it for 25% less than the previous owners had paid for it only five years earlier. It must have cost a fortune to have built it in the first place; it had massive iron girder frames, thick brick walls, solid floors on both levels, and vast amounts of landscaping and earthworks had been done to dig into the side of the granite hill. It had six bedrooms, and large architectural features including a large triangular shaped roof front which led onto a rooftop patio area looking out onto the river valley below. There was a spring in the garden that emerged from the hill itself and was channelled down small waterfalls and ponds up the hill into the woods of the garden. The spring was useful for providing drinking water which was much better than having to drink what was being piped through the taps in the house. It just meant you had to collect it in glass bottles every week and store them in the larder.

The house also boasted a large inglenook fireplace with a wood burner, and an ample supply of wood in the form of fallen branches from the surrounding trees, which just needed collecting and chopping up in his more active male hunter gatherer moments.

It was set in a tranquil spot, and nestled well in amongst the trees. The small road that led to it was lined with the original Victorian gas lamps, which was some historical vestigial feature of a bygone era. Indeed, along the path in the woods that led up the hill at the end of Sam's new drive there was one solitary gas lamp, reminiscent of the one described in *The Lion the Witch and the Wardrobe*. Which was perhaps not surprising since this was where C S Lewis used to walk during his college years after he had turned his back on religion and become an atheist and developed an extraordinary interest in mythology and the occult – and where, in hindsight most of his inspiration came from. J R R Tolkien also spent a lot of time in the same spot and it was perhaps therefore not entirely coincidental that they became good friends in later years whilst both studying at Oxford.

The old Victorian train tunnel went through the base of the hill and underneath the house several hundred feet below, and gave the occasional distant rumbling sound as trains went through. The view was spectacular and spanned across the wide valley some thirty miles over to the hills on the other side, through which the great river ran, spanned in a few places by ancient bridges around which small towns had formed. These hills were steeped in history, and Sam felt very content to be living near them again. The hills were reputed to have been at the centre of the 'perpetual choirs' which related to a circle of ancient sites - that included Stonehenge - and was also the location of the 'White Oak' and an ancient pre-druidic religious site, but these things were always open to interpretation and mythological elaboration just like the ley line that ran straight through his new property. The whole area was littered with historical creativity; it was jam packed with music, art, theatre, and writing. All gathering inspiration from - *somewhere*.

It certainly had a very strong effect on people, without most of them ever even realising it.

Sam and Brina had immersed themselves in work for the next

few months and made the most of their spare time with evenings at the theatre and planning short trips abroad.

They had thought about going to Egypt for a week's holiday, the idea being sparked off by a TV documentary about the Great Sphinx of Giza. It was claimed that archaeologists believed that they had discovered a small square room in the ground under the front feet of the Sphinx, with walls set distances apart and a sloping ramp down to it underground and that this rather excitingly eluded to the fact that this space contained the source of all knowledge - a room that had been described in ancient text as 'The Library' – but sadly it had turned out to be confusingly empty and plain.

As Sam had watched the programme his mind began working again. That space was probably where the priests wielding snake adorned staffs would have gone to draw in collective knowledge in their Mind Palaces -almost certainly with the use of shamanic drugs, rituals, or a particular variety of mushrooms – which they would have then presented to the awe of the masses that fed and supported them with their hard-earned grain rations and gold. It must have been very exciting and hypnotically impressive, all those shows, rituals and impressive effects and yet curious as to why nobody ever bothered to check on results, or place any accountability or responsibility to them - or even had any real clue as to what they were all really dealing with, and tapping into.

No change there then Sam had thought.

But their plans to get away had not seemed sensible in the end as there appeared to be a lot of unrest with the 'Arab Spring' in full flow. Indeed there appeared to be a lot of disturbing world events unfolding, a lot of change happening globally, and, it seemed that the trouble was mostly occurring in places that they had both visited in the past.

A similar event applied the Delphi Oracle site – and in Greece in general. Sam had listened to a brilliant audiotape by an archaeologist who had worked on the Delphi site and he appeared to have established that the Revelations and Oracle premonitions had been generated by certain volcanic gases that emanated from a crack in the ground at the site in ancient times. This was originally thought to be the case but was dismissed in 1927.

However, this team of archaeologists and scientists had

discovered two faults meeting below the site and traces of ethylene gas in the water systems - which was the missing link - and following simulated tests were the cause of the shaman-like hallucinations, and possibly had given access to the collective unconscious, or the 'Mind and Will of Apollo', such as it was then.

The *Akashic Records* or the collective memory being the source, but like any library, it held lots of information we had written, and so it was not necessarily right about everything. It was only the summation of what 'everyone' knew 'at the time', and somewhat open to interpretation and translation issues.

At Delphi, the priestesses that were known as Pythia - and there was always a clue in the name - had been trained to inhale these vapours whilst sitting in a seat that stood over the crack in the earth. From there they received divine guidance from the god Apollo, who, legend has it, had defeated a great snake or python or dragon in ancient times.

Statements would be issued forth such as 'Go to war then a great king shall die', which were just as vague and unspecific as always, unhelpful, and yet still hedging its bets, just in case.

Oracle priestesses such as these, were also known as the Sibyls, and were shrouded in ancient mystery, oracles linked with ancient gods at holy sites in Mesopotamia, Persia, Greece and Rome.

It's always snakes Sam thought, *Snakes, dragons and serpents.*

A scene from *Raiders of the Lost Ark* came into Sam's head - the scene where Indiana Jones looked down into the cave and then up to the stars asking "Why does it always have to be snakes?"

But Sam knew that was always the way, these things were fascinating until people wised up and gained greater understanding to see through these myths using science and evidence. It also all made sense when you realised how the mysteries and legends had originated - mostly from strange things that people hadn't understood at that moment in time — and yet it all still continued today in more and more refined methods having moved on from mad ravings of prophets - until uncomfortable and contradictory and awkward embarrassing evidence gets dug up, as with the Nag Hammadi scrolls that were discovered in Upper Egypt in 1945 — these ancient documents highlighted what had been changed over time from the original 'word' - which were luckily saved before certain belief and control structures were able to sweep it under the carpet in embarrassment.

So now it was mid-spring 2011 and Sam was making the most of a fresh, bright, sunny day and he had taken the dog out for a long walk on the hills again. All of his thoughts about what had happened, and all the ideas, concepts, research and experiences he had had were coming to a point of understanding. It was, or felt, as if he had been given time to ingest it all, process it, live through it and work it all out, to a point where it all made sense.

It was one of those long walks where you weren't really sure where you were going, or how long it had taken, until your legs or stomach reminded you, and the dimming light made it hard to see where the track was, and you had to find your way home again.

Sam and the dog continued on their walk down to the path that led back to the house down the long line of Victorian steps laid down the slope in the woods. It invoked a certain feeling in him, thoughts of ancient peoples and travellers and stories and myths. He hummed the Elgar tune to the hymn *Jerusalem* in his head, "And did those feet in ancient times ... Till we have built Jerusalem..." and then he couldn't remember the last bit. The steps he was walking down had been nicknamed the 'Pixie Path' - so named because of all the sightings of fairies and pixies and 'little folk' that people had 'seen' there in the past.

He stopped by the now unlit gas lamp next to the path in the woods. "So have you seen any fairies lately?" Sam asked his dog. But he dog just looked back at him blankly and pretended not to have a clue what he was talking about. But then the dog had become very good at lying these days and had also, rather suspiciously, put on a lot of weight on lately.

Throughout Sam's life, something had been persistently trying to get him to follow a pattern, a storyline for something that had occurred in the past for a role that he was being expected to fulfil - the classic 'Hero' journey that had been defined in the past for when a change had been required. It was very determined and was generating a lot of energy into making sure it happened in the 'right way' - like a reoccurring program that had to 'improve'.

The concept of 'playing along' had been the best policy to follow at this time. It had given him time to work things out, and for the moment, being what 'IT' wanted and what he was 'supposed' to be and do, was working. It was probably a lot safer to do this than taking on the dragon without a sword or with very little idea of what he was letting himself in for, or indeed as to what the hell was actually going on. Even though IT was probably busy somewhere 'working' on the problem, most of it seemed to be being applied in fast forward, as if he was being rushed along throughout his life along some 'Classic Hero' tour ride which was short of time and had a lot to cram in, stopping to see all the instructional, educational and informative scenes, getting it, and then not bothering to stop at any of the entertainment venues. It was like being at an amusement park just before closing time.

It was all giving more weight to the concept or idea that whoever, or whatever, was 'arranging the tour' was probably female in nature. Yet whereas a real woman organising, say a tour of Pompeii, would be smart enough to include a stop and viewing of the brothel - this one was more likely to avoid it and focus more on the volcano.

It was probably best to 'play the game' as he had done until now, but he had decided that it would be on his terms and that it would play by his rules for the moment - or at least that was the idea - without getting too carried away or fascinated by it all or being drawn into too much stimulating excitement in the act.

He had only been away from the house for a few hours, and all those thoughts had gone through his head in that short time. *So much for taking a rest* he thought

Sometimes he wished his brain had an on 'off' switch, or at the very least would just concentrate on one thing at a time.

Sam arrived back at his house and the dog automatically made his way to the side gate, waiting to be let into the back garden.

Then once let through, the dog walked around the back of the house and stood with his nose pressed against the back door, just as he always did, the next step was to be allowed in, have a biscuit and then to settle down on his basket.

It was good to keep daily routines going all round - it helped everything flow and to be safe without having to think too much.

Routines helped just let everything drift on, so as not cause too many ripples, and to help keep his thoughts and ideas to himself.

CHAPTER 6 - GAME CHANGE

And then, one day late in the summer of 2011, it all changed.

It was a hot night, if felt close, humid, oppressive, and it held that feeling that a thunderstorm was on its way.

There was some sort of shift, a change in the air, as if something was about to happen, and it made Sam uneasy. He had been unable to settle in bed with Brina, and had crept into the spare room during the night, so that he didn't keep Brina awake. He had eventually nodded off to sleep about midnight but woke up suddenly at around 2 a.m.

It was one of those nights where everything felt out of sync, awkward and disjoint, as if there was something going on but you couldn't figure out what.

There was a vibrational sensation, everything was still and dark, even the owls that usually hooted around the woods in the night were silent.

The air outside felt close, unnerving, and Sam felt as if he were under threat or open to attack from something non-specific.

He had been very tired before he went to bed but he couldn't stop the thoughts going through his head. He was now just lying there, looking up at the ceiling, and trying different positions to get comfortable. He felt vulnerable somehow, exposed, as if someone could break into the house at any minute, and every noise was a potential threat.

Eventually after half an hour he drifted back into a hypnagogic state. However the feeling only got worse, interspersed with half dream or half-conscious thoughts that reinforced one another and created confusing scenarios of illogical concepts.

Then it came.

Some form of structured information started coming in that was impossible to describe or put into words, but which was trying to take form, and meaning, but could not.

There was a feeling of an external growing approaching menace, some indefinable fear that was increasing and moving towards his awareness. It wasn't something you could visualise or describe in any words, but it was powerful, unhuman, feral, and able to tap into his darkest and most terrible fears.

Thought forms started to develop in Sam's mind; menacing, tricking his imagination to work against him.

Then there was a thumping, banging noise, which Sam knew was probably just the dog leaning against the conservatory doors or the wind rattling them, but it was very loud, echoing, terrifying and his imagination worked on it, reinforcing it into a whole manner of threatening fears.

Bang, BANG, BANG! .. and then again repeatedly.

It was as if something was trying to get in, get at him, get inside the safe bubble of his home.

There was that sound too, a high pitch frequency like the sound you used to get when the TV was showing the test card, but it was more dense, focused, drowning out the silence. Just the same as the high pitched noise you got in your ears after you have been to a rock concert, or after an explosion, and with the same aftermath intensity and emotional intensity, but oppressive and threatening.

It felt uncomfortably familiar.

Sweat was pouring off him, and at that point he rationalised himself and dragged himself awake. He sat up, the fears and anxious feelings still raging through his head in the darkness.

It was as if all his protective layers had been removed, he was vulnerable, defenceless, all of his egoic immunity and self-defence had gone, and had been replaced with a paranoid feeling of insecurity.

But oddly he was aware that this was happening, as if he was both observing himself and having this happen to him at the same time. In so doing it made him conscious that it was something outside of himself that was causing it, and not in a delusional way.

Sam reached for his dressing gown and stood up. The wind had got up outside now, and was rattling the windows and the doors in the conservatory, which is what he was hearing, along with creaking and whistling through the trees outside.

Sam went out of the bedroom and along the corridor and made his way to the kitchen, concentrating as much as he could on not thinking, not letting it get to him, not allowing the fear to take him.

As he passed the dark conservatory the double doors began to rattle in their hinges in the wind.

Then all the heat and energy seemed to fade from him, drawn out. He was distracted, he decided to face it and check what was in there, make sure it was all OK.

He walked up to the glass panelled doors and peered into the blackness of the conservatory where the dog slept.

Then it came, again.

Beyond the glass images appeared, forming in his mind's eye, violent and powerful dark shapes manifested, feral and wild with an edge of unrestrained animal ferocity about them.

His dog was there still, but now it was being held by the indistinct shapes, then Brina was there too, violently restrained by these forms in the indistinct darkness. Yet it was all in the periphery, unspecific at first, shapes of his family, people he loved, not quite there but referenced as information without emotion, so that he knew what they were by an associated link or meaning.

The menace and fury started, the dog was torn apart, and then eaten alive by the black shapes in a vicious feral fury of focused animal depthless evil rage.

Brina was screaming in silence as her clothes were torn off and then unspeakable things were happening to her, to her body in graphic detail, drawn from his worst fears and tortured inability to control or intervene or stop what was happening, subjected to the horrific enactment that was drawn from the worst of every human imagination.

Then also to everyone else he loved in there, in a violent unrestrained evil –focused, unrelenting, unlimited, unbounded, utter rage. The images were all indistinct but he was given the knowledge of what was going on, the unspeakable things he was 'supposed' to be seeing fed into his mind directly, consciously, in hard-wired parallel.

All exactly his worst fears and nightmares, mirrored back to him, but in graphic vivid detail with no unconscious barrier or safety bubble of mind, or any measure of human constraint, guilt or compassion. All so that he knew what was happening, so that whatever this was, it was using him against himself allowing his mind and imagination to fill the gaps in the worst possible way, and then relaying that back to him in horrific forms and unfolding horror that no film or normal situation could possibly replicate.

This scene was also combined with an defenceless feeling of impotence - an inability to do anything about it, held, constrained, bound, tied, forced to watch like a child puppet, tortured by uncaring, unconscious malice that had refined itself in capability and technique over millennia - and it was only just getting started.

It was pure unrefined industrial grade evil, with extreme energy, and it was coming from something, or somewhere external to him, his mind, his body, his ego, his soul.

Whatever it was, was using his mind, and elements in his supressed shadow psyche against himself, trying to convey evil in information form to him, and then hypnotically manipulating his mind to see and construct it into his worst nightmare, but not in a dream experience, not as in a nightmare - this was hard-routed directly into his conscious mind.

It all had a different frequency to it too, not a vision or a dream nor reality, a sort of forced delusion, *something* else, *something* entering into his sphere from outside.

An evil or negativity with pure controlling energy not originating from him or his mind or his shadow mind or any part of what he was on any level. It was harsh, ice cold darkness, undiluted and raw, there were no natural safe limits applied here, no moral values, no guilt or conscious constraints, this was pure unconscious raw negative evil, and it was attacking him with a ferocity that would shame a rabid dog.

This was being translated through him, forcing its way through his protective immunising levels of his mind like a hot knife.

It was using any negative elements that it could find on the way, any back doors, any open windows, any manipulative tools, and then translating itself into a formation of his worst nightmares, but magnified a thousand fold, and also amplifying it using elements of everyone else's along the way.

Slicing through his rationality, mental maturity, and any ego he had left. Something very powerful, soulless, unbounded by human limits, had penetrated his mental and spiritual system, breached his firewall, and had infiltrated his mental software, and like a virus had scanned him for his worst nightmare scenarios, and was now reflectively broadcasting that back to him on the inside of his bubble's inner surface. In a torture-like manner, while he was held immobile and powerless.

Sam was frozen, like a five year old boy, forced to watch, eyes wide, a scenario of clips of the most horrific video of film scenes that humanity had ever produced. Yet recast with all the characters and things that he cared about and loved, with every evil action explained as knowledge directly into his mind, just to make sure that the little boy 'got the meaning', 'got the message'.

Unable to react, unable to protect, defend, scream, or rationalise in the face of such dark evil terror, and forced to watch the torment, immobile. His mind manipulated, warped and used against him to exact the most horrific events and worst fears he could imagine summoned from the depths of his unconscious mind and then reinforced.

With at the same time, the oppressive noise ringing in his ears like a mallet smashing down repeatedly on an anvil in quick beats. 1, 2, 3... then a pause… 1, 2, 3... and again, and again.

It was all too hard, too perfect, too believable, too real, and the hypnotic effect wasn't working, because it was just that.

Then an instant later there was a rippling effect, a wall of transparent shimmering formed in front of his face, it was like a bubble of water forming around him. It formed just to his side of the doors, like a shield, an immunising iridescent translucent bubble, a firewall filter, protecting him, reasserting the correct perceptions of the images, which all then gradually vanished as the bubble expanded out and through the doors into the room, dissipating the image, purging the scene, back to reality.

It was all gone. The only thing remaining was a cold, stark, dull, blank void.

Slowly his eyes drew in the real images the true physicality, the images faded and were replaced by two blinking worried eyes looking at him questioningly from the dog basket. The dog now was alone in the darkness at the back of the room. Then slowly Sam's eyes got used to the perception change, and the shapes of the furniture and the walls came into focus.

His body was filled with an electrical humming sensation which made him shake violently, adrenaline raking though his body, made his heart pound.

He isolated himself, inoculated his thoughts to the terror - management and levels and layers of protection kicking in fast and hard in his mind. He was immunising himself from what had gone on, restoring his system.

Programs and functions hammered into him in waves, masses of data poured into his mind. "Get to the fridge, get yourself a drink and walk around, check everything and it will all go away" he reassured himself.

His body went into autopilot, he stepped back, moved away from the scene, and turned and walked calmly into the kitchen.

He opened the fridge got the milk out, poured it into a glass, replaced the bottle, closed the fridge, drank the glass down and placed it in the sink.

He backed away and tried not to think about anything, focusing inward and on himself. He walked past the microwave and the now bright illuminated LED light on it flickered on and off, dimmed and then went out, but he ignored it.

His body walked calmly back to the spare bedroom as if he were on autopilot and he climbed back into bed. His mind was then slowly shut down, systematically, as if he was being controlled by some remote device, switching him down in levels of awareness until he lost consciousness... Then it was over.

However just before he drifted off to sleep, he sensed something, a surge as if something went absolutely totally nuts at something else, something was telling something off in a way that had no words, or description or context or describable level, and which he was not part of.

Something was turning its attention away from himself now so that he was safe, and focusing towards something else, something much larger.

It was vast, powerful, with a fury and rage, and it was probably just as well that he was not party to, or involved with what was about to happen.

It was as well that he was asleep for the rest of the 'conversation'. Something was giving something else absolute hell for 'unacceptable behaviour', for letting something in while it had been busy elsewhere.

He woke up later in the morning exhausted, totally without

energy, lifeless, and it took him hours even to get enough energy to get dressed and showered.

The world spent the next three days apologising to him in any means that it could find to do so. From random people in the street stopping him, signs, newspapers, and on TV and news broadcasts. It was more than obvious, there was no subtlety about it, it was just prolific, but it didn't make him feel any better.

He would also still be numb to any synchronistic messages for weeks to come. But then it could have been nothing of the sort.

It may all have just been him believing that IT had some responsible feelings, some sense of guilt, some conscious idea of being sorry or caring, or another part of the unconscious control game.

Frankly Sam didn't really care anymore and he wasn't prepared to give it the benefit of the doubt, and he as far as he was concerned at the moment neither IT, nor the level above IT, was exhibiting any sort of conscious self-control or responsibility, and the higher up the hierarchy or layers that you went, the more unconscious and feral it got. Along it seemed with increasing levels of power and danger.

The memory of the event would stay with him for the rest of his life. It was too strong to be erased from his system completely or be deleted from his hard drive like some dream.

But it was now isolated, immunised to some extent, made impotent, inoculated. It would no longer affect him, and he would be able to isolate himself from it and its effect over time.

It may even serve as a signifier, a piece of reference material to point to, highlighting what could happen, and also a reminder of what he may be dealing with, and the levels of protection he had around him.

He had been subjected to something that he shouldn't have been, and to something on various levels that could make mistakes and errors and produce glitches.

Yet there was no evidence, no way of demonstrating it, no way of explaining it as it had just happened to him within his bubble; the experience was not shared, and a blown fuse on a microwave was the only physical trace of the whole episode.

CHAPTER 7 - TWO SIDES OF THE SAME COIN

But then there were always two sides of the same coin, two ways of making you do things, getting you to move, do something, control from every perspective.

Good and evil, love and fear, master and slave, male and female. All integrated into control and belief structures, all evolved ways of manipulation through hypnotism.

The 'Love of God' and 'fear of the devil', angels and demons, or whatever devised and imaginative concepts could be translated by your psyche for interpretations by the collective unconscious.

Reward by encouragement, bribery and placation. Punish by fear, manipulation and threats. There were tools and tricks used on both sides of the same system.

These slavery techniques have been designed to control and manipulate blind fools, of which we are all guilty, driving them forward, upwards, over each other to work for our own 'collective' benefit, well that was the original idea anyway.

It was a driving collective unconscious process that worked because we had no choice; when you are part of something you cannot get out of - well not without some spaceship or some external perspective anyway.

It is all unfair, but then life and nature are never fair, and lack of fairness is not the same thing as cruelty.

The line down the middle seemed to be the best choice, being on the edge, seeing things from both sides, but not falling for or being driven by either subconsciously. Being outside of any hierarchies.

But this had come from beyond all of that.

Protection for Sam was essential though. This was a very, very big and powerful 'coin', and the scale of what was on either side was too much to even think about and the line he was on was very thin, and from this perspective neither side looked very attractive, not when you knew where it was all coming from and what it was about.

Collective religions always offer a reward for good behaviour -

hard work, compliance, and following the rules will eventually be rewarded at the end with a place in 'heaven' - the concepts of which in themselves over thousands of years have evolved in line with the increasing levels of intelligence and knowledge. But they still avoided the trap of being technically specific, a 'something wonderful just around the corner', the 'end of the rainbow', a 'promised land', an unimaginable Christmas present in a bygone Bedford Falls, that nobody ever seems to actually receive.

However there was always a newer and better reward waiting for you when you saw beyond these things, a new higher, more sophisticated 'get out clause', some ascension concept in many forms to some higher more sophisticated paradise or heaven, and depending on your choice of prophet, something for you to believe in, that made perfect sense.

Until it didn't, and then some newer, even higher technically sophisticated previously well-hidden concept would appear.

And yet at the end of that you would still find several large logical gaps along with a range of dragged in 'fringe' alien and dimensional concepts thrown in for good measure to account for the conspiracy, and it would all be too hard to get your head around the complexity of what was going on, on the other side of the mirror.

While here on the physical earth of course everything was getting progressively worse and getting further and further away every day from the paradise that it used to be - the paradise lost.

But that didn't really matter as you were leaving it all behind anyway, and it wasn't your problem, and certainly of course not your fault, and besides it was all too big, difficult, and complex to fix anyhow.

Somehow 'heaven' and 'paradise' had to be returned to earth, before hell on earth was reflected into the out of body dreamscape of 'heaven', and somehow make the concept of 'ascending' to here and where we are, more attractive.

Since physical reality was being projected from within a set of fields that contained it all, you weren't really ascending to anywhere, you were already there, just linked to it, in another state.

Nor would you would be 'coming back' if you weren't really going anywhere in the first place, it was just that your association with the physical biological device wouldn't be there anymore.

If you could get the idea of what you really were, rather than applying concepts of your physicality and self and ego to it, then it would become clear,

So it wasn't just 'amnesia' due to the limited bandwidth and reboot/reborn process that was making you 'forget' your 'past lives' - especially if you were one of the thousands who through regression had discovered that they used to be Henry VIII of England - you really had to rethink about what 'you' really were, and what made 'you' up.

Sam thought about where Brina fitted into all of this from this perspective; what was driving her and where did the energy and drive originate from, and did IT know what it was doing in getting her to do the things she did?

She would often seem to be there just to distract him, keep him busy, and go round in circles, trying to find what she needed to do, or discover what was wrong or might be attacking them.

Yet in the end she always managed to do the right thing, or give him what he really needed.

When she wasn't with him she was 'just a girl' - a device with a dormant program in it - pretty, kind, attractive to people.

Someone who everyone wanted to hug, found interesting, living her own life, but dormant, waiting for that something.

When she was with him, the program was active, a flame fired up - it is what had driven her to find him, seek him out, then protect him, love him, but also get him to do things in line with the information she was receiving.

When she was with him it was one of the most powerful programs that had ever existed. And when she was not with him it was all meaningless.

That probably applied to him too. That was the probably the key, but some days it just seemed all too much.

It all worked on several levels though, with differing priorities, duties, responsibilities and objectives, his and hers, and theirs. Lots of things coming in, things happening, information, work, needs and demands.

All of which had to be managed, prioritised, and planned in the time, energy, and capability that they had available.

But then that was life.

But he liked love. Love was good - but it was a love between two individuals, two programs, two 'higher selves'. Sam knew that he was easily bribed, but he was not easily fooled either, and so it took a very special kind of love to fool him, one that he was always happy to let win - well eventually anyway.

It was too easy to get fooled these days, to get worn down by the endless barrage of hypnotic sales methods, charlatans and stage magicians that would try to entice you to part with your money, energy, and time.

If you stepped back it was easy to see the type of people doing it, the character, the nature the routine. He had seen through so much over the last several years online -there was so much competition around for the small minded, the naive looking for the answers to the gaps in their beliefs, an explanation to cover and give meaning to their experiences. The totality of which they themselves couldn't get their head around.

These people would have experiences themselves up to a certain 'level' - maybe vivid dreams or revelations, meditative enlightenment or drug induced shaman like trances - none of which Sam had ever had or done.

The commonality being that they weren't actually conscious for these experiences, or were perhaps in a hypnotically suggestive 'tuned in to listen to the god channel' state, and then believed everything that they were 'told' without questioning it in logical intellectual terms, and without any integration to the state of 'reality'.

This was then translated into the priest-like, white robed, evangelical style glossy TV image, setting the stall out and the 'buy into me', with a repetitive charlatan, beguiling hypnotist, selling mode.

They all used the modern professional marketing and styling techniques to give credibility and sense to what they believed, all of which had their own 'take' on what was going on - what they were 'prophesising' - but none of them claimed to be influencing any of it, changing or effecting the obviously disastrous course that 'god' was steering, but hey salvation and ascension were just around the next corner.

Until it wasn't and a more appealing rabbit hole for the millions of followers, the now obviously illogical one they have just jumped from now appeared with even more improved selling techniques.

There were even ones admitting that these techniques were being used by religions and others, and explaining the methods, in an attempt to show that they were different, before then delivering the same selling and hypnotising methods all over again.

It made the street prophets on their soapboxes in the *Life of Brian* look very lame.

Yet they all had a similar approach, a common goal, and were probably all well-meaning, but the types, the approach, the pitch, the look, the nature were the same.

Almost as if they have a role they are fulfilling, backfilling, catching the unwary unintelligent, and how they all have something different at the end some totally illogical concept in a cul-de-sac that doesn't stand up to any logic that they cling onto.

They also used scientific references, stepping stones of logic to reinforce their stands in just the same way as theoretical physicists created imaginative concepts, say with string theory or infinite dimensional universes, to explain something which fell down as soon as you thought about it logically, or cross referenced the ideas, or looked for logical gaps, contradictions, or just used common sense.

They were all trying to give some explanation to the inexplicable, some description or image to the indescribable or some new way of thinking.

There were vast amounts of channellings, mystical revelations, alien concepts, visions and interpretations of occult and pseudo-science on the internet.

The key was to look at the end of what they were saying, see what collection of rubbish was being gathered together at the end of their explanation, like bundles of grass for the sheep.

The use of terms such as 'ascension', 'Illuminati', aliens or dimensional beings being bandied around, together with an array of symbols and imagery and meaningful scenes from popular films.

Which is what all these people were seeing on some higher channel, the 'channel' obviously having moved on from pixies, fairies, elves, and demons, which were more popular and now more believable, summoned from the not so distant past.

One in which none of this curiously existed, but then perhaps not that curious that you would want to bother checking, obviously.

Yet also many things that were believed in in ancient times were surprisingly persistent in their form and structure and words, being brought forward through collective symbols, imagery and legacy concepts and integrated with present day understandings.

You had to wade through so much chaff and fluff to get to some of the nuggets of useful information that was coming through.

It had been getting much noisier over the last several years, so much more imaginative, more complex and 'fascinating' - as if something was stirring it up, trying to keep pace, and trying to dynamically compete and adapt.

It was very difficult though to get out of that hypnotic trap though - to see beyond what you wanted to see and what felt safe, combined with the bribery of love, and the threatening stick of ever present dark hidden menacing nameless controlling evil.

It was what people wanted to hear - they wanted to know that there *was* a heaven, they wanted proof. They wanted to know there was a god or creator that was looking after them - and you could be very popular if you sold that idea to them, without obviously going into any detailed eye glazing explanations of the technicalities.

Yet there was always the key problem of physical proof to back up any part of these religious ideas, and frameworks of belief.

There was no real physical world evidence at all, or even anything that had a measurable cause and effect to back up the theories. ..... Nothing.

Sam couldn't even begin to describe how far beyond all that he had seen, or of what he knew.

But equally it was an easy trap to fall into and it was best to not believe in anything, especially with so many powerfully reinforced symbols and controls in place within the collective mind - you either knew or you didn't - and 'gap filling' was easy to do but without real proof and evidence it was always open to traps and 'suggestions'.

Indeed it was easier to define it by what it wasn't, and so far it wasn't described or defined by any subjugating religion or belief structure or science concept that he had come across, not by a long way.

He suspected there were, but with the way things were, those that knew what was really going on were hiding away, and the books that these people should be reading are the ones that no one is allowed to see or understand.

People were protected inside various immunising bubbles that surrounded them, whether it be by their religion, culture, language, geographical positioning, work or academic structures, family, academic structure or in their own homes.

It protected you, shielded you against the realities of life that you didn't want to see or know about, kept you safe from too much of whatever was outside, the REAL.

It was a natural thing, an evolutionary thing, it was what you grew from and expanded out into.

The bubbles themselves worked to keep you inside them too, the more the merrier, the larger the bubble the more energy and impetus it had.

Religious bubbles were self-sustaining clubs, cultural belief structures turned into control structures, keeping those inside seeing what they were meant to see on the reflected inside of the bubble walls so that nothing outside made any sense, was alien, incomprehensible, especially from the language side of things which governed the rules and structure more than people realised.

The 'I can't see how you can believe what you believe, why can't you see and understand what I can see?' idea.

Bubbles competed for energy, dominance and control of each other, extensions of the natural human biological animal condition. Which was fine up to a point. The problem was there was nothing influencing the top, nothing for this bubbly macro human life form to shape or control it.

Unless there was something outside of it doing that, and if the ecosphere it existed in was no longer capable of doing much about it. Well not yet anyway.

That was, however, the problem with Sam; he wasn't really part of any bubble, or belief structure - or at least he had been to and seen so much of the world and he knew so much - that he wasn't bound by any of these control structures or belief bubbles.

Which was not necessarily a good position to be in - rather exposed in fact - and if you *knew* everything rather than *believed* everything, then 'everything' had a somewhat different perspective.

The difference was that he knew what it all was. He knew how it worked and how it was structured - but without proof and evidence it all meant nothing, and he was just the same as everyone else.

Of course though, if some other idea arrived carried by a beautiful topless blonde, with a large symbolic suitcase full of cash, then he would be happy to believe in anything.

It all still left him with an uncomfortable, unprotected feeling though, as if he was out in the cold, vulnerable, and outside the safe warm immunising bubble.

There was something behind this whole process - and it wasn't just money, it was something more profound than that - they all seemed to have an underlying role, a function and they were all too 'samey'.

Yet despite everything these people said, everything they could 'see' and envisage, they were all still inside the same human operating system bubble, the same sphere of influence and control and hologram perception within the planetary fields.

Sam closed his eyes - he was now looking at the sphere in the dark of his conscious mind - it was in trouble, it was dying, and it was too blind and immature to see that for itself.

He wasn't competing with anyone outside of it here, but then there was nobody to help him either, or to share the same perspective.

Unless they were hiding somewhere like hermits like Max, attacked for what they knew, being a threat, a danger to the unconscious for what they knew of it.

He needed help.

The following morning Sam woke up early, put the dog in his cage in the boot and got in his car and headed off for a walk in the local common on the other side of the town.

He parked his car right next to the common and stood behind his car waiting for a gap in the traffic to safely open the rear car door to let the dog out.

It was still 7.30 a.m. and the sun was bright and the greens of the street were alive and fresh.

A man emerged from a house on the opposite side of the road wearing a brown suit, a shirt and tie and carrying a briefcase.

He appeared to be in his mid-50's, academic looking.

He was clearly in a hurry as he seemed to be still trying to get into his jacket while running and holding a half-eaten bit of toast in his hand. He was heading off in the direction of the train station which was about half a mile away.

It may have all been part of his daily routine, or some one-off conference that he had to get to, but Sam wondered if this was a good way to live your life.

Was whatever he was going to worthwhile, would it achieve anything?

Was it worth eating cold toast for?

Why take toast with you? It must have been something in the man's programming that meant that he *had* to eat the toast, his breakfast, he was in some sort of bubble, some sort of autopilot, unaware of what he was doing or what he looked like or that he now needed to brush his teeth.

It was a symbol - the toast - something he was subconsciously clinging on to.

He had been sold it in his mind, something to grab, something that was there, to take with him, hypnotised into believing it was doing him good or fulfilling something, a gap to be filled in his belief, unable to step back from himself and see what was going on with himself.

Sam had seen much of the same in London, but there it was very difficult to step back and see it for what it was, one giant bubble that achieved nothing, just drew people in to make money out of each other, consuming mountains of toast and growing none of it.

Sam was half expecting his mobile phone to ring and the man then putting the piece of toast to his ear in his confusion, forced then to buy a croissant on the train to go with his customary latte so that he could get a free napkin to wipe the butter away from around the inside of his ear.

The big question was, was anything he was doing necessary? Did it have any meaning, purpose, any point, or was the job he was rushing to also just a waste of time?

Was he working flat out in a career that was pointless, of no value, in some autocratic paper shuffling machine, or devising more entrepreneurial ways of selling things to bored women who themselves didn't know what they really wanted?

But then you could argue that about anything anyone did.

You could argue that making plastic flashing toys to give away with fast food, was as equally as pointless as sweeping the streets, or moving large organisations from one part of a city to the other.

But then Sam had been there, been that man, when he had been much younger and had a different naive perspective of the world.

He never ran anywhere now, and Brina never allowed him out of the house until he had finished his breakfast, and checked him over, and made sure he was ready in good time, and safe.

In a world where everyone was running blind, it was a good idea to take your time.

As the old saying by Erasmus went, "In the land of the blind, the one-eyed man is king", or at least be very wary and careful not to run, and especially not in the direction everyone else was going in, just in case there was a cliff there and you found yourself in front with a lot of weight behind you.

In the land of the blind slaves, anyone with one eye could be king - even if that sight was obtained out of the protective hypnotic bubble though drugs or insanity.

Even if they were pre-programmed with existing belief structures formed by previous 'seers' - people who didn't know or understand what they were perceiving - or more problematically what they were telling or reflecting back into the 'virtual' REAL world on the other side of the mirror.

Giving IT, in effect, all the wrong ideas and perspectives.

CHAPTER 8 - SELF FULFILLING PROPHESIES

Sam was now spending a lot more time researching relevant subjects and talking to individuals who he considered to be the most intelligent, or at the forefront of various scientific and spiritual domains and fields.

Perhaps the right word for these people was 'enlightened'- depending on your point of view, on both sides of the mirror.

He felt that it was now really important to find those who were trying to connect fields of study together and synthesise understanding between these areas rather than just taking individual compartmentalised views.

He couldn't seem to find anyone who had a complete across-the-board synthesised perspective though, someone who may have had a complete picture or overall working model or understanding of what was really going on.

This was probably due to the fact that everything had been stove piped into specific manageable compartmentalised areas of scientific knowledge, or religious beliefs, or spiritual departments, or had blinkered understandings of historical and cultural evolution.

Also combining that with what was being discoursed from the unconscious in the form of art, films, and stories, which was a biological feature of the collective mind-set and macro-organism.

It was difficult to even know where to start each time, but somehow, almost as if he were being directed, he found that he was able to go straight to the right place or person to get the next piece of the picture to fit together with the others - it was a sort of synthesising process helping him to build up the overall shape and nature of the thing, and build on the work done by others, to save him time, energy and effort. Like a crumb trail.

It was hard work though, taking the highly intelligent perceptive views of different people who were experts in a broad range of intellectual disciplines, and then combining the correct parts that made sense to him, and what he knew.

Synthesising different areas and using that to help describe a working logical model that made coherent sense and fitted in with his experiences and knowing of interpreted true reality, the REAL. Trying to match up the theories with the thing he was dealing with.

That combined with the gnosis information coming in, and correlating that with what people had experienced as 'prophets' in the past - but at the same time remembering that the original interpretations, and also his interpretation and knowledge, were all still contained within this field based biological operating system, and so may be wrong in itself, or wrong in its interpretation. IT after all, was living and learning just as he was. IT only knew what we knew.

What he really needed was to take it one step further and locate the books of others who had also tried to do the same synthesis work over many areas in recent times.

He needed to find those who had already done the work for him by compiling all their research into a meaningful set of volumes, integrating and amalgamating of science and spirituality, or a correlation of religions and their similar foundation structures.

Then he needed to somehow link all of that together with what he knew and understood, and had written down in his journals and then put it all together into some structure, some form, something all encompassing. A logical, working, provable model.

Which Sam knew would be totally impossible.

Also it was important to not keep getting bogged down with all the legacy interpretations that, although useful, had their own 'if only they had known what we know now - they would have realised' baggage.

It would be a bit like going back in time to the beginning of Microsoft Windows decades ago and engineering it for today's understandings and technology - but of course that couldn't work because you would only encounter the same problems again, having introduced self-affecting feedback.

One thing Sam had noticed recently though was that the amount of information on all of this stuff now available, thanks mostly to the internet, was vast and increasing all the time, and also that there were increasing levels of interest in all things spiritual.

On the scientific side interests in understanding areas such as consciousness, quantum mechanics, mind functions, and DNA research, was exploding.

When he had first started looking into it all several years ago there had seemed to be very little information - no real answers, or depth of understanding or energy - or if there had been it had all been very well hidden in secret schools of wizardry and academic ivory towers.

Now it was all everywhere, books seemed to be being published daily, websites, people, experts, concepts and groups.

It felt as if it were almost trying to catch him up, fill in the gaps behind him.

But Sam knew really that it was more likely that he hadn't been looking in the right places, or hadn't looked hard enough or had searched for the wrong things, or used the wrong keywords before.

It was almost a reverse déjà-vu feeling, a 'hang on a minute I don't remember that being there' feeling, as if a piece of code had been added retrospectively to the operating system, a lost memory that was now there, and always had been there.

But whatever was 'going on' it was getting very 'busy' especially as it was coming up to 2012, with a whole new set of 'takes' on what was going on, what it all meant, and it was now hard to see the woods for the trees, and filter the 'chaff' from the wheat, and there was certainly a lot of chaff to sift through, which was probably only easy if you knew how.

There were certainly still a lot of colourful rabbit holes for the unsuspecting to fall into, and to part with their money for, to enjoy and be caught up in the show.

But still nothing much that came close to what he knew. Perhaps those people, like Max, who were close to the working 'coalface', had hidden themselves away, or had been forced to be that way, and were keeping quiet. It certainly all seemed to have progressed very quickly in just a few short years.

A lot of building blocks were now being put in place, and tools for establishing ways of working - the internet had evolved a lot since then too, along with information handling software and management tools, and even recording and tracking what was going on all over the world.

There were many comments in the lead up to 2012 appearing on the possible disasters foretold by ancient prophesies, and people had tried to make sense of them with possible dates, locations, and scenarios.

It had all clearly been fascinating to many people, and in itself created quite a lot of concern and global tension. Like a form of self-creating collective stress or self-fulfilling prophesies in the same way that crowds behaved in uncertain situations.

People started to seek answers and tried to find some meaning in what was happening around them.

The problem being of course that these prophesies had a tendency, when collectively programmed into the collective mind, to become naively self-fulfilling, especially with the reflective nature of the self, and the controlling hive mind nature of the human macro organism, like mass neural linguistic programming.

In fact the same could also be said for philosophies in general - that those generating philosophies could, if they were 'giving it ideas', cause the philosophies themselves to become potentially not 'how things are' but ever more the case of 'how things are going to turn out'.

Becoming self-fulfilling philosophies.

Just in the same way as telling a child what it is, and how it should behave - which in the case of people like Friedrich Nietzsche could have had drastic potential consequences.

In the future, Sam thought, it should be made a prerequisite for all potential philosophers to have at least a basic grounding in systems control theory; to understand the effect of negative and positive feedback loops - and more importantly - parenting skills - preferably with first hand exposure. With electric cables wired to their academic chairs, and online bank balances.

That may encourage them to have more of a positive mental attitude, and some cause and effect accountability! The same concept as someone being made to change a baby's nappy when they have been feeding it all the wrong food.

This thought brought Sam's mind back to all the strange personal events over the last few years that had also interlinked with a lot of things in the news that had a sort of energy associated with them, feelings that 'something was going on', that some big change was happening in the system everywhere.

He had noted all of his ideas and thoughts and concepts in his journals as they came to him in waves of understanding almost every day. But he found it hard to merge it all together into a coherent picture.

Also having looked at what others were coming up with on the internet, both from a scientific perspective and from a spiritual or consciousness side, he had found that there wasn't really an overall answer that worked or logically made sense. Combined too with a distinct lack of evidence to back any ideas up with.

It was all so incoherent, as if he was party to some giant dream that was going on around him, of something vast that was dreaming this physical reality in which we were consciously living in as individuals.

He received snapshots of what IT was thinking and what IT knew, even though IT, in itself, was unconscious, like a giant child computer. With us a robot ant programs running around inside it.

There had been a lot in the news over the last few years about the Arab Spring countries, the changes, the political issues, the spontaneous evolutionary forces happening. Nobody was sure what was causing it, what was driving it, or how it was all happening almost in parallel. It seemed all spontaneous.

Sam remembered that when it had started in 2009, he had even given Brina a verbal list of the countries that somehow he knew would be involved.

He had also spoken to her about it a few weeks ago when there had been yet another incident and he had mentioned the list to her again.

She had helpfully commented that he had got it in the wrong order, the wrong sequence of countries - she was always a bit dismissive of these things like that, always carrying a disassociated position trying all the time to keep him real.

She was like that when she wanted to avoid the nature of the conversation, like a failsafe, but he wasn't sure if it was her being protective, stopping him from being delusional, or if it was some unconscious process going on covering over the history, the process that went on, sweeping it under the carpet somehow.

The current events in the Arab countries, were very similar to the changes that had taken place in the Middle Ages in Europe, with a culture resisting dictator control systems, being overtaken by democracy and cultural shifts in consciousness, and a need for change.

The reasons were there as to why it was happening, why it was necessary what had to happen. But what wasn't clear was why now, and what was causing it.

It did feel almost personal though. It was almost as if it had something to do with him, as if something was showing him things as a sort of running commentary.

Almost testing his views as to whether the things that were going on were right or not, unconsciously verifying. But it was easy to become delusional about it, and maybe he was just being stimulated by the news events, the interests that he had had and the synchronicity of the events themselves.

There were a lot of change events happening in Egypt too, which again was a country that they had both visited. Been to several times, and seen the various tourist and archaeological sites together and had met many people there.

It was sobering seeing the same places on the news, it gave him a connection to them, a reference to the culture, the people.

In all these places he had met lots of great people, all friendly helpful and kind, all trying to make the best of their lives in the environment they lived in, and the situations they found themselves in.

The same was also the case Tunisia, which is where the Arab Spring seemed to have started.

They had spent a week or so together there before they had gone to New Zealand. He had gone there to visit some of the more remote archaeological sites there such as Dougga for a few days. However as a compromise, he also had to book a 5 star hotel on a beach so that Brina could do a little relaxing in luxury. He found one situated between Sousse and Hammamet which was close enough to visit the sites he wanted to see.

He had found the people there to be very friendly and helpful, he had even struck up a friendship with a young lad who brought him ancient coins and lamps and intaglios from the Bedouin who found them by chance in the dirt.

Sam had admired his entrepreneurialism even though he didn't buy the goods, but the lad's persistence for a sale all went slightly too far when he managed to work out which hotel Sam had been staying at and brought round a selection for him to buy as he sunbathed by the pool – much to Brina's concern!

It had been a great week though and they had covered a lot of ground and sites, and done lots of sunbathing and they had managed to combine the solitude of the remote ancient sites with the impressive museums - including one with a vast array of beautiful mosaics - which must have taken ages to construct originally and then piece together like a jigsaw in modern times from the confusing ruins – with a relaxing break from normality

The same sorts of feelings also surrounded what was going on in Greece with the riots, and the news concerning the financial austerity and hardships.

It had been going on since May 2010, and month by month seemed to be getting worse with the country spiralling into depression, and political unrest with its membership of the Eurozone body under question.

There were more large scale protests planned in Athens and the Greek Islands, and there was seemingly no way out of the debt situation other than never ending bailouts from the rest of the EU organisation.

He and Brina had a trip planned for Greece in the following year. They were going to Crete for ten days, one of these off the beaten track customised archaeological guided tours.

Thinking about Greece made Sam think of Max, and he wondered how he was managing on his island.

IT seemed to have a soft spot for Greece a sort of nostalgic, clinging to ancient bonds feel to it - invoking ideas of Atlantis, myths and legends, which made it almost forgivable for anything on a collective level.

There had been so many documentaries on the TV too over the last few months on ancient history. However that was probably more to do with the number of new history channels available that sold on their productions.

So many places that he had visited - it was almost as if he was watching a series of holiday videos, or being 'stalked' by some global entity that was following him around and showing him where he had been, and more importantly the things he had probably missed.

There was one programme about the Egyptian temples which included the strange monolithic looking one at the Osirion - which looks very like Stonehenge and very similar to the ones in Malta and Göbekli Tepe.

The temple at Göbekli Tepe in Mesopotamia and its surrounding area, was now part of southern Turkey. It seemed to be the 'ground zero' or originating source for most of these symbols and designs and images that had spread throughout the ancient western world.

The original monolithic temple 'roof supports', along with its icons, signifiers, symbols, astrology, animal drawings had all originated from the human need to get together and have a chat, a party, in combination with various forms of intoxication.

All carried forward into the consciousness of the migrating populous from there outwards. All moved on by post-Ice Age warming, surviving the floods, and onward into ever evolving and competing cultural programmes of consciousness structures, city states, religions, and civilisations worldwide.

Just in the same way that the evolving DNA migration of the population could be mapped over time.

Other cultures such as the Aborigines and Native Americans, and certain Eastern ones that had not passed through that Mesopotamian forming or 'birthing', would not share or suffer the same historical programming or the same processes of change.

Yet as a result they would subsequently be identified biologically as a threat, an ancient alien 'them' to be moved on, attacked, defended against or over-coded.

Just in the same way as nature had always done, just in this case at a macro level. And yet if you were to go back a hundred thousand years you would discover that it all had the same source code.

If you did your homework you would also find that it wasn't difficult to track down where all the so called ancient aliens, the gods, the symbols, and the divine beings had come from. But rather than having a 'them' program feel to them, sadly they all had more of an 'us' nature and ancient or modern cultural archaeology feel to them.

With all of us now full of the successful winning programs and traits and habits. Such that within the system and interpreted by certain psychological types, almost everyone would appear 'alien' to them in their various shapes and forms, but which were really just different interpretations of programs and functions within us, at ever increasing levels or scales and sophistication and complexity.

Yet even using the word 'programs' as an analogy was wrong; it was way too complex to just do that, but that didn't stop people over the last fifty years attributing imagery to these 'alien programs' imagery and story that was associated with either fear, or had historical origins and symbolism, or shared the same nature as the originating group psyche structure.

We had been doing the same thing for millennia.

All the other links were there too; the pyramid temples in South America, with the references and worship of snakes and serpents, especially at certain times of the year, and the associated Kundalini type symbolism and meaning, and hints at secret knowledge from the gods and certain rituals.

All mysterious, but all with simple answers if you knew what was going on. Questions being asked such as 'How can this have happened?' and 'How can so many things have occurred all over the world at once?'

It would be very boring to say that it was reinforced symbolism and knowledge structures in a collective mind, supported on a field based information framework, the biological operating system hive mind dragon, sitting on the planetary field intensity server. Or also boring to say that it was just transformational change caused by the biological processes.

How interesting would that be ?

The masses wouldn't fill the coffers with that concept.

Equally you wouldn't win many high priestesses over with those ideas, that was for sure.

Or of course you could just blame it on ancient aliens. Ah yes that was the best solution, always better to blame a 'them', or demons, or the devil rather than 'us'. Especially if it was, well all a bit complicated and technical to get your head around.

But hey give it a few more decades of pseudo-archaeology and tenuous unscientific ancient aliens documentaries to keep the storyboard and plot rolling.

Ones that ignored any contra evidence, so you didn't have time to stop and think or question the logic. Look for any real evidence or check the consistency of the whole thing, and before you knew it you would have your very own new religion.

Just like all the previous ones, and their also rather insubstantial, illogical, and irrational documents of truth.

Ones that all sort of looked like some child had put them together in a rush but had come up with something that seemed to be very believable.

But ones though as an adult, when you stepped back from them, looked at them closely, and of course when you were awake just seemed a bit lacking in something. Mainly logic and evidence.

If there was something that really got genuine trained archaeologists angry about it was to see these 'spiritualists' trying to shoehorn anything they found into their own belief structures and legends.

Taking anything that emerged out of their spiritual 'channelling' derived through and from the collective historical myths, like say Atlantis, or the more recent ancient aliens.

Then trying to force the archaeology and science to somehow fit that picture. Blindly ignoring the hard scientific facts, evidence, and above all ignoring them and their list of academic achievements and then selectively reinterpreting and shoehorning what was there to suit their own agenda and mental picture. Even though it was wildly illogical, irrational, and in many cases self-contradictory.

But hey it made fascinating watching.

This was also a situation that the US military and government and defence industries had also fallen foul of many years ago.

In the 1950's and 1960's they had initially been very interested in this new 'alien' phenomena, and had secretly used what was being 'learnt' to generate ideas for technology and craft that people had 'seen' and had allegedly been inside of.

Just in the same way that geniuses were given ideas from the collective mass knowledge base, the collective could also use its unconscious imagination to come up with the most believable and imaginative new technology and theories.

But also in parallel would try to figure out what this really was, why it was evolving, and where these virtual 'things' really came from. This was all reinforced by the collective post-war fear and the massive explosion of war driven technological advances and theoretical scientific concepts and strange new things appearing in the sky.

Because they knew the facts, these organisations became very secretive of it, and tried to collect and gather and utilise anything that they could from people who were sensitive to it all.

Unfortunately and embarrassingly though it took a long while before it was realised that these were ideas that IT had got from within itself from sci-fi books, TV series and films, and its own collective virtual dream world rather than anything that was actually alien technology that had been channelled. All the ideas of which were then amalgamated with the most advanced scientific thinking and technological concepts at the time from within itself - its own collective mind's imagination. Yet oddly nothing that would get off the ground – well for very long anyway. With lots of holes in the logic as well as the ground.

Post-World War II, the world was a very uneasy place everywhere. There was a lot of secrecy around and experimentation going on. Air bases in the US with odd looking craft with new shapes - the ones of which that did get airborne came crashing down, along with their non-human rubber and plastic pilots, inside roundhead riveted craft.

All ending in embarrassing non 'alien like' crashes and expensive failures, and some very upset and confused people wanting to cover up the embarrassment. Fuelling ever more conspiracy theories, and ideas of secret alien agendas.

It had then gone 'back to the drawing board' again for the last few decades, with more of an emphasis on scientific and conscious reasoning than on the unconscious childish collective imagination. The collective 'us' turning out to be not the most reliable of sources for scientific advancement.

The only conspiracy therefore, ended up being the amount of money wasted ,and the lack of control of departments and defence organisations, which had all been given blank cheques and carte blanche restrictions with no attributed accountability or coordination. Along with storing compartmentalised intelligence, which was out of the control and out of sight of senior government.

All that combined with what the Russians were doing and being done to, along with their own set of secretly squirrelled away German scientists - who were somehow at least ten years ahead of everyone else with their designs, technology, and new spacey sci-fi concepts.

Kids with new toys eh? Just as well 'God' is keeping a careful caring eye on everything he thought.

Sam could see it all now. He could see what was going on, why, and where it was all going, and it made him so angry.

No one person or group knew what was going on with these virtual 'Aliens' - no one had seen the bigger picture or worked out why this had occurred, or even realised what was really happening or why, and they still don't really completely understand even now.

There were just so many groups and departments jumping to conclusions, and some exploiting opportunities at all costs, and some covering up the chaos.

The truth was out there, and he knew the answer, it wasn't them, *it was all us*, and it was all from a species point of view - very embarrassing.

But then we are very good at covering up our mistakes, especially irresponsible and really embarrassing ones. Ones that had also in themselves compounded and reinforced the problem of the mess we were now in.

With hundreds of types of 'alien' now rather than just the four that we had in the early 1960's - but then sci-fi too and technology and collective imagination had come a long way since then as well.

Yet still nobody was asking why this was actually happening in the first place. What was being gained from it, and why it has so much control over people and the system, or why so many people were searching for evidence to back up this ever evolving new religion. What was causing the underlying drive.

Sam rubbed his face with his hands in frustration.

He really had to pace himself though with what he watched and read. It was all very well watching a documentary or reading a book and then fitting it all into the map and structure in his head of what it all meant and how it all worked.

But when he went to sleep at night he would dream some very vivid dreams, as if gluing pieces together and making it fit and opening things up to 'more stuff'.

The following night he woke up slap in the middle of a 'conversation' dream in which he found himself on a flat map of the world which showed the layout of night and day and the Pacific letting the world sleep - but not these days.

It was an Old World map, showing that the Spanish invasion of South America had switched off a light.

The Sun was rising in the East and setting in the West as normal, but the map was indicating that there used to be a dark area over the countries while the Pacific Ocean was illuminated, the words **'just need sleep'** appeared - which seem to imply that IT used to sleep, but that it was now kept awake permanently with 'people' awake 24/7 with the formation of cities on the West Coast of America and the East coasts of the Pacific.

The rhythms of the world had gone. It all seemed a little tenuous to Sam, and there was no idea of knowing if this was correct, or some idea that IT had invented for itself, or if it were just a dream.

It was re-enforced a few times after that with images and things in the news and magazines, but it was, as far as Sam was concerned it was IT's own stupid fault, and not something he could do anything about, and so he wasn't exactly brimming with sympathy.

There was just too much knowledge and too many ideas and events coming in too fast, too much waking up in the morning with 'stuff' in his head, and walls of synchronous events happening every day.

It was all just too much to deal with at the same time as trying to have a life of his own, and it wasn't benefiting him in any way either - quite the opposite in fact.

It was like he was in a never ending unconscious diametric game, developed and refined by people from the past, just learning more about it all the time, and yet playing against an opponent that seemed to always be one step ahead, and who always knew what move you were going to make - in a game we were forced to play.

Something had to change.

It was now mid May 2012, and early evening, and Sam was watching yet another documentary about the current research taking place at the Large Hadron Collider at CERN near Geneva.

He had his feet up on the coffee table and was sat on the sofa reading some notes that were rested on his lap. The dog was in its basket next to him - as Brina was out of the house for the evening he was allowed to' get away with it' in a male conspiratorial setup, the dog had that 'smug' look about him but kept a slightly nervous vigilance for the sound of the front door.

Sam was going to complete the conspiracy by have a sneaky beer but as he had to concentrate on the work notes had decided to put it off until later.

The documentary was fairly innocuous and it primarily focused on the projects currently being worked on and some of the history of the development of the site and how the LHC worked, which Sam had seen in a few magazine articles a few years before.

The documentary then focused on the work going on looking for the Higgs Boson particle and the extensive studies and investigations that had been carried out and where they were with their research.

It briefly explained the standard model and the historical theories behind their work over the last century. They showed the construction of the LHC and the inside structure of it with the large tubes coming out.

Sam had this same picture as a poster on his office wall and he had often thought that it looked like the underside of a giant metal octopus – and there was a small man in the photo wearing a hard hat placed in the photo to demonstrate the size and scale of the LHC which always amused him.

The film also showed the exploding animated diagrams of what happened when the particles impacted and the swirling exploding mass of particles and energy spirals came off them.

The octopus shape stuck in his mind. It was a concept he had had before somewhere, an analogy for the collective mind, how we were cells within it, organisations as groups of cells, and countries or cultures were like organs, and tentacles were various religions, functions, and the way everything could operate independently but also as a whole.... A giant metal machine-like octopus.

The focus of the documentary then changed to talk about the investigative work going on at that time, and the collaborative work where they were exploring the potential range of frequency bandwidths in which it could exist, and how most of it had already been eliminated.

The tone of the presenter changed to that of someone who seemed tired and almost resigned to the fact that it would never be found, and as such may not exist at all. In which case it was all 'back to the drawing board', or in this case glass blackboards with lots of colourful symbols and squiggles on. All to explore other more colourful and imaginative theories to explain the effects which would take on new vigour and energy in their exploration.

"Perhaps they would never know, never find the answer, never make sense of it" the presenter continued.

It was at that point that Sam took more notice.

His head started to gain an intensity and a cold flushed feeling spread over face, his mind started to expand and thoughts and concepts started to form.

He seemed to be involved in something, some thought flows and concept analysis at many levels.

Something was 'going on'.

However he couldn't work out what the whole thing was about.

It seemed to relate to things he had seen in his so called cosmic consciousness experience, that 'vision of the true Reality' and knowledge download that happened many years earlier. All combined with what was being shown here, and thoughts that he had had since then, knowledge and information he had read casually in various scientific magazines and journals over the last few years. It was as if he was being shown something tentatively, or being asked if something was correct from what he had been show or worked through or understood.

The documentary then began to draw to an end and the only two remaining frequency bands were highlighted on a diagram.

"These were the only remaining places that the particle could exist, and equally they were the hardest ones in which to carry out tests and experiment in... " went the commentary, "...but it is unlikely that anything will be found now considering the amount of testing that has been carried out so far..." it went on.

Energy flowed up his spine and around his body and his head ached for some reason.

Sam was getting angry, and he didn't exactly know why.

Pulses of tingling energy coursed up and down his body.

"But that's not possible" he mouthed.

It had to be there, he knew already, he had seen it.

There was no other alternative that made sense either, it had to be there, he had already visualised it, understood it in its field state context, perceived it working. He had 'been inside the knowing of it', and experienced it being described in conjunction with many other things, and how it operated with the quantum gravity field along with other particles, and other fields, to store and manipulate and evolve information.

He had seen it all and understood it all in context, in parallel.

He had been 'in it', or the collective understanding of it, in flowing knowledge form in that experience years ago, he had interacted with the immediate combined knowledge described from and by and within fields. Been 'in the know'.

There were too many other interactions and functions that meant it *had* to be there too, or they all wouldn't operate.

There was no other explanation or solution, it just couldn't be described in 'real' physical or mathematical terms, you had to be 'in it' to understand it, and 'know' all of that at that moment.

He knew it was there, and how it operated and how it interacted with everything else.

Although he didn't know how he knew, or was able to describe it, he just did. He just knew and it was all still there, in his mind.

Although he may have been getting a little rusty on the words and terminology of quantum physics, and complex quantum mechanics concepts these days - he was sure on that one, and he was sure that IT knew it was there too.

But that wasn't the point here.

It didn't matter if what he 'knew' was correct or not, whether it was right or not. Especially since it had come from, and been derived within the collective mind, it could well be wrong anyway.

That wasn't the problem though ..... The problem was one of control, and being conscious or aware of the process happening.

The same thing had occurred with many people in the past, such as Wolfgang Pauli, who had been shocked to find that 'god' had led him down the odd rabbit hole or two or quantum physics to try and see what was right with enlightening visions.

There were probably several people around now at the front end of the quantum physics heated debates that were sure that it wasn't there, that another solution was right, and would continue to be sure for some years to come, having been thus illuminated by 'god' or divine enlightenment or revelation or gnosis. While IT busily covered all the rabbit holes in, and as far as divine driving forces around at the moment trying to work it all out and what it was, this area was the hottest.

Everyone was trying to be the 'one' divinely driven to uncover the answer, the truth, the meaning of life, a unified field theory, and the answer to life, the universe, and everything.

But not until IT had worked it out first. But as we hadn't even proved the existence of gravitational waves yet, that was going to be a chuffing long way off, especially as the theoretical physics approaches were just creating more elephants in the room.

Sam knew that IT knew, that IT unconsciously knew what was going on, and that IT was manipulating the situation.

He also knew that IT didn't know everything.

The real question was - what the hell was going on here? What was really happening? He knew that IT knew all of this, and so it had to be manipulating the situation unconsciously, playing some sort of recurring game with everyone, with the scientists, exploring and trying every avenue or path or rabbit hole. Before being allowed to move forward, by being given proof and evidence.

Sam took his feet off the coffee table and sat upright, and narrowed his eyes.

"What the hell is going on here?" he said out loud, and he made the dog jump in surprise.

The dog first looked at Sam and then at the TV, and then looked confused as if he wasn't sure if he were meant to be doing something proactive, and looked round as if to check whether a squirrel had run into the living room.

Information and knowledge started to flow into Sam's mind.

They were deliberately being held back. People were being kept blind until the last possible minute just in case IT was wrong, forcing us to use our imagination to come up with other new imaginative scientific concept or possibilities, even though IT already knew.

Something knew it was there - but only very recently, within the last decade – something knew how it fitted in, how it worked, and how it integrated, and how it was derived from a field structure.

If of course those were the even the right words to use.

IT had known for some time. It had even been found before now and the evidence had been conveniently lost or 'not seen' from other experiments. IT kept spinning people around in circles.

But this wasn't deliberate - it was just a subconscious process, like a discovering dream journey, a macro mind that was exploring pathways and elaborate dreamlike ideas. Thoughts and collective neural directions that we were expected to work on, and scientifically rationalise and prove in physical reality.

IT needed proof, but wasn't willing to let people find it until everything else had been exhausted, every other avenue checked, all the other moves played out.

IT knew what was in the cupboard but it didn't want to face the reality, just in case the consequences were something that it didn't like, and then that opened up another doorway to something else that perhaps IT wasn't prepared for.

Sam was sure that IT did this with lots of things, and that IT had done so throughout most of history - stringing things along that it had seen through us in our minds, or had worked out collectively but not individually. Concepts where no individual had subconsciously joined up the dots or had all the pieces and had the whole picture, but IT was able to within its own macro context.

The obvious was there to be seen, but only rationally obvious in a collective state-based information system, where all the gathered data was there all at once.

But until it was rationalised from that form into an individual form, and was then tested and visualised, it remained in that uncertain, un-rationalised, unobserved form until verified and confirmed and processed into knowing.

The human mind would operate in much the same way - denying things in its mind that were in plain sight, until it could form a recognised pattern, and see beyond its own hypnotic protocols of perception, recognising, and rationalising.

Sam wondered how many other things in its collective memory IT had seen or witnessed in the ancient past via some person or group - some observation, some happening, or event that had now been lost and forgotten. That was now unseen, which had now become myth, legend, and then used in an ever expanding collective imaginative story, with ever more complex possibilities and outlandish theories and dreamy non logical emotional inventive ideas.

'Planet X', Atlantis, aliens, the Great Flood, the list was endless, but all with something at their source that IT had seen and remembered through us in some form, or through our interpretation, but didn't know the logical provable rational answer, and so was, like a child's imagination and dreams, trying to find every possible imaginable option as an answer that made sense to explain what it was perceiving.

The documentary on the television then finished by showing a large group of scientists in a lecture room discussing various theories as the presenter carried on discussing what future work would be done at CERN.

It is all wrong, thought Sam. IT should not be behaving like that - it was lazy, manipulative and wasteful. IT was applying a control structure to these people, and to all of us, so that it was always at least one step ahead in the unconscious game.

This was fine up to a point, but it was now just looking after its own interests at our expense. The balance was wrong, there was nobody consciously taking the wheel, and it was unconsciously and constantly outsmarting us as ourselves, and rewarding those that supported that controlling process.

Yet ultimately there was no direction, no plan, no conscious awareness of what it was doing.

IT had to wake up and smell the icebergs.

Sam was now stepping back from it all to figure out what was going on. It was 'unacceptable behaviour'. His mind started doing things that he could neither latch onto or describe.

It was as if he, or his 'higher self', was scolding something, and he felt himself getting angrier and his anger grew way out of proportion to the situation and then he remembered the night-time incident in the conservatory and all the other things that he had been subjected to and then fury and rage welled up inside him, and he felt the top of his head ache and his spine tingle with energy.

He seemed to be telling something off and snapping it out of some state, but he seemed to be doing this at a very high level.

Yet he could only do this because he knew what IT was, and was able to see and know what was going on. It was as if he was forcing self-awareness onto IT – like an ant shouting at the colony that it consciously knew that it was in.

As the documentary finished and the credits and music started to roll, Sam's eyes flicked down at the dog in the basket - which was now looking at him with an expression of surprise and nervousness.

He kept repeatedly looking up and down, first from Sam's eyes and then to the top of his head again repeatedly, with a 'do you know your bloody head's on fire?' sort of urgent look.

Then the TV switched onto the adverts for chocolate, fizzy drinks, cosmetics, shopping malls, and cruise holidays.

Sam switched the television off using the remote control.

He got up and paced the room trying to calm down, energy still pulsing from him his mind racing, thinking, working concepts out.

He then walked out into the garden in his socks and onto the grass and the dog followed. He kind of wished he had had that beer earlier on now. But at the moment he didn't feel like anything, he just wanted to clear his head, calm down. So he just walked around the damp grass breathing in as much of the air as he could, filling his lungs, his heart racing.

Nobody was stopping to ask why, or stepping back and looking at the bigger picture - why are things like this obscured, why are things made difficult to see, compute, or interpret?

The Higgs boson particle was only a theory for 50 years or so. Why should it be so hard to find, why when the alternatives just did not make any sense? Why did we exert so much effort in coming up with alternative solutions, especially when the solution could only make sense with it in, and why was it in the very, very hardest and very last place we looked?

Sam also suspected that if you were to look at some historical experimental data now, you would discover that we had actually found it quite a while ago but somehow hadn't noticed it - which was probably the case for quite a number of things.

Something was unconsciously, yet deliberately, making it difficult. Something was controlling information in a need-to-know, protective, academic, compartmentalised manner.

IT was not allowing people to see the bigger picture, not allowing them to understand until it had moved on to the next level, an unconscious control structure that was always one step ahead.

Yet this was a necessary, if naturally selfish, mechanism for control that was going on within the collective subconscious.

Information evolving into knowledge within the subconscious, within the information field structure it existed in, and projected from. Fed into the minds of its components which was then translated into serial logical interpretation, processed into thought-form and then reintegrated as a co-evolving macro form.

Consequently IT knew far more of what was going on than we did, but it was knowledge in a different form. It was correlated information but without reference or conceptualisation or perspective of physicality and interpretative meaning. IT knew all that we did and more but in a different state, form, parallel, and context.

But Sam also knew that IT didn't know everything, which is why we were being driven unconsciously down every blind alley, every rabbit hole, constantly seeking possible knowledge and understanding and potential philosophy and theory on ITs behalf.

All this going on before allowing us to move forward. Always keeping us one step behind in the direction IT was being driven and trying to grow in.

But we didn't have enough time and resources to hold things back to be blindly kept dumb in this way. We did not have enough energy to waste, being sent off needlessly down cul-de-sacs. All just in case IT wasn't right or it had missed something, and all for ITs benefit rather than ours.

So it was the collective mind of humanity that was the problem - what IT had evolved to become, and us following this unconscious never ending phoenix cycle. The problems we were encountering were all due to this diametric hive-like collective nature, this unconscious cold, harsh, feral, brutal, virtual machine like, yet biological, operating system behaviour. IT was software stumbling around within the planetary server, and over coding all the other eco operating systems without any external control and guidance.

Many analogies came into his head at once trying to picture the problem from many angles, and get the right interpretations, understanding, and perspective from many different ways without actually having to be it all.

The *Pinocchio* analogy came into his mind of IT being Pinocchio. Did he have to become a Jiminy Cricket to the wooden clockwork child, and make it feel guilty or should he call for help from outside from the Blue Fairy?

There was just too much coming in too fast, at too many levels.

He then imagined himself as Jiminy Cricket wearing Neo shades, standing in front of the screens in *The Minority Report* with 4 screens for the various psychological types or the suits of cards in *Alice in Wonderland* or from tarot cards. This was integrated with dozens of Precog feeds coming in, all displaying many probable futures, this being rationalised and made sense of by large groups of compartmentalised technical departments to help him understand what was going on, on the screens.

His mind was racing to keep pace with the conceptual ideas flowing in, drawing on all the physical perceptions to bring them together to rationalise and make sense of the concepts he was trying to form.

Something, just as the situation and plot in the *Minority Report* film, had made him angry too, and he was now having to channel that anger into a choice that consciously changed things.

But also he had to get others people to do this work too, do what he was doing right now. Be consciously aware of the game.

The analogy wasn't working - there was too much information flowing in to try to deal with so he tried another concept.

It was a game, so he had to think of it all as a game, like a game of chess.

Sam had played chess a lot as a boy.

He used to be very good at it and he even played at National level in various Congresses all over the country.

He once played against Nigel Short, a famous very young Grandmaster - although he had been several years older than Sam at the time. To Sam he seemed a bit like a computer, and Nigel had admitted to him that most of how he played was unconscious; he could just see the board and interpret it, and the ideas of which moves to make just came to him in his mind.

But to win at the Grandmaster level he also had to apply a conscious rational logical element to that decision making process, based on his opponent. Otherwise he would just end up playing like a computer and losing – but you also had to know your opponent, figure out what they were thinking, where they were going, and judge their capabilities, nuances and habits. So that after a while it became more like poker.

A few months after this particular chess match, Sam had sort of given up playing, and he went on to computers and studying operating systems, and computer role playing games.

Thankfully this phase occurred well before he grew up, and he had to face the far more complex game of 'girls'.

Then, all of a sudden, Sam thought about the *Titanic* analogy and he formed the concept in his mind again. He again imagined it being driven by an unconscious computer - that was our collective human unconscious - in a dark room, that was operating like a chess computer, simply becoming more intelligent as we tried to outsmart it.

Which of course we never could as it was us, all of us, individually, culturally and humanity collectively.

In effect everyone was playing chess against themselves, and ourselves, on many levels, through their psyche and collective layers.

Some weren't even actively playing they were just going through the motions. They were so blind, zombie like, hypnotised, they weren't even aware they were just moving the same pieces back and forward all the time, in their own mind, their own reflective containing immunising bubble.

The analogy started to form in his mind, and he tried to wrap the problem into the analogy.

But it was not easy. His mind was still wandering around thinking of other things, problems, concepts, ideas.

He knew IT could only go so far unconsciously. What needed to happen now was that it needed to have self-awareness in macro form. In ITs own mind's eye it needed to overcome the reflective nature of consciousness at all levels.

IT now needed conscious elements to not only make decisions for it, and within it, based on what is going on in physical reality, the physical *Titanic*, the human planet, but also on the virtual ship too the human collective mind, which were in reality all one together within one system.

But not just that - we also had to fix all the programming errors, glitches and lack of balance between the unconscious 'sides', wake everyone up to what the hell was really going on.

In this particular case, it seemed particularly poignant that the Higgs boson had been nicknamed the 'God' particle.

It was in essence the link - among many links - into and from the unified field, the universal etheric field of consciousness, the other side of the mirror where information went to and from, in and out from the physical devices and structures to and from the virtual 'other side' which was in actuality all part of the same thing.

The information didn't go and come from and to anywhere else - it was all the same system, with the physical drawing the short straw as far as information percentages went, which in itself was deliberate to maximise the errors and glitches, required for evolution, along with the bandwidth limitations back and forth – a lot of which IT hadn't worked out yet - and as a consequence neither had he.

But that wasn't the issue in this case.

Even though IT had the knowledge that was there in its mind, it was sending people off in all directions, lots of fanciful ideas, theories, and concepts.

IT already unconsciously knew it was there, and Sam knew it had to be there, he had seen it, in IT's mind, which was one of the things he had seen too much of, which is why he was dangerous.

But that in itself wasn't the problem; the problem was that this had been going on for far too long, this unconscious direction and control, and its manifestation into belief structures, control structures, thoughts, ideas, ways of working and so on.

It all had to change, IT had to become conscious of what it was doing and more people needed to become aware of this, be the conscious self-aware self-conscious mind's eye of ITself.

This was on a macro-organism level, it was totally 'unacceptable behaviour', and the only thing to do was to tell it off, wake it up to what it was doing, make it conscious of itself.

So many thoughts went through Sam's head, *God particle, why wasn't it Goddess particle?* What were these feminists playing at, missing an obvious thing to attack like that? Or perhaps it was a double bluff to throw every one off the scent.

He thought for a moment about when he had read about Parmenides, the ancient Greek philosopher, and his encounter in the dark with the 'goddess' - which was obviously an early discourse of what was going on in the collective human mind translated through his own psyche - well, what words in poetic form that actually still survived that is, those that hadn't been swept under the carpet like so many others.

Even then IT had admitted it had been deluding him, outsmarting him and everyone in a diametric process. But of course he couldn't understand what that all meant, it was all long before we understood evolution, quantum physics, bio mechanics, religion, psychology, and all the elephants in the room caused by trying to describe reality and the REAL from the wrong directions, and obviously a long time before IT realised what was creating itself either.

Yet it was still giving us the drive and urge and need to find out what it all was, how it all worked, what it all meant, and still growing in size and appetite.

It was time to stop all these games of chess, all these 'riddles in the dark', especially as 99% of the players now seemed to be offline or just playing games against themselves, asleep, or playing *Call of Duty 7* with all their Metis, cunning and outsmarting ability, channelled into nothing, diverted away from the reality, away from the real games, away from the real tables where you could win real inflatable elephants.

CHAPTER 10 - CHESS WITH THE GODDESS

So now Sam felt he was ready, he had all the concepts and thoughts in his mind now.

The sun came out now too and bathed him and the grass around him in warming energy.

He closed his eyes and let the energy and flow of the feeling well up inside him. He allowed all the knowledge of what was going on come to him, into him, what it all meant, the gnosis of data. All the learning and the understanding he had gained over many years and since his experience in New Zealand. He focused on what he had seen, and what he had been involved in, and what was wrong.

He drew together all the analogies and knowledge in his mind and focused on the messages and concepts that he was trying to convey, and needed to somehow direct.

He created the scenario in his mind of the *Titanic* again, with the chess computer on it, and everyone, including him, playing chess against themselves. Games which were all being unconsciously controlled by the ship's computer.

He imagined himself sat at a table, and he made a move in his mind 'Knight to Queen-10'.

He drew in a few mythical analogies, ancient roles, a connection to ancient Tarot concepts and the psychological structures. With connections to rabbit holes, films, books.

All the ones he had read and seen, all the ones that had meaning. All the ones that had scenes that could be used to integrate as a message, like the use of chess in *Blade Runner*.

Anything to try and construct a meaningful yet conscious message, but one that was a step away from the game, and out of the controlling rules, archetypal manipulation, and hypnotic levels.

He knew this was an illegal move, since there were only eight rows or columns on the board and he also knew that this notation contravened the algebraic naming convention for describing piece movement, the language by which we were bound, controlled and described by.

But nothing came back, it was an illegal move, it was not

something IT could process, or understand.

IT, like him, had to play within the rules of the biological system and the laws it had evolved within.

He then tried amplifying it with 'conscious override' added to it. This was directed not at his 'self' opponent, but at the operating system behind it, the thing that was pulling the strings.

But that had no effect either.

He then tried making the same move, but on everyone else's boards in his mind, but the same result came back.

He realised that to some extent that he was now able to influence the moves of other people through the system, but that he was still not changing the situation, that was still 'within the system', still unconscious behaviour, falling for the trap of 'becoming Illuminati' and influencing the unconscious but yet still being driven by it, hypnotised by it and its aims.

The key was to force the system to make conscious decisions for itself, as a macro-organism, as one mind, see and know itself, and hand it the wheel of the ship.

He tried to visualise it another way.

He closed his eyes and imagined himself sitting at a table with a chess board set out on it with pieces in play again.

He found himself opposite an Ancient Greek goddess, and realised that this was a game that he could never win as the goddess was one that had evolved as part of his self - a psyche interface control program, to and from the architype formations in the unconscious.

The trick when playing chess with the goddess is to realise that you can never win. The only way out is to not play the game, to ignore it, walk away, or if that failed, to lose in a certain direction.

The more you play to win, the smarter the game gets. Then just when you may think you are winning, you discover another more sophisticated level, in an ever evolving game of deception.

In Sam's case though he had somehow found himself in a place in his mind that everyone was trying to get to.

He had seen what was there, he knew it but couldn't describe it, and now he was trying to work out why it was playing games with everyone else, and why nobody else could see what he could see.

The room he had now created on the ship was vast and full of dozens of similar tables that filled all four corners of the room.

All the other games related to the academic, cultural, scientific and spiritual rabbit holes, in never ending ever evolving, outsmarting, unconscious, political and controlling, yet compartmentalised processes.

It was a ballroom with giant chandeliers hanging and swaying from the ceiling. The games had been going on for millennia with numerous players, all getting so close, all seeing parts of the picture, but never quite making it, never quite working it all out. Never figuring it all, yet oh so very nearly there.

Then for those that had seen too many of the games being played, seen too much of the same repeated scenarios, synthesised the picture from many angles, got close to the sharp edge of Occam's razor, they had been immunised, isolated, with any evidence hidden away or burnt, or even more extreme measures being taken to cover it what they knew. Always covering its collective arse.

You could never get past the opposing goddess or god, not from this direction; you could never overtake the tortoise in this 'almost there' never ending story. Sometimes you may see past one game, win one battle or see more than you should in one compartment, but you would then simply be drawn to another table to try to solve the overall riddle. Always trying to get the bigger picture, to get at it all, see it all, fill all the logic gaps, and somehow know it all.

You could only move say from the spiritual experience table to the quantum physics one, to mathematics, to religion and so on.

In an ever evolving field of play.

Until you ended up at the table in the middle.

Sam in his mind now spent a lot of time watching the games on the other tables, seeing what was there, the state of play, the same patterns and processes. He saw the structures, saw the other areas 'trying to work out what it was' from both sides of the mirror.

In most cases, he could see what was missing, and he could now see what they couldn't see, why they had not quite come at it from the right direction, or why they weren't allowed to see it all from a different objective view, or be able to make the connection and come out of their compartments.

Some of the games had come to a grinding halt, and no one was playing at them anymore. Instead people were favouring some of the more exciting, lively and interesting tables, the ones with more energy and money associated with them.

He was also aware that he was being prevented from being involved in actually playing at the other tables and was not able to interact with the players, nor they with him.

Which in itself was telling him something

But he had seen it all now, he had it all in his mind, the reality was in his head, he could understand the whole thing.

His main failing was his descriptive ability and correct technical or scientific vocabulary, and he wasn't that great at using the right academic terminology either above Degree level.

He didn't have the depth of study, vocabulary, and tenure in many areas to compete at the front end on many of these games from the bottom up. He also knew that he was still out of his depth on some areas, just like when managing an organisation.

But then he didn't need to now, and he was coming from the other direction. So he didn't need to play, but he still had to try and help, try to describe it and work it all out.

He could already see what was going on, see the answers, see why people in all the areas were getting stuck, contained, beguiled, unconsciously unable to see what they were in, or why they were being driven, and why certain areas were so popular.

They were all competing from different sides and for different agendas, but they were all still unaware of what they were in.

But no one was able to see the whole thing, or influence it, or do anything about it all.

But hey when the ship went down there would at least be plenty of people around who could describe it happening from their own perspectives. They would all be there to say 'see, we told you so', and showing and explaining from their crumbling ivory towers why it was all happening.

But then it was always all too difficult, all too big, all too complex to do anything about, and even if you tried in parts it would unconsciously work against you, or belittle you, with plenty of condescending snorts of overinflated academic pomposity, and hierarchical shielding.

People throughout history had desperately tried to work it all out from so many different directions, without realising that they were in a game, a game in which they could never win or see the whole overall complex system.

Area after area, rabbit hole after rabbit hole, the same process the same journey, the same outcomes and individual role types, all just helping IT to work it all out for itself, unconsciously adding to ITs knowledge, its controlling and manipulative devious collective 'us' in capability and self-shaping nature at the same time.

Fresh new players were coming and going all the time with at the end of each game, all the pieces and all the money going back into the box on each table.

It had all started long ago, with just one table. But there were so many now. Yet that was part of it too, it was compartmentalising the problem to make the whole less easy to see beyond. And all the time it was making what was really very simple as complicated as possible.

That was nature for you... Which was fine up to a point. Up to the point when it was no longer 'fine'.

Which was right now...

Besides he didn't really need to be able to describe it. Sam *knew* it, and he didn't need to be able to articulate it in great technical, academic and scientific detail. He didn't need to write down a theory of everything, of unified fields, of life, of it all.

When he could do what he could do, it was much easier to apply the approach used by experimental physicists rather than theoretical ones.

The sort of 'smash it and see what bits drop out' approach and work out what IT was from that. With what it was becoming glaringly obvious.

Or even using the philosophical and technological approach of 'keep bashing it hard until it starts working again' method.

He settled himself down in the seat a little more at the table that nobody else wanted to play at, the one in the middle of the room.

It was the one that others got to sit at if they had seen too much, or seen past the goddesses at the other tables, who were all still one and the same.

The game, he noted, was already in play again.

This version of the goddess he was sat opposite already knew what move he was going to make, which piece he would choose and where he would move it. She could work out all probable futures, she knew what he was thinking and she was also partly him too, yet in another context.

She made her move with a somewhat nervous expression on her face. It was the expression of someone confused as to why, when they had been playing against the greatest and most powerful minds in history, geniuses, mystics, and prophets, was she now sitting opposite a strange five year old boy with a smile on his face?

A smile that looked suspiciously like he was about to do something mind numbingly stupid.

Which of course he was.

She also found it disconcerting in the way that he sat on his hands and jigged his feet back and forth, tapping his heels together impatiently waiting for her to make her move.

But nothing would catch her out or confuse her, not even the kicking of the table, or the fact that, for some unknown reason, he was wearing bright orange inflatable armbands.

The thing that did concern her though was that the usual group of followers were not standing behind him.

In whatever form they usually took, they were always there behind each game in the room, from Initiates all the way up the scale of Tenure, all following the person who was playing the game against her at that moment in time.

No, there was just one woman - who seemed to be dozens of women all in one - and there was something odd about her.

Normally whoever was standing behind her contestant was there to serve the goddess, to identify the best player to help compete in and improve the game, fulfilling a role, an unconscious need, and keeping a controlling eye on them.

But this one had her arms folded which meant that she held some authority. It was if she were wielding him, bringing him to the table, but that she didn't quite know what she was doing.

Neither did she have the usual keen, enthusiastic, hypnotised hungry energy there either - she was more angry and frustrated.

At first it almost seemed as though it was an expression of 'What are you going to do about it bitch?' look -but it wasn't - it was more of a 'this has to happen' look, a sort of motherly insistence.

Yet for some reason the goddess couldn't work out where that element within the woman was coming from, and it wasn't archetypal in the same way that everything else on the ship was, she seemed to come from - elsewhere.

Sam could sense this in his mind, and what his mind was creating as part of this imagined scenario, and oddly he didn't know either - but it was there - something that came from outside of the ship, outside of IT.

The goddess though knew her game, so she ignored it. Avoiding distractions was important. She leaned forward and concentrated on her opponent. He was different, and so interesting enough to play with, and he was able to recognise her for what she was.

There was nothing, nothing, he could do to win though, but she would learn, adapt, deceive, and outsmart every move he made in this unconscious reflective game.

Even when the pieces on the board switched between black and white, and from whichever side you started playing from, it made no difference to her. She could play and be the opponent on both sides, that was all part of her, it was all for her benefit in the end, as well as ours too, but only up to a point.

She was constantly becoming smarter, more sophisticated, more knowledgeable, and more complex in her game. It didn't matter to her that there were fewer players now, making fewer moves, with less enthusiasm and energy - she just carried on blindly playing to the same patterns, habits, structures, and rules.

Even the fact that he had portrayed himself as a boy would not throw her, indicating that he could not fall for all her usual charms, bribery and methods of persuasion. Even the neck brace he was wearing would not work, a clear attempt for sympathy, empathy, caring, compassion - for which she had none - she would never let him get past her.

But this was something new, and interesting enough.

Then he made his move. He reached forward to move his blue knight, the one holding a sword rather than the other that wielded a wand-like staff.

It was the move that she had seen, but she showed no emotion.

He winced in pain momentarily as he reached forward, and he moved his hand back to rub the back of his neck.

It was a deliberate move to point something out to her. Then he pushed his chair backwards, stood up, and her eyes followed him.

For a moment her expression was impassive. He had given up. That was it - it was over, she would now just wait for the next opponent.

Sam then looked up at the giant ship's wheel-shaped wooden chandelier swinging high above the table. It looked like a wagon wheel with handles and was suspended high in the air near the ceiling. There also seemed to be similar ones above all the other tables in the room. Yet nobody had noticed them before now.

The goddess looked up too, why had she never seen that before? She looked surprised, but oddly the chandeliers looked as if they had always been there. They all had dusty, ancient chains and antique shades and old lamps just as they might have had when the ship had first been built.

Perhaps she had never looked before, never made the connection, or was it some glitch in the system, something or someone playing with her memory?

She was sure that they hadn't been there before, she was sure there had been just one crystal chandelier in the centre of the whole room, and that was how it had always been.

But she must have been wrong, these must have always been there - they were all encrusted with dust and were ancient and they sort of fitted in with the style of the ship, and she would have seen if anyone had swapped them because she was always in this room. Was this some sort of trick?

She looked back at the boy suspiciously, and also now somewhat warily. He had grown, he also looked a lot older, losing his boyish naive smile – he looked as if he knew something, something he shouldn't.

The feel around the room changed, it had a certain edge to it, something in the atmosphere that was different, and there was a high pitched sound in the air, that sort of hissing sound you get sometimes in your ears or when the TV is on standby.

The boy looked up to the ceiling and her eyes followed his.

The wood of the wheel above suddenly ignited and burned away from the inside, exposing a very solid, heavy large metal wheel inside.

It glowed silvery white, with an alchemical magical radiating heat energy feel to it, throbbing and vibrating like some giant cog, in a vast machine, a wheel that was suspended in mid-air by now creaking chains.

It had some fiery letters written around the flat curved edge, ones that he had carefully written in plain English.

He was using what he knew from knowledge he had gathered at several other tables, and he had combined that knowledge together using the same processes that he had observed on each table. All of which was key to the secret of getting through each one, seeing past the elephants from the other direction, but also at the same time breaking several rules, which was fine as he was getting a bit short on time and a little more older and wiser to be playing these sort of myth games any more.

The goddess's face turned deathly pale and her expression changed to that of confusion and fear, and she started looking around for help or some form of adjudicator, or for some explanation as to how and why he was managing to 'break the system rules' and 'change the game'.

This was certainly 'not allowed', and very 'unfair'.

Everyone in the room was now staring at the wheel suspended in the air - they were all mesmerised and were watching what was going on at his table, ignoring their own games. They also ignored the new wheels that had appeared above them all - the wheels that somehow had always been there.

The wheel above his table now became hotter and heavier, the suspending chains creaked under the strain, and the energy from it filled the air with a tingling humming radiation feel.

Sam momentarily thought about putting some large elephants on top of the wheel, to give it some extra weight, but that would have just complicating the message.

It needed to be clear, obvious, and to carry a punch.

He lifted his chair back away from the table a little more, stepped back, and then he let the wheel drop.

The connecting chains snapped, releasing the wheel, but leaving it so that the lights and shades and chains were retained in the air.

There was a moment of silence as it fell. It smashed down hard, straight and flat into the middle of the table, and then it plunged through it. Which in Sam's mind was a sort of a neutral move.

The table exploded, and the pieces shattered everywhere, and the floor gave way beneath. The heavy wheel crashed its way down through the floor to the level below, and then the level below that, and continued on its symbolic way down through the layers carrying its message with it.

It bypassed all the protocols, evolved controls, and immunising layers, in a somewhat unsubtle and noisy manner.

The crashes of breaking metal and splintering woodwork as it went down echoed like it was almost saying a new word at each layer – it sounded like **'Why, Doesn't, Some, One, Do, Some, Thing, About'**, and then finally after a brief pause **IT?**

At first there was only silence... and then gasps.

"It likes symbols" he said, looking down the hole, "let's see how it likes this one."

He had made very sure that it hadn't gone through the hull of the ship - that would have been irresponsible - you wouldn't want to suddenly plunge everyone into the REAL, into the depths of the ALL, or expose everyone to the harsh cold unforgiving depths of the bio field reality.

No - not when we had spent so long building a ship to protect you from it all, to save you from the harsh brutal nature of the depths, from the sea you wouldn't want to swim in.

Even though it was the very thing supporting you and stopping you from drowning in nature, or from smashing you against the unforgiving rocks.

The ship's alarm bells and claxons started to sound within the control room and all over the ship. The sprinkler system was activated, lights flashed, symbols started appearing, and people ran about hysterically.

The medics arrived a few moments later with a stretcher, some oxygen, and medicinal brandy for the central goddess, who was now lying on the floor in a somewhat unflattering and horrified state.

There were now dozens of people and goddesses staring down into the hole in the floor, and down through the levels below, seeing what was there, seeing what he had done, and what was happening down below. Then - as one - they all turned to look at him in both awe and total horror.

But of course now, he was no longer a just little boy. They could see him as he was - and so could she.

He looked at her frightened face for a moment. "You are going to have to trust me" he said to her clearly, but there was no emotion in his voice, no feeling, and the feeling was not mutual.

"It will be OK, but it is time for you to wake up."

The goddess had now transformed into a small terrified girl with blonde pigtails, and then for a moment she became artificial, like an android or a shop mannequin, with an unsteady and indistinct voice.

It was time to go. He had to get out fast now.

His last thought was that this probably needed to happen at all of the tables, with one of the same type of woman that had been behind him, more Brina's at each table helping forming a bypassing couple at each one.

He could suddenly see many Brina programs around the room, some clear, some vague, but quite a number of them.

Then a sudden thought came to him of other Sam programs - other male players, other people like him in the game, a brief vision came back of there being five, all from various continents and sitting at other tables.

Five left that he could see, only five where there should have been many - which was a little worrying - although he knew that the data itself could not be relied on.

He was being distracted, beguiled by something interesting, that was trying to deter him away from what he was trying to do.

So he then extracted himself from the imagined scene, to see if that had worked - which of course he knew was unlikely.

You couldn't talk to IT, 'god', in that way, with words, and neither could IT or 'god' talk to you with words either, not in visions or in your head or your mind. Just in the same way as you couldn't talk to cells in your body.

No - the only way that IT would or could communicate was in the form of world events, changes in the masses, and thoughts or feelings in the minds of everyone, and meaningful synchronicity.

In the same way that you moved your arm, or had a thought that involved many cells, IT as a macro-mind, a macro-organism, would act in the same way, and probably take a long time doing so. IT being so big and all that.

But it was time for it to wake up, and see itself, perceive itself consciously. Time for the game to change, before there was no more game left to play.

He opened his eyes to the bright colours and iridescent images and smells and sounds of the intense beautiful world around him in the garden. Standing barefoot on the grass, ripples of energy flowed up his body and arms, into his spine, in the bright sunshine.

He was so furious with it all and was in a state of rage at the ridiculous situation that we had managed to get ourselves into.

Something had to change. He closed his eyes again and concentrated his thoughts and plunged into the darkness of his mind, and immediately he could visualise the vivid depths, the iridescent darkness of what he had seen many years before. There was that feel, that intensity again and presence of vibrant energy.

He wanted to visualise the whole thing as something, perhaps shaped as a child, as a Pinocchio, or a baby. So that he could tell it off, shape it into something that was more human, give it a virtual slap on the arse, but he could not. It had no shape other than what he had originally seen which in itself was just information - a dark void with nothing but energy and structure.

He tried to envisage it all as a massive growing ball of lemmings, fighting with each other about to fall off a cliff, but he couldn't.

You could not visualise it as anything, for it was not anything that you could make sense of in any sensory formation that we had developed. You could only derive it by what it did, its process, its nature, and not by any physical or even virtual form.

Sam concentrated his mind at IT, from outside of IT, from outside the collective human mind. Which in itself wasn't the right term for IT really, it was more complex than that. Yet he didn't want to use the 'g' word either as that would have just given it shape, other people's physical interpretive forms, and other people's symbolism and meaning.

He even avoiding any basic mathematical integrated geometric shapes of its own interpretation of the unified field structure. The laws and structure it was supported and originated within. He also avoided any other biological non-human mappings of data.

He could sense IT now, sense the power, the energy, that 'in the face of the divine' everything. It was a very dangerous sense of presence and all his alarm bells went off at the same time telling him to get out of that state. But he chose not to.

He focused his thoughts towards IT, knowing what it was, and told IT off, forming the *'NO'* as a thought, while at the same time holding all the knowledge he had in his head of what was going on within IT. Presenting the why and the what, so that he could show IT why he was doing so. He also focused the rage that was building up inside, giving the message purpose, authority and strength.

He tried to remember that this was what was causing everything, keeping us beguiled, controlled, manipulated.

There was nothing forcing IT to change from outside, and this was the only way he knew to rectify that. Otherwise it would just carry on generating more and more wheels of unconscious process on both good and evil sides. All to keep people unconsciously constrained with ever more complex yet still the same scenarios. Ones that nobody would ever see past, on either side, not even at the highest levels; they were all still hypnotised and controlled by this unconscious system.

He tried also to visualise IT as an ants nest and imagined himself shouting at IT, the vibrations causing IT to finally react and become aware of something external.

He figured that there was no point in fighting parts of IT or trying to change IT from within, he would have to deal with the whole thing from the outside, make it self-aware, and all the while knowing what IT was, being a 'mind's eye' of itself.

But something would not allow him to do that either.

He repeated it again, **NO**, and directed his energy and thought towards it. But IT didn't react, and his energy was almost gone.

Then for a brief moment Sam was aware that something huge had changed. It was like a conscious spark, a shift in energy, or frequency. It had almost a guilty feeling to it, a reactive wake up call for bad dragon behaviour, for unconscious laziness and hyper manipulation, and needless undirected control and corruption.

It was a shock for something, nothing had ever made IT feel

that way before, like a shudder. Nothing had ever responded or stood up to it like that, or been able to move or see past it, and outsmart it, know what IT was, and then turn around and do that to it - whatever it was that he was actually doing to IT.

From ITs perspective, something within itself - within its own mind and yet outside of it - was telling it off, a Jiminy Cricket moment of waking up the wooden toy. Bringing the human biological operating system into self-awareness and guilt.

It was a conscience, or consciousness, directing it from outside of IT, and yet inside. Shaking or slapping IT awake from all the unconscious laziness and 'couch potato' autopilot spoilt childlike city-state controlling thoughts, that it was used to having, in the absence of anything else making it do anything.

It was a projected external, yet self-aware, thought form coming from both within and without.

He breathed in deeply and focused his mind back to the now. Sweat began forming on his forehead, and searing energy flowed through him and from this thing that he was now focused on.

It was a very dangerous thing to do, what he was doing now, whatever it was, and very hazardous - he could sense it, that edge, that warning feeling and sense of approaching trepidation and fear in his mind.

But he didn't care. It was the right thing to do at this moment. It was the responsible thing to do - he seemed to have the ability to do it - and if he didn't do it then who would?

So he then formed the thought in his mind - **_WAKE UP_** - and he directed it at IT - at IT but from outside of IT - along with all the implications of what that meant it had to do within itself. Around the thought he formed the ideas of everything that the concept entailed at every level, the waking up of everyone within it, thereby raising the levels of consciousness and awareness of everyone to what was going on.

IT actually being conscious was the key here - not going through the unconscious game, the meditations, mystic paths, visionary journeys - you had to get IT to come to you and wake up. Wake it up from outside of IT and not as a voice or thought or dream in its mind - IT now had to express itself in the physical world in a conscious, meaningful and obvious way.

He wrapped all those thoughts around and focused again at what he now perceived in his mind.

He thought of all the people who had died for what they believed in in all of the wars, the people who had tried to make the world a better place, and he thought about the crazy situation that we had now got ourselves into – of what was wrong on all sides, the mindless corruption, the control, ignorance, laziness, bureaucracy, brainwashing, and self-destruction.

It made him angry. "Wake Up" he repeated out loud, and then with more energy and concentration he thought directly at IT, **"WAKE UP!"**

And then a few moments later - he wished he hadn't.

A wall of energy hit him with an unspeakable and indescribable power, and now in the darkness of his mind he found himself fully exposed to something imminent and harsh and intense, fresh, unnerving, extreme - an iridescent depthless black. No known words or expressions existed to describe what it was like - it had no comparable physical similarity or feel, no sensory description – it was just raw energy.

Something reacted to him, and also *at* him, with a power that you could not possibly begin to describe.

His ears rang with a high pitched sound, energy totally drained away from his body, and his body became bone cold. But he would not stop until he knew that the concept had got through.

There was a pulsing sensation now too, a rippling, tingling, with walls of images, thoughts and knowledge flowing both into and out through him and around. All pulling everything from him, and opening him up to the outward cold harsh REAL, and the dark void that context or expression or words could describe.

But he would not back away, would not give up, he held strong there in the face of IT, unbreathing, until several seconds later he couldn't stand it anymore and he pulled himself out. But not in defeat, but because he knew that he had done what he needed to do, he just knew somehow that he had done what he had to do.

Suddenly his body became totally numb and his legs gave way beneath him. His body crumpled onto the grass and he rested his head on his knees, breathing hard. It was done and there was a release and a moment of resolution. He then tried to shut it all out as quickly as possible and breathe life back into his body again. Then time seemed to waiver, became indistinct, non-quantifiable.

All of this happening while the smart Earth Angel Blue Fairy, whose fault it probably all was anyway, was busy down the supermarket buying something healthy for dinner, whilst politely getting angry at the zombie sheep-le, the Burberry bag wielding women in their stiletto operated 4x4s, and the lizard men from Planet X carrying their shopping lists from their grey wives, who were always suspiciously and conspiratorially hogging the fresh fish counter, and buying out all of the DVD box sets of *Grey's Anatomy*, *Conan the Barbarian*, and the original *Star Trek* TV series.

Several minutes later he remembered lying flat backwards, and the dog coming and lying down on the grass next to him and resting his head on his thigh, and then there was nothing, emptiness. Time seemed to stop.

There was just nothing until Brina came home and got him inside the house. His mind was everywhere and nowhere. He didn't see her face, and her shocked expressions. He didn't hear her words or her crying, or see the unjustified guilt in her eyes.

In the next few days she took him to be checked over. He had body scans, brain scans, he was taken to expensive neuro surgeons, psychiatrists and therapists. Days of tests, checks, consultations, all a blur. But they could find nothing wrong with him. He was pronounced rational, sane, and all the results came back as normal, aside from his existing neck issues and associated bodily pains.

After that it would take him just over two weeks to recover safely in his home.

But still not satisfied, Brina then took him to a world-renowned specialist healer and spiritualist who she had met several years earlier. He was an expert in a wide range of 'spiritual' techniques and alternative healing tools and methods, held a PHD in physiology and was qualified in osteopathy and other scientific disciplines.

He was the one that all of the other alternative specialists and spiritualists went to see when they themselves couldn't cope with the demons anymore and needed his help.

He immediately seemed to know exactly what it was that Sam was doing, what was going on, and what was happening to him.

He hadn't ever met anyone like Sam before. They both talked and he was able to relate precisely to what Sam thought was happening and they seemed to have the same perspective view of what Sam thought he was actually doing.

Sam didn't need to explain anything to him or to try to make him understand. He explained what Sam was doing and confirmed that he *really was* doing these things.

He helped Sam with a few more sessions of treatments for his spine, and prescribed some homeopathy to help balance a few things out, and help calm the 'traffic and noise coming in'- but reassuringly he said that aside from that Sam was actually OK - he seemed to be doing what he was supposed to do.

Which at the same time seemed somewhat disassociating, and made it all feel as though what he was doing was just some sort of work or job – even if it was a thankless one, where the employer seemed to be charging him rather than the other way around.

The significance of this event would be much more profound than Sam could have ever realised though - not just the astounding significance to science of all the hard work from the scientists, but a change in the overall game plan and nature of what was going on.

He had woken IT up and had brought a tiny part of the subconscious dragon to consciousness that could be thought of as a baby, a metaphysical child that was now making its first waking tentative conscious steps, and starting to see itself with its all-seeing collective mind's eye.

All hell broke loose for the next few weeks following this event. The news was literally full of events too numerous, too rapid, and in too much depth for him to even have time to write in his journals.

Then two weeks later there was flood of announcements from CERN stating that the Higgs boson had possibly been found, in an almost excited, pleased, 'telling him' sort of way. Which in itself was only a small part of what had happened.

But it had taken a lot out of Sam both physically and mentally and he needed time to get his body and mind back together.

Yet by Christmas he had been, due to a strange set of circumstances, invited to a dinner in the Houses of Parliament by the UK Space Agency. The function had been attended by various scientific academic bodies and while Sam was there they announced that CERN had reached Level 2 of Certainty that this was indeed the Higgs that they had found.

The presenter of the news even looked directly at Sam as he made the announcement to the guests and everyone was pleased and clapped - everyone except Sam that is. The bandwidth, apparently, had been determined as 125 - which was exactly halfway between the two competing quantum theories, and which of course now ruled out both original camps and concepts.

It now meant that they had to start all over again with new ideas on theories of how it all worked. *Which will undoubtedly involve more free lunches, more grants and more stovepipes*, thought Sam.

He felt like speaking up at the event and asking if he could have a receipt for all the money that had been paid for the work gone into coming up with alternative theoretical ideas, and wanted to ask for a refund on all the previous ones.

But he hadn't had enough to drink for that.

Besides the last thing you should do is punish a child with sarcasm, especially when it is so pleased with itself.

But the alarm bells and the magnitude of what he was involved in were disconcerting, it wasn't just this one event, this was just the start...... How many more things would IT do this with?

How many things that he had seen in the pieces were yet to be revealed with proof?

But then IT probably had just as much trouble explaining and understanding knowledge in our context and reality as we had within IT's. The key was to establish the common ground, work a path through the jungle to the mountains and get them to meet in the middle, but in a balanced and fair shared benefit way.

Which just wasn't happening at the moment. There weren't enough people around who saw what he saw, knew what he knew.

This waking up process was long overdue and he didn't have the bandwidth to cope with it all on his own with Brina, he needed others and fast, and he needed everyone to be part of it, and he couldn't do that physically - he had to get IT to do that within itself and the physical world.

He had to make a Plan.

CHAPTER 11 - BACKWARDS DREAM

Early one morning at the end of January 2012, Sam woke up into what he knew was the hypnagogic transitional state between being asleep and awake. He was getting used to it by now.

He was too hot under the warm quilt and sweat was clinging to him, even though the air in the room was cold. Things were racing through his head - thoughts, unconnected worries and irrational, illogical concepts were gnawing at his brain.

The air seemed damp, still, and noiseless. The sheets stuck him as if they were suffocating his skin but he didn't dare move in case he woke Brina who was fast asleep next to him.

He watched her in the dim light and saw her eyelids flickering as if she were in the middle of a dream and she occasionally mumbled something non descriptive and incoherent.

As he lay there he became aware that he had woken up with his arm folded over the top of his head again, bent at the elbow, his forearm covering the crown of his head.

This had happened so many times in the last year or so and it was as if subconsciously he was physically trying to block something off, to protect himself from something. Like an unconscious reactive gesture you would use to shield yourself from something falling on top of your skull.

It reminded him of a night dive that he had done in the Red Sea just off Sharm-el-Sheikh a few years earlier.

He remembered that he inadvertently shone his torch directly at an octopus that was sleeping in the darkness on a reef.

The poor thing had folded all of its arms above itself and over its eyes to try and get away from the intense beam, shielding itself in vain from the intense and sudden blinding light.

Sam had quickly diverted his torch so as not to blind and overwhelm the creature, but he had felt so bad about that incident and now he knew exactly how the octopus had felt.

However he had the distinct impression that whatever was doing this to him did not have the same awareness of what it was doing, or have any concept of responsibility or care.

Every morning he seemed to wake up exhausted with an arm, or sometimes both arms, wrapped protectively around the top of his head, just like the octopus.

It was like some weak subliminal attempt to try and limit the information coming in, to filter it, or to reduce the bandwidth of data being transferred into and out of his mind while he slept.

But this situation this morning was different.

Something was very wrong, he could feel it.

There was an odd, intense vibrational feel in the air, a pressure that he couldn't associate with, or reference to, or with anything that he already knew; an unknown feeling that something was going on, something happening somewhere else.

Something that shouldn't be happening.

It was the same unnerving feeling that you get when you sense that perhaps someone is trying to break into your house, or is lurking in the garden in the shadows outside and is spying through your windows.

There was also a sense of déjà vu, not the feeling itself, but just the same sensation of having it.

A disjointed, unsettled, unnerving sense mixed in with that feeling you have when you miss a footstep on the stairs and get a sudden shock to the system and a race of adrenaline.

He closed his eyes again and he felt the warning, a concern - something was trying to warn him about something.

He realised that it related to something that he had thought about the day before, but he couldn't define it, or narrow it down, it was too convoluted, too complex and in-depth.

Then momentarily, there was an image in his mind that he had seen before, a situation from a dream that he knew he had once had.

It felt as if it was a dream that he had a long time ago — it was distant, remote, vague - but then again it could have been at any time. He was trying to explore in his mind the scene, find a path to it, with a sense of focused uneasiness and trepidation.

Then images came to him to get him to try and formulate the concept.

The images were of a farmyard and there were open barns and farm buildings all around him full of big old farm machinery.

But it didn't seem right. It was all static, as if it this were a scene at the end of the dream.

This was the end of a neural network journey, a situational memory where he would have finished up at, at the end of the dream in question. It was as if his dream sequence film was frozen at the last frame of the film or scene, and somehow he was supposed to recognise it, and remember the whole thing back regressively from that. But he couldn't.

He could now sense the things around in the virtual scene in his mind, the things that he had seen before in his dream. Remembering, recognising the familiar, the sudden knowing and recollection of items, positions, scene layout and perspective of a favourite childhood storybook.

He was also being forced to work something out and steer a route through it. Navigating or exploring how he had got there to this point at the end of the dream, winding back the images through links, connections, references, thoughts, feelings, but all in reverse.

The only way to do that was to stumble into them, the objects, the meanings, in static form and then pick your way backwards through a virtual neural memory network or maze.

But there was no logical path or connection, no flow back or journey, it was like finding yourself in *Wonderland* without a map to take you back to the rabbit hole.

He was being asked to work his own way backwards through his own previous dream, to get at some message or symbol.

This was not easy and it took a lot of focus to concentrate on following the linked data before finding doorways back through into parts of the previously navigated dream journey.

It was all going in the opposite direction to how his dream had been, and against how it would originally have been linked neurologically, and organised naturally in flowing sequence.

It was *Little Red Riding Hood* in reverse.

When he got stuck, he tried looking at each element that he had created before in his mind again and it hurt.

It was difficult, he was struggling to grab onto associations and context like a reverse maze, as if he was trying to traverse backwards through one of those scene-based computer puzzle adventure games that he had played in his youth.

Then he found an old and rusty wooden-handled scythe resting against a wall.

Then he was beyond it to a field of long grass and poppies, still and motionless. Ah! This is where the idea for the scythe had come from - he was on the right track! Again his mind was being forced back through the dream trying to get him to its beginning, to see what it was referring to.

It took him a few minutes to work his way back through several more locations, situations and dream scenes which had meaning and static feeling and emotion, but it all had no context whilst in this reverse direction.

He was getting the hang of it now, building up a technique.

The next location had motion and activities, but it was all going backwards, his mind was now able to recreate the backward interpretation for him of the scene, but it was very hard work, like following a crumb trail of clues and markers, and then having to create the story manually.

There were odd transitions of scenes now too, highly vivid and intense, with Egyptian style archways of stone blocks built into larger smooth walls. Then rooms within pyramids with vents going up to the sky, and burials inside large rock structures - this must originally have been a very long dream.

Then out into open areas, fields of wheat, followed by a series of more specific quick transitional scenes, ones that he was able to progress through quickly without having to process the meaning of.

A few more cul-de-sacs and image connections and he was there - back through his scene-based neural network dream and where he needed to be.

This was where the energy was coming from - somewhere at or near to the start of his original dream - and this is what he needed to be seeing now.

Then it was there in front of him - a building, it resembled a giant pure white masonry kiln, or a large smooth stone igloo with no windows. It was set in amongst some olive trees that swayed the wrong way in the wind, and it was whitewashed like the Mediterranean style houses, and there was a giant dome with a covered arched entrance on one side. The ground was parched and Sam was aware that there were cicadas even though it was silent.

Then the warning feeling intensified to a roaring sound in his ears. Then the shape changed, morphing in reverse, into a representation of a giant white and bright clam shell, which would have been originally closed, but was now opening to show the female figure of Venus standing upright within it.

It ended in the position as she would have started at the very beginning of the dream looking exactly the same as the famous painting by Botticelli.

But Sam could not process what he was seeing or being shown, nor could he rationalise the context of what he was seeing with what he had thought the day before.

It was all working in the opposite way to how his brain worked and how it normally processed information. He was where he needed to be to get the information and association of the building structure and the meaning of the Venus symbolism, but he couldn't do anything with it, he couldn't think, he couldn't rationalise it all and integrate it consciously.

But whatever was pushing him here was insistent that he did so, forcing him to 'get the message' - to work it out, to understand, and to 'see'.

Then it suddenly all made sense, he got it, he remembered. But he also realised with alarm that he was now stuck. Stuck by whatever was blindly holding him there in that state.

In his mind he had the image of what it was that he was being warned about, but he was locked there, repeating over and over.

He was held by the energy, not able to go forwards or backwards. He had 'got' what it was now — he understood the symbolism- but there was something physically wrong, wrong with his brain and mind - and the panic rose in his quickly like an approaching fear gathering like waves of anxious trepidation.

Sam gasped, and he realised that he hadn't been breathing, or more to the point that he had actually been breathing backwards.

His whole mind and his brain were operating in reverse - thoughts couldn't form correctly and he suddenly experienced a surge of adrenaline — he opened his eyes and, now in sheer panic, sat upright, gripping the sheets in his sweaty hands as both physical and mental terror spread throughout his body and mind.

He had to get some air into his body. He had to get out of the room, make a change. But it was all backwards and he was unable to register anything at all.

He could sense Brina react next to him, waking, responding, grabbing her dressing gown, out of the bed, talking fast. But she was saying nothing he could recognise, everything was backwards.

His body unconsciously moved outwards and away from the bed, his lungs still gasping backwards.

He bounced off the walls and slid through into the corridor. He made it halfway across the lounge before he was stopped in his tracks as he hit the sofa.

The room span, he was gasping, fear surged through him but everything was all the wrong way around.

Then he tried to move again, but even though he was trying to get to the kitchen he was actually reversing back towards the bedroom.

He froze in sheer terror again, trying to form a sentence, to cry for help, to explain, but he couldn't, and he then raised his hands in front of him as he tried desperately to grab onto some form of sanity or anything physical in any form of rational order.

Sweat poured from him, he shook violently in adrenaline fuelled shudders, and he groaned incoherently.

Brina was there in front of him in seconds, but he couldn't focus on her, or even turn his head to look at her; she was saying things to him but they didn't make any sense.

To him they were just slow groaning phrases. She put her hands on the sides of his arms and started squeezing and rubbing them as she tried to get him to look at her.

His mind had locked and everything he tried to think of, anything, was all backwards, and it would then drag his mind to his previous thought, then working it backwards to what he had dreamt.

It was as if the whole world had gone into reverse but his body was still trying going forward.

"Ba-ck-w-ards" - he managed one word in juddering gasping convulsions.

He felt Brina pause as she tried to work out what he was saying.

He held his breath - which was the same as it was forwards - he was relying on his body to force him to do what he had to do in the right way. He held, held, held and then it broke the chain of authority. Down to the raw subconscious fundamentals, his body gasped for air, and then slowly he started breathing hard in the right direction.

He rested his hands at arm's length on the back of the sofa as he stood there leaning forward, gasping and focusing, rebooting his whole system from the bottom up.

As his mind started to switch from one direction to the other in convulsions he looked at Brina's eyes - but he couldn't process her expression or emotion.

He concentrated on the breathing and nothing else; it gave him focus, energy and direction. He built up his forward thinking, and he was there, "mind going backwards" he breathed out quickly. "I'm OK…will be OK… in … in a minute" he was eventually able add.

His mind was not OK though.

It was flashing and jumping around everywhere, and his head hurt, and the terror was still with him and images and scenes and impressions flashed all over the place in his mind.

It was a slow process but after about an hour, and with the help of some tablets, he was calm enough to go back to some form of sleep.

It was one of the imprinting experiences though, and the feeling of it would stay with him for the rest of his days.

It was not something that he could describe to anyone else, nor could he express the absolute animalistic terror that it had invoked. It had shifted something at his very core, reversed his poles at the base level if only for a moment.

Or at least, that is how it felt, and the dangerous power that he now knew was there was not something that he could easily ignore.

The next day, in order to try and understand what it was that he had been 'told', Sam went back over what he had been researching in his laptop the day before.

As he ploughed through the history of his searches - the image of the International Academy of Consciousness and the buildings they had created in Portugal were presented to him from one of the websites – but he couldn't even remember that he had actually looked at that website.

It was so obvious – the buildings in the photograph staring back at him looked exactly the same; they were surrounded by woods, the same shape, everything, exactly as in his re-engineered dream, along with the opening and the female element of power and knowledge that had been represented.

But he wasn't being warned about the organisation itself - he was being warned not to attempt to try to recreate what had happened to him before.

Trying to repeat that cosmic consciousness experience by force would be highly dangerous for him, if not fatal. It should only be used when necessary and naturally in conjunction with events and processes.

Going on what had happened the night before, Sam was now quite prepared to take IT's word for it, even if in doing so it had nearly caused the same situation to occur.

He had no recollection of having had the original dream before though, nor any idea of when it had happened in the past, but he knew a warning when he saw one, and was smart enough to take it on board.

He had the feeling that there were a lot of things in place at many levels that were protecting him and his mind, like firewalls and guards, immunising layers and bubbles.

Everything happening without him even being aware of, just as with the immunising and protective biological processes that went on within your body.

So taking stupid blind trips and trying things out just for the sake of experimentation didn't sound like a very smart thing to be doing.

Not to mention the fact that processes that were busy working hard filtering, refining and translating the information he needed to do what he had to do and that he was actually insulting the very things trying to protect him.

This was just IT's way of telling him that sticking his mind and brain into the nuclear blast furnace of the collective human mind operating system was something that should only be done as part of a process. Something you should only do in line with other things going on, not something you should force to happen or chase after. It wasn't a game at that level.

Unless of course you were happy with the risk of carrying your brains around in a bucket.

A few days later, after he had recovered, Sam had wanted to talk it all through with Brina, to attempt to explain in detail what had happened, what he had gone through and what he had figured out.

Again though, she didn't seem to want or need to know.

She just wanted to make sure that he was OK, safe and well. It was just as before, as if somehow she knew what was going on unconsciously, and knew that her job was just to look after him, to let him work things out for himself and for him to do what he had to do and she would support him in that.

Which was probably just as well as it was all so complex anyway, so vast, that finding the right words to explain it all would have been very difficult, especially without any sort of evidence or examples or context to refer to.

CHAPTER 12 - SYNCHRONISED

Then during February events started to become more 'well defined' more graphic and 'evidential', as if something was waking up. Something was now making moves to express itself, form coherence and connection, so that it was more obvious as to what it was 'saying'.

It was early morning in the middle of March 2012 - almost 7 years to the day since 'his Experience' in New Zealand.

Sam had been sleeping in the spare room again and the morning light was creeping in though the curtains. He felt lousy, like he had been asleep for only a few minutes rather than several hours.

Again, he felt worn out, tired, weary, as if something had been using his mind and brain all night as some sort of knowledge processor, and it didn't feel in any way that it was for his benefit.

Lying there half awake, he could hear the noise of the TV in the master bedroom - Brina had obviously woken early too, but was making 'I'm awake so everyone else must be' noises - showering, cupboard doors opening and closing, singing quietly, and full of annoying female energy, a busy-ness that hiding under the quilt could just about protect you from for a while.

Ten minutes later she came bursting into the bedroom, stopping herself momentarily in the doorway. She had checked her enthusiasm when she saw that he still had a pillow covering his head.

He lifted it and looked sideways at her, which was obviously a mistake, and she bounced into the room and knelt by the side of the bed, bursting to tell him something.

He groaned, but still managed a smile at the same time.

"I have just seen this horse, and I KNOW it is going to win the Gold Cup at Cheltenham this weekend" she said "I have seen it, I have seen it" she was almost shaking with excitement. "I want you to put a bet on it for me."

Sam closed one eye, but that didn't seem to make much difference, it still all looked too much to cope with from this angle. So he sat up slowly, grabbed his dressing gown from the end of the bed, and steered himself wearily out of the room and into the other bedroom.

"Look," she said "you watch the TV and I will get you some breakfast." He sat on the bed and watched, but the television was now showing some report about the National Health Service, and how there were so many problems with it, and what was being planned to resolve it all.

His whole body felt like lead, he just wanted to sleep, and wake up happy, healthy, refreshed, and energetic like he used to.

It almost seemed as if Brina had worked out a way of, or was unconsciously, stealing all the energy from him in the night, and breakfast was her subconscious way of making herself feel less guilty about having done so.

It seemed like the deal was that he went through industrial scale gnosis, processing it all in his mind and within the collective unconscious, she got the results she wanted and then she made the breakfast - it was a fair swap apparently.

Ten minutes later the whirlwind arrived back in the room. "The horse is called *Synchronised*," she explained excitedly, "It jumped out at me because of all the things you have been telling me about synchronicity and events!

"It was almost as if something was trying to tell Sam something, that IT got it, that it understood, it understood the concept of synchronicity, it was a message or something, as if IT understood what was going on, like an operating system realising what it was and what it was doing, and synchronicity was being generated from within it as an expression."

It seemed a bit far-fetched to Sam to think that IT was capable of being that refined, that it could use a horse to do that, or that it could be that specific.

But he was happy to go along with the idea anyway.

So later in the week Sam signed up to one of the online bookmakers. One of the ones that were offering free bets and promotions and various event based incentives for the Cheltenham racing festival, all to get punters to part with their money.

He created an account with a couple of them, and put a small amount with each on the horse named *Synchronised* that was to run in the Cheltenham Gold Cup.

As the racecourse itself wasn't too far away from where they lived, he had briefly thought about taking Brina to see the race - but he the remembered how busy it was there these days for that event, and it was all very weather dependent, and frankly he was just knackered, as it would appear, were most of the horses.

Besides he wasn't sure how he would cope with the drunken mass of Irishmen stumbling into him - his tolerance levels weren't that high at the moment - but then knowing Brina, she would have been fine, she seemed to be able to deal and cope with anything and anyone these days. More so than he was.

So for the Friday, the day of the race, he had gathered some work together that he could do at home, and got up early so that he could get it all completed by early afternoon.

Then after lunch he settled down to watch the races on television in the lounge with Brina. He carefully placed a few notes that he still had to read next to the sofa - which were there more there to placate his guilt at not working, and to give the false impression to her that he wasn't that interested in the race.

It was strange, but watching the event 'live' on the TV gave him a feeling that there was an energy associated with the event itself. Something was definitely 'going on'; there was a certain feel to it, a connection, a focus, a meaning, a lively excitement.

The race started without incident and Brina's horse wasn't mentioned for a while. She started to look quite despondent, almost confused. At one point, she thought that a horse that had fallen badly at one of the first fences was hers, and she looked quite lost - as though it was wrong.

She was very relieved when she eventually heard her horse's name again, and realised that hers hadn't fallen.

Then the commentator mentioned her horse briefly again after several more fences had been jumped - it was towards the rear of the field, but the words made Brina sit up and edge forward on the sofa, her hands clasped together staring intently at the screen.

Sam glanced sideways at her, the horse was miles back, it hadn't got a chance in hell.

Again there were a few more mentions of her horse's name as things progressed, and when they eventually turned for home with two furlongs to go, her horse was sixth and not looking very promising. The commentator gave the names of the horses in order and said "...and *Synchronised* is once more wanting for pace."

And then it all changed. It changed, and he felt it change.

There was a change of energy in the room too, a tingling energy. Sam felt it going through the core of his body, precise and focused, it made his body tingle, starting from his thighs and working up his body and spine. Thoughts and concepts and perceptions became clear. It was a 'not on my watch it doesn't' feeling but it was not coming from him.

Everything became vivid and intense.

Sam placed his working papers down on the carpet next to the sofa again, and began to watch everything that was happening in front of him very closely. The horses jumped the second to last hurdle and everything changed - all of the other horses suddenly began to look as if they were running through deep mud, and they all hit the last fence like it was ten feet high.

All that is – except one.

Her horse suddenly seemed to take off and it went past the rest of the horses as if their legs were made of lead, and they were just standing still.

Brina screamed at the TV, her eyes wide, "Yes go! Yes, yes... go on...go!" louder and louder in an increasingly wild voice.

Her horse, very obviously, won.

"I saw it..." she shouted excitedly

"I saw it! It was all just as I saw it!"

Sam was speechless. He hadn't seen Brina so emotional, or seen such an obvious sign as that before. It was so direct and clear, so 'in the moment'.

He looked sideways at the screen and was aware of an uncomfortable feeling in his throat, but he snapped out of that quickly and became happy and excited for Brina.

He tried not to think or process what was going on; instead he just let himself be caught up in the emotion of the moment and her happiness.

After the race had finished, Brina was absolutely thrilled and unable to sit still or control her emotions, and she started crying and hugging Sam.

She kept kissing him repeatedly and pacing around the room,

somehow unable to know what to do with herself. Sam was also now thinking of the practical side of things, the winnings at 8/1, the bottle of champagne in the fridge, and the rewarding evening ahead.

After fifteen minutes or so though, he decided to try and get her to calm down a bit, he felt that she was a little too drawn into it all, and he could sense that the emotion and energy were making her a little uncontrolled and erratic. So he went into the kitchen and made her a cup of tea, it was also so that she could watch the follow up of the race by herself and enjoy the moment.

Sam was really pleased, really happy for her - she had done something, something powerful with evidence, and she knew it, and he had 'seen it' and 'got the message'.

It was just a shame that he could never experience anything like that for himself, but somehow he knew that was how it was meant to be. He would always be deprived and isolated from that emotion, it was part of what had to be.

A few minutes later she was in the kitchen doing things again, this time taking over the making of the tea, and quickly emptying the dishwasher. Busy 'doing things' again at speed.

In an attempt to get her to calm down a bit he suggested that she go and watch the parade for the next race instead.

Which she did.

Ten minutes later it had gone very quiet,

He carried the tea back into the lounge. He stopped in the doorway and looked at Brina - she was sitting forward on the sofa again, quietly focused on the television screen, her hands clasped in front of her, rocking slightly.

She was intently watching the horses for the next race go around the parade ring.

She didn't look at him as he quietly placed the tray on the table in front of her.

"That horse is talking to me" she said a moment later without taking her eyes off the screen. Sam looked at the TV, and there was a horse looking at the camera and nodding as it walked around the parade ring. Then it looked away.

"Talking?" asked Sam.

"Yes you know - saying things with its expressions and looks -

sort of communicating in my head" she replied.

Sam looked at Brina, and then back at the screen.

"Did it sound a little hoarse perhaps?" he asked jokingly, trying to break the intensity of what was actually being said.

But she didn't really hear him - she was just fixated on the screen again. "Can you put some money on that one for me?" she asked pointing at the screen. Sam worked out what number it was, and took his laptop out and put just £25 on it to win.

The race came and finished, and her horse won easily, but Brina was quite different in her attitude this time. She didn't have the same level of excitement and emotion as with the previous race, it was as if she knew already, and that it was now just a process.

It was a process that was involved collective emotion, it was as if she was now drawn into a connected surreal process which was detaching itself, and her, from reality. There was excitement there but it was detached somehow. It was more something that he had to see going on and so it was allowed to happen, and it didn't matter how obvious it was.

Over the next three weekends they watched a few more races, and she repeated the success in all the races she chose to bet on.

She would not bet unless she was sure, unless she could 'see the horse' unless it was 'talking to her', and on those occasions, that did actually seem to be the case. It was quite extraordinary, and the margin for delusion or probability of 'this not really happening' disappeared into finite improbability.

Sam had never been very good at betting on horses, he usually went on the name or something in the name that had some connection to him.

This though, was a whole new ballgame. Actually getting the horse to tell you if it was going to win or not, was certainly a novel approach. It was a sort of 'equestrian conspiracy', though something you would expect Jilly Cooper to write about rather than Dan Brown.

The following Saturday was Grand National day, and on the morning of the race Sam noticed that *Synchronised* was due to run again. Sam looked over the list of runners, and chose one for himself so as not to be outdone, even though he knew the odds were stacked against him, as they always appeared to be.

He offered the newspaper to Brina at the breakfast table, and mentioned that 'her horse' was running again. But for some reason she didn't want to look - she had to 'see' them, there had to be some connection, apparently.

There had to be some link, either on the screen or in the parade ring. That was how 'it' worked, apparently, this oracle thing, you had to 'see' them.

Half an hour before the race began they sat down in the lounge and got ready. Sam had the laptop logged in to his online bookmaker account. He had set it up so he could put any bets on that she wanted instantly, a sort of 'in the now' referral process, as she was assessing and 'talking' to the four-legged 'hopefuls'.

It wasn't quite the same though - everything had a different feel to it, there was something different in the energy level, the focus.

Brina seemed a little agitated as if she was putting herself under pressure to perform, as if she was trying to impress him, to show what she could do.

She watched the screen intently, every horse, every action, every look, trying to decide the right option.

"None of them are talking to me..." she said, "and I can't see all of them, there are too many." "They haven't shown all of them" she kept looking for certainties, and doubts started to creep into her mind, and she became more and more agitated.

After ten minutes the horses came out onto the course, spiralled around in circles, and then began heading off to the start.

There was too much information coming through, too many horses, too much being said at once. She couldn't filter the information, and she was now putting herself under pressure to live up to his, or her own expectations.

"Do you want me to put some money on your original horse?" asked Sam unhelpfully as it appeared on the screen and began its long run up the course.

"No it's not talking to me" she said very dismissively "I don't want that one."

She waved her hand irritably and abruptly, her manner was uncharacteristically brisk, as if she was trying too hard, and had become irritated that it, whatever it was, this 'oracle' 'pre-cognition' feature, wasn't working, or not being clear enough.

Then suddenly as the horse moved forward to the starting line to inspect it, *Synchronised* gave a strange jump, as if it had received a shock or seen something on the ground. It then stopped suddenly and twisted to run away, and then dislodged its jockey from the saddle.

It then started running around the course, rider-less, looking quite agitated. The camera followed it and people ran about trying to catch it.

Then the camera focused back on the other horses moving onto the course, and panned through the backfield of other riders heading to the start.

Brina looked again at the horses and all of a sudden one stopped and looked as if it were listening for something and turned towards the camera. It started jogging its head. "That one." she said. "That one there - the yellow one with the red star."

Sam looked it up, it was called Neptune or something, the betting odds were 33/1 but he didn't mention this to her as he didn't want to put her off by its overly long odds.

"Are you sure?" he asked. "Well yes" she said, "but it's hard to tell, but that is the only one talking to me."

"Ahh... Yes" said Sam under his breath "but it could be saying "I really only have three legs" but thankfully she didn't hear that.

Sam just put a £20 bet on it, and left it at that. It was getting quite stressful now and not at all enjoyable.

They caught the horse *Synchronised* and the jockey remounted it and they trotted up to the start line to take another look and re-join the other horses.

Then it turned back again and still looked quite distressed and unsettled. Even the commentator made the same observation – the horse didn't seem right – and then it caused all the other horses to be turned back as a false start.

Brina was unconsciously tapping her leg with her hand in an agitated manner. "They shouldn't make it run" she said "Don't make it run" she told the TV abruptly and then she repeated it again "DON'T MAKE IT RUN!" so loudly that it startled Sam as it was very out of character. She had become quite unaware of herself.

The horses turned again and then started and this time there was no false start and thus began the biggest and most dangerous race that those horses would ever run.

But they still ran - after all they had no choice.

It all felt quite uncomfortable now, wrong somehow, as they headed off on their long *Titanic* journey over so many high and difficult fences, it was as if the pieces in the game were now set in motion, and there was no stopping it now.

There was a surreal feeling to watching it, as if it were now some film or process being played out in front of him, it was not enjoyable at all.

Then several fences into the race *Synchronised* had a dreadful fall and threw its jockey - Brina saw it - it was in full view on the screen in front of them.

It didn't get up.

She stared at the screen, unblinking.

She knew, somehow she already knew what had happened; walls of understanding came to her, what she was involved in, what was happening, what she had invoked, what she had done, or more to the point what IT was doing.

It all came to her in walls of realisation and energy and horror, and a few moments later she found that it is hard to see anything with your hands over your face when you are kneeling down and screaming into the carpet.

Her blonde hair was spread out over the floor, and her body position was awkward, and momentarily animalistic, as though her image and poise had suddenly been dropped several notches down the priority list.

She screamed. Then after a minute or so she sat back onto the sofa, white faced, tears rolling down her cheeks and completely speechless.

The race continued, and the horse with the star that she had chosen won. But she was too shocked to say anything, and there was no enjoyment in the victory this time.

She already knew the fate of her original horse.

As the race finished she put her hand over her mouth, pale, and ran to the bathroom and stayed in there for half an hour.

All the while graphic images still being relayed through and into her mind of what she had 'seen', and what she had been involved with.

There was nothing Sam could do.

She may have been through her 'training' for her 'role', and she may have done what she was supposed to do, and had found what she needed to find.

She may also have subconsciously followed 'the process', and she may have felt ready and excited by it all, intrigued and curious, but she wasn't aware of what was really going on, or the level that things were at, and happening.

Nothing, nothing, could have prepared her for the depth of energy and intensity and magnitude of the experience - the nature of the information coming in, the power, the game of fire that she was now playing around with.

What had just happened, and what she had been exposed to - and the harrowing reality and scale of what it really meant - had shocked her to the core and rattled her confident composure.

She had got carried away and strayed into regions, depths and areas, that she was not meant to go into. That she could not manage.

It was somewhere where even angels feared to tread - and for good reason.

She went right off horse racing for a very long time after that.

'Angels' were sensitive creatures or programs. That was sort of part of the function of them, it went with the territory as it were.

She at least had some idea now what he was doing, what she was dealing with, and the level or depth or scale of what was going on.

Yet it was just as well it was only a horse this time, and not some of the things that he would soon be dealing with. It would be a responsibility level way beyond anything she could deal or cope with, she just had to support him, protect him, and understand what he was doing, and do her part in what needed to be done.

She could not go where he went, nor do what he had to do.

Yet it was all a team thing.

An hour later, when Brina had recovered, Sam found himself looking out of the lounge window at the view in front of him. He then remembered part of a dream about a ship that he had had a few years ago.

There had been a room in it, one in which Brina had not being able to go into for some reason, because of their separate roles, purpose, and functions.

These were just glimpses for her to briefly see into the system.

A system and process that she sometimes needed to see, to do with her role and her abilities, but which she only needed a taste of to understand.

It also made him very aware of the massive levels of protective programming, understanding, and capability that must be in place to allow him to cope with it, and to do the things in there that he had to do.

Much the same way as willingly sticking your head into a nuclear reactor to fix the broken rods.

Getting your wings singed is one thing, but Sam had the feeling that he wouldn't have the same tolerance level afforded to him.

He realised that if he didn't tread carefully and keep in step along the razors edge, and in pace with whatever was going on, he would wind up just as a small lump of carbon.

This was not a great feeling to have, especially when you have no idea what you are doing it for or why, and not something you would go chasing after to get involved with either, unless it was absolutely necessary.

Following that day, there were significant changes made to the Grand National race. It was talked about in the news for several months afterwards, and well into the next year. There were discussions as to whether it should be banned altogether, or if fences should just be made safer.

People even said that *Synchronised* seemed to almost 'know' what was going to happen, and they talked about the cruelty, the cost.

It was all improved but it didn't stop though - it was hard to change things that people wanted. It was an institution after all, like so many others.

Change after all was a process, something though that sometimes, had to be managed.

The horse with the star that won for Brina was retired after the race, a gelding, his racing days were now over, and he would now be performing in a dressage ring for a woman rider. Sam felt this was a good lesson for Sam, a gentle reminder of the slippery slope down which it was so easy for the mighty to fall.

But hey that was life too.

Equally from then on the format of the live TV horse racing events changed, such that there was now much more focus on interviews with the jockeys, trainers, and pre-recorded discussions with the owners, along with carefully timed adverts.

Anything rather than actually showing the horses being paraded live on TV, and shown to potential gamblers to 'see' before the race. Any views of the horse parades that did appear were pre-recorded, and were shown just before the start of the race.

It was an interesting responsive biological effect to something external. Something you could see happening everywhere, if you were awake enough to see it.

Sam had done quite a lot of extensive research on synchronicity over the year before, starting with Carl Jung's work, and interestingly from his more recently published Red Book in 2009. The book opened up a lot of where all Jung's ideas and experiences had come from, and of his visions before, during, and after the First World War.

He remembered the synchronistic example he had given with the example of the beetle, and his work and letters over many years with Gustav Pauli. It was a very complex area to get your head around, and it was a much more modern phenomena, something that had started in the twentieth century and was now quite common and observable, and even testable.

An interesting phenomena, especially when it became meaningful and provided a form of communication, but not something you as an individual could cause to happen.

For Sam though his days would be filled with several such examples of this occurrence, even before breakfast most days, over the next few years With everyone else now experiencing this sort of synchronistic event all the time.

Yet it is being aware of them, recognising the meaning and context, in conjunction with everything else that is going on around, that is important.

It was like an operating system making itself ever more obvious to its programs and devices.

Yet, thought Sam, it is only when these 'happenings' are

perceived, and interpreted with other connections and structure that they can make sense.

Just in the way that the Chinese see events that occur in a timeless manner.

Happenings that are by association rather than linear, as with events occurring, for instance, in the Year of the Dragon, where you might get some feel for the field-based, no-space, no-time context of the information, which is how it exists, in a state form, a state machine operating system.

It is when you apply meaning to these events or synchronicities that context and organisation are then realised, causing change to occur and be realised in the system, and also hopefully invoking a natural evolutionary process.

Looking at how much 'synchronicity' was going on these days it was clear that IT was evolving quite rapidly now which was an indication that something on a large scale was waking up, something at a higher level was starting to communicate consciously and applying meaning to what it perceived from its collective unconscious foundations, and interpreting from the underlying server or 'hardware' structure.

The key though with it, from what Sam could understand, was to try to make sense of the information, and to understand the nature of the information coming from a collective perspective with events, a stateless formless field, as is the case with everything we perceive.

Just, as an analogy, in the same way that a program receives information from an operating system, and the program puts it into context, with what it is involved with, doing, and sees by putting structure and order to it within its sphere of influence.

Just in the same way as cells do in the body. If the program then indicates back that it has received the information and that it makes sense, it is able to correlate it, and process it and then respond.

Once you know that and are consciously aware of that process, the ramifications can be immense.

This, he thought, is in effect how IT could begin to consciously communicate. A hive collective mind forming conscious communication or meaning through synchronicity; all being external to the self and the ego. This is why Jung realised it was so important, but he was unable to replicate it or able to force it to occur.

It was not the visions, the voices in the head, the 'out of body' or near death experiences that meant anything, and he had realised that.

This synchronicity, this expression into the physical, was the key. But it also had to be interpreted in relation to everything else, to make sense of it, with gnosis and technical understanding, to rationalise it, process it, and then consciously make sense of it all.

But for Sam now, it was happening in bulk, every day, and it was starting to make sense, with knowledge that he was receiving through world events.

That along with interpreting the visions and dreams that people were having around him, in relation to what was going on in the physical - a world which IT too was projecting, interpreting, and perceiving through us.

He now also realised that reality was in effect an evolved expression of perception derived from this information field, this *in-form-ation*.

You could almost imagine yourself in some *Matrix*-like existence, or being within an evolving computer game and you could see how information was projected and perceived 'on screen', as it were, in our minds, to a definition level that made sense, as with pixels on a monitor. But that was again, just an analogy of how it all worked.

Things therefore only exist to us when they are perceived, not in 'physical reality' but within this informational field — of reality, of which physical perceived reality is but a part, part of something much larger, a picture within something more complex, of which the picture is all we can, or have need or benefit, to perceive.

We have only seen, or choose to see, that which we are able to make sense of, and have grown the energy needed to manifest.

Sam looked out from the window at the trees swaying in the breeze.

We as individuals, he thought, have also evolved to describe this picture with language, meaning, structure, thought forms. In the same way that programming languages like Java has evolved, they evolve and define as a language to give shape to what is perceived in order to describe it, in an evolved way.

This also applies to spoken languages; English, Mandarin, Japanese, Arabic. Giving things meaning to structure the perception within a set of rules and agreed protocols, of a culture or organisational psyche group.

Sam shook his head, he was thinking too hard again.

Yet this 'horse thing' wasn't just another 'normal' synchronistic event to IT like those he had seen numerous of over the last few years though.

This was a conscious representation of something, i.e. IT was trying to convey something meaningful of the understanding that IT had.

It was a conscious representation with meaning, not just an expression from the collective unconscious, this was the problem, the confusion, and IT was in effect, trying to 'speak'.

Sam had also noticed that these synchronistic events occurred mostly around late March or late September, at the equinoxes when things were most 'agitated'.

This was something else that IT didn't understand; the effect on it by something external. It was something 'external' to IT, that affected it, that IT couldn't perceive, that gave IT direction and influence. A guiding organising force, information with energy like the swing of a pendulum for a collective mechanical machine.

IT was now trying to communicate with him, like a macro-organism baby trying to talk, expressing itself in the only way that it could.

Over the next year the 'meaningful synchronicity' would become very obvious, as would the things IT was worried about.

But now Sam had decided to try and keep things calm for a few weeks, and to try and not 'get involved' with too much thinking.

He tried to make it clear in his mind, as much as he could, that he and Brina needed a break, that he had understood the 'message', but now he needed a rest.

Over the next week he spent a lot of his free time doing DIY jobs and Brina spent a lot of time in the garden 'tidying' and creating.

It all helped him keep fit too, especially the planting of the trees in the garden.

He also spent a lot of time late in the evenings when Brina was asleep writing up his journals with records of the events and things that had happened.

It helped a lot somehow, just getting it all down in some form, recording it, expressing it in some form of discourse, getting it out of his system. Putting down ideas from his mind onto paper so that it was 'there', and out of his head, which was getting somewhat 'full'.

It wasn't easy though, finding the time and energy to write it all down, and finding words and means to express it - nor was it easy collating it all with the physical and process evidence he had to back it all up.

It was hard juggling with working it all out in his mind, and then writing about it all at the same time, as well as dealing with the 'living through it all'.

Not to mention the problem of even being able to describe and articulate the complexity of the information he had coming into his mind - and creative writing had never been his strong point.

Yet it meant that by doing that, he didn't have to keep all those thoughts in his brain as well, or dwell on the thoughts in his mind.

It was all recorded, logged, and he could move on, not think about it, or worry that he might forget it all.

He also recorded what he thought it all meant and how it was all fitting together, how the picture of the whole thing was starting to take shape. The connective meaning, context and form.

Bit by bit it all formed into a coherent working scientific and 'spiritual' model in his mind, and he knew that he had backed it all up with recording both the evidence, the process, the context and the examples. It all made sense.

He also had started putting it together into a fictional form, using some of the analogies he had come across or invented.

It was a way of explaining what he was going through but expressing it as a virtual character and it was also a way of explaining the transitions, the events, and the feelings Brina involved, rather than the hard facts or non-fictional impersonal concepts.

It helped, and it also helped keep him sane - which looking at what others had done in the past seemed to be the tricky part.

But unlike others, he had something that made absolute sense, a philosophical model that was not just logical and worked, but was real, meaningful, and backed up with evidence and science. He would also be able to describe it, yet maybe not very well, to anyone if he were ever allowed to.

Fortunately for them both, everything really calmed down in the following week, both with information 'coming in', news, and most importantly the effect on Brina had slowly dissipated and she had now moved on to other things and other 'jobs' and 'role functions'.

There seemed to be a lot of anxiety around, and in, the news about the safety of the forthcoming Olympics in the UK in July, about the risk of potential terrorist attacks.

He really hoped that especially after what he had been through in the last six months, that nothing like that would happen, and it was also quite important to Brina - she liked the Olympics and was very patriotic, and just in the same way that she kept her house and garden tidy, she would be upset if anything messed it up.

He just wanted peace and quiet - he didn't want anything to happen - and he just wanted it all to go well.

Which later that year 'coincidentally' it did, in fact it went extremely well for the GB teams and individuals in their various events.

There were no terrorist attacks or any major problems at all. Which in itself was quite remarkable - amazing in fact. Nothing went wrong at all, and surprisingly nobody commented on that either after the event.

Even the weather was great, but he was sure, with the reputation of the UK weather, that in this case that part of it was just pure luck.

The same would also likely occur for the 2016 Olympics with the UK doing exceptionally well again, along with no terrorist attacks or anything going wrong.

But that was what could happen when you could turn dreams into reality, especially Angel ones. Yet that was the case for everyone, if they realised that they could, and set their mind to it.

Thankfully though now, IT had calmed down somewhat, and they had, for a while a chance to rest and recover for a few days.

Which was just as well considering what they would be going to go through a week later, and for the rest of the year.

CHAPTER 13 - HOSPITAL AND BRIGHTON

It was Sunday 22nd April 2012. They had both had a good day and had both finally managed to relax somewhat.

Sam had even had a couple of glasses of organic wine with dinner that evening and they had just sat down to watch a film together on the TV in the lounge.

They hadn't relaxed all week, and this was the first time they had actually had a chance to, with everything else now being out the way. It was great to finally capture a bit of peace.

About ten minutes into the film the phone rang.

They both knew that there was something up. The moment and situation had that odd energy feel to it. Even the ring on the phone had that determined and persistent manner about it.

It was Brina's mother.

Brina got up to answer it with an annoyed look on her face, having already done the maths as to who it was on the other end.

Sam thought about pausing the film, but after she had picked up the receiver and confirmed it was her mother, Brina casually waved at him to carry on with the film from the other side of the lounge, so she could continue watching it while she carried on with the conversation.

Sam listened to the dialogue on the phone that seemed to follow the same normal patter about her telling Brina about her week, who had said what, and who was causing her trouble. Dramatized dialogue on who had done what, and who had said what to who, all in a created village busybody sort of way.

Then ten minutes into the conversation, the tone switched abruptly. Brina's voice had changed and the 'Mmm's and 'Yeah's had stopped. Her mother had said something offhand, but clearly it had clicked a switch on in Brina's alert system, and she went quiet and stood up straight and was now no longer watching the TV.

Sam switched the sound on the TV to mute, and then paused the film. He stood up and walked over to Brina. She looked shocked, her face was red and she was listening intently to the words her mother was saying on the phone.

She saw Sam come over and pushed the speakerphone button on the phone so that he could hear what her mother was saying. She was learning. He needed to hear this.

Her mother's voice started mid-sentence on the speakerphone, it was talking about possible angina, hot flushes, out of breath, pains in shoulders, visit to doctor, something that had been going on for a few weeks.

There was, according to her, 'nothing to worry about', but she needed to go in the next day for some 'silly tests'.

It was like a list of things that she hadn't been able to talk about for weeks. Guilty secrets that were all now coming out in one go, bottled up, contrived, manipulated, and then landed firmly in Brina's lap.

She was apparently having to go for tests at the hospital the next day. It was hard to pick out the details but it sounded like she had deliberately been keeping this problem from Brina for some time. She had 'not wanted to worry her', 'not wanted the fuss', but she was now 'fessing up to it all as she had to go to hospital.

You could almost hear the cogs whirring inside Brina's head as the drama her mother had created was now being played out in front of her. Presented subtly like some deviously clever time bomb.

It was a control thing. Her mother was unconsciously and unintentionally manipulating her daughter, taking away control, but at the same time loading her with emotion, drama, and then handing over 'the problem' and responsibility to her.

But Brina couldn't see this yet, her mind was still being manipulated, hypnotised and blackmailed by her mother's subconscious, and it was drawing her in with every moment.

Brina asked her mother for the appointment times, asked her to call her when she had got home, asked her to take in some clothes and an overnight bag just in case, trying to think around all the eventualities in that moment that she had open to her.

Her mother retorted with a 'It is only a set of tests, don't fuss', and a 'I'm fine' series of control countermeasures.

But Brina was adamant about her having to take in the overnight bag, and her mother relented.

Brina also offered to drive down and go to the appointment

with her and support her. But curiously, Sam thought, she refused. She didn't want Brina to fuss, it was all fine, she had already booked the taxi, and she had some friends or neighbours who had agreed to pick her up, so Brina didn't have to concern herself.

Obviously, thought Sam, Brina was being unconsciously placed into the guilty camp of 'those that didn't care for her' but could be psychologically bullied into doing so.

Brina just had to be guilty and powerless, and yet her mother 'didn't want to be a burden to her'.

What her mother had actually done was unconsciously created a maze for herself, a 'poor me' maze of complex problems, situations, scenarios, people and conditions, and placed herself in the middle of it so that she could draw Brina in.

Yet Brina was now 'subconsciously' supposed to navigate her way in through all the turns and complex created barriers and situations. Overcome the lack of knowing of what had happened, what was going on and what was 'in there', and 'get her mother out safely', even though her mother 'really didn't want her taking any trouble', or to 'put herself out'.

The problem with doing that is that this clever little created unconscious maze game, can quite often collapse. So that instead of a game, it turns into a major rescue operation requiring earth moving machines, teams of medical and emergency operatives, and a lot of inconvenience.

With all the drawn in *Alice in Wonderland* maze of characters then suddenly divesting themselves of any responsibility, walking 'off set', leaving the sleeping Alice in the middle of it all still completely oblivious to all the helicopters and sirens going off around her.

'That's the evening gone', thought Sam, along with anything else that may have followed later. He knew now he would spend the next three hours talking around the problem, going through every possible scenario, and explanations as to why her mother hadn't told her before.

Sam knew the answer to that but he didn't think it was a good idea to go into a critical personality and psychological report of her mother at this time.

Sam could feel something coming. He could sense the scenario forming, he couldn't define it in real terms, but he knew something was being 'created', and that ultimately he was the one being pulled into it all.

The following day on the 23rd April the phone call came mid-afternoon. It wasn't from her mother, it was from a neighbour who had been in with the said mother, and had been given the task of 'phoning, just to let you know'.

Her mother had had a scan, and various tests including an angiogram, and she had been identified as having a serious blockage of one of her arteries along with deterioration of the artery walls from her heart.

She was being kept at the hospital, and not allowed home. The neighbour had no idea which ward her mother was in. The only thing they knew was that her mother was being scheduled in for an operation at some point, probably at Brighton hospital some fifty miles away from the hospital she was currently in.

Brina thanked the neighbour kindly, put the phone down politely, and then went absolutely nuts!!!

It took two hours of phone calls for Brina to find out where her mother was, what was going on and what was due to happen.

It was all starting to play out.

Sam had already begun going through his diary, sorting out what could be moved or cancelled for the next two weeks. He rang his parents on his mobile to ask them to come and pick up and look after the dog. By late evening he and Brina were both packed and ready. Then very early the next morning they were in the car, and driving down to sort out the created mess.

After four hours of driving they got to the hospital that Brina knew that her mother was in, and they made their way to the ward.

It was a few minutes past the end of morning visiting time now but looking at Brina's face none of the staff or nurses thought it was a wise thing to mention.

Sam carried their bags in, into which Brina had packed an assortment of essentials, and anything she thought may be useful.

To Sam though at that moment it seemed curious, there was an odd thing going on. It was to do with the timings, the overall scenario. It was like something being enacted, a program of events, a play unfolding with scenes and situations, being set up and shown to him.

He let Brina have time with her mother on her own, and to have a conversation with her in private. It just seemed the thing to do.

Seeing it from here, it wasn't an animated conversation, or loud. Brina had seemingly gone straight into care mode, taking charge, being now 'in control', working out what had gone on, who had done what, and what had to be sorted out.

It was just like watching a mother coming into school to take care of a child that had had an accident in the playground, not concerned with the how's, or the why's or the other people, just focusing on what was needed now.

There was a slight touch on the side of his arm. He jumped.

Sam turned abruptly to look into the eyes of a young nurse. She had dark hair tied back in a ponytail, was slim with plain features, and she was about six inches shorter than Sam. The touch felt unusual, Sam wasn't used to people just making physical contact him out of the blue. It just didn't seem to happen to him much these days, other than via handshakes, or with Brina.

"Just so you know" the nurse whispered "visiting time is finished now, but as you have come a long way I have put you down as urgent so don't worry, so you can stay on and nobody will bother you."

Sam thanked her and nodded back to her.

She smiled and stood there in silence looking toward the bed where Brina and her mother were.

"You must be very busy" Sam said to make conversation. She nodded, and then she went on to explain to him in detail about the changes going on and the demands of the day-to-day running at the hospital, the pressures of funding, the communications.

It was like a prepared list, a report, that she had to convey to him. A list of issues and problems and situations that he had to listened to. A sort of Situation Report of changes that were happening 'in the system'. It was somewhat surreal in that situation, and the manner she conveyed it. It was as if it were all coming from someone that had known him for a long time.

He didn't mind, she was pleasant enough, and anyway he didn't fancy talking with Brina's mother.

At the end of her ten minute report, she looked down at his hands, and in a completely different voice said "Would you like me to get you a vase for those?", and she pointed at the flowers he had picked up from the petrol service station on the way there.

Sam looked down at the flowers that were now dripping water onto the polished floor.

He followed her to the kitchen area just off the ward, and she took them from him. With expert efficiency she opened the wrappings, snipped the stems, and placed them in a glass vase from a selection of various shapes and dimensions on a shelf. She quickly arranged them and put some water in the vase from the tap.

She then curiously held onto the vase of flowers, holding them at her waist in front of her like a bridesmaid, looking up to him smiling, presenting them to him. Her eyes - there was something about her eyes. It was as if he was looking into something, or seeing something through them, but not anything you could describe, and he couldn't look away.

Whilst still holding onto the vase of his flowers, she then continued with her list of problems with the Health Service, and what was wrong. The various issues with hospitals in the area. She was only in her mid-twenties but she seemed very confident, knowledgeable, and committed to being whatever it was that she was, and was doing.

She then led him back to the ward with the flowers, and walked him up to where Brina mother's bed was. She then spoke to Brina's mother as if she was a slightly deaf five year old, explaining what she was doing.

The nurse then placed the flowers behind the bed on a shelf, smiled briefly at Brina, and then left. Sam surveyed the scene and then smiled at Brina's mother nervously, but she didn't really notice him.

"Ahhh, they must have given her some strong drugs', he thought.

Half an hour later, Sam drove Brina to her mother's house to fetch a few things, and to turn off the water and the heating in the house. They left a few lights on to indicate that someone was in, and put the valuables away.

Just the basic things so the house was secure for the next few weeks or so. They then returned to the hospital later in the afternoon, with a bag full of some more of her mother's things and clothes.

Brina then spoke to the consultant surgeon again to get his views, and spent another half an hour with her mother, and then they both left for home again. It had all been a bit of a whirlwind.

The problem was that her mother was 'in the system' now. She had taken away the option of choosing private medical care. A subliminal way of eliminating that means of support from Brina.

They could not take her mother out of the state health system now, or bring a private surgeon in, or apply any sort of control. All those options had been taken away from Brina by her mother now, in what she had subconsciously engineered.

Two days later, Brina had a call out of the blue again. This one was very early in the morning from the hospital to say that her mother was already being transferred to the other hospital in Brighton, and was being operated on that afternoon.

It was all way too sudden, there was no warning.

Then followed an hour of organising, repacking, and phone calls. Sam tried to get a hotel room booked in the centre of Brighton, but they were all full. In the end he had to book one near the Marina a mile along the coast from the hospital.

There was then another half an hour or sorting things out, along with arranging for the dog, work, and securing the house, until they got in the car and left.

The motorway that led down to Brighton from the north, tuned into a dual carriageway a few miles before it reached the small city. Sam had visualised in his mind the route map from the internet, and knew where the hospital was in relation to where they were staying, and where they were now.

However the road system itself was a little complex with roads and turnings that just didn't flow in the logical directions. There were one-way streets and bends, as was the case with a lot of Victorian towns and cities.

He was also planning to call into the hotel beforehand, so they could check in and unpack, so he was also trying to work out in his mind where that was too.

He could visualise it all in his mind like a plan, seeing the map in his mind, and where they were on it.

It was just that he didn't know his way through the maze of

streets, and one-way systems, all of which seemed to be taking them in the wrong direction from where they needed to go.

So as they came off the dual carriageway heading south, they found themselves heading into the main part of the city and towards the seafront. All the signs indicated the opposite direction to where he thought he should be going. They seemed to want to send him right instead of left, in the opposite direction to where he knew in his mind he needed to go, and he became disorientated.

He asked Brina to get the map out of the glove compartment to ask her which road they were coming in on, and work out a way around the strange one-way system that they were being led around.

She looked at the map. "You want to go straight on here, and then left when you get to the sea - we will go to the hospital first" she said.

Which all seemed logical, but the road became a one-way street a few hundred yards on, and they had to turn right instead.

Sam could feel in his mind which way they had to go, and he could place where the hospital was so he needed to get around the roads somehow. After about half a mile of going the wrong way, he stopped the car and parked in a layby next to the curb.

Then he had a feeling that something was very wrong. It wasn't the direction, it was the feeling itself, he sensed it, something was wrong, a presence, something dark, menacing, threatening, he felt all the energy drain from him.

Something here was wrong, bad, something that was against him, in this specific physical area of buildings and streets. He turned to Brina, she had gone white as a sheet, and looked cold and weary. She was experiencing the same feelings and she gave him an acknowledging look as if to say so, without words.

He drove on for a few more streets and he could almost pinpoint the source of whatever it was to a few hundred yards, a few blocks of buildings, a specific neighbourhood. He had to stop the car, they didn't know what to say to each other. Then Brina put her hands over her face and leaned forward.

"I am not putting up with this, I don't have time for this rubbish." said Brina, which was very uncharacteristic of her, almost as if she were stepping out of her character or role for a moment.

She seemed to take on a resolved stance for a moment, and then inhaled a few times and then lowered her hands, colour coming back to her cheeks. "Drive towards the sea" she said "and then along the coast road, we will go to the hotel first, now."

Sam followed the instructions, his head couldn't seem to do anything else. After a mile the feeling and the presence had gone, but they still didn't talk. They didn't have the energy.

They parked in a multi-storey car park and checked into the hotel which was next to it. They unloaded their bags into the room, and then drove off to the hospital, without a word.

The environment was very different from the local hospital they had been to a few days before. Sam noticed it straight away; the attitude of the people around was different, the visitors, the staff, even the drivers in the hospital car park behaved differently, impersonal, a totally different ethos, culture, and psyche.

Things were harsher, more selfish, too busy, uncaring, and bleak. He had dropped Brina off at what he assumed was the Main Entrance to the hospital, and spent twenty minutes in the car park driving around looking for a space, and then another ten minutes finding a ticket machine that worked.

As he walked into the hospital everything became very confusing. Even the few information signs that were around were short on 'Please' and 'Thankyou's' or any useful information.

There was also no information on where he was or where he had to go, and nobody seemed available or willing to be asked - and that was just the other visitors.

It was all very inhuman and machine like.

Sam finally managed to work out which ward Brina's mother was on, and pressed the button on the door to buzz the reception desk inside to be let in.

He hoped he was in time before they wheeled her off to surgery. As he walked up to the desk, all the staff on the ward seemed very busy, this was a surgical ward, and so the formalities and niceties were replaced with functional practicality.

Sam spotted Brina and walked along the corridor towards her. Her mother was there in a Pre-Op bed, and she looked as if she had been heavily drugged in preparation for the operation.

Brina was already in conversation with the Ward Registrar, who was explaining something to her, and was gesturing with his hands. He looked to be apologising to her for some reason, and Brina began to look more and more exasperated as the conversation went on.

As Sam walked up to them, the Registrar cut off from talking to Brina, and rapidly explained to him that her mother's operation had been cancelled as there was no bed available in the High Dependency Unit for her mother to go into after her surgery.

So despite having transferred her mother from the other hospital to here, lined up the operating room, surgeon, and staff, they had wasted everyone's time and money, just because there was no follow-up bed available.

It didn't make a lot of sense to Sam, it just sounded like a mass of mindless bureaucracy.

The Registrar continued to apologise to Brina, and went on to explain that it would now be another week before another operation could be arranged, and after a few minutes more of talking, he excused himself and went off out of the ward.

Brina turned to look at her mother who was only partly aware that she was there. Her mother did not look well at all, her colour had gone she looked weak and drawn, as if she only had a few hours left, which was probably the case.

Suddenly there was now a different sort of Brina that was now in charge, and had been landed in it big time. "I don't bloody well believe this" she exclaimed to Sam, "I shouldn't be having to deal with this all this rubbish".

It took Sam by surprise; he hadn't heard her swear like that before, and it was very uncharacteristic. She walked over to her mother's bed, sat down in a chair next to it, took her hand and started to cry in absolute frustration, she turned to Sam with tears in her eyes, pleading with him, with an expression that seemed to say 'why doesn't somebody do something?'

Sam didn't know what to do. He turned and walked out from the ward, and back into the corridor, he looked around at what was going on in the ward. He saw several staff behind the reception desk, the whiteboards on the wall, the signs, the other beds around.

He felt quite isolated, alone. He looked down the corridor to where the operating theatres were. He felt lost, unable to know what to do, trapped by crazy mindless situations and red tape.

It was then that one of the side doors to the operating suite opened, and the surgeon that he had seen at the other hospital came out, and he was putting his coat on to go home.

Having already prepped for the operation and then being stood down, he was now dressed in his normal clothes and heading off home.

He caught Sam's eye as he passed, and Sam smiled at him, but the surgeon didn't recognise him. The surgeon just acknowledged him as another human being, and walked towards the reception desk.

Sam turned and went back to where Brina was. She was just sitting, talking quietly to her mother who was not really able to hear her, so he kept several feet back, and stood in the middle of the ward.

It was as if everything around him, all the situations, the problems, the issues, the people, were just being used as an analogy for what was going wrong with the planet, with humanity. As if he was being shown 'things that were wrong', like a child showing him, and presenting it all to him as list of issues and situations, and using this whole organisation as a model so that he could 'see'.

But with real people, real situations, and physical places and events to demonstrate it all with and through.

It was as if this Health Service organisation was being presented as a model of what was wrong with the evolving yet decaying Western cultural structure. The caring but inefficient controlling unchangeable bureaucracy, all filled with red tape, and corruption. All badly managed, and creaking at the seams trying to cope, with too many people playing political games with it, or failing to fix it.

Yet it was also full of caring individual people who were just trying to help other people, and work, and make life meaningful in the face of unconscious blind ignorance, legacy, and the vast status quo.

Which was all very well, but it didn't really help him and Brina, and it was all frankly getting well out of hand, this 'showing' thing. There was only so much 'messaging' that one could take at any one go, and this was more than enough, especially as it was over coding their lives.

He closed his eyes and concentrated, he relaxed and focused his mind into the darkness.

I am not prepared to put up with this, I have understood, and I have got the message, thank you, but that is enough… he said in his mind.

He went through his thoughts; what had gone on, what had happened, and what was going on. He focused on the situation and what was around him and the area. He spent several minutes just concentrating; oblivious to what was happening around him. He didn't care what he must have looked like standing there with his eyes closed, it didn't matter.

Then he felt the energy in him build up, and he focused it though his body, and through his head. He didn't get angry he just focused and worked with the thoughts that came in and out.

After a few more minutes it went still around him, and also strangely quiet.

He opened his eyes, and walked back into the entrance of the ward. After a minute or two he took a few paces up to the end of the bed and stood there.

Looking over to the bed he could see that Brina's mother had now gone to sleep, and Brina was looking at him. Well not directly at him, more past the right side of him.

Then she looked at him again curiously, and then to whatever it was that going on behind him toward the corridor.

"They are behind me aren't they?" he said quietly. Brina stood up and walked towards him. Sam turned at the same time to see the Registrar and the surgeon he had seen several minutes earlier and another surgeon, all coming their way into the ward, all with folders in their hands.

It all happened very quickly, the Registrar was smiling and explained that there was now a bed available in the morning, and that her mother's surgeon had arranged for another surgeon to take on the operation.

He gestured towards the other man who would be able to do the triple heart bypass operation in the morning. The new surgeon then quickly explained that he wanted to see her mother beforehand to check a few things over, and to just run through a few tests.

It was all happening in fast time now, discussions and decisions were made in minutes, arrangements by people and medical checks were carried out minutes later, and information was passed over and exchanged.

It all went like clockwork, it was all totally surreal, and in complete contrast to the situation earlier. Within twenty minutes all the staff had been and gone. Everything going from abject chaos, and an impossible emotional cul-de-sac, to 'fine', working, polite, efficient, and how it should be. All done and dusted.

Brina finally turned to Sam, but didn't say anything, she just looked grateful, and utterly bewildered.

Sam wasn't aware of what he had done, it was just an 'in the moment' thing, several things had just come together at once, and it had involved him and Brina to do these things jointly.

They were just part of something that was happening, a process, so that they were able to influence something that was there and going on at that time.

Before they left the hospital later in the evening, Brina wrote a letter to her mother who was now asleep again.

It was just some information so she would know what was going on when she woke up later.

They made a few final checks, and then left for the hotel.

CHAPTER 14 - STATE OF HEALTH

Everything that happened after that had a somewhat surreal and detached feel to it and there was energy flowing everywhere around them. The night-time lights along the Marina seemed dreamlike and virtual as they walked along the jetty from the hotel to a nearby restaurant. The conversation was equally surreal as if they were in some sort of film or play, it was hard to know what to say to each other, and there was a buzzing electric energy in the air.

They walked in the approaching darkness from the Marina along the seafront promenade at the back of the beach that led along the coast to the Pier for a brief time. The city seafront was visible in the distance with its long Pier and illuminated Victorian buildings.

It was still cold, and the sea wind had that salty harsh edge to it, but it was pleasant enough. Brina had begun to calm down a little now too, but she was still apprehensive for the following day.

They stood a few hundred yards along from the Marina on the beach looking at the lights in the distance over the beach. Brina's hands were cold, he became aware that she wasn't thinking, almost in some drunk state of mind, unaware of where they were, what they were doing, and confused as to what was going on.

It was as if the whole experience had fazed her out, and she had become numb to everything. So he put his jacket around her, and led her back to the hotel.

The operation was scheduled for 7.30 a.m. the following morning, which was well before visitors were allowed in, so they had decided to get to bed early, and be at the hospital for 9 a.m. in good time for when her mother came out from surgery.

It was the morning of the 27th April. In the hotel room at 7 a.m. Sam had put the news on the TV while Brina was in the shower. The local news was alive with three major incidents that had happened overnight in the city.

A hotel fire had occurred in Brighton city centre, in the same area where they had stopped their car the day before.

A woman's body had been washed up on the beach at a spot where they had been walking the previous night. She was a middle aged woman from the same area in the city where they had encountered the negative feeling. There had also been a break-in and knifing in an apartment just around the corner in the same block of buildings.

It was too improbable, beyond any possible coincidence for it to be not something relating to him and Brina. It was all something to do with the negative energy that they had encountered from that area the night before.

Something had occurred and had made all these things happen, all three from the same area at the same time. Sam could feel that something had gone on, something in the background stepping in and influencing things. He had no idea who the woman was or her background, or the occupant of the flat, or the situation in the hotel, or who was there. But it certainly felt personal, as if they were somehow 'not on his side' and negative, dark, destructive, a potential threat to him, and his life.

Yet, he needed to know what was going on.

Sam closed his eyes and concentrated and got 'into the zone', *I need to know what went on with these events* and he formed the ideas, and then he thought of the three synchronistic events.

The was a pause, nothing, nothing come into his mind.

Not specific enough he thought. He applied a sort of kinesiology-type mechanism in his mind to start things going, *Were these events related to me being here?*.

'Yes' came the response.

Were these people causing a problem for me and Brina ?

'Yes'.

Attacking me? Nothing. No reply. Then he created the thought *Was it anything to do with Brina?* 'Yes' came the answer.

Was it to do with her…her 'higher self'? and he inwardly cringed at not being able to get a thought form that was any better to articulate what she was, and what he meant by that.

But the positive feeling came back as a 'Yes'.

So, she took them out at distance? There was an uncomfortable silence, so that question obviously wasn't right or clear enough either.

OK then - did she cause something to happen indirectly and unconsciously that caused this action? 'Yes' came the reply.

She invoked unconsciously some form of overriding protocol? There was a short pause then a 'Yes'.

Then information flowed in, a knowing, the impressions of what had gone on, the knowledge and the events flashed into his mind one after the other.

Brina's higher programming, or some part of her, or protecting capability within her, had acted to protect him. Something was invoked that had, under pressure of too many things going on, acted with unfettered extreme prejudice.

It was because he was left vulnerable, and he had been brought into this 'alien' city bubble with a lot of confused and counterproductive programs in it, and she had, for want of a better description hit the big red virtual panic button.

So he asked his original question again in a slightly different way, and the answer came back, 'yes'.

Immediately there was an image in his mind of a panic stricken 'higher self' Brina pressing a big red panic button, with the implications of what that entailed laid out in front of him in a miniature LEGOLAND-style landscape, and something fairly graphic happening to part of it, and to several of the tiny characters. Situations and scenarios being acted out for him to see and understand, with all the information of what was happening fed to him in parallel.

Blimey thought Sam, *that's a bit worrying*. And he made a mental note not to ever do anything to upset Brina, at all, ever.

Sam also decided not to mention the news on the TV to Brina, well not for a few days anyway, she had enough on her plate at the moment.

The whole thing that they were being subjected to, and having to experience, was just starting to seem to be a long list of problems that he was being presented with, a series of scenes, a storyboard of issues and concerns. All the things that were wrong with the system, but demonstrated in a real physical situation. Translated into a living form of drama.

It was like being involved in a play, but one in which you were the lead character, and around which the play revolved. But unlike everyone else in the play, you had no lines or any idea of what was in the script or what the plot was meant to be.

It was all artificial too, as if a child was presenting a list to him of problems it was having, with say part of its body. Trying to describe or explain something like teething pain or colic, that it couldn't fix for itself, or see. Where it didn't know what was happening, nor able to describe it, and yet was expecting him to somehow resolve it and come up with a solution.

It was a 'see this,' 'see that', 'show you this', 'describe it in this way.' Then the next scene, with new characters, then onto the next crazy, bizarre scenario.

When it was all placed together it became totally surreal, and impossibly implausible. A set of dream scenes, and yet it was being played out by real people, real places, real situations, and real physical events and dangers in front of them.

Also, just as in a dream, it was presented as a flowing set of synchronised scenarios and information created specifically to 'show him', 'make him understand', see the problems, interpret, and then feedback what had to happen next, like some conscious functioning part of the brain or mind in a body.

But this did not relate to the event or scenario itself, not to what was happening here in this small city. With these people and organisations it was a model or microcosm for the whole thing, the total system or subsystem. It was connecting the parts of the macro into a micro-flowing journey of knowledge and understanding, application of experience, intelligence and thoughts to rationalise and articulate and perceive the problem.

Then using that process to decide what had to happen, based on his knowledge, intelligence, experience and thoughts. Which all sounded a little mad, if it wasn't actually happening before his very eyes, again.

They left the hotel for the Hospital at 8 a.m. By the time they arrived on the ward, her mother had already been taken through to the operating theatre as planned. Many things had gone on in the background and the process was going through the motions, and they were now out of the loop for the moment while the curtains were drawn on the stage.

It was as if Sam had put a halt to the play and everything had been cleared from the stage, and now the props, scenery, and characters and events were being repositioned behind curtains ready for the next 'act'.

There was nothing to be done, so they went out of the hospital for a walk along the Brighton promenade. The cool sea breeze and sea air though were failing to give them any purchase on reality.

Sam steered her away from the part of the beach where the police cordon had been erected, not that she seemed to be able to notice much of anything around anyway.

"I need to get her some things" Brina said abruptly after half an hour of walking and 'not saying anything'. They had reached a point a few hundred yards from the main Pier, and there was a shopping arcade nearby along the seafront buildings. They crossed to road, and stopped outside.

"You don't need to come in," she said "just sit on the bench there overlooking the beach, and I will be out in a while." Sam crossed the road and sat down on the bench which looked over a low brick wall down onto the beach. He stared out at the grey sea, over the features of the beach.

There were quite a number of people walking, cycling and running along the promenade and along the beach itself at that time of day, all getting on with their day-to-day routines. They all probably had the thoughts and imagery from the local news going through their minds. It all just felt totally surreal, so utterly detached from reality, like waking up to find yourself in a TV soap opera.

After twenty minutes of 'thinking' Sam got up. The hard metal seat of the Victorian bench was starting to make his arse numb. He paced up and down for a moment and looked around.

Most of the promenade was ornately Victorian, with ample amounts of cast iron metalwork heavily overpainted, along with a lot of now seemingly purposeless decorative architecture.

In the height of its day it must have been magnificent, with thousands of fine London ladies and gentlemen strolling and taking in the sea air along the fashionable promenade.

People who were all much hardier than folks these days, he thought, and probably underneath their finery still had arses like leather if they were happy sitting on these benches.

He tried to envisage what it must have been like, the clothes, the lack of traffic, no noise, just the happy voices, the seagulls, the fresh paintwork, and smells.

Now it just felt like a legacy relic, a too-nice-to-change piece of nostalgic architecture. It was much easier and safer just to keep painting over the rust than to pull it all down and start again.

The little train that ran the length of the beach trundled past on its narrow-gauge metal rails. It was loaded with half a dozen tourists, who were now just there to use it for what it was, rather than what it had been put there for originally. To just go from A to B and then back again, because it was there and interesting.

It rattled off further down the promenade towards the Pier on its repetitive journey.

All this wasn't really helping him get a handle on reality, so he decided to go into the mall and look for Brina, who was probably now looking for a suitable new nightdress for her mother. But rather than ringing her mobile Sam decided to use his 'in-built' radar to track her down.

Well, it was something to do.

He could always somehow sense where she was, but it was only precise enough or specific enough when he really needed her.

So he just concentrated for a moment and let his unconscious compass do its thing.

He knew she was in one of the ground floor shops, and he narrowed it down from the forty of so that were there to within just a few. He walked into a clothes shop, he could sort of sense her towards the back of the building.

When he got to the back of the store she wasn't around, but he could still sense her there somehow, so he narrowed it down to the changing rooms at the back wall. Which is where he thought she must be, but they were all empty, and then after a moment he zoned into a wall of shoes in the area next to the changing rooms.

Odd, he thought.

Rather than messing with the process he just got his phone out and called her number. He could just about make out the sound of her phone ringing somewhere. "Where are you?" he asked when she answered.

She described the shop she was in, some outdoor supplies shop where she was looking for a small rucksack or bag for her mother. Sam could still hear her voice when he moved the phone away from his ear.

"Hang on" he said "can you hear this?" and he went over to the shoe wall and knocked on it hard. There was silence from the other end of the phone, then "Was that you knocking?" she asked.

He put the phone away and went out of the shop, walked out of the mall and around the corner to the row of shops that backed onto the mall, and into the Outdoor Supplies Shop in which Brina was now in.

It sort of broke things up a bit, injected some form of connected reality into the scene. Brina bought a bag, and they went to get something to eat.

He chose an evil unhealthy pizza, he was after all in a rebellious mood. Half an hour later, and after some more going around in circles, they walked back along the promenade to the Hospital to wait for her mother to come back from the operating theatre.

Brina's mother emerged an hour later mid-afternoon. The operation had taken seven hours. She was still unconscious, on oxygen and surrounded by machines. With attached wires, tubes, and drips, tended to by a kindly middle aged nurse.

Her mother looked ancient, like some white ghostly prune. A body that had been drained, and was now being filled back up again.

Fortunately, Brina was too busy talking to the surgeon to see the expression on Sam's face as he looked at her mother. He listened in on the conversation - it had been 'touch and go', there had been several problems, finding viable veins, the levels, the strain, and it had all almost been aborted twice. Brina did her usual thing of hugging everyone, which was a bit of a shock for the surgeon who didn't seem to be a 'huggy' sort of person at all.

Sam looked back at her mother again, who was still unconscious. He tried to see her in some way, see inside her, visualise her, but he couldn't see anything. There was just nothing there, just an unconscious body surrounded by machines, drips and full of drugs. He noticed there were some bruises on the side of her upper arm, and also on her hip and thigh, which were slightly visible under the gowns.

It seemed as if she had been dropped or knocked into something when she was moved around. It reminded him of his operation a few years before, when he had come out afterwards, and had similar bruises on one side on his shoulder and hip from being laid on one side on the operating table.

When you were asleep you could avoid all of that, your body was still aware enough to move or respond to touch. That was the subconscious doing what it did to protect you. When you were totally unconscious you were at the mercy of anything that came along, and you had no way of reacting or protecting yourself or of feeling anything.

It would be several hours yet before she would be moved out of Intensive Care, and into the High Dependency Unit. Sam knew that they wouldn't be going home that day, even though they were both exhausted.

Before they left for the hotel again late that evening, he leaned over to Brina's mother, and spoke gently to her even though she was still asleep.

"You are fine" he said gently, "we are going to be back in the morning, I need to get Brina back to the hotel to rest."

It seemed important somehow to say these things.

The nurse in attendance leaned over to him and whispered, "It's OK, she can't hear anything - she is still sedated."

Sam nodded and thanked her, "I know" he said "I was just saying it for my own reassurance really."

The nurse gave him that 'Ohh bless him' look.

Otherwise she may have been a little shocked if he had actually said "I wouldn't f**king count on it !!"

Brina spent the rest of the evening in the hotel packing the things she had bought for her mum, and writing notes to her, so that when her mother was more awake in a few days, she would know what was going on.

They called into the hospital the following morning and dropped the things off, and made sure that she was being cared for.

They were both still in emergency mode, and they had to get back home. Back to somewhere where they could organise things, reposition themselves, get things set up and organised in place of the chaos that they had now been landed in.

Brina slept in the car all the way back.

CHAPTER 15 - ANOTHER SCENE IN THE PLAY

Two days later they drove back down again to the hospital to be there mid-morning.

Brina had now re-engineered or remodelled herself into a different role, gathered herself, regrouped, she was back to the organised, professional confident, 'no messing with' woman that she was, and had to be.

Brina was now dressed smartly, looked well-presented and as though she had slept well. She took a deep breath before going into the hospital ward.

Her mother greeted them from her bed with a pleased but pained smile inside her oxygen hood. After several minutes of greetings and updates, Brina left Sam to continue chatting with her while she went off to get a situation report from the nurses.

Sam sat down on the chair next to the bed, and held her frail white hand in his, while at the same time lifting the plastic oxygen hood up slightly so she could talk without having to raise her voice.

She was still very 'high' and vague, and started chatting to him quietly in a stream of consciousness. Telling him straight away of things she has seen, visions, out-of-body type experiences, tunnels, lights, a whole array of spiritual experiences that she had had in the last few days, and also during the operation.

"Even last night," she went on "I was lying in the dark and I could hear a conversation going on at the end on my bed, but there was nobody there, some gangster type talking to another chap who was going to frame this woman for a crime he had done, and they were going to blackmail someone in America. But it was all real, it was a real conversation, I could hear their voices so clearly, but there was nobody there." She went on to describe several other similar experiences, some were brief, fleeting images and events others had gone on for up to half an hour as journeys or progressive stories.

She also recounted a conversation she had had with her own mother, who Sam knew had died in 1973, it was all very vivid, and real to her. Sam just sat there listening to it all.

Sam had heard quite a bit about Brina's grandmother, she had been very close to Brina when she was young. She had that kind loving empathic nature.

It was something genetic, and sometimes missed a generation. Her grandmother had been one of these supressed medium types, very in touch with the spiritual, and had a knowing sense or feeling about her, an Oracle, or pre-cog, Sibyl type – just like Brina.

Brina had recounted quite a number of interesting stories about her grandmother, interesting abilities that were only hinted at, supressed by the attitude of others around her and culture she lived in. It was something that 'went with the territory' in those days.

But in some cases, as with for example Brina's mother, it was much better to bury it away, occupy yourself with organising tea parties, church fetes, school fundraising bazaars. Competing in the village community politics, status checking and management, and the usual bored female local hierarchy battles and positioning.

This was probably Brina's mother's dramatic 'outing', the drug assisted opening of the spiritual closet that her mother had been supressing all this time, in response to domestic pressure in her own upbringing.

Brina had been given assurances by the nurses that her mother would not be discharged until they had spoken with her first.

Brina had to have time to get things ready at her mother's house, which is where he and Brina were off to now. It would take her at least ten days to arrange for the house to be ready, support in place, food, care, and people who could look after her mother.

On the way to her mother's house, while Sam was driving, Brina phoned a few people in her mother's village. From what Sam could overhear of the conversation it had all gone pear-shaped in the village, apparently the vicar had been to her Aunt's house as everyone in village was very concerned about not hearing about how she was, and everyone was now worried and upset.

There then followed a list of instructions and explanations, and some fairly swift organised co-ordinated communications. It was all done in a fashion that sounded quite alien to Sam, a way of operating that he wasn't familiar with, it was 'how things were done in the village'.

The village had all been 'kept out of the loop', there was news to be had, to be worried about, and nobody had been 'told' for days on end. After all, what were they to think?

The village was the classic archetypal little ancient English country village, full of all the required ticks in the boxes for 'Olde Worlde' style quaintness. The church dated back to Saxon-Norman times, gothic with vast stained glass windows, ancient grey stone walls, square stone grey bell tower, long aisles and Templar history and whitewashed walls.

It was large and surrounded by a peaceful ancient wooded graveyard, full of large stones, some tomblike, with carefully positioned layouts, and metal fencing. All echoing the long gone battles of the village hierarchy, status, importance and funding.

There were two or three fruit farms which generated the work for the villagers. There was a manor house, a few shops and a couple of public houses, and the whole place was surrounded by fields and woods for miles which undulated over green countryside, crisscrossed with small country lanes which led to the next villages in any direction.

This village was made up a three or four hundred houses, ranging in date from modern to several hundred years old, all spread along several narrow country roads. There was a village green, and a playground where all the metal chains and swings had been replaced with plastic ones as thieves had stolen the metal.

There was an old brick village hall, and a Primary school. With one main road coming through which went into the village bubble at one end, and out the other, with a sign at each end warning you of which village you were entering.

It reminded him of those BBC crime dramas like *Miss Marple* or *Midsomer Murders*, where people driving along the road and seeing the sign for the quaint little village of *Midsomer* would immediately apply the brakes on the car, leaving black skid marks on the road.

The name *Midsomer* meant that you were entering a village where you were 2 million times more likely to either be murdered, witness one, or be blamed for one. If you had seen the TV show and knew what was going on there, it was all fairly bloody obvious. Yet there was still no telling some people.

There were no skid marks on the road in front of this village sign. No, the village was far too clever for that, far too subtle and devious. It had spent many centuries refining its immune system, its defensive firewalls, culture and nervous system, and the communications protocols were quite unique.

It had that quiet, quaint, picturesque archetypal unsuspecting country village look about it, hedgerows, flowers, orchards, red post-boxes, village hall, ancient inns, telephone boxes, and narrow hedge-lined lanes with cottages and footpaths. Structures and legacy from bygone eras that somehow lingered on under the surface, formed and mapped the psyche of the hamlet, evolved and reinforced over the centuries.

It weathered change and adapted around it, folding it into its life, absorbing it, using it.

Underneath the surface though lay many secrets, history, unspoken dark truths, hushed scandals, and 'goings on'. Just like Brighton this village had its own collective unconscious identity, and macro-culture.

One it shrouded and veiled under the surface, and buried in ignorance. The buildings themselves seemed to hold its memories, its programs and routines. You could feel them at work on people, changing them, forming them, hypnotising them, immunising them from the outer reality, and holding them to task within its bubble of unconsciousness.

They became 'people of the village', a tribal identity, branded, and encoded and recognised as such by other 'villages'. There were though some unusually powerful programs here at work; ghosts and demons in the walls that sought to manipulate, possess, and draw you in like a game of chess into its network of repeating scenes and dramas.

Just like *Hotel California* in the song, or the 'Overlook Hotel' in the *Shining* film, it would even create fairy-tale princesses to be sent forth from its kingdom, to 'marry well' into other kingdoms, carrying its code into the wide world beyond, and to hopefully return with their catch.

The unsuspecting boy 'prince' would then be drawn into the game, being dragged to the village device by ancient and refined and maintained programs, to play within it. To relive its saga storylines, enact the scenes of the gameplay in modern form. All the while unconsciously and cleverly disguising its hidden nature and structure from those beguiled within it, and the casual lazy eye of the passer by.

But unlike in the *Shining* film, Sam was no naive little boy on the tricycle with a wooden sword. The village was in for a shock, and unlike the song *Hotel California*, he wasn't going to have any trouble leaving it. But then of course - you could just see it as a quaint old village with people living in it.

In any case he quite liked it, it was charming.

He had visited the village to see Brina's mother a number of times, invited at times that seemed very coincidental with certain garden parties, fetes, and 'get-together events'.

Brina, or 'Sabrina darling', as she was known there, was the young maiden princess done good, 'married' well, ignoring the obvious minor technicality of the ring.

Having found a 'nice young handsome man' who was 'well to do', and brought him back for them to approve of.

With little ladies stroking the side of her arm in reassuring gestures, emotions that no words could convey, but which didn't stop them trying anyway. The youthful internet-driven adjectives of 'churching' and 'shipping' didn't mean anything here, or translate into village speak, this was a place that didn't need adjectives.

But Brina loved it, and it loved Brina, and it would do anything to bring her back into it again, especially now she had brought with her that 'nice young man'. Their Sabrina reverted back to being the role they always knew and loved, a polite gentle kind loving 18 year old, from whom everyone wanted a hug.

When he had been there in the past, he had done his best to be the handsome polite and bright chivalrous knight in smart casual gear. Conveying that all elusive air of breeding and groomed yet interesting attentiveness. Which of course he was anyway.

When he went there he could almost sense the village collectively talking to him, like a razor sharp 'Miss Marple' in her tweed jacket, walking stick and muddy boots. Surveying his looks, his manner, his mind, and bloodstock, and poking him with a stick.

Which was fine, just so as long as they didn't start checking his teeth, and running their hands over his fetlocks he would probably cope very well.

Every time he visited the village the program would restart again in a different episode, firing into action with a new drama, with new and old characters with some other implausible illogical 'story' lesson to be played out at the touch of the button, having led dormant in freeze-frame for months.

However in the last few days the role of 'Darling Sabrina' had now been recast into the new role of 'that Brina girl', along with the guilty until proven innocent verdict, of 'causing untold grief' to the concerned neighbours and friends of which there were now it seemed, many hundreds.

Midnight had arrived unexpectedly for *Cinderella* in her blue dress, and now she was back in rags, as a badly behaved serving-girl-come-stepdaughter, with a mountain of cleaning up, fixing, and sorting out to do.

In this playhouse the scenes changed pretty fast around here.

The actual physical house preparation and clean-up of her mother's cottage took several hours. It now had to be made suitable for someone who would potentially be in a wheelchair for some time.

It was Friday night when they got back to their own home. During the night Brina had a violent nightmare, from which she woke up crying.

In the vivid dream her mother was on the ground; there was blood everywhere; but Brina was helpless and couldn't stop her dying. Sam had spent half an hour trying to calm her down, but before Brina could settle down or even think of going back to sleep she made Sam go through the scenario of what to do if it happened in real life.

So, rather than arguing over the illogic of it, he went through with her what to do. He explained that she should to try to stop the immediate bleeding, then to ring the ambulance, but he kept reassuring Brina that the operation that her mother had had wouldn't create that kind of situation, and that there wouldn't be any blood, so she just had to stop worrying.

She obviously had some 'message' or translated image in her mind of something that was wrong, and the only way she could deal with it was to keep asking him what to do, in a range of situations that somehow made sense. It made no sense to him though, but to her it was very vivid.

CHAPTER 16 - CONSCIOUS INTERVENTION

It had now been five days since the operation, and they now figured that they had a week left before her mother would be out of hospital. They had done all the tidying-up of her house earlier in the week, and made a whole string of other arrangements that needed to be done so now they just had to wait. Sam had even scheduled some time off from work over the end of the next week. They were both exhausted still, but at least had a long quiet Bank Holiday weekend to look forward to.

The next morning they were woken up at 9 a.m. by the phone ringing. Sam handed the receiver to Brina and put it on speakerphone, and put his head under the pillow again. It was one of Brina's mothers relatives just letting her know that her elderly husband had offered to pick Brina's mother up from the hospital that afternoon as her mother had called them and asked them to collect her. She, apparently, had done so as she didn't want to cause Brina any more trouble, and her mother had convinced the nursing staff at the hospital not to call her.

Apparently - as she could now walk – she felt 'fine', and there were plenty of people at home in the village who could look after her, she was now ready to go, and so was being discharged later that morning.

There was a long pause in the telephone conversation as the relative waited for Brina to respond.

Sam put his head further under the pillow.

Five hours later they arrived at 'the village' and to her mother's house, to try to get things ready. Half an hour later she arrived in the car, along with a large quantity of pharmaceutical products, paperwork, and no idea which planet she was on.

Her mother got out of the car with a walking stick in hand, and thanked the aged 'uncle' for the lift.

Brina had been outmanoeuvred again, and the only thing to do now was to play catch-up and to try and make the best of the situation, without resorting to screaming at her mother.

Her mother hobbled slowly into the house, after handing over her bags that she insisted on carrying out of the car to Brina, and walked into the house breathlessly. Sam walked beside her to make sure she didn't fall, until she had settled herself into her comfy reclining chair in the kitchen with an 'I'm home' smile.

She looked very nauseous, pale, and dizzy, and more like someone who should still be in a hospital bed with lots of cables and tubes attached.

How the hell had they let her out of hospital? he thought, *She is in no fit state to come home.* But then these days there was so much pressure to get beds free, get patients out of their responsibility, off the books as it were. As long as you could walk a few steps and say you were fine to go, then you could go.

Once home now she immediately started complaining that Brina had moved things, that she had tried to change her house around. It took her a while before she had calmed down and relaxed back into being 'back at home' and safe.

From the following conversations it was obvious that her mother's impression of what had been going on at the hospital and what he and Brina had been going through was very different to reality. She kept saying how nice everyone had been, the doctors, the surgeons, the nurses.

She then went on about who had sent her cards, flowers, almost as if she was relaying the story to a friend who had popped round for a cup of tea to get the news. She seemed to have completely forgotten the stress, the awful events, the situations and the chaos, and the life threatening danger that she was in.

Sam listened in silence just nodding here and there. She recounted to him again some of her spiritual experiences too, with suitable additional colourful embellished touches added in.

Brina returned to the kitchen and made her mother a few drinks and a light supper and put her to bed early using the wheelchair that her Aunt had helpfully thought to provide. Brina checked on her regularly in-between getting her own things ready to stay, and sorting domestic things out and talking with Sam.

A couple of times that she checked on her she had dropped off to sleep, and fallen sideways in the bed and gone quite pale. Something was obviously not quite right, but Sam had to go, it was getting late and he had a long drive back home. This, again had caught them off guard, he had things to get back at home to do.

Brina was concerned. "What do I do?" she pleaded with him. But there was nothing to be done, there was nobody to help, no support, no doctor, it was a Bank Holiday, and there was no plan, no medical help, advice or anyone coming around to check.

He had also not brought any clothes with him for himself. Brina had packed some things for herself in preparation for the following week, but he had just assumed he was going to drop her off and go back home. It had been such a rush, he hadn't had time to think.

As time went on he realised he couldn't do that now. He had to stay, but there also wasn't really anywhere to sleep, she had her little room with the single bed, but that was it. For him, it was going to be a long uncomfortable night on the sofa.

About 1 a.m. he woke up in the dark wearing just his boxer shorts, with a sheet and knitted blanket over him. He was oblivious to where he was, and why everything smelt different.

He slowly orientated his mind to his situation. There were noises and voices coming from Brina's mother's bedroom. He quickly pulled his trousers on, and blearily stumbled out of the lounge, into the corridor and then into the main bedroom to see Brina trying to lift her mother up, to help her to the bathroom.

Sam was very nervous about lifting Brina's mother, but in the end he didn't give her any option. He just lifted her into his arms and carried her slowly to the bathroom, into which he lowered her down gently and stepped out of the door. The lock clicked shut.

"I am just going to straighten the bed and sheets" Brina whispered to him still shaking her head, and walked back along the corridor sighing loudly and tying up her hair back as she went. Sam quietly waited listening as politely as he could.

After a few minutes the toilet flushed and the seat slammed down with a bang, and it made him jump.

"Umm, are you OK?" asked Sam through the door with a short nervous cough. There was just silence. Then a few thumps as something fell heavily on the floor.

"Hello?" said Sam. But there was no reply, he tapped on the door. "Hello?" he said again. There was nothing, just silence.

Immediately several nightmare visions went through his head. He tried the door which was definitely locked. He was wary of forcing it open in case she was immediately on the other side. He took a coin out of his pocket, and used it to turn the spindle in the lock. There was a click and he opened to door. Brina's mother was on the floor unconscious on her back in a heap. She was ghostly white, and her mouth was open. He started talking to her as he knew he was supposed to from his first aid training, he knelt down to check her breathing and pulse.

She wasn't breathing, he gently felt for a pulse on her wrist, and placed his hand on her heart area. There was some sort of pulse or beating, but it seemed to be fluttering, vibrating, and sporadic.

"Shit" said Sam under his breath. "Oh bloody hell!"

He tilted her head back and checked her airway which was clear. He remembered all his first aid training, and his Rescue Diver course procedures, but nothing had prepared him for resuscitating someone who had just had major open heart surgery, or how to avoid the cuts and fractures all over her ribcage. He laid her out straight, tilted her neck back, pinched her nose and breathed into her mouth to gently inflate her lungs, as much as felt safe.

He touched her gently on her chest, but it was just too fragile to do any compressions, he could feel the heart fluttering under his palms, it hadn't stopped - it was trying to do something, but it wasn't pumping. He tried another breath but he knew that would be no good if the blood wasn't flowing.

He stopped to try and think, he closed his eyes and concentrated and allowed his mind to clear, sweat pouring from his forehead in panic. What was going on in her body formed in his mind, and he translated it into something he had to do, in a way you couldn't describe in words. He lifted her neck up and raised her back up gently off the floor, and slid himself behind her propping her up and pushed her ribcage up and outward away from him, so her neck and head bent back slightly and he rubbed her back hard. It was all he could do to get whatever it was working or moving again.

There was a change, and he felt her heart start up, rapidly changing from a fluttering to a rapid beat to a more measured stable beat.

She started breathing in a slow rasping stuttering rhythm, and then it all picked up together and she began to come back.

It had all happened in just over a minute, but it seemed like several hours to Sam. Brina appeared in the doorway having heard the noises, her eyes bulged and then her face went white.

Sam put his hand up to stop her coming any further, he didn't want to add any variables to a fragile situation. He left his other palm on her mother's back feeling for the rhythms, and he helped with the breathing motion.

It was a further two minutes before he felt that things had stabilised. He moved himself round her without disturbing her position, and picked her up again in a straight lift. His legs by this time were cramped and shaking. He instructed Brina to put all the pillows at the head of the bed so she could be propped up, and carried her back to her room, laid her into the bed, and left his hand on her back a minute more until she had settled down.

She was still unconscious and oblivious to what had gone on.

What the hell are we to do now?, he thought and he suddenly realised it was 1 a.m. on a Bank Holiday Sunday morning, and the chance of getting an ambulance out here now was going to be pretty remote.

It also dawned on him that this was no mere coincidence. That this was happening now as part of the crisis scene, and that the whole thing was starting to shape up to be Act Two of the Saga that they had been through the first part of a week before.

Now that Brina's mother was propped up, the colour started to return to her face, and she started to sleep more peacefully. Even though Sam had known what to do, and had responded to knowledge and instinct in his mind of what needed to happen, that still didn't give him the answer as to why this was happening.

Also he did not know what it was that had caused the problem and why it was no longer there. It was very confusing.

They were both already very tired, and there was nobody to call, they had no numbers to refer to other than the emergency one which he knew would be futile. Eventually he tried calling the ward at the hospital she had come from, which ended up being entirely pointless, unhelpful, and with him just getting angrier at them with the fact that she had been allowed to leave in the first place.

There was nothing to be done for the moment, other than making her as comfortable as possible, and keeping her upright. It was going to be a long sleepless night for both of them.

By 8 a.m. of the Sunday morning, they had managed to get through to an on-call doctor service, it was the only option available.

Her mother was awake now but feeling very giddy and sick. Two hours later, the doctor turned up, and apologised for being late only he had been flown in from Delhi two days earlier, by the contract agency that filled in for Bank Holiday services for the health service, and he was still suffering from jetlag.

Sam tried to explain the situation to him but he could only speak very basic English. He ran over the details of the operation, the situation and what had happened, and her symptoms, the dizziness, the vertigo feeling she had, and her collapsing.

Yet amazingly the doctor diagnosed her on the spot as having Norovirus. He had come to that conclusion within a few moments, without having even examined her. She, apparently, must have contracted at the hospital, it was very common *apparently*.

"Errr no," said Sam to the doctor "I don't think so, she doesn't have any of the symptoms of Norovirus", and he gestured the doctor into the bedroom to actually see her.

The doctor examined her mother for about two minutes, talking to her briefly, and then stepped back out into the corridor with Sam. He then became quite dismissive, and said that she had picked up what he had said before. There was nothing he could do.

"Look" said Sam, trying not to lose his temper, "Can you at least just give her something for the moment to stop her feeling giddy and sick?"

The doctor reluctantly opened his bag and got out a syringe and a small bottle labelled *Stemetil*, and went back in to give the injection to her. He came back out and then gave Sam two sachets of powder. "It is for the diarrhoea" he said.

"But she doesn't have any diarrhoea" Sam explained again. The doctor picked up his bag and went to go.

"Hang on" said Sam, "that can't be it surely not after what I have just described to you as having happened". The doctor looked at him blankly and started to leave, trying to ignore Sam. "Can you at least suggest anything we should do?" the doctor stopped and turned.

"You just have to keep her lying down flat until the vomiting stops, and the dizziness goes away, in twenty four hours she will be fine." He was completely ignoring everything Sam had said about what had gone on. He turned again and left, leaving Sam in a bewildered state of confusion in the doorway.

This was clearly some guy with only rudimentary health knowledge, and yet somehow had the required credentials and paperwork. Imported by a local health service agency from India to provide cover for the UK health service over the Bank Holiday.

He probably had all his flights and expenses and a nominal salary paid for and in return they would be charging him out for a fortune every hour to a bureaucratic health system, that was being held to ransom by itself.

It was insane, totally insane. Fortunately though Sam was not, nor was he stupid, and he knew that he was the only thing keeping Brina's mother alive. He knew he had to keep her propped up and supported. If she were to be laid down now as instructed she would be dead in minutes.

After an hour her mother started to look much better and less light headed and sick. It appeared that whatever had caused the problem had now dissipated. It was also clear that Sam wasn't going home that following night either. The rest of the day dragged on and into the night, with various phone calls trying to get help, and unhelpful callers to the house who had to be turned away.

Brina was spending all her time nurse-maiding her mother and trying to get a few hours rest.

By the Monday morning, things were still pretty much the same, they were coping and things were stable, but they were now way beyond exhausted. Sam had that sweaty weak feeling all over from lack of sleep, he felt hollow, numb, and had nowhere to relax or get comfortable in an unfriendly stressful environment.

By mid-afternoon her mother had decided that she was well enough to get up out of bed by herself.

They were both in the kitchen talking when they heard the clatter come from the bedroom. They got there in a few seconds to find her mother on the floor again on her side. Sam followed the same process as before, and eventually lifted her back into bed unconscious.

That was it, enough was enough. He dialled for an emergency ambulance, the point had been reached.

Sam managed to negotiate through the question and answer system for an ambulance to actually come, and got to the question as to whether her life was in immediate danger. He stopped to think, she was sat up in bed and fine now, propped up and with them both looking after her she was OK, she wasn't going to die.

But he knew if he said "No", there would be no ambulance or at least not one for a long while, not today. He felt himself wanting to say "Hang on a minute I will just go off and lie her down for a second and then be back with you."

His voice stuttered in a confused set of mumbles. The operator repeated the question, adding that she could only get an ambulance out there immediately if her life was in immediate danger.

Sam could feel himself in a position within a flowchart. One answer simply meant that nothing would happen, and there would be a slight chance of getting an ambulance several hours later. Or the other option meant that he would get what he needed, or at least the next step along the process in the game.

The operator asked the question again. "Is her life in immediate danger?"

"Yes" was the answer that he gave, and the operator got him to confirm it. It was something he was being shown that he had to do but on a larger scale, just like Brina pressing her override button.

Then everything happened, quickly.

The ambulance arrived ten minutes later, along with a paramedic in a car, sirens blazing along the way. They could hear them coming from miles away. Both the ambulance and the paramedic had managed to get lost in the lanes in the village, trying to find the badly signposted road and house.

Several 'helpful' village bystanders, who all happened to be coincidentally walking their dogs just outside their houses all at the same time, had offered help with directions, and Brina went outside to wave the ambulance in. She also gave reassuring smiles to the small crowd of people with their dogs now forming at the end of the lane.

All the while Sam had been on the phone talking with the operator while the ambulances came. Brina, before she went outside, had been getting her mother awake again, and propping her up and talking with her.

As such, by the time the paramedic and ambulance men arrived into the bedroom she looked 'fine', and smiled at them warmly when they came in. In fact she was at pains to tell them she was 'fine' and they shouldn't have troubled themselves. The ambulance men carrying their Medipacks exchanged glances with Sam, and he gave a brief shake of his head to them. Obviously they had also been briefed on the way by the operator as to what to expect.

Sam explained in detail about the situation, about the operation and leaving the hospital too early, her symptoms and that he couldn't work out specifically what was wrong.

He also explained about the visit from the doctor the following day. The two paramedics just exchanged knowing glances but didn't say anything. They started to go through their diagnostic process and attached sensors and an ECG machine to her. It was obvious by their manner and conversation and questions that they were highly competent and knowledgeable.

But they we also still at a loss to work out what was wrong. All of which was not helped by her mother, who kept reiterating that she was 'fine'.

Brina stood in the doorway, arms crossed looking pale and anxious while several more minutes passed with various checks, tests, and questions.

"Let me try this", said Sam and he gestured his head to Brina to follow him to the head of the bed. He removed the pillows in front of the headboard, and eased Brina's mother down onto her back.

The various machines that her mother was attached to by cables, all lit up like Christmas trees, and alarms went off loudly. Things started 'beeping' urgently, her mother went pale immediately, and then lost consciousness.

Sam sat her up again, and then after a minute she recovered slowly and was fine.

"It's a sort of feature", said Sam helpfully, "do you want to see it again?"

The paramedics scanned over the readouts and printed graphs.

Her heart had indeed stopped pumping and her blood pressure had fallen down instantly. Now they were all talking through various options and diagnosis with each other. Sam listened in.

He looked at Brina's mother sitting there in her bed, breathing rapidly, and colour coming back to her cheeks again. An image of a marble inside one of those old Victorian glass bottles came into his mind, one that would act like a stopper, and then when it was released would rattle around in the tube at the top.

"I think she has a blood clot" said Sam to the paramedics abruptly. They both stopped and looked at him.

"Yes, that is the most likely explanation", said one of them. "A post-operative blood clot blocking one of her tubes either to or from the lungs to the heart."

They didn't ask him though how he knew, or if he was medically trained. They carried on talking for another few minutes and then turned to him again.

"The problem is" one of them said "that we can't take her back to Brighton hospital, to the ward she came from, we have to take her to Accident and Emergency at the local hospital.

"The difficulty with that, is that today being a Bank Holiday, it is currently seventy deep in people waiting on trolleys in the corridors waiting to get in. If we take her in she will be waiting in the ambulance for half an hour, and then two hours on a trolley even as a high priority. They also don't have any scanning facility available and even if they did there would be nothing that could be done until tomorrow, when everyone else gets back from the holiday break.".

Sam processed what they were trying to explain to him. "So essentially what you are saying is that although this is their busiest day, the bulk of the staff aren't there, and there is nothing than can be done anyway, and she would be at risk, and very uncomfortable being taken there?"

They nodded. "We can take her in but that is the situation."

"But she will most likely die if that is the case" said Sam.

There was silence.

"So" said Sam "the best option is to try and make it until tomorrow here, keep her in bed as we have done, and stay as calm as possible. Get an ambulance out in the morning, and hope the backlog has cleared."

Neither of them said anything, and it was clear that the choice was his, but it was a fairly obvious that he didn't have one.

Ten minutes later the ambulance left. But the paramedic stayed to complete the tests, check over the bruises from the falls, and provide a few helpful pieces of advice.

Aside from several other 'interested well-wishers' calling, the afternoon, evening and night went through uneventfully. Sam and Brina took it in turns to cover the nursing shifts and get what sleep they could.

In the morning they both knew what was coming, and so decided to get prepared for it all as much as they could beforehand.

So before calling the ambulance, Sam decided he and Brina should have a shower and at least try and freshen up, and prepare for the long day ahead.

Unsurprisingly the immersion heater had decided to break, and there was no hot water. It was the one thing Sam hated, cold showers in the morning, and he was sure Brina was the same.

A hot shower was the one thing he wanted, and after all they had been through it was more than coincidental, and almost too much to bear.

Sam called the ambulance again, and went through the flowchart again to get what he needed. It arrived again about twenty minutes later. By which time Brina had already packed her mother's bags, and explained what was happening to her. The ambulance men wheeled her out along the gravel path, and into the back of the ambulance with her legs covered in a blanket.

They both just stood outside and watched her go, unable to speak. It just seemed surreal.

Then Sam went into the house to get the car keys, and lock up the house, before he and Brina following her to the hospital in the car.

Many of the occupied trolleys in Accident and Emergency were still there from the previous day, with people still waiting to get to see a specialist or surgeon for ongoing treatment.

Fortunately her mother was taken straight through to the Resuscitation Unit, and propped up in a bed, the Unit having been briefed on the situation beforehand.

After an hour she was wheeled off to a bed on a critical care ward to wait for a scan, but moments later she was wheeled back again - someone having beaten her to the bed.

The long list of crazy situations was getting so beyond surreal now that it was no longer logically acceptable or possible, but there was still nothing they could do. Even though it was total madness, and totally fabricated like some unbelievable play, they could not get out of it, they were trapped in the process.

They were also becoming emotionally numb to it all now too, detached from the reality of it, mindlessly watching the next demonstrated and organised scene of the fiasco play to be acted out so that they could 'get the message'.

It came over now as a virtualised set of flashcard scenes, each with its own problem, issue, problem, or concern within the culture of the macro-organism health system, which was in itself being used as an *exemplar* of something much larger.

It was the same sort of scenario as you would get in an office, with him as a brand new senior manager coming in and having a series of representations from different departments, all showing him what is going on.

Groups of good hard working people, arriving in front of his desk each with a set of papers and lists of problems from each department of the organisation, explaining why it was all such a disorganised bureaucratic mess.

At the end of the day you open the drawer of your desk, and find the plans of several other previous managers, and then you realise that there is no point in trying to do the same, you have to get to the source of the problem, and get to the unconscious agendas much higher up, that are blind to what is going on.

The play continued to be drawn out, with several more problems shown to them of errors, and issues in the system as the day went on.

Four hours later after a scan they were informed that her mother had a large blood clot in the tube between the heart and the lung, and that she would have to be put on strong anticoagulants to dissipate the clot.

CHAPTER 17 - THE VILLAGE CHURCH

Over the next few days her mother's condition in the hospital deteriorated to the point where she was even visited by the village vicar. Which was always a key indicator in the village of what stage 'things were at', and also the state things had reached with the funds for the church roof.

Everything had started to become a blur now. An emotionless series of events, a slideshow presented to someone who was bone tired weary, and strapped to a chair unable to get away.

Even events such as her mother being laid down by staff who hadn't been made aware of her condition, due to poor communication, causing her to crash and be resuscitated again. It all just seemed to be distant now, and in the background.

Over the next week all the travelling to and from their own home, the visits to the hospital, the talks with specialists, the reviews of what had gone wrong, the ignored complaints, the apologies, all seemed to become like echoes in a detached existence of aching weary blurred sleeplessness, and a constant clammy unwashed feeling.

Things had now improved for her mother and she was eventually allowed home, along with another bag of heavy duty drugs. Sam picked her up this time from hospital, and left Brina at her mother's house cleaning again.

Brina had arranged for several people to look after her mother over the next few weeks, and had decided that she and Sam needed to get home and get out of the crazy environment and situation. She knew now her mother would somehow be fine. It was if now that the play had ended, and they had been shown all they needed to see.

Later in the afternoon at her mother's house, and before they left for home again, Sam decided they should go for a short walk together along the footpath that led to the village church. He had never taken the time to look at it closely, and it seemed like a good excuse to get some air, and for her to show him the places that she had grown up around, and had told him so many stories about.

The churchyard was idyllic, bathed in dappled warm sunshine which shone through overhanging trees onto well mown grass. It was one of those ancient little quintessentially English village churches, set in its own space and time.

It was empty, quiet and peaceful, aside from the gentle birdsong and distant occasional traffic noises from the main road in the distance. The ancient church was irregularly shaped, evolved and built on over a thousand years from its small humble Saxon foundations. A Norman tower had been added, tall medieval glass windows and flint stone walls, and a high Victorian clay tiled and leaded roof.

Sections had been added at times when the village had been prosperous, or local landowners had sought to buy their salvation out of generosity or guilt.

It sat in the middle of the tree lined acre of land, with grey tombstones and worn mossy graves, all surrounding it like sentinels.

Brina led him round the outside to the back of the church, and showed him the wall where her father's grave was. It was a simple unimposing marble square stone, laid into the ground a few inches from the flint wall of the church itself. There were roses behind it, climbing up the wall in the sunshine, and the stone plinth was surrounded by multi-coloured wild flowers, and alongside it was her grandmother's grave.

Sam remembered Brina had told him that her father had only ever wanted a simple grave, nothing fancy, but in that specific location on the back wall of the church, and next to his mother's. With provision on the other side, made for his wife - Brina's mother. It was apparently how things were done here.

The sun shone down on both graves, and made the inclusions in the polished marble sparkle, which highlighted the names and dates and inscriptions.

Brina had mentioned her grandmother briefly to him, with memories from when she was young and the attachment and connection they felt, but she was very small when she died. Yet certain smells, tastes and events would bring those memories back to her in moments.

She just stood there quietly with him in the sunshine, her hand in his.

After she had laid a few flowers on the graves, they went inside so she could show him around the church. Just like the graveyard, it was empty, but dark and cold. The air inside was still, dank, quiet with a sense of serene reverence. The grey stone arches supported by tall stone pillars, towered up and over the isles of wooden benches and heavy flagstone floors.

It was cooler in here and slightly musty with echoes of movement. It was an old ancient smell with a sense of the history of the place and the village. The weight of memory for so many events and passing years etched into the stone walls, pillars, and dark grey floors and wooden boards.

It had all the smell and feel of history steeped and carved into it, like patination on an ancient wooden throne.

It was also a focal point, a meeting place, an iconic image for the village, but somehow distinct, preserved in isolation within it, like a holy central shrine in a temple. One that observed and recorded the proceedings in a timeless, implacable manner.

There was something here, something in this place, he could feel it.

In a quiet voice Brina talked to him explaining what she knew of this place, walked him around the aisles and pointed out the key aspects of it all. The history, the font, the nave, the altar, the inscriptions, the organ, the archaeological work done on it, the high vaulted wooden roof, the windows.

She also mentioned the ancient Templar markings on the walls that her father had remembered seeing when he had been a boy, but which had been whitewashed over many years ago for some reason. He had spent a lot of his time looking after the church, keeping the hedges and grass trimmed, and helping keep the building maintained, sort of acting as its caretaker in an unofficial capacity in his retirement.

It was as if it was now kept in suspended animation since he had gone, the same air, the same sprinkling of dust, with a few weeds starting to appear here and there on the paths. With small rodents and birds making their nests in and around it in quiet corners, and in the roof. It had been frozen in time, just sat there waiting, dormant, inactive. All left in a state of suspended animation, waiting for something to happen.

Sam placed his hand on one of the stone pillars. He could almost feel the walls in the church storing all of its history, recording things away like some giant filing cabinet. Information preserved as if in some archaic library.

There were so many things here hidden away, secrets being recorded subconsciously, all adding to the unconscious mind of the village and perceptive views of how they saw and remembered things in this building.

This was a powerful place, far more so than the people in the village realised, or were aware of, with the subconscious effect it was having on them. All its inherent unconscious programs, reinforced functions and archetypal symbolism and structure.

It was also drawing powerful 'spirits' in, if that was the right word, to reinforce it, play with, grow with, and manipulate and evolve it. But in his case he had the distinct feeling it had caught more than it had bargained for, and was not sure what to make of him.

He closed his eyes for a moment with his hand still on the wall, just to focus on what was going on under the surface of all this, what was here, and what was going on.

He had the image of himself as a little boy in his mind now, with a sword and wanting to play in the graveyard, from some distant ancient time. Yet also eternally, summoning myth programs, processes in ways words could not describe to try and interact with it, engage with the structure, the history, the nature of the building and its spirit or soul held within its walls and projected by the people in the village.

He could see now that it was trying to draw him in at a subconscious level, with outdated games, mythical structures and methods and tricks.

Ones that may work on others, but not him. He did not want to play old hero games, over and over again in repeating loops, nor was he a naive child. Yet there was no evil here, no demons in the walls, no malevolence. It was just old and empty, and yet protecting.

Energy flowed through him and around him, but there was nothing threatening him, so he just continued sensing, and exploring in his mind.

Brina had walked to the back of the church and was writing something in the Visitor's Book next to the entrance doorway. Sam decided to move around in the empty building and he walked along the aisle slowly to the front of the church with the altar and the large stained glass windows and then he moved to the right and into a side nave.

He placed his hand on the cold carved stone of the back wall, and closed his eyes.

Power surged up through his body in tingling energy.

It came up through his spine and surrounded him. He emptied his mind and just allowed what he needed to do happen, over coding, re-coding, re-alignment, and structure modifications.

It took just a few moments and was not related to what they had been through for the last two weeks. No, this was something very different.

He breathed heavily out, and then a few moments later he lowered his hand again, and opened his eyes, and then walked out hand in hand with Brina, before driving the long trip home.

Two weeks later the whole plan and programme of what needed to happen for the National Health Service would manifest itself into a presented system-wide reorganisation and regeneration, a country-wide plan.

The list of things to be resolved delivered by the Government at the press conference read like a list of diary or journal entries, a 'to do' fixing list of everything he and Brina had been through over the last few weeks.

By the end of the year it would be converted into a plan, put forward in Parliament, and then it would begin to be implemented the following year.

But all these things needed fixing at the same time as everything else needed fixing - just like one failing organ in the body - you couldn't just mend that in isolation, you had to fix everything all at once. Manage the whole system.

The only way to do that was to tell it, direct the system, tell it what it needed to do, so that it could consciously fix itself.

Just in the same way as homeopathy did. You couldn't fix it all yourself - you just had to give it the information it needed to sort itself out, tell it what was wrong, and give it the information it needed to respond against.

Then you moved forward with it, until it faced its next perfect storm, the next 'management review phase' to be tied in with everything else that was changing. It needed to be a direction that avoided the icebergs, at least for the moment, dealing with the here and now, with a mind on the destination, a plan.

For Sam though it was also so easy to get drawn into the whole thing, the 'Am I really doing this?' thing , getting caught into the delusional trap of it all, and the reflective nature of consciousness.

It was so easy to forget how simple it was to fool yourself, and also to change your own perception of reality to fit in with what you believed to be happening.

Even if he was making these changes happen, even if he was influencing the collective mind, changing the field to influence our physical reality, it still meant nothing without proof, without real evidence.

For the moment he just went along with it, and if they were doing this thing or not, it was the right thing to do none the less.

However even if he, or they, were 'Doing this thing', the whole 'thing' still seemed too big, too complicated, with too little cause and effect or bandwidth capability that they had available to them to avoid the inevitable though. There was just too much to do.

Just doing this had nearly killed them, and the scale of everything else that needed fixing was just vast.

There needed to be dozens of him doing this, and dozens of Brina's, all singing from the same hymn sheet, as it were, to make it work, to make a big enough difference.

There seemed no way that that was likely to happen.

CHAPTER 18 - CITY STREET MATRIX

It was now the end of June 2012 and another day like every other so far that month, which by then wasn't saying very much as far as 'normality' was concerned.

Sam had woken up exhausted with masses of complex thoughts and information flowing through his head...again.

Yet again he had been disturbed in the night a few times, waking up in one instance with images of masses of dark snakes writhing over each other a few feet away from his closed eyelids.

It took him a few minutes to dismiss the phantasm, and dissipate the imagery before he could go back to sleep.

He had got up showered, had breakfast, and then just sat down. He really just felt that he couldn't concentrate or summon up the energy to motivate himself to do anything, as if he had already worked all night and hadn't slept at all.

Brina had decided that rather than wasting another day in limbo they should both get out, get out and do something productive, like say shopping.

So in autopilot mode he drove them both to the local city of Cheltenham to do some shopping for clothes and new bedding.

It was a rather cold and wet day for June, and everything seemed to have an edge of bleakness to it. He didn't mind, it was something to break up the template of monotony, something to get them doing something that needed to be done. He was a fit and healthy guy that would normally be full of energy - he shouldn't be feeling like this.

It was as if he was being used as a processing device, to resolve things - but he didn't know what, or why, or even how he was doing whatever it was that he was involved in.

He drove carefully and deliberately being mindful of everything around him; people, other cars and situations that may suddenly throw themselves at him.

He was used to this situation, this heightened state of alert, that level of intensity of whatever it was that was going on - you just had to be that bit more aware.

Yet he wasn't in the mood for 'additional information' in the form of 'people messages' coming in in the shape of attacks or hassles or situations, so he was being overly careful, and gave himself a cushion of defence against anything that may occur.

The multi-storey car park was one of those designed for city centres, laid out economically with the size of the parking spaces minimised, so that you had to squeeze a large car in and around concrete pillars, but leave just enough space to open your door and squeeze out – but only if you were a stick insect.

Sam drove carefully around and up five levels until he eventually came to some free spaces, ones that weren't reserved for local companies, all of whom clearly only employed staff that could manage only one or two flights of stairs.

He began reversing into a space carefully, and just as he was almost fully in place a car drove past in front of his quite quickly.

His attention was drawn to it due to its speed and odd behaviour. It was some small plastic bumper-car style one, with a lone young blonde woman driving it, and Sam noticed that she had a phone pressed to her ear using one hand, whilst steering with the other.

It was at that point that he realised that he had not left enough room on the passenger side to allow Brina to get out past the wing mirrors, so a few moments later Sam drove slightly forward to allow her to be able to get out more easily, before reversing again.

Brina then opened her door and stepped out. It was at that point that he noticed the woman in the car that had just driven past – it had stopped about 60 feet further along but then started to reverse back again quickly, as if the woman had seen someone else about to come out of a space and she was too hurried and impatient to check behind her.

It was all too obvious, and he could already see what was going to happen. He tried to reverse out of the way, but realised that Brina's car door was still open so he could only go back a foot without it colliding with the wing mirror of the car next to him.

Luckily this was just enough - the woman's car reversed past him and only glanced the front edge of his bumper, rather than smashing right into the side of it.

She had only scraped the front of his car bumper, a glancing moment, but the force was enough to crack the plastic on her rear side bumper, which unclipped and started dragging noisily along the ground.

She stopped her car several feet further back and got out and came towards them. She was in her early 20's, already red faced and starting to cry, and the phone that had been pressed to her ear had presumably been guiltily thrown down somewhere in the footwell of her car.

She was shaking and panicking, and clearly in a rush to get somewhere. Sam got out and checked the front of his car, which was becoming somewhat of a habit. There was no damage save for a long black plastic streak mark along the front.

Brina was already busy consoling the woman and telling her that it didn't matter - Sam did the same but the woman was frantic. She then ran back to her car and began scrabbling around in the glove compartment of it for some insurance documents, and with shaking hands tried to pass them to Brina, who politely refused them.

"It's OK" said Sam "there is no damage – it's all OK, it's fine." The woman then started to unload her situation to Brina - the interview, the directions, the job, not concentrating as she was late, and she thought he had parked already, it went on and on …

Sam walked over to her car and clipped the cracked bumper back onto the rear frame of her car and checked that it was secure.

"There," he said "all OK now." The woman looked at him blinking through red eyes. A smile tried to stretch across her face.

"It's not important" said Brina "these things just don't matter, they're not worth worrying about" and she gave her a hug and then the woman started thanking Brina and Sam.

He then closed the doors on his car and parked it, and she got into hers and drove it a few hundred feet and did the same, and then ran off down the stairs thanking them again as she passed by.

Hugs were a big thing with Brina, and she didn't give them away lightly, but for some reason, and they didn't understand why, everyone seemed to want one from her.

Then after getting a hug from her, everything seemed to be OK with them and their lives were now much brighter - but it all seemed a bit one sided though.

He didn't know if she made it to her interview, or how it went, but they did see her in the town later on sitting in a café drinking coffee with the phone on her ear again.

She still looked stressed, but it was hard to tell if that was to do with the incident or the interview, or if she chose to permanently live her life that way.

But she was young and had plenty of time to learn.

The streets in the city were very busy and damp with shoppers moving around quickly between the tall terraced streets of beige and grey Georgian style stone. All the shops and department stores were on three or four floors. It was similar in style to Bath, that Georgian English spa town look.

The sky was still heavy and dark holding the potential for more rain. Everyone seemed to be focused on themselves, introspective, with their minds set on getting to where they needed to go.

There were a couple of shops that Sam didn't want to go into - the smells of chemicals, perfumes and LED lights were just too much for him to deal with, too much sensory overload.

So while Brina went in, he decided to just wait outside on the other side of the street, in the open air, with his back against the massive thick old stone wall of the HSBC bank on the corner of the High Street, and just avoid doing anything.

The bank was very much in the pseudo-Roman style, with stone carved pillars, and impressive thick beige monolith like walls, high windows, and a tall roof.

The building must have stood there for a hundred years or so, deliberately grand and imposing, instilling an image and sense of regency, security and permanency.

How much must it have seen over the years, been through, and contained? Existing and witnessing all the wars, crises, weather, people, changes in the street. He stood and watched the hundreds of people walking by - so many different personalities, shapes, ages, faces, directions, journeys and cultures.

His head was already crammed with thoughts and concepts and flow of information traffic, knowledge and ideas.

The more he thought about things like that the worse it got, but he couldn't just stand there with his eyes closed as that would look odd, and he didn't want to go in shops - that would just add to all that and overload his senses with fake information and ideas.

Brina, he thought, also needed to be on her own for a bit too, to do some shopping in peace, have her own time to explore and think.

Being around so many people was so hard for him when he was so tired -he seemed to pick up so much information from everyone all the time. When he was tired he was exposed, open, lacking in bubble-like immunity.

It was as if they were passing him all their program information at once as they passed by.

Ideas, thoughts, beliefs, understandings, knowledge. Meme data arriving in packets as concepts that his mind would then assemble and integrate and work on in this state.

This would normally be OK as he could shut most of it out or be able to process it naturally, but when he was tired it was a struggle, like being at one too many dinner parties, and his tolerance for pleasantries and social interaction, was running a bit low on steam.

His face felt flushed, and a cold sensation spread over the front of his face. His cheeks and forehead felt slightly numb, as if he were inhaling cold fresh air through his sinuses, and it was all concentrated at a point in middle of the brow and forehead about a centimetre beneath the bone.

He also had a throbbing, aching, pain inside the middle of his head, between the two halves of his brain - he could feel it even though he shouldn't have been able to – and the pain ebbed up inside his head and translated to a bruising, aching feeling on the top of his crown, which was now hot and sensitive to the touch.

He was getting used to this sensation and the effect it had on him and his thoughts - it wasn't pleasant though as it gave him an intense, vivid, heightened perceptive, alert, awake feeling.

There was a vibrational sensation associated with it too, like you got when holding an electric razor, only this was a higher frequency of vibration. Awake and alert to every sense, every datum of perceptive information that was coming in.

His mind started racing - rapid thoughts and information sparked into his brain and his mind felt clear, sharp, fresh, and alert now.

He could sense he was 'doing something' again, processing some information, but he didn't know what, and as he watched he became somewhat detached from everything going on around him as though he were observing it, but not actually in it. He was a 'fly on the wall' of the street, or just observing a created scene from a construct program of a virtual street and program people going by as in the *Matrix* film.

Then everything started to slow down, the scene around him began to freeze, the sounds died away, and it seemed as if people were walking in slow motion, slower and slower, then almost stopping, but not quite. Just as the sequence in the *Matrix* film.

He knew it wasn't actually happening this way, it was just that his mind was suddenly working very fast, so fast that everything was being processed much quicker, so that it appeared that everything around him had slowed down almost to a halt.

His senses were still feeding information in at the same rate, but his brain was processing it at vastly increased speeds, utilising dual pathways of conscious and unconscious perception.

It was also doing this to convey some interpretation of external information coming in, and at the same time he was aware of not being delusional about it; he was not seeing it as real but was interpreting it as messages and information, rather than the misleading interpretation.

In effect he was observing what he was seeing, rather than believing that he was seeing some real phenomena. There was also ringing sound in his mind - like a television that had been left on standby - which he assumed was blood circulating in his ears.

The definition of everything became intense, vivid, and appeared to be in exquisite detail, as if he had all the time in the world to examine and perceive every colour, texture, fibre, line, and facial expression.

Even the pigeons slowed down as they took off and landed - as in fast frame capture film photography - which clearly indicated too that there was no form of mass human control going on, and that pigeons were really rubbish at playing games and at keeping secrets after all.

He watched the effect for a few moments and realised how much it resembled many scenes in some films that he had seen.

It was fascinating, and then slowly everything started to speed up again, and the sound returned with a rush, along with the sensation of the air and temperature, and after a few more moments everything was as it had been before.

Then there was the rushing roar of the present and the air and the noise all returned.

Except that he could barely stand because he was so exhausted.

He leaned back against the hard stone of the building and waited, trying not to think too much or faint.

He closed his eyes and just stood there trying to concentrate on shutting everything out.

It seemed to Sam as it was another half an hour before Brina found him, even though it had probably only been a few minutes.

Without talking, she just walked close to him as they returned back to the car park. She didn't ask him what had happened or what he had seen, she just supported him gently as they walked and then she drove them both home.

It was important not to read anything into these sorts of events, these happenings. He had come to jokingly call them *Matrix* moments due to the alarmingly coincidental similarity to situations and circumstances in the films.

He had learned to step back from himself and not allow himself to be drawn into the delusional nature of these experiential things, which, due to the discourse nature of what was happening, would have been easy to do. Which was what was happening to a lot of people who believed the film was how things really were.

The collective system would unconsciously reinforce that within them, making them believe they were in a virtual computer generated world and fighting some AI machine.

But just as with all these things, the films were based on the state of philosophical play and understanding at the time that they had been made - based on ideas from Jean Baudrillard and others - ideas which in themselves had been fed into the system unconsciously, and then reinforced in such a way that they were what IT thought it was, but of course it wasn't, IT was no *Clockwork God*, it was us, on both sides of the mirror, just two ways of seeing the same thing.

We are just limited by our physical 'side' and by the naive way that we have evolved our perceptions and senses.

This physicality and interpretation of it is just an evolved translation of what we have been able, up until now, to perceive, and that which was useful to us to evolve and survive.

In effect it is just the same as in the *Matrix* film, but there are no machines on the 'other side', we are just perceiving an interpretation of a field-based biological state based information system. It was all just one system, and it was us rather than 'them'.

It is just one way of describing it - as software in an operating system in which we are contained and have created and built up, all based on whichever particular state we have found ourselves in.

We have created perceived concepts of time, distance and dimension to give that data meaning and context as it appears to us, and it is the change within an information system - the reality - that we have to try and make sense of.

The reality though, probably wouldn't make a very good film when you described it like that, but then people don't like reality that much, it is boring, and difficult to deal with or understand.

In essence it is that perceptive limitation, only what we can sense, how we interpret it and the language we use to describe it with, that is holding us back.

We had learned to use and see only what is useful and that which makes sense from a natural advantage perspective. We have not evolved to see this all as a matrix, we have no need or sensory means to, nor any way of comprehending or processing it into logical meaning, and no evolutionary advantage in doing so.

Sam's mind wandered at this point to a scene in the film with the Oracle in the kitchen with Neo, and he then thought how amazing it was how Brina had always been fond of making cookies - all the while he had known her she had made them - and they were exactly the same as the ones in the film.

It didn't seem to bother her all these similarities, these synchronicities, these bizarre happenings.

As far as she was concerned she was just doing what she did, just as Trinity did in the film, protecting him, taking care of him, having faith in him, and being her part in the story.

The problem seemed to come with the practicalities of living up to the dreamlike aspirations of the myth, in whatever it was that was doing the dreaming, when the dream was manifesting itself into their real lives. The practicalities of living the roles.

Cookies were just a message, a link, and a connection to something that he was meant to understand the meaning of, along with a dozen other things that day.

He did however enjoy Brina's cookies, in fact he loved all her organic, healthy cooking. To be honest there didn't seem to be anything about her that he wasn't in love with.

When they got home she just put him to bed and he slept for fifteen hours straight.

This phase continued over the next few weeks. It was some sort of new transforming process going on and energy came in and out of him in waves and changes occurred physically too.

He experienced energy spontaneously flowing up his spine in twin snake-like rhythms, and the top of his skull ached like mad and was even visibly bruised.

The front of his face continued with that fresh sensation, as if it had been exposed to a harsh frost. He had been through this process many years before - it was known as Kundalini in Eastern religions - a re-potentiating process for the mind and body.

And yet he seemed to be going through it again, as if somehow he needed to - to run through it again from scratch before moving onto another phase another level- a reprocessing.

It was, however, not a pleasant experience.

He would still wake up exhausted every day, and it felt as if his mind was working flat out, and yet there were no meaningful or vivid dreams to speak of except for one - which seemed to repeat itself several times - of him running up a very steep grassy hill.

It was as if he was being elevated up to another level again, another sort of frequency in the range, and at the same time resyncing all the other stages, as if he were being rebooted.

As far as he was aware it wasn't him causing it and the medical professionals that he called upon were less than helpful.

Whatever it was that was causing it was impolite and unhelpful and he experienced physical symptoms ranging from aches all over his body, to streaming sinuses, to a stiff neck and back.

A few weeks later it all began to ease off, and Sam began to notice some very odd external things happening.

On July 1st Sam had woken up exhausted at around 8 a.m. having spent most of the night vividly dreaming with lots of information coming in and 'telling him things' that were translated by his psyche into some story that he had to somehow decipher into 'real' context.

Brina had brought him breakfast in bed on a tray again, and she put the television on for him to watch while she got showered.

The breakfast TV show from the BBC burst into life in front of him in its usual excited fashion. This channel was a little easier to view than the garish orange spray-tanned presenters and décor and subjects on the other breakfast TV shows. It was more structured, gentle and professional, with scheduled reports and news items where the discussions had been carefully synthesised and selected for particular audiences.

However, this particular series of news reports seemed to be synthesised into a childish form of story, and more worrying than that - they seemed to be talking directly to him.

There was a whole string of news reports; DNA discoveries, Bank crises, the Grand National potentially being cancelled due to safety concerns, extreme weather in the USA, elections, issues in the Middle East - all of the subjects which were curiously already in his head, already in his thoughts, but not just the subjects - the actual words and phrases they were using all seemed to be related to him in some way.

It was all very odd.

Once the shower was free, Sam went in and tried to wash the thoughts and connecting ideas away with a steady stream of hot water flowing onto the back of the neck.

Half an hour later, he had loaded the dog into the back of his car and was driving up to the hill to take it for a walk. Suddenly he came headlong up against a large group of people jogging in aid of some organised fund raising event - each of them wearing different T-shirts emblazoned with the names of various health and children's charities - there were hundreds of them.

This would have been fine if they hadn't been running in the middle of the main road and that no one had thought to stop the traffic from entering from the side roads. The mass was collectively unaware that it was heading towards moving cars.

Sam stopped his car and put his hazard warning lights on. People flowed around the car like a river, a spectrum of T-shirts flashed in front of his eyes with numerous messages, group names, organisations. People were shouting words at him and making gestures towards him in the confusion.

It was very intimidating somehow. Even though he was safely inside the metal bubble of his car it felt as though he was in some bizarre safari park with herds of mindless animals blindly flowing around him, all telling him different things.

Twenty minutes later, after having been told off by some guilty sounding organising official, Sam managed to navigate the car up to the top of the hill - his back window now having been steamed up by the dog.

Sam desperately wanted to avoid meeting anyone else on the walk, but today for some reason this appeared to be an impossible task. He was inundated by people who wanted to stop and talk, mainly about the news and their problems, and of course the weather which was, as usual, blowing a gale.

He had encountered it before, this feeling, this bizarre set of scenarios, something trying to get a message to him. This 'why doesn't someone do something about everything?' thing.

After their half an hour walk, Sam and the dog drove down from the car park on the hill, back towards home, but as he turned the bend he found that there was a fallen tree blocking the road that must have fallen in the strong winds a few minutes earlier as there were already a few stationery cars in front of him.

There was just enough space to drive around it, but only if you drove over onto the other side of the road, which a few cars had already successfully done.

However a woman in the car at the front of the queue now seemed unwilling to attempt this manoeuvre.

Perhaps she couldn't see past it enough to ensure there was nothing coming the other way, or maybe the whole situation had spooked her or she just didn't know what to do.

A man wearing a reflective jacket appeared from around the other side of the tree and started waving his arms at her, but she still didn't move. He then flapped his hands in a downward motion, and then did the cut motion with his hands to indicate that she had to turn her engine off.

Twenty seconds later a wall of people appeared around the tree and started flowing past the cars - the same set of charity runners as before. It was herd mentality gone mad. Nobody was stopping to move the fallen branches - which several people together could have managed quite easily — no one was thinking about what they were doing individually either, they were all running blindly around the tree and potentially straight into the oncoming traffic.

It was just like watching ants.

Yet somehow, for some reason, because there was a large group of people all doing the same thing. It must have appeared to have been safe as it made sense to everyone. Nobody had to think as an individual, the herd was doing all that on its own, in a nutsy sort of way. Because there were so many people all doing the same thing, nobody stopped to question anything, nobody took charge or stopped to think, it was what everyone else was doing, and it was a race after all.

It was seemingly what this 2012 thing was all about - those self-fulfilling prophesies of disaster.

This was also all about us as humans collectively. Of us being capable of being much more than we are individually - we should all be much fitter, healthier, intelligent and wiser - especially considering the capacity within our brains - and live with more energy.

We could all be much more enlightened, switched into the collective mind and integrated with one another if we just all woke up to it, and became aware of the effect it was having on us and our lives - just like the runners.

But we aren't and we are just getting more stupid, fatter, sicker, poisoned and lazy, both individually and collectively.

It was simply that we had nothing to compete against, nothing forcing us to evolve, either as individuals or collectively as a species.

There is too much unconscious influence going on - the

blindness to the tree in the road, nobody stepping back and looking at the situation and directing things.

Nobody being in the driving seat, with no 'hand on the wheel'.

Something that perhaps dolphins, for example, would never suffer from.

As he sat in the car waiting for something to happen, someone to do something, Sam thought about things - like dolphins, his dog, and why they were all a lot happier than he was.

Had anyone tried to communicate with dogs and dolphins to see how they thought, and why it was that they were so happy?

He sat and closed his eyes, just for a little while.

The thought of a *Sea Life*-style pool filled with dolphins came into his mind, and a wise man dressed in robes stood by the edge of the water trying to talk to the dolphins.

The man was trying to talk to them using his mind, using telepathy, and they were clicking and nodding and laughing back at him in their dolphin manner. So to try and establish a rapport, he had offered them tuna fish to bribe them into telling him their secrets.

The thoughts of the dolphins came into the man's mind, and the thoughts were all full of fish, open waters and sunlight and friends, and also of darkness, killer whales and hunger, and that their 'spiritual' world was the same as their physical one.

They were laughing at him because he was stupid and worked for his food – to them it was amusing that he wanted to know everything, and wasn't happy just living and being.

So finally, as promised, the man threw the tuna into the pool and told he them that he was doing so because he wanted to share the world with them, to learn from them, understand them, and this was his offering to them in gratitude for their wisdom.

The dolphins stopped laughing at him and then a question came into the man's head telepathically from them, and the question was "…Yes, but how do we get the tin open?"

Then the man smiled back, and said in a smug plain English voice "Well, if you think you are so bloody clever why don't you work it out?"

Abruptly, there was a loud horn sound from the car behind and Sam jumped and opened his eyes again.

Flustered, he fumbled with the key in the ignition, and then he started the engine. He put it into gear and drove ahead in the road past the tree that had now been moved to the side of the road.

By the time Sam got home he felt as if he were ready for a holiday, but the rest of the day still had a lot of things to say, and for hours he was bombarded with numerous other synchronistic examples of things he had to connect and understand and see.

It was all getting too much.

The following morning Brina had got him up early and he found himself sitting up in bed with his breakfast watching the television again.

Once more it seemed to have a curious energy about it, and he started to notice that it was almost talking to him, just like the day before - the thoughts and knowledge in his head from the last night seemed to relate again to what was coming up in news articles, events, and to what was being said - they were using his words too and his expressions again – which was disturbingly odd.

It was as if the news was reporting to him on what had happened as a result of his thoughts, his ideas, and decisions, and was relaying it in a way that was personal to him, and timed in such a way as to make sure he would see it, and recognise it, but only in that moment in time.

After his shower and checking his emails he decided to go for a walk on his own to clear his head again. He decided not to up on the hills this time, he was feeling exhausted and his legs didn't feel up to the climb and so he got in the car wearing his well-worn jacket, work jeans and old boots.

He loaded the dog safely in the cage in the boot of the car, and set off for the local park reserve. It was a bright crisp morning and it was quite busy there, so he kept the dog on the lead and kept well away from everyone else and their dogs, all of whom seemed to be causing chaos.

There was a woman in one of the fields who had some annoying whistle and about five dogs all running around her completely out of control – she was one of these middle-aged brisk country estate pseudo-upper class tweedy types.

One of those 'the father couldn't marry her off as she looked too much like the horse' types. She just seemed to be looking around and moving unconsciously towards other groups so that she could cause chaos and get angry with them.

Wide berth, thought Sam - and he was right on both counts.

He just wanted to keep himself wrapped in his bubble. He kept the dog on a short lead and walked slowly round the wooded paths in the peaceful sunshine, not wanting to bother anyone or be bothered.

Walking back to the car park, he approached the latch gate that separated the reserve from the car park itself, and he noticed that there were a few people milling around and talking on the other side of the gate.

Then a dirty black BMW - that clearly hadn't been washed for a long time, so much so that the number plate was hidden, probably deliberately - pulled up and parked over and onto one of the curbs and then along the pavement and grass verge, not bothering to wait for a car parking space.

A slim blonde 40-something year old woman - wearing sunglasses perched on the top of her head, with white shirt, tight light brown corduroy trousers, and totally inappropriate high heel leather boots - got out of the BMW and opened the back door of her car. A madly excited brown and white Springer spaniel leapt out of it, and went running around the car park, frenziedly introducing itself to all the people and all the other dogs.

The woman leant forward into the car and picked out her mobile phone from its holder to continue the conversation she was obviously still having, and then leant in again to grab a half-full takeaway Costa coffee cup, and token dog lead.

She used her arse to slam the car door shut, and then took the phone from her ear to shout at the dog - it was called Miffy or Zippy or something like that - it wasn't a telling off sort of shout, it was a sort of 'come here' encouraging high pitch shout - that had absolutely no effect other than to indicate to the other people there that she was 'trying to do something about the situation'- which was obviously not the case - responsibility not being something that featured very high on her list of priorities. A placatory call was enough to show everyone that she was trying to 'do something' and abscond herself of any guilt.

She then walked up to the gate that Sam was now approaching

from the other side, and the spaniel came dashing up to it in front of her. It started wagging its tail and nosing at Sam's dog under the gate, and then crawled underneath, and rolled onto its back in a submissive action, wagging its tail.

Sam's dog was obviously very interested, and started getting excited. Sam pulled back on the lead to get some control while he tried to open the gate and get through.

"Not without a pre-agreed and signed consent contract and a good lawyer these days I'm afraid mate" he whispered under his breath jokingly to his dog.

The woman walked through the open gate with her mobile phone pressed to her ear with one hand, and holding the latte in the other. She glanced at Sam for an instant but it was with total indifference, and a short fake smile, not thanking him or having any care for the chaos her dog was causing.

She carried on the conversation on the phone "I know..." she said "...it's crazy isn't it? You would think someone would do something about it, letting it get to this state, these politicians eh… I know, what can you do though?" and just walked on leaving her dog to spin madly around his.

Sam went through the gate pulling the lead, and her dog followed them back through. A few moments later she gave another shout of "Tiffy, Tiffy, come on, come along Tiffy!!!!" and it got off its back, turned swiftly and bolted off, with a few looks behind as it went to check to see if it was being followed.

The other people in the car park were still talking to each other - a couple of pensioners, a 'plain Jane' thirty-something woman and an older woman who was now pointing at the black BMW.

Sam smiled at them as he walked past, and his dog exchanged sniffs with the bored looking fat chocolate Labrador that was standing with them.

Sam stopped and looked at them and smiled - they were commenting on the rudeness, the lack of consideration of the woman. "I know," said Sam "you would think someone would do something about it all" he said. They nodded for a moment agreeing with him, and then paused while it sunk in, and then didn't know what to say next.

"It works on lots of levels you know," he said "several in fact, trouble is where do you start? Is it supposed to be happening, and what are the consequences of changing it? It's a management thing you see, cause and effect, chaos and control. You have to work from the top down, but then also see and monitor what is happening."

They looked at him highly confused, but the 'plain Jane' was smiling in a polite, yet confused, manner.

"Tell you what" he continued "why don't you let her tyres down, or let me be the hero and tell her off when she gets back eh? Or call the police, or have her shot, bring down the government for letting it get like this.

"But no all of that that would be wrong - and that is the difference, knowing right from wrong and doing things about it in the right way, and at the right level.

"So either do something or don't, just don't waste your energy standing here talking about it. But equally you should know that I understand it all already, so you don't have to all create this just so that I get the message."

They all looked at him confused, and wordless, and even Sam's dog looked embarrassed.

Sam walked on now and loaded the dog into the car and drove home. He understood everything, he knew everything that was going on, but he couldn't understand why these scenarios kept happening to him, why people weren't allowed to 'see' him, understand what he was saying, act or integrate with him. Not this situation obviously, but generally, with everybody.

Was he that dangerous to the system, that much of a risk?

Was he being immunised, or was he perhaps so key to everything that he was only being allowed a few people to interact with - just those who could advise him, or help him make the choices and decisions that had to be made? Was it necessary, or was IT just shutting him off ?

Whichever it was, it certainly felt as though he was being picked on, supressed, hidden, and piled high with responsibility, and, more than anything else, he couldn't see how the any of it was helping him in any way.

In fact, again, quite the opposite, almost as if by interacting with IT he was making himself open to attack by some dark unconscious collective shadowy over-mind that didn't like change even though it was about to hit an iceberg, and yet was consciously worried about the possibility.

Over the next few weeks it didn't get any better.

He tried to record the events as best he could in his journals but there was so much of it, and the information came in so many forms, it was hard to get it down in any coherent recordable form or meaningful structure or description. It was all just so complex, vast and involved, and there just wasn't enough time to get it down before IT was onto the next thing.

There seemed to be so much going on everywhere with news events, a sort of collective worry, concern, stress, that was being translated into events, catastrophes, or riots, and he could sense it everywhere, and in the attitudes and feelings of everyone around him.

Late one night a few days later on the 13th July Sam found himself just lying on his back in his bed. He was in a very deep relaxed state, with Brina tucked under his right arm next to him asleep.

Again he tried to maintain that state between sleep and awake - that hypnagogic state - trying to maintain that detached state of consciousness.

When he closed his eyes now he could see, or perceive, a vibrant darkness with depth and perspective, a void of emptiness, not just blackness but something that was there that he was trying to generate some perception of.

The air was very quiet and still and the pillows behind his head put a mild pressure on his neck. It was a fine balance to maintain.

The void of deep black changed in intensity, frequency, and then he phased out until he became totally unaware of himself or his body aside from gentle surging energy pulses up his spine and body.

He had no control of what was going on he could only observe, passively condense the nothingness, form the information, but in an observational way.

He could also sense the approaching presence of something, an intensity of power, energy, overwhelming trepidation and alarm, which he had to work through to avoid it panicking him, and consequently forcing him to shy away from it.

The blackness started to take form and depth like a dark sheet shaping into an old man's face several feet in front of him - a grey indistinct outline as if it were a shroud covering the front of a head, and profiling it in negative relief - the same effect as he had seen on the Turin Shroud.

The features in the image of the face changed as if it were trying to form some recognisable visage, some archetype, or some god-like representation that he had probably seen somewhere before, it was hard concentrating and focusing on what was going on in front of him without being drawn in by it, or allowing it to manifest itself into something rather than him being observational of it.

Sam then dismissed the image, knowing what was going on, and he slowly overrode the energy and information behind it, to force it to take some other form. It was hard work though, and it wouldn't disappear completely, and continued to try and latch onto other facial forms.

To break the pattern Sam decided to ask a question in his mind *What am I meant to be doing?* which he realised was an odd question to ask, and he wasn't sure where it came from.

The image cleared quickly and a new shape formed in front of him. It was a large drip of water, a tear shaped drop in perfect high definition, with its surfaces rounded and transparent and reflective in the darkness. Again it was a few feet away and a few inches wide like some ultra-high-definition graphical image on a black 3D screen, and it was also falling.

It fell downwards in slow motion into a flat calm watery surface into which it entered, causing, just like any drip falling into water would, a reflective spike of water upwards tipped with a smaller drop, which fell again downwards. This was then followed by dark ripples slowly fanning outwards in silver circles over the dark glassy surface in slow motion like some time-lapse scientific experiment.

Then it was all gone, and he gradually returned back to full awake state.

Whatever was being 'said' was typically ambiguous, it could have meant anything, was he the drip causing change, and creating ripples in the system, creating waves of change? Or, which he assumed was more likely, was he just a total 'drip' in a big pond.

Or was it a hidden message? One, for example, that was saying that he had left one of the taps on somewhere in the house and that this was just his way of reminding himself.

That was the problem with these sorts of visions and vivid dreams; it was information coming in and being translated and perceived, but you had to know where it was coming from, what it meant and what relevance it had, and at what level it related to. If anything.

In this case Sam had no idea, and as it hadn't any energy associated with it or any lottery numbers alongside it, unless he really knew, it wasn't worth worrying about.

In the morning there was a parcel from Greece on the doorstep with a return address label on the side with Max's name on it.

Inside was a letter from Max, and also a thick heavy book – *The Exegesis of Philip K Dick*.

This was the new book that had been produced from the masses of journal entries recorded by Philip K Dick, the famous science fiction writer, many of whose works had posthumously been made into films; *Blade Runner, The Minority Report, Total Recall, Adjustment Bureau, The Man in the High Castle* and so on.

Sam had read a few of his books from when he had met with Max a while ago, but this was new, something that had been carefully and methodically put together from his own private journals and notes and diaries.

Works which made up tens of thousands of pages of philosophical, personal, metaphysical and religious observations.

This exegesis was a synthesised collection of 1,000 of those pages – it was a thick impressive book, and it made Sam's three or four journal folders seem quite inadequate next to it.

Whoever had put this work together deserved a medal.

Phillip K Dick wrote in copious amounts, he had so much stuff coming in from the collective all the time, and he had been driven to write it all down, expressing and discoursing it into words, stories and journal entries.

Sometimes many dozens of pages a day.

He had somehow tried to articulate and channel what was coming into his mind, and get it into some form that made sense –

or even just out of his mind in any form - expressing ideas that he generated, and in many cases revelations in his, sometimes drug induced, states of consciousness.

States that often he wasn't even aware of himself, and discoursed ideas and thoughts and concepts that he was totally unaware that he was generating into his writings. With occasional odd out of context comments that seem to come from nowhere and just placed into the middle of the text, in a short story. Like clues that you had to piece together, to solve a riddle he was unaware that he was writing.

He was like some shamanic author, and it took decades after his death for him to be understood, the concepts of which were then grasped, and transposed into film with many of his theories and ideas in many cases being manifested into reality years later, like the internet, and computers and robotic concepts.

He, like Sam, seemed to have received information coming in through a form of gnosis, with ideas, thoughts, concepts, and knowledge seemingly appearing from nowhere.

All of which he had tried to make sense of with extensive study and research.

PKD was a genuine 'genius', and his turning point theosophical experience - as highlighted by the date on the spine of the book - was on the 2nd March 1974, and it involved a woman at the door, and a reflected beam in a similar situation to that of Jacob Boehme.

But it was nothing on the level of what Sam had had or experienced, nor did he have Sam's scientific background and working experience.

None the less, PKD had made a great effort to express what was going on within him into fictional form. Which in itself, was very valuable in demonstrating the process of what had happened, and what information had been generated, processed, and how it had been presented to him.

So, unlike so many cases of others before, here was tangible evidence, and a documented discourse of what had been going on with him at the time, and the complex nature of the process itself.

Here was someone doing the best he could with what information and knowledge was available to him at that time.

Sam pored over the book for the next few weeks, and by the

time Sam reached Page 888 - Feb 1982, shortly before P K Dick died - it was obvious that he had not been able to form a coherent logical philosophy for 'what was going on', or what it all meant and how it all fitted together.

He had touched on a lot of what had really going on, and had sort of mapped out the concepts, but somehow hadn't been able to string it all together into a coherent workable model or logical understanding. He had relied too much on other people's views and ideas, and of those who had similar experiences in the past.

Probably, like everyone else, he had looked for answers too much from others. He also hadn't realised the possibility that the thing itself maybe evolving, or that it had a hival biological nature.

Also he would have been unaware that he was also partly controlling the process, the information flow coming in, and that he himself was influencing it in a reflective manner and thereby stimulating it and engaging with a system that responded to him in a diametric way.

In many cases that were documented, it appeared obvious that he had actually influenced things in the system, and had given it ideas.

Ideas that would eventually become manifest, along with events in people's lives, strange synchronicities and mythically enacted concepts.

Sam had probably reached the same point quite some time ago, but now was much further forward, and had a fairly clear idea of what was going on.

With this in mind, Sam was now very much aware of what he himself thought, what he wrote about in his own books, and what constructive and conscious direction this may take things whilst keeping a conscious eye on the potential effects and what people may be getting in visions, 'illuminations', channellings, vivid dreams, and spiritual conceptualisations. Then seeing the effect of that in measurable events. This, along with also what was going on in terms of news, real world events, situations, and the general direction of things.

Everything these days though, all happened so much quicker, and it was much easier to spot this sort of effect going on with the internet and simultaneous news reports.

But not only that, once you knew that this was going on, you could prove it, try out the effect, put information or ideas and suggestions into the system, and see what happened.

It was starting to explain why everything that was going on in the world was the way it was, and equally why it was all mad.

Nobody had realised this was happening, everyone was led to believe it was something else, rather than 'us'.

Yet it meant too, that we could realise this unconscious effect, be - for want of a better word - conscious of it, and break away from this cyclic mythical unconscious repeating wheel.

We could use the process itself to change our direction, instil ideas into the zeitgeist, and at the same time collectively wake us all up to what is going on, create a new level, a new paradigm, a new hope. Give 'us' conscious awareness.

Or then again you may not, and you may just end up making it all worse. In all likelihood and looking at what others had done in the past, trying to help IT wasn't the best approach, and due to the reflective nature of consciousness and the hival controlling nature of it all, it was likely that doing what IT wanted and helping it was the wrong approach and you could in fact make the whole situation worse.

What was needed was a whole new concept of dealing with IT, a more parental or management orientated and balanced strategy.

With the amount of immunisation and control that Sam seemed to be experiencing, he had to be very wary of what he wrote and how his thoughts and ideas progressed. IT was picking things up from him all the time and he had to be careful of thoughts, analogies, and ideas in case they became manifested in the system.

The *Exegesis of Phillip K Dick* shared so much commonality in it with his own life process, the journey, the thoughts, and inner experiences, almost as if his life were being driven by it, and what ideas had been written into it in many instances.

As if the system was getting a long list of 'nice to have' qualities and experiences for the next poor unsuspecting 'one' or 'ones' in line. His prophesies were in effect - giving IT ideas.

Sam could sense the frustration in what PKD was writing though, the not being able to quite get the picture, work out what it all meant, even though the guy was clearly a genius he hadn't stumbled on - or wasn't able to get to - the fundamental perspectives.

He had almost immersed himself too far into it looking for answers, too far into the ancient texts, reading too much into what people had written, finding hidden meaning, finding religions and psychological, metaphysical, and spiritual integration but not something that worked or made sense. He had missed the few basic obvious logical simple concepts.

But in those days there was no internet to help his imagination follow through into the in-depth science that is only just being proven today.

So even though he had perceived it, opened a door to it at the same level, despite not being able to write it down or describe the experience or retain the knowledge, it was there, unconsciously nagging him to understand.

Which was the same for several others who had had intense cosmic consciousness or extreme near death experiences that Sam had read about in the past.

It was that inability to describe, that disassociation with the body, a program conscious of itself and integrated with the collective, free from physical constraints, but in a field based environment that was impossible to describe in physical or verbal terms. It was the same as a caveman trying to describe Windows 10 to the rest of the tribe.

There were certainly a lot of uncomfortable similarities and coincidences with PKD in what Sam was reading to his own mythical journey, and life experiences.

Especially in a lot of his later fictional books, and specifically in the *Flow My Tears, the Policeman said* book. It was as if the system itself was using the ideas that he was generating to refine the journey Sam was being subjected to, and that they were being put into more contemporary terms.

A few days later, Sam was in the spare room bed listening until the early hours to the *VALIS* series in audiobook form. The setting for the book was all envisaged as some sort of computer information system.

Sam had listened up to the last book, *The Transmigration of Timothy Archer*, where one of the characters was describing the experience he had had - which was clearly the same experience that Sam had been put through - put into fictional form, even down to seeing the pieces and the inter-connectedness.

As he listened to the words in that part, everything seemed surreal and uncomfortably accurate in its description, but there was also the frustration there, of not being able to write it down, describe it, define it, articulate, and remember.

It was almost as if PKD wasn't being allowed to, and had been limited and constrained - he also referred to a Bodhisattva, a Buddhist term for someone who turns away from attaining Nirvana, one who goes back to help other people, a concept which seemed somewhat familiar to Sam.

There were even references to things being observed in tanks, just as Sam had used in his analogies - and one of the characters was even an Angel - it was all a little uncomfortably prophetic.

Philip K Dick seemed to have tried to put so many things in the stories all at once, like throwing everything at it to see if somehow it would make sense and magically re-arrange itself into something meaningful. Like going to a postgraduate Philosophy exam with several books, a shredder, and some glue.

There was even a story about a journey by one of the characters to Jerusalem, which incorporated ancient beliefs - the hill where David, Solomon and Muhammad had all had the same experience and who knows else.

Sam had read about people going there to integrate earth fields, which was probably correct, it was probably a hub or focus point, or at least had been in the past.

Again PKD had also seemed to be aware that mountains seemed to have that focal gravity and spirituality associated with them.

Dick, within his exegesis, seemed to go through a whole series of 'I have it now' epiphany moments, only to later be unable to get a satisfactory logical philosophical model or workable perspective for the whole thing.

He just had not got quite enough pieces to make it work, probably because he had too many ancient concepts and religious naive patterns filling in the gaps in his mind, too many existing belief structure and concepts at a time that had no idea of evolution and a vast range of things and ideas that we know now.

Yet everything was there in what Dick wrote, and in what he had channelled. If you took the whole lot of what he produced together, and say used a pair of scissors to form it into something else, you had all the workings of the correct solution.

All the right words and ideas and philosophical concepts were there but just not necessarily in the right order and shape. He had just not started from the right place and had used too many of other people's ideas and thoughts, rather than his own.

It was almost as if Dick was listening in to the thoughts of IT, our collective mind, like a baby in the womb. He tried to work out what IT was, whilst IT was feeding him ideas and thoughts and taking him into and out of spiritual, metaphysical, philosophical, religious and scientific concepts.

He had tried to work out what made sense and what didn't in some progressive process of revelation, interpretation, processing and discourse which incorporated the world view and situations that were present at that the time. At the same time as dealing with his own paranoia, drug use, political views, fear of authority and government control.

It was useful to read it though, and to learn from what he had been through and tried to do.

But Sam was sure that this time it would be different.

Sam could put it all together, work it all out, so that it did all make sense. Well, sense probably wasn't the right word, a logical 'dog's breakfast', was probably a better term, or even two - a real one and a virtual one.

Yet Sam could only do that by stepping back, and working out what made logical sense and what didn't, and by taking a scientific and management perspective.

But he also needed to look after his own mind and body at the same time too.

The key was to take, or view, what was coming out of the system objectively, for what it was, rather than literally, and at the same time be aware of what was generating it.

But over the last few decades we have come to know so much more about the brain, the mind, information management, quantum mechanics, Field Theory, biology, collective behaviour, physics, philosophy, and belief structures - alongside nature and changes in culture, social and religious control - you can add so much more 'up' these days, join the dots as it were, and see past it all.

Information was instant now too, and easier to find, put together, search, correlate.

News was there straight away, projected to you live and in the moment, so that it is a lot easier to see, even though the problem itself has grown much larger - almost too large to get your mind around and deal with - you could create a working logical model from both sides, scientific and spiritual, if the system itself allowed you to.

Yet without what Philip K Dick had done, without all the effort he had taken to actually write it all down, and express it in some form, Sam would have missed several important things from a management perspective; it was 'work', and there was a cause and effect process to it. It had been written down and it was there to see.

Very useful information when you realise that you are trying to do the same thing. In many cases it was almost as if he were trying to talk to Sam directly without the concept of time, as if he were connected to him in some way, sensing him.

There were lots of mental cul-de-sacs that Sam didn't have to waste his time going down now too, rabbit holes he could see to avoid, and missing connections that were mentioned that he was now able to fit together and learn from.

But it was also useful to see that someone else had gone through this navigation process, and he had learned from it - even seeing the importance of simple things like adding dates into your notes and journals.

The people that had put the exegesis of PKD together had done a great job; it must have been very hard.

Sam thought about his own notes and made a mental note to date and label everything and keep it in some order. All part of learning lessons from those in the past.

At the end of the book, there was a review by a psychologist, who referred to PKD as a 'garage philosopher'. Sam thought this came across as very condescending - and the whole attitude of the psychologist was derogatory and belittling - almost 'holier than thou'.

Note to self, Sam thought and he wrote in his journal, '*Psychologists are compartmentalised controlling small minded condescending ...*', and then something unprintable. He clearly marked the date next to it. But he had only written it in jest, he knew some very able and intelligent psychologists, but as with everything in life there were good and bad ones everywhere.

What also worried Sam, just as with Jung's *Red Book,* was the amount of time after PKD's death that it had taken for the exegesis to be published. It was also curious as to why Dick's work was only becoming so popular now, over the last few decades, as if something was trying to cover its tracks.

Yet without people like Dick, we would never change, never move forward, and 'errors' would never occur in the system, and everything would be very boring. Nature was never boring.

But then again it was all just words, ideas, integrated notions and concepts. Many big name authors were still doing it today, with symbolic titles and hinting at hidden mysteries, but his was different - he had just been trying to make sense of an experience just as Sam was, and had been coming from the other direction rather than trying to work through a maze of a jungle to get from the physical to the 'other side'.

What was also needed now was proof, evidence, scientific structure and models, and cause and effect of putting ideas into the system and structured thoughts and those then being manifest into reality - or at least ideas that everyone else was getting.

Sam remembered a phrase that PKD used in his books a number of times, 'hysteron proteron' when the thing to be demonstrated is in the premise - that was something that was in the book a lot, and it stuck in Sam's mind.

Ironically that is exactly what seemed to be happening when IT demonstrated conscious behaviour rather than just unconscious, just as would appear to have been in Phillip K Dick's observations of IT at the time.

It was also interesting that Carl Jung had been through a similar process - as described in his recently published *Red Book* - and that some of the key French philosophers were also generating their works around the time of Dick's death, seemingly picking up on changes going on in the system as it was discoursing information to them in the form of visions and gnosis. Like some form of interpretive dialogue of the state of the system, and what IT was thinking.

There were indeed quite a lot of gnostic elements and concepts to PKD's work, and his use of terms such as 'Hagia Sophia'.

But what he didn't realise was that it was all just our collective knowledge in integrated field form, not divine knowledge, just 'ours'.

Dick had no way of getting his mind around that concept, it was a long time before information system architectures would be developed that could simulate those ideas.

Sam knew all that now, and he also realised that it was evolving and growing with us. The key was to get the right information into it now, rather than blindly and naively filling it with rubbish.

Much of what Sam was going through indicated that he was on a similar 'journey of gnosis', receiving sparks of inspiration, genius revelations, and concepts that he was able to link together with his intelligent understanding of the world, and through his academic readings of the various associated subjects.

Although Dick seemed to take on a gnostic perspective overall, he did seem to switch between religious positions almost every dozen pages or so in his journals, which was quite frustrating, but also an indication of his personality.

PKD was obviously getting a lot of information coming into his mind as visions, inspirations, and gnosis, that 'knowing' of knowledge, combined with his extensive reading of philosophy and psychology.

The trouble was that, like everyone else in history who had tried to work out what it was all about, what it all meant, they had assumed that the thing, or the source, that they were getting this information from, knew what it was itself in the first place, or that it knew more about what was going on than we did collectively or as individuals.

So even though you 'knew', and you were 'in the know', that didn't necessarily mean that that knowledge was correct, or actually right. Just because it was 'god' and it was telling you this or giving your that divine illuminating insight, it didn't mean that it was actually correct or accurate. Or that it knew everything about absolutely everything - and equally it was naturally geared up to make sure, unconsciously, that you as an individual didn't see past it, so you were hypnotically bound to believe it.

Suffice to say that the life expectancy of an ant that could outsmart the colony it was in was an interesting, but short one.

Sam had read quite a lot of what other people had thought of PKD - even Jean Baudrillard had made several in depth observations of him, and of what he had written or discoursed - and he had then applied his own interpretations to that, i.e. explaining what was going from the information given in his fictional work.

But that was before this exegesis had been published.

Now it was all there in black and white – everything that had gone on in his mind, the thoughts he had had and the information he had received, were all there in his journals, rather than just in the fictional presentation of those ideas and re-engineered mythical legends and concepts.

There had obviously been some stimulation of the collective mind going on from PKD - IT had obviously got a lot of its ideas from him and the thoughts that he had generated. Cultural stimulus, agitating the zeitgeist.

He had almost been operating as some sort of device, receiving that gnosis knowledge coming in, processing it, refining it, and then influencing the system with what he produced, effectively writing back into IT. But still with only half the picture, half of the pieces of the puzzle, one that Sam now had joined together. PKD was even aware that he was doing this, that he was discoursing a stream of consciousness from the collective, but that it was incomplete or only half of the logical map.

It was just the same concept as program receiving data from the operating system, processing it, making sense of it and reflecting it back into the core system as ideas and thought forms.

Whilst also discoursing that in the physical form of books, which in turn would be used by others as their own starting points for say films, with their own discourse added to them, as with Ridley Scott and *Blade Runner* and so on.

Also like many others, PKD had had real trouble finding anyone he could talk to about it all, or find anyone who could understand the process he was going through at the time without being put into a position where he became controlled by the system itself or by psychologists, doctors, police, and the other State control structures.

It seemed that unless you could find others with the same level of experience and gnosis flow of information, then everyone else was just unable to 'get' or understand what you were saying or understand you, or have your point of reference of the system, or what it all meant.

Just like Carl Jung, PKD had been very attractive to women, having had five wives and many relationships. Being surrounded by women seemed to be key to the whole process. It was that female energy thing again.

Sam wondered how many other people were living parts of their lives in the dreams that Philip K Dick had created - that mythical reinforcing conceptualisation into the collective. Giving IT unconscious ideas and synchronistic events IT could act out in the future for people to relive, just as it had in the past with so many other things.

These reinforcing and cyclical mythical legends and stories like the *Epic of Gilgamesh*, Greek Myths to Shakespeare, all the way to the present day with the *Star Wars* story, *The Matrix* films etc. all continuing, being re-engineered, continually re-lived and repeated into modernity.

How many other people around the globe were aware of playing out these parts, these pieces in the play, for this *VALIS* collective entity, all blindly acting out their parts, all being part of the puppet play they were in, and all interpreting and seeing the drama from their own individual perspectives and interpretation?

All thinking that they knew what was going on, and all unconsciously hidden in plain sight.

Until now that is. Until someone realised what was going on.

Then Sam looked again at the date on the spine of the *Exegesis of Philp K Dick* - the date that he had his experience March 1974 - and Sam remembered certain events going on at that time in his own life, when what had gone on when he had been a small boy.

His eyes narrowed.

He also remembered many of the uncomfortable references in the book to both him and Brina, almost as if his life were being mapped out from its pages. References in there that seemed to point to his life, what he had studied, where he had lived, events, direction, thoughts.

It was the process, or journey, for their lives, and it had almost been written in that book, in conjunction with several others.

Almost as a list of 'wouldn't this be a good thing to do, have this character person to know, have to go through, and have happen to them, and then understand?'

It was just a stream of them; cybernetics, operating systems, myths, gnostic processes, and real life events, just too numerous to be coincidental, and almost one on every other page.

It was as if a whole series of thoughts were then manifested into 'being', set up, giving IT ideas of what should happen to him and what he needed to 'be' and 'do'.

The difference now was that Sam was conscious of that very fact, aware of this progressive myth evolving process, it was there in black and white, and you could see it in action now, literally.

He re-read a section in the book - 90:E-8 – with the little boy, the Spinners and the poisoning by the heavy metals on the farm, and realised that it almost exactly described Brina's father's village.

It was also now that Sam realised that he was being shown something, the paragraph had energy associated with it.

He also re-read section 3:38 with the notes on the Divine Child coming to England and the impressions Dick had received from the David Bowie film - *The Man Who Fell to Earth*.

Sam though in hindsight wished they could have made it say Fiji, and landing in a gold mine rather than a lake. But then sadly that of course wouldn't be believable or in any way reflect the nature of real life, or even make a very good story.

Even the only children's book Dick ever wrote had Sam's name all over it as it were. It seemed to be about him, his life story and some demiurge-like collective entity.

This was linked to another book called *Galactic Pot-Healer* and was about someone who reassembled the pieces of a collective unconscious planetary mind together, for the same demiurge-like entity. Along with many other uncomfortably familiar references.

Sam wondered just how many other books his life been written into that he hadn't read yet, and how many other people were having their lives mapped out for them in books and films and collective mythology, and if it were possible to change the process, and evolve the story?

Just as with the *Matrix* film and so many others that had given IT ideas in a cyclic mythical recycling refining feedback loop, it was easy to see where a lot of the 'alien' conspiracy concepts had come from, and putting imaginative ideas unconsciously into the system could be naively 'read' or channelled by others and then taken literally.

Once you knew that you could affect the system in that way you could change it, make a difference, pass things on, and then the possibilities were endless and you would no longer be stuck in that unconscious mythical loop.

What Sam needed to do now was to also pass that concept into the system and get some evidence that IT had got it, that IT was listening, to get others to see what he saw, see what could be done, and get some more people at the wheel of the ship.

Except that it wasn't quite a simple as that - the whole thing was vastly complex with so many levels and information bubbles, loops and controls and counter objectives, and you could get negative and positive signals at any time.

It was a very tricky process to manage and understand. You didn't want to have just anyone doing that. The only way to do it was to get the system itself to consciously choose who it needed, give it a sort of homeopathic or kinesiology suggestion, using what he knew to find what it needed for itself, rather than you trying to do it all on your own, and to also follow some plan.

Recognising this as an ongoing process also made him aware of the shape of IT, what IT was, its nature. IT was all of us at a macro-level. Such that being part of IT we could all put ideas, thoughts, and processing back into the system, and give IT direction.

This would then be manifested into reality, and into people's lives. Just in the way that you as an individual thought about things, thought positively, creatively, and with a life plan in mind.

Seeing that going on and realising that it's *you* doing this, was a step up in macro-level self-awareness too - people actually being IT's mind's eye, being the all seeing eye of IT-self.

But again it wasn't that simple - the whole thing was a complex integrated mass of different levels of bubbles and bio information systems, so just by influencing IT and giving IT ideas you could be changing anything - cause and effect, feedback loops - and cause harm when you were trying to do good, chaos when you were trying to calm etc. So that the only way to sort it all out was to then make IT self-aware of itself, get IT to see itself, wake IT all up, and to do it all in a joint benefit way, before the ship hit the iceberg.

Sam's mind flicked to a scene he remembered from the *Monty Python's Life of Brian* film where the character Brian was being chased by followers - "He has given us a sign, he has brought us to this place!" one follower said and then Brian responded with, "I didn't bring you here, you just followed me!" And then the crowd shouted "Oh, it's still a good sign by any standard."

And it was – it was incredible the whole thing.

Dick had spent his life searching for what Sam had in his head - the answer to the picture of what was going on and how it fitted together into a logical philosophy and structure.

In the end though P K Dick didn't come up with any form of working logical model or philosophy. The interesting parts of the book from Sam's perspective were what he had been through and what he had managed to discourse into words. From this point of view to him it was invaluable - as it was happening to him too.

Maybe if Dick had lived another twenty years he may well have pulled together some of the more advanced philosophical ideas, and joined up the dots. But to Sam what was more interesting was what was being channelled through him, what he was discoursing in his works and stories that he hadn't even been aware of, and probably what something was unconsciously feeding him with.

Equally things had taken a lot longer to percolate into, through, and out of the system than now, so he possibly would not have been aware of changes that he may have affected, or what drug induced perceptions of the world he had related back into it.

These days IT was much larger, more refined, sophisticated and integrated and its thoughts may now only take weeks rather than years to be observed.

It all made Sam all the more determined to get what he knew down in some form - a 'story of his life' as it were - with all the ideas embedded in there, along with a set of structured and dated journal notes with the more complex allegories filed away.

He needed to get it all organised into some meaningful structure with the ideas and concepts well defined, as well as he possibly could given the constraints of time and his own descriptive ability.

If we were the world we created with our thoughts and ideas, then he had better think of a better way forward. He felt it was important to get this all down, especially for those who would follow him - after all that was what life was about, building on what others had done, and passing it on.

What was important now was that Sam knew that this was going on. That he understood that what you wrote, thought, envisaged, generated as a story at this level, in conjunction with the collective mind discourse and focus, could and would, be manifested into reality.

That this process was going on with many others, without them realising it.

We could become what we thought, and it could change, in a managed way.

People everywhere could get his thoughts, his ideas, words, his concepts, and change.

By feeding this information into the operating system at this level, he could instil the same ideas in everyone else, start to make IT conscious of itself, and bring these people together with the same ideas, direction and words, just like any programme of change in a large organisation.

But it had to be done in a beneficial way to all parties, on all levels, and all perspectives.

The best way of doing that was to use the *Titanic* analogy concept - that we were all in the same boat together both physically and spiritually, individually and collectively.

So that instead of unconsciously and selfishly competing and fighting and using up all the ship's stores, and having nobody at the wheel, it would force the whole ship to work together, integrate and avoid the inevitable icebergs floating on the ocean that it was on. Without also the 'unsinkable ship' having a beguiling effect on all the passengers.

But he had to get it all written down - probably in some fictional form too - get it out there. Besides, even if nobody were allowed to read it all, it would still make him feel better knowing it was recorded somewhere, and not just all stuck in his head.

Like a giant mass of scribbles on Post-It notes crammed into a bucket. Which also aptly described the product and efforts of his creative writing skills.

For the whole of Autumn 2012 Sam wrote, read and studied.

He gave up on his normal work, and totally focused on getting his mind around whatever it was that was happening to him and to Brina. To help him figure out what was going on.

At the same time, a whole array of unusual events continued to unfold around the world. News items that he seemed to be being shown, synchronistic occurrences, and the continuous stream of knowledge kept pouring into his head every day.

The more he worked and thought, the more intense it became, as if he were generating the workload for himself in a reflective manner, stimulating the very thing he was trying to describe.

He was now reading and studying 'front end' science on a whole variety of subjects, to try and contextualise, from his perspective, what was going on in logical terms and to also to learn the correct terminology, grounding in the state of play, and latest analogy concepts.

He learned about Peter Sloterdijk's bubbles, froth and foam philosophical concepts and studied John Searle's mind/body philosophy, and read about a range of other professors who specialised in subjects ranging from biology to metaphysical research.

All different ways of trying to describe that which was hard to define or articulate, in the same way as the original 'tree of life' had been used as an analogy, with us as leaves, on cultural branches stemming from the trunk of humanity in a forest of species.

At the same time he kept his eye on the internet to keep check of what was going on at that time in the 'spiritual' creative game-scape and read work from some people who he would class as geniuses - those who had extracted themselves from the controlling academic systems to try and independently articulate what was going on and use cross-the-board understandings in various areas of study to give a synthesised yet highly intelligent interpretation. People such as John David Ebert.

He had to approach it from several directions this zeitgeist thing

- this collective consciousness, god, field of existence, hologram projecting information metaphysical system 'thing'.

But more importantly he had to see it all and figure out how it fitted together into his own perspective, rather than just from theirs. He wanted to be able to take a synthesised perspective view from many others as well as his own and to also get into that terminology, that tenure of scholarly articulation of being able to define and describe IT.

But to get to conceptualise the whole thing he had to go beyond it all, see past everything, past all the hypnotic self-interpretive 'takes' on it all, and make his own damn mind up.

He had to go past the real 'god' we were busy unconsciously evolving - and had been blindly refining ever since Mesopotamian days — and see what was going on from dual perspectives, the physical and non-physical paradigms.

In Sam's case it was more about turning around and coming back the other way having already gone way too far, and seen too much. He had to at least try to find something that went some way to describing what he knew IT was.

He could see how easy it was to get beguiled by it too, to be hypnotised into self-immunising belief structures, and get drawn down the rabbit hole of some story that claimed to explain it all.

Which was all part of the biological hival control process - whether it be a religious, or occult, mystic, or individual interpretations reinforced through psyche archetypal embodiment and manifestation of thought forms.

Or even New Age type elaborations, with more colourful fluffy visual dynamics, which floated further along more imaginative dimensions, incorporating more energy type ideas and physical body patterns and information protocols, and some science here and there, both pseudo and real.

But they were mostly drawing on ancient 'wisdom', symbols, some alchemic concepts, and folklore. Just more and more layers of fluff being padded in all the time to hide you away, and protect you from the brutal reality of the thing and its nature.

All though still a long way off even touching on the complexity of the thing. Sam also spent a lot of time looking at all of the various newly forming religions with various virtual 'alien' explanations of what was going on, different groups, races, locations, influences, with fear control and manipulation, or *Matrix* style dark Artificial Intelligence concepts.

All these with a never ending expanding story of what 'they' were doing, and what 'they' had done or had been responsible for in the past, and how 'they' were controlling us with genetic manipulation, abductions, and secret plans - most of which all still seemed to contradict each other at basic levels, be lacking somewhat in logic, rationale and any consistency or evidence.

But hey at least it was entertaining and becoming popular, much to the annoyance of the hard working 'grey' academics, and their tenure based hierarchy, rigorous scientific disciplines, and closed shop condescending status protocols.

Not to mention all the politicians and bankers with their lizard brain draconian mentalities.

It was important to observe it though. This was a reflection of what was going on in the collective imagination, IT's dream world.

So even though it didn't make any logical sense, you could see ITs attempts at forming new religions, new consciousness structures - in line with the progressive evolving and adaptive consciousness structures from before as described by Jean Gebser - or in the forms of biological rhizomes explained by Gilles Deleuze and Félix Guattari in their book '*A Thousand Plateaus*'.

Just like any evolving macro-life form would do, and what we have done. None the less, these things *were* going on in the world.

Evil was happening everywhere, there were bad people, there was corruption - and on a vast scale - there was something unconscious manipulating things in a controlling manner, and something was making life fairly unpleasant for many people.

It was something that was mindless, toxic, and just didn't make any sense over and above the logical explanations as to why things were the way they were.

Something that was seemingly almost demonic was at the heart of everything, controlling, and also rewarding those willing to take gain and benefit for perpetuating that unconscious controlling mindless system. Just as you had in your own body.

But now there was not enough balance. It had become all too one-sided, and happiness, freedom, good news and positivity, were all becoming overwhelmed by the bad, and the controlling and the negative, and the corrupt and toxic.

Something had to change it.

But then Sam knew that there had always been those cycles, the rise and fall of cultures, phases - it was just that it was more obvious now, more global, more extreme, and more apparent if you knew what was happening, were awake, studied it, and were not still being hypnotised by it.

It was just that the scale of it was all too much now for even for governments to cope with. There was nowhere else to go, nowhere to get away from it, it had reached its limit globally.

Yet even the new religions, like the ancient aliens ones, all had the same ever present origin elements in the system; attachments to legacy symbols, icons and structures that had existed for millennia.

They had the same processes, the same journeys, the same patterns, mythology, phases, and bio-processes woven into them.

All the same hypnotic mechanisms of how we were driven and controlled, but these days with a more modern terminology, language and *Star Trek*-like stories behind them.

The questions were really more about where had 'they' come from and were 'they' really these extra-terrestrials or multi-dimensional beings, or were they just something that we had created collectively to divert us away from seeing the real problem, to focus on the 'them' rather than the 'us'?

The answer was fairly obvious really.

But it was not right to just ignore it all nor to dismiss it or label it as 'crackpot', 'loony' or as the ravings of the mad.

This information was there and therefore they existed in a form with all the gaps in the logic being progressively filled with ever more imaginative science fiction.

The interesting thing was that many scientists knew what was going on - even Jung took an interest in the UFO phenomena in the 1950's knowing full well what was really going on.

They were observing this post-New Age religious phenomena but were not doing anything about it, they were simply studying it and keeping it inside their academic ivory towers.

But then when you had no 'skin in the game' all you could do was analyse the players, the rules, the scores, and the moves; you couldn't actually get in there and change what was going on, down on the pitch.

Yet to the people involved in channelling and visioning and being subjected to this, it was very real and reinforcing, and there was a lot of commonality in what they 'channelled', which inferred that the collective source was becoming much more evolved in its unconscious thoughts and adaptive fear control methods.

It had all evolved so much from the 'good old days', when you may occasionally have got a few 'enlightened geniuses' having the same idea at the same time, or different societies all building pyramids around the world in isolation, or sharing religious symbols, or the same ideas of 'what came from 'heaven' or were 'demons'. It was slow and steady.

This now was on a whole new level though, and was being fuelled by the 'internet' - which in itself emulated the information dynamics of IT, but only as would a plastic leaf emulating a forest.

Even the academic organisational structures that were trying to describe it, to work it all out, were still a long way from doing so.

They were limited by only having physical descriptive capability, physical mechanisms, and understanding. The physical world was all they knew, had language for, and could assimilate to.

Physicality was also all they could relate to, and describe from, even though at the quantum level it stopped making any sense.

In essence they needed to come at it from the other direction, and meet somewhere in the middle, connect the two paradigms.

We had come so far in increasing our understanding and perception of what the physical world and universe was, how it was made, how it worked and what its rules were.

But that was only a subset of the picture, and an interpretation from that part of it that we had learned to interpret, and what we experienced and sensed with and from.

We had only learned that physical domain or context, a context that was now just leaving bigger questions to things that no longer made sense, things that no longer had any reasonable logical answer to in so many areas, down into the quantum level, through and up to the impossible infinite on the other side.

To get your head around it all, you had to have in-depth understandings of both sides - both perspectives and contexts - to be able to even start to form a non-naive cohesive big picture.

It was always that 'elephant in the room' problem again, no matter what physical discipline you started from, whichever academic line you took.

It was that hitting the wall of perception, trying to see through that tiny hole in the wall which was the size of a quantum spinning subatomic particle and projecting it all out onto the 'other but same yet different side', and back again. All very complicated.

We were not yet physically equipped to experience, perceive and understand the different context of everything from the other perspective, from within the 'spiritual' - the REAL field domain structures - from which the physical world we saw was being projected from within.

IT was all a completely alien context to us.

It was too intense, too extreme, held too much information, and in the wrong form for us to make physical sequential sense of all at once. We had in effect become desensitised to it, protected, detached. There was no benefit in it, no evolutionary gain in making sense of it compared to making sense of the physical perspective.

But that, after all, is what we needed to do now to evolve.

So far all we had were impressions, snapshots, 'out of body' experiences, channellings, discourse and spiritual tools to try to get glimpses of the content and nature of what was there and how it worked. The other difficulty was that at the same time as trying to work out what was there we were also changing its content.

Then again if we only existed and floated around in the REAL, only in the context of the field, then there would be no evolution, no drive to change, no need to work things out.

There wouldn't be any errors, we would see it all and be it all at once, and as a result we would be nothing at all.

We were nothing without the physical device, that driving force of change that created rational, logical structure and context, with its rules, constraints and shape to the REAL, which was then reflected back from within it.

You couldn't have a radio or TV show without people making it, and a station to produce it.

Everything, including biology, came from the REAL and was

energetically projected through constraints and laws and structure into what we sensed, perceived, and represented as the physical part of it. Which by virtue of those laws and errors and limits it could evolve and interact with the information structured it evolved in the unified field.

Science was all about being correct, testable provable, but it was only seeing part of the picture, only seeing it all from a limited context and naive perspective.

A perspective in which we were limited by our understanding and physical way of thinking, in the 'REAL', in the bigger context 'operating system'. Yet when you were in the bigger picture, the wider context, everything made sense because you perceived it in a different way, and with different informational state context.

It all suddenly made sense if you could see all of it. Such that distance was not distance, time was not time, all that we knew was all there in the 'now', an immediate state, and everything was just immediate information and knowledge.

Having seen it, been in it, and experienced it, Sam frankly preferred the physical paradise we had on earth, the physical bubble and perception of what we were in, and especially the physically soft and 'touchable' Brina.

He liked everything as he had always known it - rather than as virtual information - and all that knowing, divine bliss and hypnotic virtual drugs, frankly got on your tits after a while.

He didn't like the idea of being information in a field - he liked being physical, it felt real, it felt good, it felt right.

He preferred his body as it was, he liked being in it, experiencing and discovering things, not knowing things, and having surprises.

We had spent a lot of effort building up the physical, nature, and appreciating it all, touching, tasting, smelling, being, and having emotional feeling, so why would you want to go anyplace else? Which meant that there had to be a reason for it - this physical side to things - a purpose, function.

So given the choice he would rather stay here. It was also probably why 'dead people' were so keen to come back - not that anyone actually 'went' anywhere anyway. How could you transcend, or ascend to somewhere with no space or time context?

The key was to make 'here' somewhere you would want to

come back to, or at the very least, to be unselfish, be somewhere everyone would like to live in the future.

The other problem Sam had in explaining things to them was that people were so unconsciously controlled by the system itself, and unable to move freely outside of their belief structures, that they just couldn't see outside of their boxes, irrespective of whether their boxes were religious or academic.

He had attempted several approaches with people to get over this effect. He tried to give in-depth explanations - which just ended up in people's eyes glazing over, and they then just snapped back into their safe box of belief and understanding.

He had tried being confrontational, sent polite e-mails, reviewed academic papers, books, but in many cases people seemed to not being able to see him at all.

He had even offered to help people, people who were writing books, and who were looking for examples of the experiences he had had. Even discussion groups, and scientists looking for research material – but <u>nothing</u> !

It just seemed that unless he found someone who had had the same level of experience as himself then they just couldn't see things from his level of perspective, couldn't understand what he saw, was going through, or see the whole thing from the outside.

It was as if they were all still somewhere inside the spiritual field system itself, contained within it, or in some compartment of it. Still behaving like programs in an operating system that could always bring them under control at whatever level they thought they were at.

He had sent out hundreds, if not thousands, of emails, contacts, notes, even copies of the chapters of the book he was writing.

But nothing. He even tried taking the 'dumb', the 'trying to work out what was going on' approach, and still nothing.

Something was deliberately, yet unconsciously, stopping him from being seen by people. Immunising and isolating him.

It wasn't even subtle about it. He had no one that he could really discuss things with other than Max, who had now pretty much taken himself out of the game, and couldn't be contacted except by letter. It was getting quite depressing, and it made him start to wonder if he was completely barking mad, or just barking up the wrong tree, or perhaps he had gone down his own newly invented rabbit hole and was stuck there, or just delusional.

The strange thing was that he could put himself into other people's perspectives, either scientific, philosophical, or spiritual.

He could see where they were, see their compartment, and see things from their perspective with what they were saying. He could see how what they were saying fitted into the larger picture, even though it was just one part or naive element of it.

But nobody could see him, or his overall perspective at all, it was as if he were somewhere, or at a level of understanding, that they couldn't or weren't allowed to go.

Eventually Sam found a guy who had left the UK to live in the West Coast of the US a few years earlier.

He and his wife and had moved there to be closer to his children and grandchildren, and he was twenty years or so older than Sam. He had had very similar experiences, as if he was satisfying a checklist of prerequisites to be whatever they were, and had been through a journey of discovery, and research and been involved with a lot of interesting people for the last fifty years. He had produced a blog which tried to encapsulate his ideas, and he had read just about everything from both sides of the fence.

It was like pushing on an open door and all of a sudden here was someone who 'got' everything. He also seemed to get what Sam was saying, and what's more he would point him in a lot of directions for things to read and research that would save Sam a lot of time, and he very usefully pointed out which rabbit holes Sam should avoid, both scientifically and spiritually.

Sam's first communications with him cascaded forward like a stream of consciousness, reactive and unstructured - but after years of banging his head against a wall of trying to get others to see and understand it was quite understandable.

Interestingly he had also kept a set of journals in black leather folders and wrote with an old style fountain pen, and they shared a string of other similar 'life' commonalities.

It was a remote friendship that over the following years would help Sam a great deal - without which he would probably had fallen by the wayside, smothered by the collective shadow, and become a hermit like Max, on some remote island with Brina.

It was reassuring to know that there was a least one other person who could see past all the fluff, the chaff and controls and structures in place to manage the ants.

It was also interesting to discover that there had been similar people in the past too, and to find out what they had done, what they had expressed as 'going on' and 'what IT was', what their influences had been and what they had been subjected to.

It helped to explain and see why it was so hard.

It was in effect a situation where you were potentially being subconsciously considered as a threat to the system, an element that was trying to change something in something that didn't want to. Something trying to organise something that wanted to do the opposite. To try and save something that didn't understand what it was, or what it was doing, and it outsmarting you, beguiling you and giving you the impression it knew everything when it didn't.

It wasn't exactly a job you would rush to submit your CV in for, especially with the health and safety risks, responsibility, lack of salary, and zero job security. But then you could also say that for any parent. There also seemed to be a correlation with these people in the past, the 'kundalini' with the cosmic consciousness transformation process, and their partners bonding with them to provide the 'second snake female energy'.

Also geological situations or locations seemed to be important, along with cultural climate and social stress and unrest at the time. There were also factors relating to the individuals' personality, intelligence, background and age.

The effect they had also depended a lot on their mental state, and the influence they had depended a lot on their psyche and upbringing and experiences. In some cases it could create a 'spiritual' centre - usually in a mountain area - with a lot of conscious 'gravity' focal points - Tibet, Jerusalem, Northern Mesopotamia, Greece, Rome, South America - or within groups, for example the Cathars near the Pyrenees, or ones in India, China, and Arabian mountain caves.

It never seemed to be somewhere in a flat desert, jungle, or icy tundra, no — but that's usually where they eventually ended up, as hermits, trying to get away from the bloody thing, or going off on some journey quest, following the same hero story program.

A saviour, messiah, prophet, someone being the godhead for a time, Christ-consciousness, Brahma figure, hidden or ascended masters - all invoking change and broadcasting their interpretation and meanings of prophetic channelling into their own cultural virtual structure, hopefully with some positive new direction and change, rather than instigating another world war.

Sam could understand why historically it had been so hard to write about, describe and articulate what IT was, and the why the evidence of the first-hand experiences of these people were very hard to find. The information was always second hand, written *about* them, or discoursed in the form of poetry, legend or myth.

But then it was like trying to write a book about motor racing while you were actually driving the car around the track.

He remembered again Jung's *Red Book*, and other 'bibles' and prophetic works that had been hidden away. It was not easy to get this stuff down, nor was it any easier once you understood all of the technicalities, the science, the psychology, the mysticism, along with the more recent interpretations, and philosophy.

The more you knew the more complex it got and the harder it became to describe or encompass in words.

He was quite glad now that when it had happened to him originally, that he had just walked away from it, and had left it alone to sink in for a few years.

He was relieved that he hadn't gone off diving down rabbit holes to try and work out what it all meant. But then he hadn't needed to, he had seen enough of it at the time, and taken in so much of the information that he knew what it was, he just couldn't describe it, he didn't have the words or physical context with which to articulate it all. He could only describe it in analogical terms so that it could be understood.

But that didn't mean that it wasn't fundamentally very simple, and manageable, nor that it wasn't possible for it to be sorted out.

You just had to break it down into manageable chunks, pieces, quantify what you could change and what you couldn't, and manage the problem. You had to keep to what you were able to influence and observe, and not expect anything but grief, hassle, and ingratitude in return.

But what if you didn't *want* to be 'doing this'? What if you were quite happy living in blissful ignorance, wondering why the human world was in such a mess, and trying to make the most of it as best you could? What if you were OK with just the simple night time dial-up modem dream interface, rather than the ultra-fast 24/7 superfast broadband, with an access all areas internet pass?

Could you get out of it all, avoid it? Could you switch it off, delete or disconnect the connection mechanism?

Especially if you were just destined to repeat the same journey, same process, respawning the same routine or scenario with the same characters, events, situations, and personalities.

All programmed again but just in a more modern setting, playing the same song for an operating system, invoking that 'Fifth Element' function when something went wrong, to fix and make a change from an 'observer' 'external' perspective.

How could he break out of the groove of the same record path that he had been set on, escape that 'ring of ouroboros'?

How could he extract himself from that saga journey defined for his program 'role' within a cultural mythical or magical consciousness structure? It had all been patterned and derived and evolved from earlier and deeper layers of collective psyche that had previously been successful.

Could he drag it out of the darkness into a more mental consciousness structure, a thought based one, a more conscious stage or level of awareness, one of real choice rather than unconscious habit? Even just letting the system know that you knew the game it was playing would be a start.

The overall problem seemed to be that we had evolved too slowly - both physically and mentally - in comparison to the growth of the collective knowledge base and the cultural structure of 'programs' and functions that made up its system.

Because there wasn't anything for the human race to evolve against, nothing forcing it to cope with, adapt to, survive against, both individually and collectively it was becoming corrupt, poisoned, and those individual human 'ants' that were exposed to, or were aware of, and had woken up to it, found it very hard to cope with both with bandwidth and processing capacity and learning and understanding wise.

It had become dangerous to associate with the information – it was highly volatile and too much to process safely at its raw level.

The whole system was also more reactive and hypnotically controlling, without become self-aware of itself, or of what it was doing, both on a cultural and collective humanity level.

It was like having to be a new brain cell inside some giant abandoned baby that just wanted to stay asleep. IT having convinced itself that its 'parent' would soon arrive soon and sort out the problems it was having, and yet fought any brain cell that tried to get it to change.

It was easy to see where the concepts of heaven and hell had originated from too. Both were two sides of the evolving collective subconscious imagination, that dreamscape virtual shared world of the Robert Munroe style 'out of body' and 'near death experience' virtual landscapes within IT's mind.

All maintained within the database and human operating system, the zeitgeist. It was supported on and within the planetary information field, translated through your own psyche structure interpretation mechanism, growing and adapting all the time with people's new ideas, thoughts and concepts.

Thousands of years ago when the collective mind hadn't been so advanced, this 'Garden of Eden' virtual land that we had created from what we saw around us, the level of collective knowledge had been bearable, even with later Dante-style additions.

It even shared the same ideas, spiritual icons, symbols and story structures between cultures and across continents from the Mesopotamians, Greeks, Minoans and Asians.

But in recent decades it had evolved into a much more ominous grey, building- filled environment, likened to reality more and more, full of dangers, and virtual 'people' not seeing each other, and which was just like the real world.

One in which snakes and stolen fruit were the least of your worries. It now required you to stand well back from all of that and observe and interpret. You had to have a plan, and be very careful how you went about it, or what you did.

It was intense and extreme. Like any cell in a unconscious body you have to be careful what messages you are giving out, and be aware of what others cells and subconscious systems there were around – particularly ones that you might upset, and come up against, with their naive perspectives and agendas.

It was easy to see why there were so many different ideas, conspiracy theories, hidden dark secrets, mysteries and fears of the unknown. That unimaginable divine 'something' that was there, all hidden by secret government organisations and covert societies meeting behind closed doors.

Yet with all Sam's knowledge, understanding, scientific and management background - plus a lot of common sense - it was easy for him to see beyond all that. It was much less frightening and clearer to Sam- but daunting nonetheless.

Sam had noticed that over the last six months or so the level of intensity of spiritual 'talk' and chatter, discussions, and interest on the internet had grown substantially.

There were now vast amounts of 'traffic' and 'theories' about.

It was as if the whole world was being excited by its own interest in the 2012 'End of the World' thing - the prophesies of a foredooming apocalypse, originally prophesied from the ancient Mayan calendar and writings.

It had also sparked off a whole library of books to be written on the subject, along with many individual's 'takes' on the concept.

All fuelling the fire of the collective nervousness and worry in its imagination, or at least in the Western cultural side.

The whole thing would obviously end in disappointment for the few who were so convinced of its truth that they were even now making last and final pilgrimages to certain geographic locations around the globe to confront the dawn of the apocalypse - again, but *really really* this time.

From Sam's perspective he was quite happy to give the thing reassuring advice to assure IT that this wasn't going to happen, and that the anxious and irrational imaginative ideas it was having, were just figments of its own imagination, and if anything did happen it would just be as a result of its own self-fulfilling prophesies.

A bit like the idea of collective positive thinking - but in reverse - sort of self-fulfilling disasters, which of course we were much better at having.

None the less he had a feeling that the end of 2012 was still going to bring some anxious news and events as a result of the collective stress that was underway that IT was creating for itself.

CHAPTER 21
THE TOO CLOSE TO CALL LANDSLIDE

And around the 19th October things did start to change. There was a different feeling in the air, a sense of 'something going on'.

He woke up exhausted that morning with so many mixed up concepts and information whirling through his head.

This particular morning it all felt very focused, and he had even woken up to white snakes writhing around and a weird firework display of lights in front of his closed eyelids. It was as if so many thoughts were being overlaid at once, too many parts of a picture spread out from different levels.

It was as if there *was* a real problem - but one that existed in many contexts and perspectives so that it was too difficult to articulate.

All that day both he and Brina seemed to go around in circles, just not really achieving anything, unable to concentrate, or focus.

In the evening he watched the news as usual and all the stories - although minor and innocuous - seemed to be saying the opposite to what he thought was right or logical.

The next day was the same, and all the events and news reports were progressively inclined away from what he would say were balanced or fair, and more towards injustice, illogical subconscious actions or fear based choices.

The emphasis was on drama, greed, sensationalism, and a mismatch of reactionary choices rather than mature aware logic by adult people. But not just in the news, it was everything going on around them.

By the third day it was getting fairly intense. He had spent four hours just driving around in the afternoon, trying to avoid traffic jams, cancelled meetings, people everywhere just seemed to be milling around confused, uncertain.

He also had a feeling of disconnection, as if he were missing something, like he was detached or out of range of whatever he should have been in touch with.

Brina was the same, he tried talking with her but the

conversations would always be interrupted or distractions would occur, or someone else would find her something meaningless to do.

By the fifth day it was getting serious, and way too obvious, it felt as if there were a couple of bumper cars banging together in his head, the top of his head ached again all the time and he had that same cold flushed feeling on his face and it all made him feel uncomfortable, under pressure.

Brina had a letter arrive that was asking her to attend Jury Service, he had a phone call from the new power and gas company that he was switching to saying that they had got the wrong house and had switched the house further along the road by mistake, and now all the bills had got mixed up.

It went on like that for another week, meaningless letters, phone calls, and bewildered people everywhere, event after event, situation after mad situation.

By the tenth day everything had got very agitated. People now seemed very aggressive, he saw two people almost get run over and small children screaming and people being highly agitated everywhere in and around shops.

He couldn't concentrate on anything he was doing, and he just couldn't work. So he decided to have a week off and stay at home.

There was just too much going on, too much information coming in. He felt that he was being expected to do something, or work something out, but he didn't know what.

It made no sense, there was no logic to any of it, it felt chaotic, and irrational.

The next afternoon he just sat at home in the front room, making the most of the early winter sunshine streaming in through the windows and enjoying the warmth from the open fire, and he started to write up his journals.

There were lots of news reports on the television so he just left it on quietly in the background while he sat there with a cup of tea and his papers and books.

The stories seemed to be focused on 'cleaning out of old baggage' in institutions, like the police forces, the BBC, removing corruption and stamping down on injustice.

There was also news on the ongoing progress in the cases of

child abuse from old celebrities - both living and dead ones. People saying, 'How could people not see what was going on?', 'How could people have let this happen?, and 'Why didn't anyone say anything?'.

Lots of old skeletons being let out of the closet and buried. But whatever was going on - Sam knew that it didn't seem to relate to those reports.

Sam thought that the problem may be related to something that was about to happen in Syria within the next few week - to finally close off that situation - but as he thought about it - that didn't seem right either.

Then the news changed and he looked up from his journal as an American reporter's voice kicked in with a much more of a jolly, brash, polished tone.

It was a report on the up and coming US presidential elections and was about what was going on with each side; the lobbying, rallies, the personalities involved, their wives, what they were saying, and how 'close' the result was going to be.

The energy came in and the boxes started being ticked - what had been 'said' through gnosis over the last few weeks, the created situations, and what people had been saying to him. Suddenly it all made sense.

He now had everything in his mind that was going on in the background, everything that was happening at all levels; the people involved, the group psyche of the country, the effect on the local collective subconscious, the games being played, the manipulation of the unconscious, the fear, the confusion.

All the suggestive ideas from groups, hypnosis of the masses, it was all very strange. It drew him in, he was fascinated by it.

He knew what was going on.

Sam felt his mind being involved, drawn in, working things out, processing things, seeing, focusing, and feeding back what he thought.

Whatever was going on here he felt as if he were being asked to involve himself.

It was crazy he knew. But somehow he had the clear idea in his mind that it knew the whole situation was being subconsciously manipulated by various elements and groups involved in this US election, but it was all going on unconsciously.

IT was worried because it knew it was wrong, and IT was now either awake to the situation, or IT didn't like it, or maybe it was frightened. It was a bit vague at the moment.

Which in itself was interesting.

Yet why should he care? It had nothing to do with him, this was all going on in another country after all - it wasn't his business, his concern or even his responsibility. But it was there.

He turned the TV off and went for a walk. He decided to try and clear his head, and stop thinking about it.

In the evening Brina seemed much more content, settled, and happy, as she always did when he had 'got' something. They had a couple of glasses of wine and relaxed, and went to bed early.

At about 4 a.m. Brina woke Sam up, she was talking loudly in her sleep next to him, obviously having a vivid dream about something.

He let her carry on for twenty minutes until it became clear that she was getting upset, at which point he stroked her arm to gently to wake her up.

She jumped and sat bolt upright in bed.

After a few minutes calming down she went through her dream. She had dreamt that Sam had been taken away by some 'strange' people into a hole in the ground and that there were lots of different types of people. And then she continued to describe her dream in greater depth...

...She had then had to go to a hospital where he was being held, and she was out of control and nobody would let her do anything or allow her to take him away. They had taken away his black T-shirt, then they told her he was dead - even though she knew he wasn't – and people then started singing folk songs to try and cheer her up, and then they locked her in a cupboard for her own protection.

Sam listened to what she was saying and when he matched her dream up to what he already had in his head, it was as if she was seeing several elements of what he already knew but had woven them into a story that he could then translate and interpret it all with meaning.

He could then apply that to connect them together into a more complete picture, such that she was seeing something that he needed to get or understand, and that this was her way of receiving and conveying the information.

It was a very graphic and very vivid dream, and it was another half an hour before she went back to sleep.

In the hour before the sun came up Sam managed to drop off to sleep. Then it was his turn.

During that hour before he woke up he had a short but vivid dream. It was about a boy who was blindfolded inside a Coptic-style church, and the boy was choosing the new Pope by picking balls from a globe.

There was a voice talking over the ceremony - like a news reporter - who commented that 'If only the US president could be chosen in the same way, by a child'.

There was also some strange grouping of people in Syria that didn't make sense, and some cure from Australia for colon cancer. Which to be frank all sounded a bit mad - but then mad these days was getting to be the norm.

Sam woke up in the morning on his own in bed with the light streaming in from the window. It was Tuesday 6th November. He was tired, and the waking up at 4 a.m. had taken a lot out of him, and he also now had lots of information flowing in and out of his head.

He looked at the bedside clock and saw that it was now 8 a.m. and he could hear Brina in the kitchen making breakfast - twice by the sound of it, the sound of the bin opening and closing indicated that the first attempt had failed.

It was an indication that she would be going round in circles again all day, probably finding things for him to do at the same time, to keep him busy and out of trouble.

He got up and had a short shower, letting the heat from the stream of hot water work its way into his neck, his back, and all over his head to try and improve how he felt.

He didn't bother getting dressed, he just put a dressing gown on and went into the kitchen and sat down at the breakfast table.

He knew enough from what was going on in the room not to say anything, and just accepted breakfast in whatever form it took.

He also knew not to try and help or make conversation, she

seemed happy enough. He picked up the freshly delivered newspaper off the sideboard and pulled out the free supplement magazine inside.

He waded through the gardening and cooking articles, the discussions about makeup and current affairs and which new movies were being showed at the cinema.

He then turned a page, and a full page advert leapt out at him. The whole page had energy and synchronistic indicators printed all over it.

It was a picture of two stiletto shoes facing each other on a marble background. One was black and the other was leopard skin. Above the shoes was a message "Can't decide which to choose?"

He stared at it for a few moments - it was clearly a representation of the two sides in the US election - he knew this because of several other news feeds that had come in in the previous days, or more specifically representations of the two wives involved and their association.

A minute later a plate appeared over the top of the advert with breakfast on it, and Sam moved the magazine away, and thought while he ate.

He didn't feel intimidated by what was going on, he felt detached, as if he we just being asked to make a decision based on an independent objective view and was seeing what was happening in physical terms.

He wasn't really in the mood though - he was tired and he needed to get out, and so did Brina.

They decided to do the weekly shop early at the supermarket, which turned out to be a mistake, the whole place was full of zombies again, bumping into him, and crowding them, with things trying to 'tell' him information relating to the same subject everywhere.

By the evening they were both irritable and tired. Brina had decided to go to bed very early, and Sam just sat and watched the early evening news to see what was going on.

The news was relaying what had been said the night before in the US - how the opinion surveys were indicating a very close result - too close to call 50/50 - with some polls indicating a slight lead for the leopard skin wife Republicans, over the existing black president. They were talking about change, and the possibility of having to have a revote. It was all very disconcerting.

So he turned the television off and went to bed early too and slept in the spare room.

Sam just lay there in the bed in the spare room, with his hands tucked under his armpits again, trying to empty his mind, but it was still firing away in lots of directions. He knew what he was being asked now, and what he was being given to work out, but he was just so worn down.

It wasn't for him to make these sorts of decisions, interfering wasn't the thing to do, things had to be done properly, people given the right to choose, make an informed choice.

He had no opinion either way, he just wanted stability, continuity, calm, and this was just all confusing change.

Then he closed his eyes. Images came to him, information, flashes of thought, along with knowing packets of data, all the references, links, and context.

Then it hit him clearly - he could see what was wrong - something wasn't allowing that very choice to happen - that freedom to choose - there was subconscious interference going on, that was why it was so close, why it was 'too close to call'. Something or some group had set this pattern, this narrowing of margins so that it could control things, exploit the situation, some group or groups of controlling 'elite' or such bodies that were trying to manipulate things within the unconscious, but who themselves were controlled by the system itself.

A manipulating force influencing the collective unconscious mind was using all the old tricks of symbols, hypnosis and fear – well, at least the US part of IT anyway.

Something was trying to push things the other way for some reason, apply pressure subconsciously within the US subconscious mind set, or the US part of the collective mind psyche structure and its data. Something was applying fear, influence and hypnotic suggestion to it to manipulate the vote.

It was complicated but the whole situation was being unconsciously fabricated by a group, or programs within a group, of people who would gain by doing this.

Things like this had been going on a long time, but somehow

this was different. IT was conscious that this was happening, and it didn't like it, and it was unsure what it meant or what it was meant to do.

IT was frightened by it, confused, uncertain, and anxious. IT knew something was wrong but didn't know what it was, or what to do, or what was happening, or how to overcome it.

Sam closed his eyes and focused.

Show me, he said slowly and calmly in his mind, and energy started to tingle through his body, surging up from his thighs and up his spine and body into his head.

There was a little confusion at first.

He concentrated. He was now able to see them as a group of a dozen or maybe as many as twenty or so. They phased in and out seemingly trying to take some form that he could interpret and accept, programs becoming something perceivable. IT toyed with the idea of representing them as 'aliens' in varying forms but that quickly stopped, and it thought better of it.

Sam could then see them as faces, people, all men wearing dark suits, white shirts and ties. He had no idea who they were - he had never seen them before or ever met them, there were faces but they were not their faces. It was confusing. Programs within people, unconscious programs existing within influential people.

Then comprehension slowly dawned on him, information came through as to what they were, programs, higher selves - if that was the right term.

They were not specific individuals although they were associated and supported within individual bodies, human devices. They were working together to influence that cultural part of the collective unconscious to manipulate the election, yet they were also unconscious slaves to IT themselves, even though they were operating at the highest levels.

He tried not to let his own imagination or mind expand on the concept, he just let the information flow in and build and try to explain itself to him in the best way it could.

Manipulation of everyone was going on globally in the form of unconscious control, belief structures, and ever evolving systems of hypnotic manipulation. This occurred either within that specific geographical area, e.g. country, or in a cultural area.

But this situation was more obvious than anywhere else, and as such had made itself obvious to the overall collective human mind, which is why there was so much interest in it in the news globally, and within the minds of everyone.

Sam had no idea who these people in suits were, how they were represented, or why they were doing what they appeared to be doing - all he could sense was that consciously this was wrong.

IT, through him, was worried about it, and now that it was self-aware, again through Sam, IT could see that it was wrong too.

But IT didn't know what to do or what needed to happen. IT didn't know if it should be doing something, or whether this was even supposed to be happening.

Like a child it was worried about it, and it was pointing this out to him to process the problem, and asking him to work it out, tell it what to do. IT seemed to trust him and was looking for a perceptive answer.

Sam saw straight away that this wasn't about making a decision on which way the election had to go, he didn't care. It didn't really matter aside from wanting things to remain stable at the moment and the need for balancing out both sides.

This was about doing what was right, and overcoming subconscious influences, and all part of waking up.

The decision didn't affect him personally, either. But he was being asked for his opinion, and he now needed to decide.

What was important here was not the choice of one or the other side or individuals.

The important thing was the ability of the collective mind to overcome its own subconscious when it needed to, when it knew something was wrong.

IT needed to overcome that fear when it was being manipulated by the thought of the virtual spider in the corner of the room, the noise from the mirrored wardrobe, or in this case the 'bogeymen'.

It was as simple as the little girl taking charge of the dragon.

Sam concentrated and focused, and energy surged in tingling waves through the core of his body.

Overrule he thought – he drew energy through himself and it surged up his body and through his head.

Massive levels of thoughts and concepts and intensity passed through his mind in seconds, and he inhaled deeply. He concentrated on why he was doing this, maintained the corresponding thoughts in his mind, and focused his energy in the darkness into what needed to happen.

OVERRULE! He repeated the thought only this time as a command.

The faces looked surprised and shocked as if nothing like that had happened before. Energy surged though him, and focus, thought, and direction were applied to it.

Then in an instant it was all gone, the pressure, the fear. There was a sense of determination, direction, and change, and IT was gone from his mind, it was done.

If of course he had actually done anything – he may have just been deluding himself. That was it though, the concept, that was the important thing here.

IT had to overcome its own subconscious influence, make a conscious self-aware decision of its own - with his help for now - to not be influenced by subconscious manipulation within itself or parts of itself. That was the only important thing here, the election itself was secondary on the scale of things.

IT had to grow up, change, evolve and become aware of itself rather than drifting on in an unconscious manner blindly supressing anyone trying to do anything about it.

In a few moments he fell asleep into a dreamless night.

The following morning Brina was very cheerful and full of energy, in stark contrast to Sam, who was frankly totally wasted, and could barely move.

"I can't take much more of this" he said to her at breakfast. "I am not sure I am doing anything or making any difference – it's just too much."

During the day Sam decided that if the election were to go the other way from the views he had in his mind, as now seemed to be indicated by the morning news reports, then he would emigrate to New Zealand and live on some remote island with Brina, and he told her that and she seemed quite happy about it.

They stayed at home most of the day and just tried to switch off from it all. That evening however, he turned the news on the television to see that the 'too close to call' poll had changed into a total landslide result.

Nobody would ask why there was so much of a change in the electoral vote, how a set of polls 50/50 could change to 60/40 overnight or how the blues had won by 303 to the red's 206.

It was just surreal. It was all just accepted that that was the way it was - there was no real investigation, no shock, it was just how it was, but the polling companies came in for a lot of criticism.

Which over the next few years would happen a lot.

But he was not influenced by these events personally, it did not change him or affect him, something was immunising him against the emotions or the involvement or the 'thrill' or the excitement.

It had taken a lot out of him, physically, mentally, and energy wise. Not to mention all the time that had been involved, and he had not gained anything by or from it.

Brina was much calmer for the next few days and the world seemed a better place, but it had completely exhausted Sam and it took him a week or two to recover.

Yet it was just the right thing to do, there was no feeling of power there, no feeling of awe or excitement. It was just part of a process, just part of what he had to do, and needed to be done.

He could see from another perspective that these things that were wrong, or felt wrong, were only obvious that way when you could see them.

Sometimes advice from an imaginary friend can get you through these things. You can overcome your fears, see what is happening, and understand things that are going on within yourself. Like Jiminy Cricket was for Pinocchio.

It was hard work, but then growing up always is.

A few days later when Sam and Brina sat and watched the evening news together, there was an interview with the President and his wife.

Brina turned to Sam and said "Well at least they get to stay there, and they won't have their vegetable patch dug up to build a new swimming pool and spa area", which had apparently been suggested by the other 'side', and Sam thought that it was such an odd thing for her to say.

Brina was also tired and went to bed early again without him.

He knew what he had been involved in and what he had done,

but he still felt very distant from it, as if he had served some function or purpose or role, but that he wasn't involved emotionally or even in a human way.

It made him feel cold, alone all of a sudden, as if he were in some place that nobody else could be. It didn't seem right or fair, but then that is probably how IT felt now too. If indeed IT had those sorts of feelings.

He didn't seem to have a choice for the most part about what was going on, and it appeared that neither did IT, so from that respect they were in the same situation.

He didn't know - it all may have been just another means of outsmarting him, making him think it was all him, and allowing him to delude himself.

Hopefully he thought, after just one good night's sleep things would be better in the morning.

There would be other cases in the following years where he would direct the course of other elections, but for other, yet necessary, reasons.

Curious changes such as the strange swing in the Scottish Independence referendum, and the same for the following UK General Election.

This would not be the first 'too close to call landslide' that he would influence, and from now on he would back it up with physical evidence, and recorded traceable notes as to why it was necessary and what the outcome needed to be.

He would set out and define what had to happen, before the events. Explanations of what he had done, what he was doing and why.

Specifying exactly what the results should be, and what they were indicating, showing that IT understood, and was aware what needed to happen with a significant, measurable, and obvious defined change that he had set in the resulting percentage from the polls.

It was a way of gaining conscious sovereignty, over an unconscious chaotic system. It was just a form of communication, and a process of waking up, and a way of showing him that IT was doing something observable, noticeable, and measurable and following his impartial advice.

All of these future events would be outcomes that nobody could have predicted - not even by polling companies using oracles!

He would choose the pattern of several over the next four years, along with dozens of other events as definitive indicators to ensure that he wasn't deluding himself, and that IT could make conscious distinct choices on.

It was also a way of getting himself out of whatever he was in.

For if IT didn't comply, it meant that he was either deluding himself, or that IT was playing games with him.

Either way he had a get-out clause.

Yet sadly for him, even if IT was only playing games with him, IT would call his bluff - on all of them, every single one.

It meant that his 'Am I being delusional?' get-out clause would always be avoided, always have its bluff called...

Yet because of the way the system worked none of it could directly benefit him, and sometimes would do quite the opposite.

It was a process of working out IT's concerns over the options, clarifying them with his own physical perceptions and then linking it all to information coming on from various other sources.

Although he would not be influencing the UK European Union Membership vote in 2016, by then he had other more critical things that he needed to concentrate on even though the polls beforehand would again be 'too close to call', and he could already see that IT was keeping things that way, to allow him to choose and engage with the process.

He knew that his own personal views and preference for sovereignty would be contrary to the right direction to go from IT's perspective, and so he had to put what he felt in his heart aside, and rather than pushing the decision he would advise IT to let things remain as they were, but also to let IT make its own choice.

CHAPTER 22 - COLLECTIVE WORRY

Now though in the last few months of 2012 things had become more of a blur with events and information coming in in such high volumes that Sam was only just unable to keep pace with it.

Just trying to record the events and what he was doing – or more precisely, what he thought he was doing at the time - in his journals. Noting it all down in some form, in some way. It was all he could do, trying to structure it all somehow, log it, get evidence, formulate it at the same time as processing it all, and making sense of it.

It was exhausting.

He would be grabbing news articles in relation to news items that he was being 'shown', printing them off, jotting notes down, scribbling ideas and concepts on Post-It notes, and writing his thoughts down late at night onto A4 pages.

He was also reading books and journals and listening to audio lectures in the car.

But more now recording the process and articulating it, describing what was happening to him, and what was happening around him and to Brina, rather than trying to describe what was there, and what IT was.

But with all he was writing down, he could almost have made a whole Dan Brown novel out of every page - it was just immense, yet unliveable in practicable terms.

It was at least obvious to him now that he was doing *something*, 'working', processing and rationalising things.

But describing what was going on, what knowledge he was receiving, and how that relayed to synchronistic happenings, thoughts, and subsequent world events was very hard.

It happened so quickly, and by the time a series of events, information, thoughts and effect had occurred, it was then onto the next thing. He would be left numb for days, tired and barely able to stand or move.

Yet how could you describe such a complex thing, such a vast context, the luminosity of happenings, the energy, the gnosis, the process, the flow of thoughts, the conceptualising meaning in your mind, the integration of visions and information?

There were just no words, how could you write about a roller coaster ride when you were still riding on it?

He did the best he could, but it was not easy, and he was increasingly running out of energy, time, and mental strength.

Most of the other things he was supposed to do, apart from eating and breathing, were now going by the wayside too, and he was now finding himself desperately trying to do too many things at once.

Brina could sense all of this happening to him and she was doing as much as she could for him, but she was suffering too in her own way too, processing things in her own manner, protecting him.

It was starting to show in her eyes and her energy was waning.

Sam had been taking natural melatonin to help him set a balanced sleep pattern during the day and night, and to help, in some instances, to block out too much information coming in.

It gave him some sort of control over it, or at least a break now and again.

It was as if IT was now getting him to work things out, do things, make decisions, rather than doing them itself. Which made sense as he and everyone else was part of IT.

But it was too much for just two people to deal with on their own, and IT had no sense of their capability and capacity and bandwidth for dealing with it all. It was too demanding.

So by early November it had all reached a point where they had both had enough - it had become too intense, too demanding and they were both in danger of breakdown or collapse. Sam decided he needed to limit it drastically, reduce the bandwidth, limit the information and demands to and from him and Brina.

He had to try to get it to do things for itself, on its own, as it was affecting both of them too much both physically and mentally.

Brina was just going round in circles too, cleaning, trying to make sense of dreams. Trying to do everything and nothing, all at once, and yet also trying to help everyone else at the same time, talking to him about everyone else and their problems.

She would be trying to plan for tomorrow, see eventualities, and yet not even have enough time for the here and now.

It also seemed that they were almost being attacked every time they went out; people, dogs, cars, situations. It was just chaotic, as if they were a pair of butterflies in the eye of a storm.

So Sam made a list of what he could somehow see IT was worried about from the information that was coming in, and then from that he set out a list of short objectives.

A set of things which it needed to achieve before mid-December.

Most of what he was picking up as happening was of an unnecessary collective nervousness about the 2012 stupid Mayan prophecy thing, which in itself was in danger of becoming a self-fulfilling one, with everyone being worried about it, and the media driving the frenzy.

What he was trying to do by setting this out was to create a sort of distraction thing, to try to get it to focus on three things that he was clear about that needed to happen, and to get those resolved.

It was also to discipline itself, to establish good habits, finish things IT had started and do one thing at a time, rather than getting distracted and walking away from the problems IT had created.

That way IT wouldn't start worrying about everything else, or what else maybe in the collective wardrobe. So by giving it things to do on its own IT should leave him alone, perhaps for several weeks, to recover. Well that was the idea anyway.

It occurred to him as he was making the list that the thing he was dealing with seemed to have very female characteristics and nature, with its ways of thinking, behaving, and the things that IT was focusing on.

Sam knew there were problems with what he was trying to do - forcing IT to do something, could make IT react very badly against him, and if it went wrong the repercussions could bounce back and cause long term problems within itself too.

But he had no choice, and he had to know what was going on, what he was influencing and what IT was capable of - besides he and Brina couldn't go on like that, at this rate they would be dead before Christmas.

He decided that one of the three things would be to resolve the situation going on in Syria. There had been a several reports and news items on what was going on there, and he knew it was complicated.

Following on from Arab Spring, Syria was the only country that hadn't resolved anything yet. It was trying to evolve from a legacy structure, form into a new consciousness structure, change the status quo, move forward.

But it was stuck, something was blocking it, the rebels, the people - the change just wasn't happening and it had reached an impasse that it shouldn't have been at.

But Sam didn't know why.

It was still part of the problem though - still part of the change that had to happen. It was supposed to have sorted out all the changes collectively earlier in the year, as part of a global change, but for some reason it was still going on in Syria.

IT had been distracted and its focus had been moved away from that area by other things, other more interesting collective events, ones that were less difficult, and with fewer confusing thoughts.

So he used the Syria situation as one area IT had to resolve, and Sam put a date down of December 10th and then after that it was to be silent for 4 days until the 15th, mainly to see if it could be.

Over the next few days the level of news reports in Syria went up exponentially, and by the following week he could 'see' what IT was trying to do.

A few days later it became apparent that IT was clearly experiencing great difficulties. IT was expressing its concerns in all sorts of synchronistic events, news items, and stress.

Brina had loads of vivid dreams in relation to it too and was generally very anxious.

Sam hadn't expected this - IT was supposed to be sorting it out on its own - but for some reason he had forgotten that he was in it, part of IT, so whatever went on he would always be involved somehow.

One afternoon it became so intense that Sam decided that he had to know what was going on, and so he closed his eyes and concentrated and he did the *show me* thing again.

Concepts and images and thoughts came flooding into his mind and he tried as best he could to stop the raw data being translated into anything that his own psyche would convert into images or stories or visions, but that was only possible to some extent.

He spent the afternoon trying to relax, trying to get some focus, and the information he needed was presented to him very clearly in the early evening news.

There was a short report explaining the rebel situation in Syria, and how they had recently made moves towards Damascus and had even taken over the airport for a short while.

The scene changed to a short video of two rebel gunmen overlooking the airport which was a few hundred yards away, and off towards the horizon was Damascus with the houses and buildings on the hills in the distance.

The words used in the report meant something too; lines drawn, barrier, bubble around the city, and the sides seeing each other.

Sam drew in on what he was seeing, along with all the context and information he had also been given from other routes in the last few weeks, from other sources.

He formed what had come into his mind as knowledge, but in varying forms and contexts, and he shaped it as a sort of multi-media storyboard that he had to interpret and work out.

Then he saw the problem.

It related to one man in a small house on the hill overlooking Damascus.

Sam could see his face. He had a light grey hair and beard, was around 75 years old, with weathered features and a long gaunt face. He was Gnostic or Sophist, or of a similar type of religion, a mystic who had been through several theophanies and gnosis processes, but with existing belief structures dominating his interpretations of it all. Which was a common problem.

He was, however, someone who was out of the game now, as it were. He had learnt all the old mystic tools and tricks, for protecting himself from the unconscious.

He was though very powerful in influencing things around him, in subtle ways, influencing the culture of the area and the minds of the people in that area.

However he was completely unaware himself that he was having this effect, or causing that influence to occur.

The character Yoda from *Star Wars* came into Sam's mind,

where Yoda was living like a hermit in a jungle on his remote planet, protected and immunised against the Empire.

But in this instance this old man didn't have any idea of the consequences or the ramifications of what he was doing, or the effect he was creating around him. He had placed his hermit home overlooking a city, and had wrapped his influencing immunising bubble of programming around a very large part of it.

It was a firewall - a sphere of consciousness structure that he had unconsciously created to protect himself.

To subconsciously defend himself within, but one that also controlled and hypnotised everything and everyone within it, and anything that came inside it, and some distance beyond to some extent.

He was unaware that the extent of this bubble, this firewalled sphere of influence would become so well defined that streets and buildings would remain unharmed within it while only yards outside streets and buildings would become rubble for years to come. All projected out by one old man, in a small house on the hill - who was totally oblivious to it all.

IT had tried to create a path for him to go, to leave for the coast, to escape from the city - a safe passage that the rebels had defined for the civilians of Damascus to travel out of the city, to flee to the coast — specifically to a place where this man had come from originally. He could have moved to a new home by the sea and retired, to be happy, out of the way and would have moved aside to allow change. It couldn't be more obvious.

He was nothing to do with what was going on, nothing to do with the change, the politics, the fighting.

But he was there - and he wouldn't move,

You could even see a change in the President when he had come from the UK and became immersed in the Syrian country state. His psyche transition, caught up in the group programming within the capital city, changed as soon as he entered the bubble.

IT appeared to have a great fondness for this old man on the hill, a loving, a respect, almost like a father, but perhaps more like a baby would have for a comforting blanket or teddy. IT didn't want any harm to come to him. There was emotion there.

Sam could see the dangers in that, the unchanging, unyielding resistance to change and movement with a wave of energy coming in that needed to over code the capital, and move the country forward.

It was almost like a bubble of wind in the intestines of a baby that wouldn't shift - but that was an awful analogy he thought.

These were all features and functions of a system that was resisting change, not wanting to evolve or move forward, remain under the quilt inside a nice 'samey' ecological and cultural niche, and couch potato mental state.

It had the same inertia, the force of 'why change?', that 'why believe in anything else?', 'why not just keep doing what we are doing?' sense of lethargy.

That's what all the control structures that existed had evolved to do, keeping the sheep and zombies asleep, repeating the same programs patterns, functions, and stories.

The same roles and jobs and functions in the machine, but always with two sides, East/West, wrong/right, us/them, good and bad. All beguiled from seeing what was really going on, and the approaching , but not obviously immediate, disaster.

But if change didn't happen soon then the problems would just build up.

The long term ramifications of this not being sorted were immense, the follow on bounce back effect of not being able to resolve this problem simply and effectively now, would grow and grow, evolve, mutate, expand and overflow for years to come.

The localised cultural reaction to this overall collective pressure would have disproportional ramifications and consequences. All this from one event, one immovable powerful yet immunised naive immovable object entity.

Sam could see what would happen in the future to some extent, the probably outcomes, the reactions.

But what could Sam do about it, travel down there and ask the old guy to move?

Sam went outside in the cold garden to get some air and stood on the grass.

All the information started to come into his mind and there was that feeling again - that 'being in the void' - intense energy in his head that flowed up his spine.

The front of his face and forehead felt fresh, cold, and the top of his skull throbbed and ached again, as if it was being bombarded with a vertical torrent of cold water.

He closed his eyes again, experiencing the darkness of void, reality, and the thoughts formed in his mind, translating everything that was coming in into instant perspective translations, into a picture, a vast set of visions like seeing a hundred films in fast forward at once at the same instant, from a parallel state virtual machine into meaningful, logical, physical, interpretive representations, yet all first hand.

All the stories built up at once, all the problems, the underlying issues, he was being given the information to try and solve the problem, make a choice based on what he knew or could understand.

This thing he was doing now, he knew was just a natural biological evolving process, something that had gone on for millions of years, adapting refining, growing.

IT had become more intelligent, sophisticated and refined as time went on through a biological device or devices - which equally had to evolve and become smarter, refined, and knowledgeable, capable of processing and learning within a set of laws and constraints, errors and frameworks.

A system that was intelligent by what was in it, and one that worked to find within itself that little bit more each time, outsmarting itself with whatever worked, towards ever more self-awareness and perception.

It was understanding the constraints of that low level guiding structure, and boundaries and laws and directions that was the key - something that the higher level collective 'operating system' couldn't obtain, couldn't duplicate or do away with, the software and operating systems governed and shaped by the limitations and nature of the physical hardware and firmware that wrote it - people.

In this case the hardware and firmware was his biology, which was capable of doing things a computer would never be able to attain, not even by using the best and most advanced quantum computers, could you ever duplicate that source nature or errors, energy and shape.

Something was being preserved from the bottom upwards.

Yet all that didn't help much in this situation. Being aware that that this was happening, stepping back from the process, knowing he was being used as a device to resolve something, didn't make it any easier.

It was still not a conscious self-aware process - whatever it was that was getting him to do this, was for the most part unconscious. If he made this decision and gave back the instruction IT would still not be self-aware because he was still part of IT. It was all very complex.

Equally though he couldn't just step back and ignore it, so he decided to try an advisory approach, and just give it advice on what to do - but allow IT to actually do it itself, as it was originally meant to in the first place.

Sam could sense the potential or probable future now, the consequences, the impact, and he knew he had to force this through.

Even though he knew the consequences of what would happen if it failed, the energy of pushing it through would bounce back and react like a tidal wave hitting a wall and take on energy from that confrontation.

The driving energy would in effect become a reactive energy, and be magnified and spread outward from the bubble with the opposite objectives, energy, and values but magnified, becoming negative, destructive and at the same time highly evolved and smarter.

But he had no choice.

He concentrated harder and opened his mind up more to the knowledge of what was going on and more about this person on the hill, and what needed to happen, and to find out why he wouldn't move.

This guy was a true gnostic in the sense that he had from an early age experienced the knowing, that exposure of his mind to the spiritual real, either through physical trauma to reconnect and repair his body, or from a near death experience or a feature of his genetic physical makeup.

So he saw what others didn't, or weren't able to see. He could see through that protective immunizing wall of their ego selves. He had also avoided descending into insanity, and he was well read and intelligent.

He had built up his perspective views on what it all meant, and how it was all constructed, but he had dwelled too much on ancient perspectives, naive analogies and mysticism, ancient learnings and religion.

All of his ideas were based on the shape of it all as it had been when he had been younger, when it hadn't been so evolved, with less refined consciousness structures, and when we had known so much less scientifically.

He had affected many things and influenced the system with his views ideas and thought forms. He had suffered too, been exposed to the shadow side of the collective unconscious, attacked mentally and psychologically from this dark entity.

He was, if you were going to use the term, one of these Hidden Masters - but then again that was a very poor term to use as he wouldn't have described himself as that.

He had also done nothing wrong. He was just trying to do what he thought was right, and had helped people in many ways how and where he could.

His wife had died several years before, and since then his gnosis - his exposure to true knowledge and mystic connection - had stopped, along with his influence and work. She had been his other half, she had looked after him and taken care of him through his dark times, and now she was gone, and now he was all alone.

He locked himself away and surrounded himself in a protective bubble of crystals, symbols, books and energy, with only the occasional old friend to visit, and his wife's family to call on.

Yet he had no idea of the effect he was having on the area or the extent to which that bubble extended around him.

His understanding of the gnostic 'demiurge' creating us - rather than the other way around - and him not realising the lack of understanding of evolution two thousand years ago, or taking on board modern philosophy, were things that he couldn't shape into the mind-set that he had been hypnotized with, as he had climbed up the mystical ladder of meditation, study and tutoring.

This demiurge was from many perspectives what 'IT' was, it had just about all the same characteristics of what he had come to know as 'IT' - our collective human consciousness structure - which was not what had created the universe, or what had morphically resonated DNA to this planet.

It was not even the field structure and consciousness of the non-living planet itself or the Gaian biosphere concept which mapped more to the gnostic Sophia figure. No - this demiurge of his was something we had created, a macro-human collective consciousness, a macro-organism, and something that existed within and part of everything else.

However this is also what all the other religions were believing their 'god' to be.

Gnosticism wasn't a religion, and more to the point, it wasn't supposed to be.

Gnosis was just a state of knowing - a snapshot of an information system - like seeing into a computer state machine with an ever evolving information structure that was ever harder to describe, define and understand, the whole being evermore complex and sophisticated.

Which made it very hard to describe it from within it, which was the whole point. Otherwise it would always be what it was, and would never expand.

Yet also Gnosticism wasn't a belief structure like other religions though - it was based on, and was from, a state of knowing - if you didn't 'know' then all you had was belief and religions to follow, which were interpretations of other people's 'knowing' from the past, which in themselves were snapshots, perceptive analogies of the state of play, but only 'at that time', and from their own cultural perspectives.

What they interpreted was then mapped into their cultural and intellectual understanding for others to follow and reinforce.

For certain historical individuals, this had been combined with a lot of rage, and very few provisos or caveats, but hey - that was the art of management, you didn't have to be right 100% of the time, you just had to be sure, and loud, and be followed around by some damned good agents and travelling salesmen.

But this particular guy hadn't done anything wrong. He was a good man. He had done what he could, and suffered as a result. But now he was blind to the reality, stuck, hidden away like a hermit keeping his views to himself, and yet in the way, blocking movement and change in the system.

If you are going to do that, thought Sam, *be a hermit, and get out of the game, then don't bloody do it in the middle of a city!*

Changes that were now affecting millions of people had reached the walls of this bubble, and if he didn't move then the ramifications could be catastrophic.

IT had tried to get him to understand, tried to make it easy for him to move, even giving him a path that the 'rebels' had set up and made safe - there was a 'home by the sea' for him in the place where he grew up - IT had shown him the way – IT had even got some of his family to move there already, and they had tried to get him to follow.

But he was old, tired, blind, bitter, and resistant to change now, but above all, this is where 'she' was buried, on the hill, in a grave, there, near to him, her grave, laid with fresh cut flowers every week.

But Sam had to try, he had to force the change, there was too much at stake. He concentrated once more and all the knowledge came to him again - the sides, the situation, the underlying games and programs at work within the various cultures and parts of the consciousness structures that were adapting.

This was still the focal point.

So he told IT what it needed to do to try to move or change the situation, and he gave IT another two weeks to do it. Any more than that and he risked damaging himself and opening himself to attack from the very thing he was trying to help. He just did what he could do with what he knew and understood.

But sometimes there were just no solutions.

It seemed to make no difference. Over the next few weeks IT seemed to be trying with several other newsworthy events hitting the headlines, but in the end nothing worked, and nothing had changed by the 10th December.

IT did manage to remain quiet for the three days afterwards, and there was very little news or information or events, but that was just possibly only due to coincidence.

It was one of those impasse situations, and it now left Sam unclear on where he stood with things and unsure if he was just being delusional.

Sam continued to look at the internet, and specifically on spiritual websites, and it was clear by the end of the year that 'something was going on'.

A lot of people were now starting to become aware that 'something was happening', something was changing, and that there had been some sort of shift, a change, an awakening.

Everyone was talking about it, and not just the '2012 prophecy' thing. In fact on the actual day in 2012 that was supposed to be the 'End of the World' it had come and gone without much press coverage or interest really.

Everyone seemed to be much more interested in whatever else this was that was going on, this transition, these movement in the fields that were affecting them - and rather uncomfortably they all seemed to be using Sam's words, and be most active when he had been busy 'doing things'.

It was all a quite surreal, and yet not unsettling.

His life was starting to take on two perspectives, one as a fictional character in some children's story, and a real one.

However both seemed to have been written by a child. There were also blurred lines between the two, and it was sometimes hard to distinguish between what was real and what was virtual - both sides had massive objectives, requirements and demands.

These blurred lines needed to be organised, made more defined and have more controls applied.

The virtual field-like dreamscape 'out of body wonderland', was having too much of the wrong sort of effect and synchronistic influence on its projected reality which it manifested into his, and everyone else's, lives. This dreamscape virtual spiritual world was affecting the physical one.

This became evident in everything around, and it was all trying to express it in the form of books, films, art, news, songs, and in what people were doing. 'Paradise', 'Nirvana', *Wonderland, Narnia,* 'Utopia', *Oz, Neverland, Middle Earth,* 'Shangri-La', had all gone 'tits-up' sometime in the mid 1980's

This had also been compounded by the cultist type groups, who together reinforced occultist and spiritual beliefs based on historical structures, and were usually led by one domineering mystic individual in a Masonic-style following group and control hierarchy.

All of which were based around naive unquestioning thinking and collective hypnosis, and the overall assumption that there was something that knew what it was doing and which was in control, and that everyone else was wrong and stupid. With, on the other side - others that they needed to free themselves from - and at the same time wondering why everything was getting progressively worse, which of course wasn't ever their fault.

Sam decided to stop everything now, and review the situation when things had calmed down. He decided to try and shut off contact, do and think about other things. It was all getting to volatile, frenetic and intensive.

He needed to get himself and Brina back to what they had been before, to exercise, sleep, and try and have a break somehow, and to just shut off from everything - news, people, and information - for a few months to try and see what the situation would be after a break.

Despite what was going on they could not risk their own health - they had their own lives too.

They also had other people that they were responsible for, and they were suffering as well as a result of what they we are being asked to do for IT.

Also they certainly weren't getting any benefits from it all. There was no doubt that this was really happening to both of them, everything could now be backed up with a lot of evidence and situations that could not be argued away.

But they couldn't go on at that pace.

His and Brina's health were suffering, they were exhausted and he was starting to get strange physical symptoms over and above the pains in his neck.

He had become highly sensitive to the new LED lights which seemed to be appearing everywhere now, especially the blue-white ones - they seemed to affect him neurologically, and he had to try and avoid them as much as he could.

It was just another factor of environmental noise, more unnatural things to surround us, invade and block our senses, stifle and confuse us from seeing and being.

Also the level of intensity of the energy flowing through him some days was so great that it felt as if he had a round metal bar pressing down on the top of his skull and that there was electricity flowing up through him and it, which seemed to generate a huge amount of heat on the crown of his head, which felt bruised, and left him feeling worn down.

It was almost constant now - the same feelings he had experienced a few months ago, in the garden, or late at night - were now there just about all the time, as if he were doing something full on and with no let up.

Sam was also experiencing a pain right in the middle of his head, about a finger length from his forehead, down in a line in his head to under his chin by his Adam's apple.

It ached and it moved laterally when he moved his head up and down, as if it were axially aligned up through the top of his head, like he had some sort of virtual rod pivoting from the top of his skull and down through his head.

There was a point in the middle of his brain that was a focus for processing, and when he closed his eyes and tried to visualise it, it gave him the impression of it being a cube of light or box, but when visualising it in his mind it seemed to be more like ten inches across, and with gravity or weight associated with it, rather than the sugar cube size thing that it felt physically in his head.

He knew that neither of these feelings were physical, it was just virtual information, some sort of plug-in device.

He had had all the scans and tests and there was nothing physically wrong with him, and there was nothing actually there.

Equally he wasn't tempted to try and make anything of it, to encourage the visualisation, or give any more energy to it.

He would also constantly wake up in the morning with his arm folded over the top of his head again, protectively, unconsciously trying to block it all out, which frankly didn't seem to be helping much.

To try and help with the situation he now also made regular trips to see people that were there to help him, healers, spiritualists, and medical people, and specialists. They managed to ease things a little for a while, balance things out, but it was all fairly extreme stuff that was happening to him.

So he decided it really all had to stop for a while, they were both being overworked, and he was fairly sure that IT didn't have an understanding of them physically in terms of their capacity to deal with this - they could both end up as blown CPU's in a child computer - a computer that was taking whatever it could from them regardless of their bandwidth and capacity to deal with it, working them into the ground to selfishly, and yet naturally, get whatever it needed from them to grow and evolve, develop and adapt.

It didn't mean that they would turn their backs to IT, but it had to work both ways, and it was not acceptable to expect them to turn into zombies in order to sort IT's problems out for it.

Looking at it from a management perspective you could only move forward with a given level of confidence, and ability to measure what you are doing.

Just as in any organisation there is no point in trying to help it if your 'advice' isn't being taken, or even heard, and if contrary things are happening anyway, or if it is not demonstrating acceptable behaviour.

The communication levels are not adequate enough to be accurate, so you have to back off and have a rethink. You must work out at a higher level if you are doing what you intended to do or if you were just being manipulated.

Sam thought that he may even have been taking it all in the wrong direction anyway in that we should really be evolving away from IT, and becoming more say, 'individualistic', getting into the lifeboats, forming isolated communes, or start again. But without the tried and failed communist and other such ideals.

Maybe, he thought, we should be attempting to become detached from the collective contexts - although that seems non-natural and illogical, a waste of capability, and not without a lot of hardship.

But even if he and Brina were to think of it as just a baby or a child, they still weren't able to continue running round after it at the expense of their own lives any more.

It had taken too much from them, and was also impacting those they were responsible for too. It was all very well being selfless, but you couldn't help anyone at all if you were dead.

For things to work there needed to be dozens of others of them doing the same thing, and they would all need to be working in the same direction.

Sam definitely felt that IT was aware at some level, but that it was only subtly capable of making change globally on certain things at a conscious level.

But this could have just been him mistaking collective subconscious suggestion into actions that appear to be coming from something that is collectively self-aware, and in effect may have just been him drawing in issues and causing things to happen collectively as a result.

In which case, that was wrong and potentially dangerous.

He was not being selfish - he was just really using his experience, common sense, logic and knowledge of management disciplines to make the right decisions.

It would be too easy to go blundering in and make the wrong assumptions and judgement calls on what was going on.

It was the same as, say, remembering to fit an oxygen mask to yourself first when the aircraft is in a dive, before fitting one to the panicking child in the seat next to you.

Especially, in this case, if the child was flying the plane.

CHAPTER 23 - THE WINTER OF DISCONTENT

By the beginning of 2013 things had become much quieter, mostly because Sam and Brina had now shut themselves away, and tried not to watch the news or get too drawn into thoughts.

They established some regular life patterns, and tried to find other things to focus on or distract themselves with - anything to limit the process that was trying to take them over.

Many things had been neglected in their own lives over the last six months or so; DIY jobs on the house, work, the garden, organising the house, paperwork, family visits, socialising, and planning their lives for the future.

The weather over the winter had been fairly harsh too, so that meant that they had stayed inside and out of the snow and cold for most of the time, and as a consequence the incentive for getting out and about was reduced even further.

That didn't mean that they weren't aware of it all still going on, things happening everywhere, and events happening in the news.

It was just that they had to try and focus on themselves for once, recharge their batteries, and come back to each other, in the face of this onslaught of archetypal and metaphysical information flowing everywhere, through them, and everywhere 'out there'.

It was the same concept as having a break from work, but it was much harder to do than just driving away from an office at the end of the week, and then going on holiday. This was very hard to get away from, but they needed to, at all costs.

That wasn't to say that IT didn't still try to get messages through to them, even taking the dog for a walk was somewhat of a step into the unknown, into the jungle of the natives.

A steady stream of little old ladies appeared keen to tell Brina where she was going wrong, in sudden yet obvious outbursts in polite conversation. People would be drawn to her, to point things out, hidden unconscious subtle messages that were not very subtle at all.

But it was still mindless, and reflective.

Statements like 'you need to plan ahead', 'think about what you are doing', or mostly they related to world problems or situations in the news, that was so troubling to them, that these people wanted to share, with them, and show concern over and highlight that nothing was being done.

It didn't seem to matter which routes they took for walks - and especially if Brina was on her own with the dog - they just seem to not be able to get away from it all.

But they did the best they could.

They had taken to keeping the dog on a lead to keep away from the few people around as much as possible, but that didn't seem to help much and nor did the dog who was always unhelpfully friendly.

Sam had suggested that he put shaving foam round the dog's mouth, so that people 'got the message', but Brina pointed out that that would only result in the police becoming involved, and it then being plastered over the front of the local paper, and visits from the RSPCA and then it would all be off again onto something else, some other 'problem area'.

The situations even occasionally became quite aggressive, with their dog being attacked several times by dogs on the loose, from owners who were usually totally unconscious.

Owners who were generally selfish women, living in some mindless uncaring bubble, but still with some apologetic 'message', from something higher up yet even more unconscious, and potentially insane.

If IT was trying to put him off doing what he was doing, it was doing a very good job.

Yet he didn't seem to have a choice about what he was doing, something in him was making him do this, and something was trying to get to him and Brina with the information he needed. It was just that IT seemed oblivious to what he was going through or what he and Brina could cope with.

Minimising it as much as possible was the key at the moment.

He had already been through the self-diagnosis, the getting himself checked out, consultations, tests, and the ensuring he was non-delusional stuff, and even the walking away from it.

He had tried all that long ago, and if it was just him that this was happening to it would be something he would have stopped if he could, but it wasn't it was both of them, and everyone around them. The physical evidence for what they were doing had built up quickly over the last year or so, and not in a delusional way either, and the evidence was piling up on their doorstep.

It all made uncomfortable sense, in a mad sort of way, but as with everything else you could only do so much with what you were capable of dealing with, and had the bandwidth to cope with.

There was another side of all this too; one thing he had observed and been aware of for a few years now, but only subtly, was that people everywhere seemed to be using his words, his sayings, his ideas, and having his thoughts.

It only started to become obvious to him when he noticed that these words and phrases and ideas or imagery seem to be being put into, or discoursed from, books, films, magazines, and other media format.

But not just his ideas and words, but also what he was going through, his life, things about him, and what was happening to him as some sort of fictional mythical journey.

Also people seemed to be starting to do the things he thought needed to be done in the world, approaching head on the problems that he and Brina knew that were there in the system; the corruption, toxins, food, organic, drugs, medical, and spiritual websites were becoming prolific.

People everywhere were starting to see the system, see what was going on, what was wrong and were waking up to it all - and it was starting to change, but slowly. There was change going on, and something happening.

It seemed to be that in the last four or five years everyone was getting into the new way of thinking, questioning everything, becoming untrusting of the system, and that they were angry at the mindlessness of the system that they were in, and were being hypnotised, manipulated, and controlled by.

Of course with that also came a wall of various ideas of what was causing it, what was controlling everything, and what these 'they' were in various illogical and inconsistent forms that were hidden away in the system. What was controlling us all over history, conspiracies, and various elite agendas, the 'them'.

It was quite hard to document this effect throughout this

process, but it was definitely there subtly. Words he had used in his journals, his ideas, thoughts, concepts and analogies he had written, being reflected back at him in the world in what people were saying, news reports, science, and events.

The amount of books being published now with images of blue butterflies on their covers was a little alarming too - he had 'got that particular message' shown to him several years ago. It was more of a 'what he was supposed to be' thing, rather than anything that he associated with or from himself.

Again he knew that this was a collective unconscious archetypal symbolic template, probably derived from a biological structure. It was a sort of metaphysical fish bait, but you had to sort of play along with the game, like everything else, without being deluded by it, always remembering that you were an actor and not the real, yet still fabricated, character in the play.

He had made the mistake of buying a few of these books and reading them, and that didn't help either, it was as if he was being stalked, and the books were almost describing his life.

Some of them were quite brilliant, he liked *The Quantum Thief* by Hannu Rajaniemi and *Out of the Darkness* by Steve Taylor - but there were so many.

Even novels like *Mind's Eye* by Douglas E Richards - a New York bestseller - which not only detailed his exact description, and that of Brina, but also many of his life experiences, academic background and situations.

The book even began with the character waking up in the darkness with an extreme experience, having the ability with cybernetic implants in his head, to draw collective knowledge into his mind, - there were black t-shirts, ants, unseen advisories, military organisations, and saving the World - all the same words, even the 'pieces in the dark'.

It was just surreal beyond words - page after page of now highlighted paragraphs and lines he had thought and written down. Even the black and blue cover was somewhat disconcerting, with the blue crystal skull and the all-seeing eye in the middle of his head.

The character in the book had to make a choice in order to save humanity, which was all very well, but in all these books they never actually gave you a clue as to what that choice was, or what was really going on, or what the bloody hell he was supposed to do.

Sam had only stumbled on the book by mistake because he was looking for another one of the same title by Daniel C Dennett.

He wondered how many other books were out there, with his 'name on it' or Brina's - however he didn't have time to look, and in doing so he knew that he would just spend too much time being fascinated by it all, and not be concentrating on what he was supposed to be doing - whatever the hell that was.

Besides in his case he had a feeling that if he didn't get it right, whatever *it* was that he was supposed to do, then there wouldn't be any room or time for a follow-on novel, or a sequel film, and it would probably be one that you wouldn't want to either read or see anyway. But it wasn't just this, it was everywhere, everywhere he looked, over and over again.

It was something he was actually living through though - that concept of entering a library, going straight to a book, opening the page, and then immediately reading the line that meant something to you at that moment.

A bit like doing some form of ancient Tarot, but with books instead of cards.

The trouble was though that Sam had the distinct feeling that if he actually went inside a real library or bookshop at the moment, he would have several bookcases land on him at the same time, and several female librarians or shop assistants scream at him for being so careless, stupid, and not looking at where he was going or what he was meant to be doing.

Yet they would all have some message, some idea of what he was really doing and what he was supposed to do or was doing wrong. All of which he was supposed to 'get', read, understand, all within the 24 million hours in the day.

The problem was that the process itself of things going on and information coming in, had got out of hand, and the bandwidth was not being controlled. It was just the same old process that had gone on through history, just scaled up a thousand fold, and now consciously observable, a mythical journey that you could now understand happening, audit, and record.

If only he could work out what it was that he was supposed to do.

His mind went back to 18 months before when he had been waiting in a newsagents shop while Brina bought him a copy of *New Scientist*. He had been standing quietly on his own and looking over the shelves, trying to keep himself to himself.

Next to him was one of these cardboard stands in which the latest new releases for that week were displayed.

One book caught his eye, it was called *Fifty Shades of Grey*, and Sam had thought that the title was funny considering the black contents of his wardrobe, the colour of his own hair, and the various other connections to his vision and numbers, and the tie with the iridescent patterning on the front cover.

He had picked up a copy of the book from the shelf, and examined a few pages - but even though it seemed to have something to it, an energy, it didn't seem to be his sort of book at all, and he had no idea what it was about.

So he put it back.

A week later he had seen the book mentioned on the morning news in relation to two other news stories that had energy associated with them, which he had noted in his journal, a connecting message, which by now he had forgotten in amongst the wall of others.

But he decided to buy a copy anyway and bought one online and had it delivered the next day, but instead of reading it himself and as he was busy, he gave it to Brina to read over the next week, to see if there was anything of interest in there.

By the end of the week Brina had grown quite cross with him about the book. She had reluctantly done what he had asked of her, but she was annoyed at the trashy nature of it, and the explicit content — which, although she was very worldly, wasn't something she was happy about, and not something she thought should be encouraged, and she deemed it 'unnecessary and irresponsible'.

She explained to Sam briefly what it was about - and curiously her explaining it to him sounded far more attractive to Sam than the book itself - but it was obvious she was uncomfortable about it all, as if she were exposing this female uncontrolled irresponsible part of society, this 'if I don't write about it someone else will' so that makes it 'OK' thing.

Even though, according to Brina, the book was nothing new in terms of concepts and ideas, it was more of a coming together of things, a signifier, a message somehow.

One that was talking to him, or trying to get to him with information, and one he had picked up on and 'seen' from obscurity.

Within months it had become one of the best-selling books of all time, it was a phenomenon. It developed a cult following and it would later be made into a movie. The whole thing was surreal, illogical, and made no sense, for some reason this book had been made aware to everyone.

But that was the problem of focusing your attention on something that was wrong, or giving it too much energy - it could go the wrong way and you could light it up like a Christmas tree.

It had taken one hour and twenty minutes of his time, and five hours of Brina's.

It wasn't just books these days though, it was also films that were starting to appear; there was an ever growing theme along the same lines, the same words, concepts, ideas, hero roles and situations and it was also what films were being planned in the next few years that was disconcerting too, the titles, the rekindling of mythical stories and awakenings.

All with a sort of global expectation.

Yet none of it was helping him, it was all just making more work for him - making his and Brina's life hell. They just didn't have enough capability to do all of these things, be all these things, play all these roles, know all this stuff, it was all just too much.

He was sure that maybe 2,000 years ago the level of complexity and knowledge of the thing was manageable, able to be dealt with and processed.

Not so today, it was all far too complex, rapid, and interlaced and advanced. There was just too much to process for one mind, one physical brain to get around.

Just trying to understand it all, and help IT, and cope with the work was one thing, but dealing with all the legacy programming and ideas and concepts and chaos that it also had within it was now impossible on their own.

Even with all his knowledge and skills and understanding, it was just too unmanageable.

He was quite prepared to lose his self, his ego and everything he had, to sort the problem out. But it was simply not enough.

He knew it was a physical impossibility for just one person or one couple, there needed to be a team of *them* doing this in a coordinated way, gradually building up a process to a plan.

What was happening to them both was an unconscious role-based biological process, that was trying to repeat itself, but without having any regard for the physical capabilities and mental strength and time and energy that the two devices involved actually had available, and worryingly IT seemed oblivious to this.

Which in itself showed that there was nobody up there in charge that knew what it was doing consciously - nor did it have any regard or conscious care - which is why everything had become so compartmentalised within the system itself.

Anyway, Sam knew that just repeating this process wouldn't help things, it just meant that they would simply move things forward for IT, nothing would really change, and it would only be harder and more complex for the poor unsuspecting mugs that would be the ones next in line, or the next generation.

That was why he had tried to do what he did the year before, to wake it up, make it self-aware, try to change the constant unconscious cycle, before the human ship hit the icebergs.

He had already tried to get this message through though, because that was the only option that he thought would work - IT just seemed to be taking a long time in doing so.

Sam knew that this process had happened before in the past - people had written books, discoursed information into the system, for those to then be used as ideas for the next round - what they had to be, who it would be and what they would need to go through.

They had fed their ideas and thoughts into the system itself, which would then be picked up next time around. But then if you knew that you could use the process, and get it to become self-aware, and self-evident, you could recognise the unconscious function at work and influence it.

Sam had seen it in some of Philip K Dicks' books and films, and had cross referenced with what was in his *Exegesis*. But also from other authors too who had gone through that 'spiritual experience' and then the mystical hero saviour role process cycle, competing in the chess game against the goddess, trying to work it all out. Then doing the 'showing and telling' thing to others.

Those thoughts and ideas had then been used to refine the game and gave the biological operating system something to add to the mix of variables and role signatures.

But nobody had ever used that process in itself as a tool.

IT was learning from games played in the past though - mistakes and moves previous 'heroes' or geniuses had made, using them to refine itself unconsciously.

IT had built that into the system, learnt more about itself, and then set up a new player with all the knowing, all the learning, all the events and situations - those *Matrix* moments - so that they could carry on that bit further, that bit more, that new unfolding chapter.

Only for these people to realise at the end, and quite often disastrously, that they were still in some unconscious game and had simply served to help make the whole thing more complex.

The game would then re-start again up the Tarot- style ladder again, for that particular area, that piece of the system. Another journey for another Knight of Swords/Knight of Wands, with a *Barbie* Princess Brinavere with their cups and pentacles, just rolling through the same script - but with new dialogue, scenery, and audience - to produce yet another enhanced, more believable mythical film script structure.

The problem for Sam and Brina was that it felt as if they were dealing with several parts, several roles, several pieces all at the same time, which in itself was part of it all.

It was only when you combined things together that you could see the joins, the gaps, the errors, and how it was so childishly naive.

And as amazing, incredible, fascinating and mind blowing as it was – it was also really, really crap.

When you knew this was all going on, when you realised that you were part of this unconscious system - this mindless biological spiritual process 'again' - you became aware of all the problems, the mess it had caused, the chaos, and the lack of top-level awareness of it all.

That's why all these crazy things were going on in the world. Everyone always assumed that something or someone was in charge and was directing it all – that there was actually someone in the driving seat.

When in fact it was just a continuing bottom- up, yet self-refining, process that was achieving nothing other than driving us forward without any conscious direction.

Nothing had ever really changed.

It was just a highly intelligent ever expanding mould, with lots of insane things going on inside it.

Nothing had ever really changed – until now.

What was equally unfair on them both too, was that by even trying to help the system they were being unconsciously identified as a threat; they were attacked, immunised, isolated.

Any time he tried to do anything these days it was like an opportunity for him to be 'shown the wrong of it' – to be identified as an external thing, with a foreign energy signature, some unconscious macro-biological self-defence mechanism kicking in, a reflex action against change or something unusual that may expose itself, and prevent it from remaining 'hidden'.

It meant they were becoming increasingly immunised and isolated. No one was being allowed to 'see' them or understand them, they were being 'unfriended', 'unfollowed'.

How was he going to be able to explain to people what was happening if nobody was allowed to 'get' what he knew?

But then if he also had to explain to people what he knew and what he was doing he would not have had enough time and energy and space to think - to effectively do what he was doing.

The situation was very frustrating and very annoying though.

Buying shares for example - it didn't seem to make any difference what he bought - even the safer ones in a market that were going up in value, they would either be used to show him some corruption, or a problem in the system, or to demonstrate to him that money was not something that he needed, in some naive conceptual way.

A few of the examples Sam received were just extreme, obvious, and totally irrational.

He knew that it was all probably linked to some reinforced misguided belief from some ancient mystical mage who had put the idea 'into the system', or some church reinforced 'gambling is a sin' or 'evil money' idealism - which perversely didn't include the legalised theft by their own institutions.

All this though was far too obvious for words, way beyond any persecution type psychological state, or delusion.

Fortunately he had taken steps years ago to safely protect the majority of his money and assets, which thankfully, seeing what was going on now, was just as well.

He also knew there was no point in him entering the lottery as it was more likely that none of his own numbers would be drawn from the dozens of lines available, and that someone who was in jail, or some mindless undeserving fat, lazy, ignorant toxic zombie a few miles up the road would win instead, just to show him the 'error of his ways'.

But changing physical things was not something IT was capable of doing directly at that level, so you hadn't to allow yourself to assume that it was doing everything, or indeed that it was even capable of doing anything.

You also had to just step back from it all and not let it get to you. You needed to understand that you were the conscious element, the 'grown up', and work around it and just try to understand that it was analogous to a child that you were a part of.

For that reason alone he couldn't just walk away from it even if he wanted to. He just had to hope that that unconscious awaking 'child' image concept that he had of IT was correct, and that it was not just some self-justifying concept he had created to get out of walking away from it.

The days were starting to get longer now. It was coming into the end of February and he was more relaxed, calmer somehow. The agitating scale and level of everything had settled down, and he had been concentrating on himself and on Brina, getting healthy, fit, detoxified, de-stressed.

He was also being careful and aware all the time to not get drawn into too many things that were going on around the world that he may get caught up in, or be fascinated by.

That wasn't to say that they hadn't been anywhere at all for the last few months. They had for example briefly been down to see Brina's mother for the day in 'The Village' on the Saturday before Christmas to see how she was doing and to exchange token presents.

Her mother, having planned their visit, had roped them both into going along to the church for a carol service in the early evening.

Sam didn't mind this though - it was a nice thing to do for Brina, and she seemed to love the singing, the festive atmosphere, and the feeling of being with all the people she knew just singing together in the church.

Sam listened to the sermons being spoken during the service. He looked at the priest and listened to what he was saying. It was hard for him now to put up with listening to it all without processing things.

He couldn't help running thoughts through his mind in a disassociated way, he couldn't help forming opinions and thoughts in his mind of everything coming in, or translating, into his own perspective understandings.

Yet equally he couldn't help his mind getting overly critical too. *How can he stand there and preach this stuff to people, these half-truths, this misinformation, telling people what they want to hear when you know so much more?* He thought to himself

It is like feeding them cheap burgers, fast food, and fizzy drinks with chemicals in, when you know they should be eating organic food and drinking clear spring water.

When you know so much more and the evidence is already there- the science the biology - why are you reinforcing belief and control structures, why are you hiding so much more information, treating them like children, reinforcing the hypnosis?

He knew the answers to it all but he just couldn't help running through it in his head.

Yet why do they do all this, when all this information is out there, available to read, put together and work out? Why is he selling this to people when he can see the logic is full of holes? Is he just giving people what they want, what they want to hear at the end of the day? After all they are just paying for a service!

His mind pulled outwards and started wandering and then encompassing what was going on everywhere in the world in the same style as all religions and governments and forms of globalisation.

All the same controlling principles, suppression, hypnosis, advertising, control. People being fed chemicals, spin, media control, immunisation, organisational corruption and how it had all become so obvious since World War II.

Then he started thinking of ants again, DNA and systems control processes.

Something, he thought, *has gone wrong during our recent evolutionary process, some change or disaster has meant that our DNA hasn't been activated properly en masse.*

Something through chance or circumstance has meant that we have evolved down this path, and is causing collective grief and illogical inconsistency.

One we now have to correct consciously, release that block, that impasse that is causing us to control, and supress ourselves, and is stopping us being so much more than we are, become all awake, active as part of an greater holistic whole.

He was obviously getting bored standing there, holding the hymn sheet in his gloved hands in the cold church.

He was used to the fast processing pace of gnosis knowledge coming in, the sort of industrial processing of information, so just being passive, having to stand still and listen and do more standing and listening was not good for him.

His brain and mind were off now trying to find fault with anything and everything, even things that didn't really matter.

He closed his eyes briefly. His mind then switched to some cellular analogy of two cells in a human body talking to each other in a complaining manner…

"Look Fred, there can't possibly be a God, how can anything allow all this crap to come in, these toxins, all this chaos, evil bacteria, sugar, artificial chemicals, and let it get to this state with all the fat and cholesterol? Nothing would consciously allow this world to get into this state. It has to be something alien doing all this, just like in those science fiction films."

"Honestly, Dave" said the other cell laughing, *"you and your conspiracy theories. It's all just fear you know, next minute you will be saying we are going to be grabbed by The Morlocks!"*

Unfortunately, it made Sam laugh out loud as he was thinking of it, which was during a quiet prayer time in the service, and everyone turned around to look at him, including Brina who this time wasn't wearing her normal understanding expression.

In fact - quite the opposite.

It was a long, silent drive home.

The Christmas holiday had been good though, there was a calm about the house with the wood fire burning away and the films on the television, and especially with Brina's cooking.

It was always odd though thought Sam, why they had Christmas then, at a time when the shops were so busy, people were so fed up, stressed, and miserable? Why not have it in March or April or whenever it was that Jesus had actually been born?

But then it was quite hard to change something like that, the things people were used to, ingrained in their psyche, even if they didn't follow any particular religion. You had to have a will to move things, change the status quo. You had to have energy, consensus, purpose, and a plan for where it needed to be from where it was at the moment.

Like an elephant.

It had been a long few months of climbing back to some form of normality.

He looked out of the window of the house into the garden, at the new spring shoots of flowers and bulbs peeking through the grass, birds and animals starting to move around looking for new things.

In the end, sometimes things didn't really matter if they stayed the same or changed.

But then sometimes, they did.

CHAPTER 24 - SPRING DAYDREAM

A few days later Sam found himself sitting alone again on one of his Sunday walks with the dog. He was feeling hard done by and sorry for himself, rather than just enjoying the sunshine or admiring the view and the scenery.

He was trying to relax on a wooden park bench overlooking a small lake that was surrounded by trees.

It was one of his favourite spots to just sit and think.

There was no breeze, the air was still and there wasn't anyone else around. He kept trying to keep his mind empty of things, stop thinking of 'big stuff' just to give himself a break, time to relax, but he couldn't - it just sort of nagged at him with a constant barrage of concerns and thoughts coming in, agitating him, nagging at him, making him feel jittery.

It's all just so unbelievably hard, he thought *when you are trying to fix a system of which you are part of, and most of which wants to stay as it is.*

Sam knew that the system itself was also designed to outsmart you, manipulate you, control you in subtle ways, get you to do things for it, rather than the other way around in a hival-type manner, and it had had many thousands of years of practise at doing just that.

Yet all the while it was regressive to you, less awake, less aware, less mature, less evolved.

It was also without direction, purpose, goal, or external influence and strategy, nothing forcing it to evolve against, or giving it a clear directive mission.

It was just what IT had unconsciously evolved into being or becoming, over time, and we were tied up inside it and were at its unconscious mercy - if indeed IT had any that is.

IT didn't seem to care about anything unless something went wrong. Like a baby IT just had needs and functions, and that was it. IT was what it was, what we had made it to be, what worked.

But if there was something wrong in the system Sam was made aware of it very quickly, he could sense it and was supposed to sort it out, see what was wrong and somehow work out a solution.

But why? He wasn't its parent, he didn't have that role, IT wasn't his responsibility. So why was he doing this, why did he feel responsible?

Was it because nothing else further up the chain was responsible either? Was there nothing else within the universe to guide it, shape it, and had it all to come from the bottom up, and fill what was there in whatever way it could?

The words Max had used came to his mind, "When you '*know what IT is*', you have responsibility, and then you have a choice. You can decide to do something about IT, or not. But, it's all just too mixed up now, too complicated, too controlling, too difficult to understand. It's just a mess and there is nothing anyone can do about it."

Sam had seen individual people achieve great things, with genius minds and phenomenal imagination. But this was nothing compared to what could be achieved together, collectively, if it was integrated properly, and we all worked together as an integrated team in a shared benefit environment.

We as individuals can dream, imagine, invent, devise, and be entrepreneurs. But collectively we can be so much more, and on levels and dimensions that no individual could think or contrive.

We should also be all much healthier, fitter, adaptive and intelligent, holistically integrated. But we aren't, because nothing is forcing us to be.

If it all just worked properly from both perspectives - from the collective side and the individual - it would be fine.

We had our individual perspectives, needs, thoughts, objectives and dreams. Yet IT, as a macro-entity, was thinking and operating collectively in different ways through us.

IT should be operating or living in ways that were mutually compatible, balancing the needs of the many, i.e. all of us, with the needs of the individuals.

But that, unfortunately, wasn't happening, it had become too one-sided.

The scale of this collective ability to control and manipulate individuals was vast, and yet very subtle and impossible to see when you were in it.

It was like a hyper-evolved hive mind. IT hid itself away very well but IT was also blunt, emotionless, machinelike, coming from a regressive naive and infantile selfish biological perspective, one that we have spent so long creating for our own overall collective benefit.

But what incentive did it have to change the way it behaved, its nature? How could you get your head around it all to envisage the whole thing with all its complexity, knowledge and intricacy?

IT would always be more complex and more knowledgeable than you could ever be, as you would always be a subset of IT.

You just could not get around that problem, you cannot outsmart something that uses you to outsmart yourself, and is itself reinforced by everyone else's understandings perceptions and knowledge.

IT was an information system that would always be better informed than you, and also in effect knew what you were thinking to some extent.

You would always be looking on the reflective inside of the bubble of your mind, or at the very most the bubble of everyone else's.

Even if you could outsmart yourself, see beyond the scope of your own mind you would still be contained in the field of everyone else's, everyone else outsmarting you collectively, knowing and using everything we had ever learnt or known to unconsciously keep it that way - inside and controlled by itself.

We were cells in a naive, blind, lemming and we were heading straight over the cliff.

Yet in its own right as a collective macro-entity, IT did not have the same mentality as us, nor the same experiences, views, attitudes, maturity and sense of right and wrong, or physical conscious perception. IT had its own priorities and unconscious agendas.

IT just was what it was.

By protecting itself, IT even made it hard for us to define it, or describe it, see and understand it, or express or define what it was, despite our best efforts.

There was no way of mapping it, drawing it, or even quantifying it in any form or nature that we could recognise – not even with the most advanced complex information system definition methods, analogies, or tools we have available.

Not even when combined with all the depth of scientific knowledge or even system architectural modelling software and methods.

That is if the bloody thing even stayed in the same shape.

IT would always cleverly avoid being discovered, drawn, shaped, modelled, seen or heard, unless it wanted to hypnotise you with some controlling suggestion.

To get around this beguiling process, this hypnotic affect, you would need to have a 'spiritual' interface that didn't just rely on individuals.

You would need a way of communicating with IT, perceiving IT, and monitoring IT, to allow you to influence and change this biologically structured, knowledge management system, without getting caught up in the unconscious symbolic and legacy informational chaos. Or, of course, be born as an Aborigine or possibly a Native American, or at least someone who hadn't inherited the Mesopotamian collective forming and programming.

The only way to influence it consciously was from outside of IT, give it a perspective of itself, and see IT from the outside, outside of its own collective mind bubble. Be a mirror to it, a mind's eye of itself.

Sam closed his eyes, and tried to put the problem into a perspective picture - an allegory or analogy - he could never work out or remember the difference.

'There was a dragon in a giant cave and the dragon was sinking in gold dust quicksand which represented knowledge. He was chained to the dragon, linked to it – he was part of the problem. The dragon knew all that you knew, and could read his mind. It was selfish, cold, machine like and had its own agenda and perspective. He could not break the chain or get away. His fate was linked to the dragon.'

The imagery in his mind was working well so far, although the dragon itself was starting to look a bit unimpressed with him, even in its allegory form.

'The dragon had reached a point where it was unconsciously worried, desperate and becoming self-aware of its situation, its fate. Yet because it could read his mind, it knew what was going to happen.

However, he knew that by its animal nature, it would pull him down in with it, drown him in trying to help itself to get out. It did not directly care about him, only that it knew that he could do things, and potentially help it out by being outside of it, and yet he was also part of it, inside it somewhere too.'

The analogy was starting to get a bit awkward now.

The dragon had an immature, feral, animal-like mind, and yet it could outsmart him at every move. The only way to get it to do things was to try and outsmart it using mutual trust, talk it out of its problem, and make it self-aware of its situation.'

He was talking to himself now in his mind, trying to reinforce the concept by verbal reasoning.

'You also know that you will fail, but the trying is in itself a direction. You must not kill yourself trying to help it. It gives you problems, and you give it advice. You cannot force it to call for help.

It does not matter what has gone on in the past, or how and why we've got to this situation, into this state that we are where in.

We are where we are now, we just have to make the most of it.'

It seemed to help - this talking to himself in his mind thing - and as long as he didn't do it out loud he was fine.

'It does not matter who did what, who thought of what or when, or what made the dragon what it is now. All that is important now is that the dragon learns; that it understands its situation and that it, and you, work together to get it out of the mess in a way that benefits it, and you, jointly. In essence it needs to learn your human characteristics, your humanity, your experience, care, respect and understanding in this diametric relationship, with, and of, us. At the same time it needs to learn more about itself all while this is going on. It needs to grow up, wake up, and be responsible. As we have done as individuals we now must do collectively.'

Sam was also trying in his mind to take account of the fact that the dragon was somewhat reluctant to leave the mound of golden quicksand that it had gathered for itself. Old habits die hard - but it also really needed to develop new habits, new myths and legends.

He could see how everyone was trying to see beyond the dragon, to see outside of it but from within it, to try and come up with some logical, or even illogical or imaginative explanation for it all - for what was going on, what it all meant, and what was happening, and why it didn't make sense.

That was the benefit of analogies - you could relate to them, build up a shared perspective understanding of a situation, an environment, a context, and interpretation. It was a story and a position within it, a page, a line. It meant you were both there in the same place at the same time, but somewhere not here and not now.

They gave grounding for a situation and understanding and feeling that was so completely different from anything you had ever experienced before. It was essential to build up that analogy picture to gain a common understanding, especially if you were both in the same place but couldn't describe it, and had differing perceptions.

But there was just too much to add in to one analogy, too many variables and concepts and ideas to all combine together and the image broke down in his mind. It was all getting too complex, too many dynamics to add into the scene and the picture - it just didn't work as a story or workable model.

So he gave up an opened his eyes.

He could see how wrong perception modelling and allegory could go if you didn't realise that was what you were doing in your mind. There was also so much rubbish being produced all about conspiracy, alien races, Illuminati - all of whom had supposedly been dominating and controlling the earth for thousands of years — these were just all just more layers of belief, new evolving religions, being generated in the same way as we always had.

The problem was that the evolving post WW2 'ancient aliens' religion that was being grown in the collective mind through channellings, visions, spaceship abductions, experiences and visualisation by certain psychological types was actually being associated with particular groups in society and culture.

Such that those groups - *The Greys, The Tall Greys, Reptilians, Anunnaki, Nordics* et al. - which generally related to 'them' in the system, i.e. still 'us' as in doctors, surgeons, pharmaceutical organisations, government controlling systems, religions, or Eastern cultures and religions, or nations such as Russia, or even other 'spiritual' groups such as New Age ones or *Lightworkers*, all now saw each other as representative associated program imagery and virtual persona within the system, rather than actual real aliens or indeed anything that didn't have very similar human physical qualities, dimensions or attributes.

Such that those alien groups identified as 'them', who were in fact still 'us' if you realised it was all going on just globally, had been as individuals categorised into form within the unconscious system just as in some virtual computer game, but instead of creating our own Facebook-like profile, they had been shaped by how others would react to us as potential threats or allies.

It was easy to be fooled by the system - to forget the reflective nature of consciousness and the inverting 'mirroring' effect of what you saw, and the energy that you had put in to cause the reaction. The positive being balanced by the negative, and often causing the opposite of what was intended.

As such most of the 'demonic forces' at work in the system at the highest levels - the conspiracies in organisations, government, religions, cultures etc. - were an unconscious reaction to the 'good' threat.

These aliens were in fact us, or interpreted parts of us, in other organisations, now or historically, being demonstrated in different forms. With the system itself creating more and more elaborate imaginings, layers upon layers of cover-ups and conspiracy theories, contra straw men, false flags and so on, all protecting and hiding and masking what was behind it all, which boringly was just us, in macro-form, or for want of a better word - IT.

Ever since the 1960's most of these people had in fact caused these corruptions in the system, causing it to react unconsciously to them.

They had created these evolving shared imaginative forms in their drug-fuelled, fear-filled, weak minds. As such the 'state', or control systems, would react to them as they had identified themselves in the system as opposed or different from them, just in the same way as a biological system would.

By trying to do good, they had formed this 'them' in their minds and they had caused the system to react to them, to shape itself in reflection of that energy, that fear, that shadow.

'One man's freedom fighter is another man's terrorist'. If you came up a level there would be no need for either.

The collective imagination, just like the bloodstream in your body, would be a very confusing place to be in if you didn't know what you were really seeing or imagining.

It made Sam wonder if he was being 'seen' by these people, and what he was being represented as in the system to them.

Were they picking up on what he did and on what was going on, and what he was influencing? And if so how would they be interpreting it in their varied alien evolving virtual-scape stories?

Was he good, bad, or something in-between, or as was most likely to be the case, invisible altogether?

He had spoken with many people who were spiritual readers, or Magi, or gifted oracles, seers, or whatever term you wanted to use, in the past.

People who were able, through using a variety of means, to divine 'who' or 'what' he really was, and what he was doing. See his field-based program structure in a form that they could interpret and translate into some meaningful form from their perspective and understandings.

The answers ranged widely from them not being able to see anything at all to him being a 'saviour', and being well protected and guarded. He had been declared as being a 10th Dimensional alien being, some white cube box multidimensional ultra-powerful entity, the Christ consciousness, a divine highest-level Archangel, and also as being something dark and mysterious and hidden, all of which was also combined with rather a lot of arm stroking and over familiar hand holding.

Well those that didn't just end up hyperventilating or running off wide-eyed and screaming, that is.

But none of them had ever met or come across anything like him before, or his 'level' or 'scale' before – whatever that meant.

The commonality of what he 'was' seemed to be rather open to interpretation, not to mention having a somewhat lack of consistency, with all of them giving a completely different answer as to what he was, and also of what was really going on everywhere.

The only thing they all seemed to agree on was that he was 'on a journey' and that he had a 'purpose' and that he had to do something very important - but not really knowing what exactly *it* was, was always a bit of a stumbling block.

Just as in the physical world if you asked a hundred experts what was going on and what it all meant you would get a hundred different answers - but with slight variations of opinion – it was the same with spiritual experts - they all had completely different views, opinions, perceptions and were wildly inconsistent in logic and, in some cases, even coherence.

The only piece of useful information, rather than interesting, was that in each case he was always slightly financially worse off at the end of it.

Although a few of them did offer him free future sessions, but which would probably have involved a lot more hand holding and reinforcing of their particular rabbit holes and spiritual perspective - which he supposed was at least one up on the service he received from his neurologist.

Sam always thought his CV was a very good one - quite clear, quite straightforward, but from what he was being told by these people, the job description, role, and plan for what was required was all a bit vague, and didn't seem to match the two arms two legs, skillset and list of hobbies in his current résumé.

So by trying to describe it all as a dragon he was just simply doing the same thing as these others, trying to articulate the whole thing into some form, albeit as an analogy.

The danger was of course that it could start to become that form to him, and also possibly to many other people just by him describing it as such.

That was the problem when people's imaginations got going with information coming in they would apply imagery and shapes and concepts from the physical world they perceived, and the language and forms supplied as information from structural information within our evolving cultures.

They would then combine it all with so much symbolism from media, films, art, visions and heightened levels of spiritual awareness and interpretation.

The trouble was that a lot of it was self-reinforcing, like a collective imagination, shared by thousands, all of them contributing to the never ending story, with ever growing complexity and yet it all reflected back at them from the inside of the mirrored bubble of a collective mind.

Many of these alien concepts had originated from the mad ravings of schizophrenics or certain psychological types or from drug induced visions. All were totally illogical, even childish, when you stepped back from them and looked at it all objectively - and yet they were also very 'believable'.

Yet there was also no evidence, or even coherence and consistency between those involved. You could even go back sixty years and see how it started, see where the ideas came from, see who had channelled the information, and how that had evolved to where it was now - just as in the same way that all other religions had done so in the past in times of collective stress and fear, and had been 'looking for answers'.

Only now the levels of communication were much faster, more intricate, and more sophisticated.

But today, it was all over the place with so many people sharing the same insights, concepts, ideas and beliefs, and all of them linking together via the internet - which was in itself now forming a new belief structure, a new religion, ever more believable, even more convincing as a form of control, ever evolving, with some demonic unseen force at the top unconsciously shaping it all.

A 'them' that was no one individual or particular physical group that could be easily identified.

The question would always be the same; how is it possible for so many people to be seeing these things, the same things, the same races, shapes, images and symbols?

Sam knew that it was obvious when you knew what was really going on; it was just the same process that had happened in the past, but it now had a more 'sci-fi film' theme to it, being watched in one giant cinema for the masses.

It was too boring though to realise that it all came from our collective human mind, the zeitgeist, just IT in itself evolving, imagining, developing, controlling, manipulating fashion, and all the cultural mind group sets within it.

But it was important to realise that these concepts existed in IT's mind - in our minds collectively – and that even though they were not physically real, they were still real in the information sense. As such they were real to a lot of people, and when they were given energy they could have real effect.

Many of these new 'phantasms' were based on ancient concepts, beliefs and theory, evolved and developed, clinging to the original source structure paths, character types, symbols, shapes, and numbers, with a bit of modern sci-fi fantasy added in.

Many were also now new imaginative concepts to attempt to explain why things are the way they are, to describe new groups within the world; scientists, doctors, cultures, and also technology which IT tried to understand and interpret in its own mind.

In the end we were just fooling ourselves, but then we are very good at doing that.

The shape of modernity?

It should be more like 'moder-nutty' thought Sam.

Yet also these collective interpretive unconscious or subconscious thoughts, collective dreams and imagination, were also becoming much more vivid for people.

They were more defined and creative, far more advanced and structured than the Garden of Eden, Paradise and the multitude of Greek gods and ancient demons. It was much quicker, networked, imaginative and hypnotically fascinating.

But hey that was Hollywood for you.

Equally, IT was very good at protecting itself, hiding itself. IT had evolved to survive as a macro-organism should, built up by us as competing cultural groups over time within a macrosphere of biological evolution, the planetary biosphere. It was all gods within Gods, within GOD, of ever increasing levels of immaturity, domination, and scale, and reducing levels of consciousness.

IT would control, survive, grow and search for knowledge and awareness within whatever it could exist and evolve into and within, that was nature. These were the increasing levels of existence within the planetary information fields.

Being outside of it all gave you the benefit of a clear picture.

Yet outside was cold dark and potentially dangerous, and of no benefit to you as a detached 'loose bubble', a wayward 'cell'.

He took in a deep breath of air and looked over the lake again, and noticed the way the light reflected off it and the images of the trees and clouds in its waters seemed so less distinct and real.

One of the odd things that Sam found that he was capable of doing was that he could easily put himself into other people's perspective.

He could put himself in their shoes and make sense of what

they saw and believed and understood. He could see where they were in the system, what they perceived, and he knew which part of it they were in.

He could see someone and understand their point of view, their fractal perception of the world with their knowledge and beliefs and compartmentalised understanding.

He could put himself in that position and see how that looked, to make sense of why they thought the way they did.

In so doing it all made sense to him from many perspectives, and gave him more of a macro-perspective, and yet with in depth understanding of the information within the other sections, including the academic control structures.

He could then integrate their perspectives to create an integrated technical scientific picture of the whole thing, as well as 'spiritual' and cultural ones. He could also see all the hypnotic misinforming chaff that was also prevalent in the system.

Since the advent of cities, belief groups had all naturally evolved and developed using the same situation - where being inside part of a macro-bubble, a herd, a group, organisation, was safer, protected - and they also reinforced that. It, whatever club or group or organisation you were in, looked after you in a controlling, indoctrinating way, and you in turn looked after it, in a blind naive way.

It operated in the same way as an ant colony, but it was now mind numbingly more complicated.

Which was all fine as long as you were winning, or merging into something bigger all the time. It was all OK as long as something knew what it was doing, and was not just competing with itself.

The problems started when everything became globalised, then you had nowhere else to go, nothing to compete for or keep you in check.

It meant that you could only see what you could see and believe what you believed. You could only learn, interpret and perceive how you thought things were in the way you had been taught to with the information you received from those around you, your culture, and collective programming information - local to you and also globally.

That information though was far from perfect. It was full of symbolism, historical interpretations, reinforced linkages and imagery, like a programming language or 'The Word'.

It all made it very difficult to see other people's points of view too. While you are inside a bubble of information and meaning and understanding that all made sense to you, but which would obviously be different from anyone else's.

Different especially at the more sophisticated conscious higher levels, the parts where we started to question what was going on, what it all meant, and what was happening, and when you weren't inheriting other peoples 'best guesses' from the past.

It was hard to change, especially the things that had been successful and had been reinforced before.

But with knowledge, learning, intelligence, understanding and science you could, with a lot of hard work, see through all that, and even past the layers of macro-bubbles that existed beyond that too. Until you *knew*, and until there was nothing that you needed to believe in - not even the fairies.

Which explained why people couldn't see what others saw, why there were so many varying objective views, religions, cultures, and consequential inter-bubble wars all competing for dominance of perception.

But then Sam was also damned sure nobody could see what he saw.

From a planetary biology perspective it had all originated four billion years ago from a program information structure, and had been doing well considering the odds, until now.

It had all come from a DNA and RNA structural template that was morphically relayed or resonated to the planetary field from the universal or galactic one.

That information had created a biosphere from the template structure as soon as the planet was physically capable of supporting it, when the water had formed and cooled, asteroids had calmed down, that sort of thing.

It was an informational pattern for life that existed within the universal field.

Even if it had arrived by asteroid from a previous solar system as crystalline information, it didn't matter. The template information with all the layering and evolving capability in it, had come from elsewhere.

It had, in effect, seeded via the field structures into physicality into this and every potentially supportive planetary server out there. With direction and purpose, and from something that was off the scale smart, mind numbingly intelligent, it knew what it was doing, but had also left it all to evolve grow and 'get on with it' by itself.

You could describe it as a sort of laissez-faire universal creator, whilst carefully avoiding the three letter 'G' word.

The planetary biosphere then formed a protective immunising womb-like bubble around itself - an atmospheric firewall - to protect itself and control that which was within it, and shield it from outside, which was then emulated by the biology and nature within it.

It then created its own evolving programme of adaptation, fitting into and shaping the planetary environment and dimensions and conditions, all the while building more and more complex lifeforms from the template, into what worked to survive.

It then adapted to use information, bootstrapping from the field based information structure, to program vastly more data in a structured growth pattern on many levels.

This allowed for more and more complex and intelligent life forms that competed with each other as part of the inherent rules and profile. Which was all fine and wonderful as long as the underlying purpose was evident, and that the elbow room didn't run out in the spherical culture Petri dish.

Sam looked at the lake again, and imagined a group of accountants clawing their way out of the water and wading through the mud still holding their briefcases protectively to their chests.

There was information in the DNA structure itself in the way that it was designed and layered and constructed. It was not just random, nor had it evolved that way by non-deliberate chaotic means.

Each element or component within it formed like pins on a communications cable interface. The so called 'junk' that was there, wasn't. It was a parameter framework to program complex life forms both individually and collectively, forming macrocosms on ever increasing levels, the more advanced the collective lifeform, the more 'junk' DNA there was.

The problem being the bandwidth, and the ever adapting error driven evolutionary capability, forced through the limiting channel to promote errors.

Which was just as well, since cloning wasn't an option for natural evolution, and at least we would never make that mistake, Oh no!

But luckily we were also now gradually evolving our DNA interface connectors to our devices, upgrading and changing it one by one from RS232 to USB with associated increases in bandwidth and data access.

We were now starting to evolve physically too.

As Sam thought of things, knowledge and understanding just seemed to come to him, giving him the ability to work things out as he sat there.

It was as if he could think of something, and would then be able to cut through all the nonsense and get to the truth, or at least the forefront of understanding, on a particular concept or area of knowledge.

It was like a pathway in his head that drove straight through the jungle and up the mountain to the top. Or like a 'mind' shaft down through all the layers of the mind down to the collective layers.

He was sure that this capability, this link, had been established by the 'experience' he had had originally in New Zealand - that 'theological moment' where programming information had passed through him creating a mechanism, a program function for translation, interpretation, and a physical link and device that he seemed to now be.

It was what may be described as a 'feature'. But not exactly a very friendly or painless one.

It was also being developed and refined all the time - this mechanism or process - through a transformation process that was taking place, a programming change of information and biology, something changing his DNA, restructuring him, refining him all the time.

IT was still using an information channel though - his body and mind - which had a bandwidth and attenuation, frequency range and wavelength that was limited, in short, by what he could put up with, cope with, and tolerate.

He was in effect allowing his body and brain to interact with his mind through to the collective mind as a transceiver complete with protocols and firewalls and protection.

A biological processing device that was processing and working, but at the same time gradually refining the process at both ends.

That description though made light of the pain he had to endure, the amount of energy required and the intensity of it all. He was experiencing a transitional Kundalini process as described in Eastern cultures, which was in actuality just something biological and natural, just something we collectively had almost regarded as redundant with the lack of need to evolve collectively.

With no external driving force of change, it wasn't really needed these days, this natural selective process was less visible or aware in the Western cultures.

The process was shrouded in mythology and hidden symbolism, of snakes, intertwined serpents, hidden ultimate knowledge, magic, and becoming more of a legend than the natural biological mechanism that it was meant to be.

It was a path through which information and knowledge flowed in both directions, sometimes in great volumes when needed. His mind seemed to be constantly training itself to deal with whatever came through and then process it and transmit it back as interpreted and 'worked' and rationalised data.

Everything was information after all.

He also seemed to have programs loaded into his brain and mind that gave him certain access mechanisms to the collective, certain influencing capabilities. It sort of trusted him.

But it wasn't an easy thing to cope with, or deal with or manage. It would be very easy to allow yourself to go mad by allowing it to take over you, get out of control, or to get too fascinated and delve too deep, too quickly, into the black void of the REAL.

It would be too easy to be tempted to stare into the face of the 'divine' for too long.

This had been the downfall of many; the trick was to not go after IT, or to try and get to IT. You had to let IT come to you, over something or for something. Or even better, try and attempt to walk away from the bloody thing.

Besides IT always knew where you lived if it needed you. As long as you remembered that IT would never help you after all anyway.

Nature was a brutal and feral thing, and there was no getting away from those basic drives and systems and functions, it all had to link back to the source codes, the basic fundamental building blocks on which it all stood, and laws and controls in which it existed. All primal biological and quite basic when you removed the covering conscious layers.

He closed his eyes and imagined himself in bed with Brina, so that he could visualise the process. Well it was after all for scientific experimental purposes, so he was sure it was fine.

After having imagined himself having energetic sex with her, he then visualised himself lying back on the bed, breathing hard - all the criteria for a successful male satisfied from a biological perspective.

The process was crude and animalistic, which when combined with certain 'features' such as the syrinx or space in the mid spinal canal in his neck, and combined DNA signature, meant that he had that ability to connect.

He imagined himself there, his eyes closed, seeing into the REAL, the vibrant darkness, thoughts and feelings flowing through him. He would feel it happening and experience it, he would physically feel the perceived virtual 'snakes', of male and female energy, spiralling and interlacing up his spinal column, and activating the virtual energy points as it passed up through the nerve endings at the disc joints.

He would sense the motion upwards at each vertebral disc nerve root, fire-like heat energy flowing upwards in waves, and then up into his neck and head - the spiralling sensation of snakes simply being the sensation of the alternating nerve root positions on either side of the spine.

As he thought about it he could feel the echoes of the energy surges, the focal point in his head, the pain, the flow from the top of his skull.

He could feel Brina cuddle up next to him, wrapping herself around him, empowering and filling him with her female energy and drawing off inhibiting, protective, energy that she wanted and received from him. She was in effect rewarding him with her energy, in exchange for her agenda, her needs, her choices, and so it was that the system evolved.

Sam became quite worn out just thinking of it. He opened his eyes and breathed out hard and looked down at his feet.

The dog was looking at him reproachfully.

Sam looked back at the lake.

It was a process though that we had inadvertently evolved away from, and was now only possible through remarkable sets of coincidental circumstances and situations.

There was no real need for it any more, women were 'rewarding' and looking for the wrong things, and men were being demasculinised.

There was a big gap between want and need these days. The system was breaking down.

Something that had been achievable and natural in ancient times was now out of reach, a gap too far to jump and too dangerous to try. It had resulted in us becoming slaves to our lazy dormant collective nature in the process.

The whole situation had been exacerbated by the use of drugs like LSD that simulated the same effect, to allow the weak minded, 'sexually unsuccessful' and the 'unfit' to influence and fake the system so that choice ideas and information being conveyed into the collective mind were misdirecting.

In so doing, this was circumventing natural selection, and diverting humanity with corrupt data along the mind path of the schizophrenic, psychotic, or in the direction of those with weak minded individual bubbles with thin walls.

Selfish we were, and selfish we had all become, and it all formed IT into the mess it was now in. There was an illness in the human operating system mind that existed in the global macro-ecosphere consciousness.

It was a very odd way of thinking, the thinking that he was doing now, he was sure he had never been able to think this way when he was younger.

He could drop down through the levels in his mind easily now, down past alpha, theta and delta but remain conscious, awake - although the temptation to sleep was overwhelming - his brain linking and bonding to his mind from physical to the non-space field in which it really existed.

It was like an electronic device communicating to its cloud drive, but open, clear, and without hypnotic misperception, allowing it to freely communicate into the raw harshness and vast human collective mind, transcoding, 'seeing' and understanding all at once. It was interesting, fascinating.

But that also meant that it was something you didn't want to mess about with, something that could blow your mind and brains in a heartbeat. Especially as one side still had the subtleness and experience of a new born baby.

Without both of them though, he and Brina, this process would not be possible. Without many things it would not be possible; physical, mental training, life, work experience and knowledge. The two snakes around the rod and the sword - in this game, it took two to tango.

You could never achieve the same effect even through years of meditation. Using mental tricks, tools, or mystic disciplines to achieve the same effect was just not possible.

The problem with doing that was also that you were fooling the system into thinking that you were not only successful, but that you also had a clue about what was going on, and that you could understand what was really happening, and that what you were seeing was correct.

You were in effect fooling the system and at the same time being fooled by it, on the way down or up, or however you wanted to look at it, at the same time.

The protocols were there to protect it. Belief and control structures were there to limit access, the reinforced archetypes and thought forms were there to be readily accepted for the unquestioning, like sentinels - natural firewalls, protective immunising bubbles and controls.

You had to have a strong mental capacity to protect yourself from all that.

Equally it was likely that meditation itself was a form of hypnosis, and you used hypnotic techniques to achieve mediatory states. As such you were in effect putting yourself in a position where you were open to suggestion, which was fine under normal circumstances where the system was helping you or looking after you, but you were also putting yourself in a position of being programmed to believe anything that IT wanted, or that you wanted to believe, on ever increasing levels, rather than what was really going on, or actually equating it with reality.

Until you had that depth of understanding, that clear depth of knowledge, that freedom from pre-established belief structure to associate with, it was very hard to define.

There was that feeling too, that 'in the zone' sensation. How could you describe it, when there were no day-to-day feelings or sensations that it was 'like'?

One minute you were 'normal' the next you could sense it like a vibrational tension in your mind and in your head, 'working' on something. You could feel your brain spinning away, processing, something happening, something going on in the system, which made it hard to concentrate on everyday thoughts.

Your face had that 'fresh cold feeling', the centre of your head ached, neck stiff, and the top of your skull was numb and bruised – really, really helpful when trying to be effective in business meetings.

Thoughts and information and concepts coming in and out all the time but in parallel, trying to be interpreted into reality, interpolated, rationalised into context and story, from a parallel operating system virtual world to a program perception of reality. Some situation, some problem, some irrational worry or concern, needing to be resolved.

The only way to deal with it was to be able to receive information in a conscious state, and build up knowledge over time using a broad connection to the 'system' that had already been established, without it driving you insane - and then verifying that - and rationalising it with your perception of reality, which after all was our hard worked best perception of what was real, or at least correct and verifiable information.

Rather than being in some dream state journey floating on the sea along with everyone else on some nice ship somewhere.

So the choice really came down to that of women and who they chose.

Which was just as well really. This was not the sort of influence to give as a reward to bald-headed meditating men who lived in caves and who knew nothing at all about management, bio-mechanics, quantum physics, field theory, evolution or even child management - but at least they could make a great bowl of boiled rice.

Or, heaven forbid, famous pop stars, film stars, sportsmen, the greedy, or just madmen for that matter. But sadly these seemed to have become the preferred option over the last hundred or so years.

With no external force shaping our collective evolution, and with nothing to compete against, there was no subconscious direction given for women generally to choose what was needed, or for them to know what was the ideal successful 'man'.

These days the hero 'alpha male' was more likely to be a footballer, film star, or pop singer, celebrity cookery show host, or anyone with large amounts of cash really. Rather than some knight in shining armour.

All fake, pseudo-hypnotic shadow concepts from the past, and not very useful types for actually saving the planet in the event of a real alien or Neanderthal invasion.

But that was what was attractive to women, it was what 'they' collectively wanted, especially now in the Western World where they had the vote, shopping malls, magazines and TV.

Yet women were still drawn subconsciously to the hero, that change enabling energy, a particular variation of it that suited them, whether it was rage driven or adventurous adrenaline fired excitement to do things, that was what they sought, and then sought to contain, have, absorb, limit and control.

But if the alpha female was smart and was aware of what she was doing, and if the hero knew as well, then you were onto the next rung up, and so on.

Things had moved on a long way since Samson and Delilah, and you just couldn't find any good priestesses that did as they were told these days either.

Still it was no wonder the world was in such a mess. But it had got humanity this far over millions of years, IT and we, had achieved an incredible job, but with so many toxins and drugs, so much misinformation and corruption going globally in everything, it was all happening too quickly for IT to evolve, and the system was corrupting itself.

We were no longer on the right path, and we were blindly following one that led to disaster - and in addition to that we had also become a threat to the global ecosphere consciousness we existed within too.

Like a culture or set of cultures competing and contained in in a Petri dish that was filling up with no way out.

Individually, most people had had to develop strong mental bubbles, mentally isolating and immunising themselves from the reality of the collective mind, just fitting in as best they could into the madness, surviving with it and the physical world.

As such those that were strong yet 'in the system' and isolating themselves, just doing their jobs, were not influencing it, not causing a fuss, they were getting on, and being fine, managing their own lives in isolation.

Which is how it should be as long as there was someone competent piloting the ship, which of course there wasn't – there wasn't even someone there that you would trust to drive your car.

It had all been going well in ancient history. Tens of thousands of years ago it was evolving properly, naturally, but something had gone wrong several thousand years ago, probably involving a natural set of disasters, volcanos, tsunamis, floods - probably one very large flood looking at the symbolism and manipulated mental concepts of ancient Atlantis's, and the missing ancient races and disasters that were common stories in most cultures.

There was a real collective preoccupation about floods, tsunamis, and the fear of them. It didn't really matter what, but something had gone seriously 'tits up' with the balance post-Mesopotamia, and now there was a lot of legacy and issues to be resolved in the operating system.

Along with a large number of other issues - so no change there then!

Sam had had enough of thinking now.

He stood up and untangled the dog's lead from around the base of the seat where he had wrapped it to make sure that the dog didn't wander off if he had dropped off to sleep.

He walked down to the edge of the lake and started throwing a few stones in to make some ripples in the flat surface.

It was all very well knowing all of this, but of course knowing what was there was one thing, but having evidence for it, and what was going on and how it worked and being able to explain it to people, was another.

The other problem was being able to communicate with IT in a way it could understand and acknowledge, and to be able to affect IT and influence it in some way, consciously, that was something else too.

There was a real difference between picking up what was going on, getting visions, revelations, expressing it as cultural discourse as art and literature, and interpreting what IT was really 'saying' through matched meaningful synchronistic events.

And then of course influencing it, working, and causing change rather than just looking at it and picking up echoes of what was happening - that was a whole different ball game too. As was knowing which direction to tell IT to go in, or what it had to do.

Also there was no point in being the exception to the rule if you didn't have a better rule, some plan, some agenda to make it all work, or if you were just changing things for the worse longer term in a naive way - which had happened enough in the past already. So if it wasn't broken - don't fix it.

Unfortunately for Sam he knew it was definitely broken.

He picked up a much larger stone and threw it into the lake. It made a large splash.

CHAPTER 25 - ANGEL DREAMS

After the long winter break Sam had recovered, and with the help of various people he had managed to get himself balanced out mentally, physically and for want of a better word 'spiritually'.

In any case, he felt better in himself, he had more energy, and felt well, and almost healthy again. It was as if he had undergone some sort of transitional, transforming phase. A regeneration, resynchronisation or re-engineering of his body, to some genetic processing mechanism that had worked his body hard to re-potentiate him.

He and Brina had managed to get out of the house and do things, visit a few places, and just focus on other things. Anything other than the barrage of stuff that had been coming in to them and at them in the last year.

By early April 2013 he was much more able to handle the flow of information coming in, decide what he wanted to deal with, and focus on things important, rather than it all being just walls of unconstructed and disassociated 'stuff', and synchronistic events happening at all levels and on various subjects. He was now able to attenuate it, and process it in a structured way, and filter out the information that was both urgent and important, things that required action and thought, time and energy, rather than dealing with everything. Just as you would do in management of any large organisation.

Brina though had not recovered so well, she had suffered physically with what had gone on in the last year, and was tired and worn down by it all. Most days she looked like she hadn't slept much, and appeared almost anaemic, with obvious trouble doing the day to day jobs that she set herself.

Seeing her this way was an indicator to him of how much she was doing too, as part of all this and of what she was going through, and how much energy it was also taking out of her. Yet she was doing what she did in a different way, and from a different perspective.

He could see her fighting it though, trying to stay tough,

resilient, trying to keep pace with it, keeping up appearances, and above all looking after him, and protecting him. For the last month or so they had both taken to sleeping in separate beds, to try and let each other sleep as much as possible, and to gain some energy. Which helped, but it meant that they were quite disconnected from each other too.

Sam had noticed that when Brina did manage to sleep properly, her dreams were becoming very vivid. At least that is, from what she told him of the contents of them, and from what she could remember. She had also had several premonitions, and other types of visionary events occurring. Which were a combination of echoes of previous events, and precognitions of future potential ones.

This was over and above the crazy level of synchronistic events and messages that people seem to want to 'tell' her, of things that had gone on in the previous months.

Sam had asked her to keep a log of them in her diary, just a brief note with dates, so that he could track them all, and maybe somehow relate them to his experiences. Correlate with the information from the gnosis type knowledge he was getting, and things going on around them, and how they may be related to news or world events. A way of interpreting and correlating what was 'coming in' or being 'channelled' with physical reality.

It also meant that as he was on his own at night he had a lot of time to get notes down, and ideas on paper, until the early hours of the morning.

Sam couldn't believe how hard it was writing all these things down in his journal, trying to articulate the information coming in, shape it, word it, describe it, and how it related to physicality and real world events.

It was so hard to express the concepts, the thoughts, the complexity of the understanding of what was going on. What he was receiving was nothing that took the form of visions, or channellings, or illuminations or revelations. What he had was just a full 'knowing', a conceptual understanding that cut through all the layers of archetypal, symbolic or fluffy naive legacy perceptions and interpretation. That was just there, in his mind.

He had read a lot of works by others in the past who had had experiences, and who had tried to express what they had seen or been 'told' or 'shown', and then written it down in mystical form, shapes, phrases, symbols, interpretations of scientific concepts, mythical and New Age type fantasies. Reinforcing and re-imagining the same storylines, the same mystical programs and structures, all derived from physical world language, types, and form.

He had none of that, this was all much more direct, it cut through all the fluffy, floaty, colourful layers of added psychological naive perceptive interpretation. Raw information from a multi field-based information structure, fed directly into his mind and processed.

Describing how it all fitted together and worked at so many levels was so hard though. It was just so complicated, even trying to express just one idea or segment of the whole vast thing, from one paradigm to another, was so damned hard.

There just weren't the words or descriptive context to articulate what it was like. What he wanted to do was to somehow write it all down at once, unload a picture of the contents of his mind onto paper, which of course was impossible.

Yet it seemed important somehow though, like a means of recording what he was going through, and putting some structure to it, establishing a reference point, some control over it. Representing it all somehow, so that he 'had it all down', that it was 'stored somewhere' recorded. Even though it was all coming out as a stream of consciousness, it was there, produced, out, down, so he knew where it was and he had something to show for it at least.

It didn't matter that it probably didn't make sense to anyone else, that it was a complex technical mismatch of ideas and concepts and ramblings, an exegesis. It didn't matter that it was like a collection of Post-It notes gathered together. A collection of ideas and observations jotted down somehow, wherever and whenever they came to him, momentary epiphanies, revelations, and concepts, when he was in the zone, in 'that state', and 'in the moment', with all the knowledge to hand.

Things that probably only made absolute sense there and then at the time, in conjunction with everything else that was in his mind at that moment. Things that later on would be meaningless in isolation, and seem strange when examined out of perspective, and away from the 'rapture' of the moment.

Which of course didn't help. What he really needed was a brain photocopier.

Yet by getting it down somewhere, it was out of his head, down on paper, or in electronic form, something IT couldn't see or take away from him, or make him lose, beguile him from, or hypnotise him into forgetting. It was recorded, logged, dated and in black and white.

It made him feel good, safer, and in control.

It wasn't written for anyone else specifically, or for any purpose it was just there, and it made him feel better knowing that. It was just 'Stuff' taken down, dated, and potentially used in evidence for later.

He had even started writing some of it as a story, a fictional version of elements of his life with an alter ego, another character going through what he was going through, and what he and Brina had experienced.

This was another person though, but one he could describe emotions for, and to live a life that he didn't have. But it was also someone else, who was somehow sharing his life, along with an alter ego Brina. So that in a way they were all going through this together.

That concept somehow made him feel better too.

He would get a few minutes here and there each day, snatched moments to write things down, jot ideas and concepts onto a pad of paper. Something scribbled in a hurry as it came in, despite everything else that was going on. It was as if he were doing it to win against the distractions, jobs, duties and things that always had to be done, like trips to the zombie supermarket.

However it wasn't just the lack of free time that was a problem, it was also the level of intensity of what was going on in his head, the level of processing and thinking. It made him so tired, he had hardly any energy left at all these days, let alone enough to be able to write about it or describe it or explain it - even if that were possible - but he tried as much as he could. If he had been in a quiet isolated academic or research environment, with time to spare, things may have been different, but he wasn't.

It was so vast and exhausting. Some days though he had no

drive or enthusiasm left to write it down, and even when he tried sometimes, more thoughts and knowledge and processing would come in to his mind and distract him or make it hard for him to get down the original concepts and understandings, ideas, and thoughts that were going through his mind. Along with all the world events that he seemed to be involved in. It was like trying to simultaneously juggle, whilst driving a racing car, and at the same time trying to write down some notes to explain what you are doing and how to do it, and with a very limited vocabulary.

It was also difficult to put any form of organisation around it, sort it all out, get your head around the whole thing, or express parts of it in relation to others.

Some days making sparse sporadic notes was all he could do, all he had energy of time for. Goodness knows what they must look like to anyone else who may eventually read them. Even when he read them back to himself a few days later, he had no idea what they meant or what they related to. The depth of concept had now gone, and the association and overlaying meanings were no longer there. All he was left with was a few paragraphs of badly worded text and poorly chosen words that were trying to articulate the contents of several books of ideas at Professor level.

He was not a professional writer either, it was not what he did, but he did his best.

He knew that he knew what was going on, and how it all logically worked, and what it all meant, but translating that into words and descriptions and contextualising it, was something else. It was not something he was very good at even by using analogies. He knew how it all modelled together and worked, but translating that into words that meant something, and then being able to put it all into perspective was not easy. He needed the long words, tenure, and articulation from fifty post graduate degrees to do any of this justice in descriptive terms.

He also wasn't some author who could turn out a hundred pages in a day. But then this wasn't about that, this was just trying to get something down, something that he knew was right, rather than some elusive idea or expressive concept, that somehow he had the urge to discourse.

He could almost feel IT trying to control him, limit him in what he wrote, wanting to know what he was writing down, what he was thinking. It was as if it was worried about what he may say or who he may show it to, or tell. Like it should be some secret for a few people who were 'in the know', which in itself was just another level of control, and a form of trap.

He knew he wasn't mad either, but he did need that writing mechanism for self-control. A way of expressing something, trying to articulate and describe something so vast and complex and intricate but without having to write it in scientific papers, or in New Age-type spiritual speak. Neither side of which would be up to the job in this case.

All the interruptions and distractions didn't help though; sometimes he wished he could just lock himself in a cupboard on some desert island and type it all down in his own time. But he knew it wouldn't work that way. He knew that he was 'in the game' and being out of it meant that after a few days he would have nothing to write about. He had to be 'in the furnace' to describe what the ever changing fire was like, how it felt, what it was doing, and its effect on him.

He sometimes felt as though Brina would be distracting him deliberately, interrupting him just as he had a concept or idea in his head, or just as he was writing something down she would give him something else to do, or ask him a question.

Either she was being influenced to do so, or she was trying to make sure he was keeping his feet on the ground, and not going off into some higher plane with all the fairies and the unicorns. Even though he was several layers beyond that, that feeling was there, that sense that there were several safety controls in place.

In any case it was working, he was at least getting it all down, and it seemed to be all coming together, and it was keeping him stable.

Yet some days she would be helping him, and he would sit there in the office and she would bring him in cups of tea and a smile, and he knew it was time for him to be writing rather than doing.

He was quite glad he didn't have any 'followers', he was fairly sure Brina wouldn't be happy making tea for followers. She was quite strict on who she thought was necessary, and who wasn't. On her list, there was really only one 'follower' he needed.

Anyway, there was a lot of blind following going on with many other people in cultural society as it was. People who had had some sort of spiritual experience were drawn to other people who claimed to have the answers from their own much 'bigger' colourful or deeper experiences. Experiences which they had converted into the form of a belief structure, concepts, ideas thoughts and cultural bias, that matched what they had seen or thought they had perceived and interpreted spiritually. With ideas taken from others that seem to plug the gap in the parts they hadn't seen, so they must therefore be true.

Sam remembered the example was of a group that had been attracted to a guy called Gopi Krishna in the 1980s, who had had a cosmic consciousness experience, and a range of other similar experiences and events, seeing the information and knowledge and structures from his own cultural and spiritual and psychological standpoint.

The problem was, that what he said, and had interpreted, were almost treated with reverence. That was 'the way it was', and nothing that anyone else said made any difference. They were blind to anything else. What he said was to be taken without question, it was the truth, and come what may they would work flat out to prove it, and show everyone else how wrong they were, and that he was right. Another case of the charismatic blind, leading the blind.

The ideas of Kundalini for example, and the idea of seminal fluid passing up the spinal cord to 'nourish' the brain, which explained some energy flow and information transfer that was occurring, was odd, and obviously wrong. But because he had said it, that was how it was.

There was no medical or physical evidence to support it, or logic for that matter. It was something that had originated in the more biological bias of the Eastern religions and practises, based on what they thought biologically was happening, or more likely what that cultural part of the collective mind thought was happening. Rather than it being the simple virtual flow of field energy and information through the nervous system.

The process itself was a natural biological one that was shrouded in secrecy in the Western cultures for thousands of years, hidden in myths and iconic imagery of snakes climbing up staffs and swords attaining knowledge from 'on high'. These concepts were created by people long ago who didn't know what it was, or what caused it, and why it had such strange 'divine' effects.

It was also something that happened in the womb during the 'programing' of the foetus. Something that started to slow after birth, something where the gap in the spinal cord closed up when or before you were born 'into the world', when you were first formed.

It would only 'open' again if you were in need of 'repair' or 'reprogramming', synergising the 'etheric' software 'body' with the physical one. Reconnecting you to the server, waking you up to the system.

This could also happen occasionally during sex, if the circumstances were right. Naturally selecting the successful 'hero' and 'heroine' and integrating that 'profile', and thoughts and mentality into the collective as symbols or models with a natural energy signature of recognised success.

A template, along with all the naive concepts that had been so successful in the past. It was all just a natural process, biological information terms, that was all, keeping the species in trim, in line with what was going on around. Or not.

Yet Sam was able to see through or past the 'God' experience, the vision of the all-powerful, all knowing 'divine' mind blowing Universal consciousness and 'oneness'. He had the intelligence and depth of scientific knowledge to see into it, see what it really was, and also see the inconsistencies and gaps, and biases in what was just us, all of us, as evolved structured information in a framework of memory field structures in the void.

It was just our human collective consciousness, existing in a different form within our planetary unified field density, which in itself was a tiny component within the universal one. But because so many people throughout history didn't understand it, what it was, and had jumped to other people's conclusions, they had just followed on with the reinforcing process, and slapped their own slightly more refined interpretation on it, based on what they knew. But also using what IT had also evolved to know and represent itself as, and what was in their own existing belief and cultural psyche forms and structure. Just in the same way as we had evolved and learned and adapted to perceive the physical world, modified it, and labelled it.

The difference with Sam was that he didn't have any existing beliefs, and he had also seen far too much of it all, way beyond what say Jacob Boehme had been exposed to as a shoemaker, even though Boehme was the only documented example Sam knew of anyone seeing beyond it, and of also recognising it as a field structure even though he didn't have the words or descriptive terms to define it as such four hundred years ago. This was all at the same time as Kepler and Galileo, and at a significant transition point of collective human evolution and thinking. Even then you could see things in it had changed what IT had learnt, all ITs knowledge that built up over a million years, and of what it unconsciously knew itself, and of itself, to be at the time and in that state.

When you couldn't see past it of course, you were just in effect making it more complex by trying to describe it and understand it, from inside the system bubble. It was just another way of reinforcing the control, and so making it harder for the blind sheep following IT, to be anything else. Everyone was hypnotised by the collective hive mind, and unconsciously reinforcing its methods of hypnotic control, on all sides. It was very hard to escape and see beyond its reflective walls, and escape the matrix.

The questions really were why were these prophets and religious leaders being followed in the first place? What natural biological unconscious process was driving people to actually do that, and what was causing the ones who had seen past it to be hidden and buried?

Well the answer was fairly obvious. The control system liked ways to control people, IT didn't like people who had seen too much, and knew what it was. That was only natural, basic biological unconscious and subconscious processes at work, and from and evolutionary perspective that was OK, it worked for everything else.

As an ant for example, try going 'out of colony' and see how fast you 'evolved', on your own in the REAL.

Except that, it was not OK now on a global scale to be in control, if it had no conscious responsibility. So because IT was unconscious it didn't, and neither did anything else. IT had got itself into a state.

It was also that compartmentalisation of knowledge and awareness for groups and individuals that protected you and the system. That was a problem too, again something biological and unconscious that was now not helping the overall change process.

It was the 'need to know' principle applied in government, defence, and intelligence organisations, and any large biological system. You only needed to know what you needed to know, to do your job, in your compartment, your 'organ'isation, that was self-influencing and self-reinforcing.

Your boss or controller would know what they needed to know, and you followed his or her instructions, and so on. Which was fine until you reached the top and found that there was nobody there, just a whole mass of unconscious demonic-seeming functions, drives, controls, bureaucracy, and mindless systems of 'it's always been that way and don't try and change it'.

Which was fine until you woke up and realised that at the very top there was nobody at the helm of the ship. That all the politicians, leaders, elite, and governments were just powerless in reality.

Yet even the process of these prophets that would appear to re-engineer the system, to 'see it all in new light', that was also part of the process at work. In effect they were setting up their new stall that couldn't move forward. Still stuck to what they were unconsciously 'told' by the system itself was the 'truth'. If only science and the rest of the world could 'see'. Until a few hundred years later they did see, and then saw beyond it, and then 'lo!' a new one would appear with a more updated mythological 'god' picture. Now revised and updated in line with modernity, but with a whole line of legacy structures still there, and yet with several conveniently removed parts that didn't quite hold up to logic or fashion, or more recent scientific scrutiny.

What was equally concerning was how these people couldn't step back and equate that what they were doing, was just the same as everyone else had done throughout history. How it was no different at all to those others who had experienced the same thing. But of course this time they were right, they believed what they saw, knew it to be true, and had been hypnotised by IT in itself.

Also those that followed them, believed them. They were also blind to the basic maths of 'well if that is the case why is this happening in the world?', and stuck to the 'if everyone just 'believed' in this and got together, everything would be fine' concept, until it wasn't, again.

Admittedly it was progressively getting closer each time as the cultural psyche groups evolved, but it was a pattern. One that didn't seem to be helping the 'state of affairs' in the world, which this 'thing' they were talking about was supposedly in charge of.

It didn't matter how you looked at it, there was nothing 'awake in the driving seat' at the moment. So the people spouting these ideas off and encouraging more people to be hypnotised by the same things were not helping. You were just putting yourself in a state where you allowed the system to hypnotise you, on many levels.

But the weird thing was that Sam could have sat and talked to people like Gopi Krishna if he had been alive today, or others that were, and talk from their objective position, i.e. from where they were mentally. He could talk scientifically, logically, methodically, and explain what they had seen, how it all fitted together, even the biology. All the evolving psyche structures, and cultural evolution patterns, field based energy and information transfer, quantum mechanics, philosophy and so on.

But even if anyone were allowed to talk to him they still wouldn't be able to move or see beyond what they were hypnotised to believe within their cultural based 'experience' interpretations.

He could walk them through that mental pathway to start to build up a broader picture. But it was like pulling on a mind-set that was held by an elastic band, and as soon he stopped talking they would snap back into their previous hypnotically set pattern, and eventually forget everything he had said.

They weren't allowed out of that holding pattern, that belief and mental structure, trapped in a cul-de-sac in the jungle. It wasn't that they couldn't see, or think laterally, they weren't *allowed* to.

It was like some stage hypnosis performance that was going on, on a global scale.

But that wasn't the case for all of them, some had tried to read around and broaden their perspectives, stand back from it all and themselves. Combining it all with more western objective views say as with Carl Jung, and integrating that with analysing the process of what was going on in others, and working out what could help with the process.

But without that point of reference, that depth of experiential insight, into the 'beyond IT' void, they were still adrift within the bubble, floating around looking for meaning and direction, and focus, latching onto any symbol, structure, link, connection and story.

Yet we should have all figured this out centuries or millennia ago. Why hadn't we? What was stopping it being so obvious, so visible to us all?

There was something beguiling people as to what was happening, a self-adapting mind structure that was protecting itself from the cells or ants from seeing what was going on, what IT had evolved from, and how it was working and controlling the system. But then that was its purpose, as long as it was working and everyone was safe, happy, and blind, that was all fine – wasn't it ?

Now the obvious answer to that was – NO.

If only there was someone who could do something about it
thought Sam,
which would of course be someone else, and not him, obviously !

For the next few months the array of synchronistic events coming in and happening to them again was so prolific and themed that it was starting to form a means of communication.

There were odd things appearing all the time within the media that seemed to link together to form 'messages', ideas, or concepts that had his name on them, as it were. As if something were taking his ideas and thoughts and causing similar themed events to occur around them. Reflecting back to them as a sort of physical response.

It was also interesting that these events seemed to be lined up too, not just a one off message here and there, but a series of them. As if IT were trying to form sentences of symbolism, as if trying to speak, but through world events and correlations, with synchronistic energy, into a shape or dialogue that somehow made sense when you joined them all up.

Then early one morning at the end of April, Sam was sitting in bed eating his cereals and drinking tea that Brina, who was in the shower, had made for him. There was a feeling of energy that came in and an association feeling and then a sort of 'deep breath' feel.

He was sort of half-awake and was listening through the weather forecast, that was being presented by a blonde woman dressed in a plain black dress. He was trying to take in what was being said, but really not listening very intently.

The screen cut back to the two presenters on the studio sofas "And now" said the female host, "take a look at this..." There was a picture of a man called 'Dave' with his World Record breaking jigsaw on display on a slanted wall that "he had spent 200 hours assembling" for the Queen's Jubilee celebrations "and now he has to start all over again." The screen then switched to showing a video of the event.

After several clips of it from various angles, with images of members of the public looking at it, there was another clip a few moments later showing slow motion images of the giant jigsaw collapsing onto the floor into pieces, with the man who had put it together pacing up and down, looking distraught, holding a rod and waving it around.

The commentary continued as the video images were relayed of the jigsaw on the tiled floor now in parts and layers, with the now agitated Dave walking around and throwing his arms in the air. The film cut back to the studio, and the female host immediately said "It just leaves you speechless, I don't know what he was thinking, he just has a week to get it back together again.

"Bits of it are still together..." she continued "why doesn't he just scoop those bits up, and sort of lay it back on the board?"

The male presenter was now looking at her with an expression that implied that that was probably the most ridiculous female comment of all time. His final comment was "Good luck Dave", and he smiled. It then moved on to other subjects that Sam had been looking at the previous day; drugs, levels of caffeine in coffee in coffee shops, EU regulations and so on.

Day after day it had been going on like that, and not just with breakfast TV, it was going on all the time - magazine covers, news, people, even conversations overheard down the supermarket. But this particular news item had real energy and focus to it, and it seemed to be directed towards him.

These were not merely coincidences, you had to know the difference, and understand it. They had a luminosity to them, an 'in the now' feel, an energy in context. But it was the attribution of meaning that was the key, that recognising that it was happening as part of something, recognising the significance and the symbolic relation in the process. But now it was also the interpreting of the information and state and then deriving or sensing a meaning that was important. Then understanding that in relation to everything else going on, and processing that within the level of what it related to, and then conveying a thought process back into the system.

This was starting to form a real means of communication, something that was a lot more recordable and meaningful, and verifiable and physically relevant than say 'voices in the head', or visions. Sam could see why Carl Jung was so fixed on the importance of this phenomena.

So it was from then on that Sam started to take more notice of information coming in. He recorded and logged things that had synchronistic relevance to ideas and thoughts that he had had as a process, and also with a view to the subsequent affect or effect, in relation to his views and ideas.

It was a process that had probably been going on for a long time but one nobody had realised or been aware of it until now, or had the means in place to recognise it, and be in a position to process the information. To 'see it', and then do something about it. A 'cause and effect' thing.

The following day Sam was presented with the exact same energy feel and synchronistic focus, in exactly the same way on the breakfast TV show with a news report that confirmed that very observation.

It started with the same two presenters, both dressed totally in black, which then led to the weather forecast, with the same blonde female weather presenter. She was now wearing a dark blue dress and gold pendant which was sparkling in the studio lights, and Sam couldn't take his eyes off it.

Images started to form in Sam's mind, sort of gnosis information from what he had in his mind from when he woke up.

The woman then used the words "Occlusion coming in" describing a potentially disruptive storm that was possibly arriving over the UK later that week. Which was an unusual phrase to use in a weather forecast, and it seemed to relate to the study work he had covered in the previous week.

One that he had also read in a chapter the night before in Philip K Dick's *Exegesis* in which he was talking about error fixing, and using the 'occlusion fixing' terminology for seeing and fixing errors in the system. He had also heard the same phrase used twice in the previous weekend.

This statement was then repeated by the presenter, and then re-emphasised, and also the spelling was corrected by the commentator, something Sam was always falling foul of.

It was then repeated twice more.

It was a sort of trigger, an indicator to make sure Sam was switched onto the news article that was coming up next, an alert. Also at that moment the presenter's earpiece fell out, which was something that Sam had used in his fictional book the day before to indicate that Brina's character on a mountain had become unconnected to the system.

What was also curious, and something he had noticed over the last few months, was that this presenter had also changed her hairstyle a few times over the last month. Every time it had changed it had changed to look more like Brina's, and she had also lost a lot of weight too. She also seem to match dress colour to what Brina was wearing each day. It was clearly something that was going on, and something that was 'alive' to them.

Today it was dark blue, last week it had been light blue, then black. Which was from an observational point of view, interesting, and remarkable to be able to see, especially as he was a bloke and usually blind to these sorts of things.

Then after a few flashcard style presentations of the headlines from all the national newspapers, including drugs from overcharging pharmaceutical companies, cures for cancer, growing Islamism threats against tourists, an election battle between parties in the UK, and a couple being found dead in a hotel pool by guests attending a Murder Mystery weekend.

The cancer drug trial headline was an attempt by pharmaceutical companies to overturn or sidestep the laws on drug trials, which would again come up the following day, and which Sam thought should be prevented. In any case it then followed on with another segment entitled 'The problem with Bees'. **Bees?**

All the knowledge and information was correlated and relevant to what was going on in the discussions going on within the current EU Parliament debate. The science, the background, the major worldwide problem, the issues, use of neonicotinoids, who is doing what, the implications, the potential use of GM foods as a backdoor excuse.

It was compartmentalised and blind, with chemical and pharmaceutical companies and government organisations 'helping' the farmers, yet at the same time overloading their customers and the planet with toxins. It was a never ending subconscious battle against 'the bugs', them, insects attacking our food supply, which we were being defended against.

However we had a new chemical arsenal to finally defeat 'them', in this war that we had been losing to for several million years. A new set of weapons to improve productivity and yield, and destroy the enemy of starvation, once and for all.

These companies in themselves were completely blind to what they were doing, and subsequently blinded and indoctrinated and hypnotised the people within them. They were also just driven by profit and 'what they did', and were investing a lot of money in PR and political influence to continue to do so.

The consequential effects being mere casualties of war. One in which in ten years' time there would be more battles to be won, more complexity, more levels of the ever more sophisticated war, until it was over and there would finally be peace. Just not one in which we 'humans', would be around to hear.

In Sam's head he had all the understanding of what had gone wrong, the how, and why, this had all become an impasse, all the structures the groups, the situations. Masses of data, along with all the arguments and understanding, already in his head.

Clearly IT had decided that the 'stuff' in the other articles reviewed in the newspapers was far less important, and this is what IT was really worried about. IT was worried about bees, and chemicals, it was quite childish really.

Somehow as the words were being spoken, and the dialogue flowed through, his mind started to processes it all. Turning it over and working through it all; all the problems, situations, science, sides and logic. It was as if he was being presented with the problem, the facts, or at least what it could see of them, and on a subconscious basis what IT was aware of and it was showing the problem to him so he could decide by giving it perspective.

Well, it all certainly made a change from ants.

The article covered the loss of bees, even on organic bee farms, the chemicals, the issues, the risk to agriculture, and the vote in the EU to ban neonicotinoids. The report then abruptly cut to people protesting outside Westminster with placards, and the camera picking out many people dressed as bees in the crowds. Then the new report switched to interviewing the staff at the government research unit, and then to interviews with the representatives from the chemical industry 'pesticide side', with all the arguments left and right being explored.

Suddenly, and whilst Sam was still processing all the information, they moved straight into the next article in the news, which was all about school gardens, and how they were being encouraged in the UK, with easy access raised beds and helping to educate children about ecology and nature and growing. It seemed to be trying to demonstrate this concept as if the collective mind were a 10 year old child trying to learn more about 'gardening', 'bees' and the emergency situation facing the world. There was even a '999' emergency number in the background built from play blocks, just to emphasise the point.

It made Sam's brow furrow and the top lip on the side of his mouth curl up in a 'what the hell?' expression. All of it appearing to his as a set of meaningful flashcards. But it didn't take him long to process it all, and make a choice on what had to happen, in a balanced way. He processed it all in his mind, closed his eyes and focused and made a choice, and then fed it back into the system.

By the following day Sam knew what was going to happen in the EU vote on the use of neonicotinoids, which was a vote for a ban but for there to be more research, which it did. That was because he overcame that 'occlusion' and made the choice of what had to happen, which was fairly obvious really, when you could see, and knew what it was that was the right thing to do.

The whole process though was quite exhausting, fascinating, but exhausting. It felt almost he was fighting a war, a battle against the subconscious, that he was constantly trying to keep IT awake, aware, self-conscious.

He had to be aware and focused all the time. The ban though would only be for two years, by the end of that time he would probably be so exhausted by other things to notice. The ban would be lifted and he wouldn't even notice or be aware; it being waived through quietly with minimal press at a time when there were apparently 'more important things going on' for the public to pay attention to.

He could only do so much on his own with the time and energy that he had.

Then one morning a few weeks later in early May, after weeks of the same sort of synchronistic incidents and reports, he was watching breakfast TV once again. There was a graph on the screen being shown during a news article about crime rates in the UK. It related to the trend of serious and violent crimes over the last 60 years, which according to the report, had doubled gradually between 1987 and 2000, and then had doubled again dramatically so, between 2000 and 2005, and how since 2005 there had been a rapid and sustained dramatic drop on the graph in violent crime in the UK since 2005 to date. The graph was very clear and obvious, and had energy associated with it, he had to see this, it 'meant' something.

It wasn't obvious what was being said on the television, or why it related to him, or why it was something he had to 'see'. So later that morning he read through the news article on the TV news website.

There still wasn't anything there that leapt out at him, it was just the graph and associated report, what did it mean? He just didn't know. Was it him causing this effect, was it something he had to do, or did it relate to something else?

The date the change occurred could have been significant, it was directly after his initial theophany experience in New Zealand. Could it have got his loathing of violence and acted upon it, changed something in response to his unconscious or subconscious feelings or biases?

But no, it wasn't that. He closed his eyes and concentrated. It slowly came in as waves of connections. It was a synchronous thing, it related to his views and yet not on his own. To invoke change, there had to be, as always a correlated perspective, a joint programming synchronisation to effect this change. It always took two to invoke change. But this time, it wasn't Brina!

He opened his eyes abruptly. This was new.

But even though it was intriguing, he didn't have time to go into the specifics there and then. The thoughts and processing had also made him tired, and his mind ached.

He went out for a walk to get some air, and tried not to think about it, for the moment.

By the evening he had forgotten all about it, and settled down on the lounge sofa, and lazily ate his dinner off a tray in front of the TV, whilst just casually watching the news.

A few minutes later there was the same graph staring back at him from the screen, with the commentator emphasising the very same points that he had seen earlier in the day, and commenting on how unusual this was and an odd, but very measurable and noticeable phenomena, and yet nobody could account for what was causing it or why it was happening. It couldn't even be attributed to extra policing staff, as quite the opposite was happening in terms of staff numbers.

Whatever it was trying to say, it was being very persistent.

Yes but so what? thought Sam. He knew you could generate any perspective these days with graphs, or choose the data you wanted people to see, even fudge the figures to give the right impression to sell to the public a particular agenda, or to back up something you were promoting. It just didn't mean anything these days, but he couldn't get away from that energy of it, that focus, that association with it, so despite his internal mental protestation, it clearly did 'mean' something.... The question was, what?

Brina had gone to bed early again that night, and so he decided to use the spare room again, to give him time to write up some of his journal notes again, and to think about the information and the situation a little more.

He sat up in bed still wearing his dressing gown and turned off the light and closed his eyes. He visualised the graph again in his mind and asked the questions he needed to know, using kinesiology to help his questioning, but not with phrases, but with just associations and connections.

It took a while, there were a lot of conflicting and confusing messages. The 'who?' was both 'Brina' and yet 'not Brina', the same program but slightly different, a different shade of blue, different frequency, a different physical person.

Somehow after thinking this through for a while he began to sense that there must be many Brina's around the world, or people with the same 'Causal Angel' program within them. The same drives, personality, psychological type, and the same mythological story to 'enact', and live through. Which in itself was a naturally invoked mechanism or function.

He could sort of sense or visualise them now, all looking for their own 'Sam'.

It was hard work, and it was not easy to see past the hypnotic beguiling images, and he needed to avoid creating his own new rabbit hole of concept. The connections were very tenuous, but he had images or references to around two dozen at least of these 'Brina's' - different ages, countries, and situations in that particular frequency band or program role set.

In so doing, he was also able to link to the other 'Sam roles', which worryingly there were very few of, the same level, same function, same mythical role, but different bodies or devices.

There were just five, from what he could gather, but there should have been more, a dozen or so at least, but there were just five. Just five left, hidden and protected. He had no idea what had happened to the rest.

Over the next day or so he used a series of techniques to narrow down this particular 'other Brina' and to establish the source or 'her' in his mind, who she was, so that he could focus on her, and how she was doing what she was doing through him.

By a series of logical steps eventually he worked out that is must have been Brina's cousin, but to put into words of how he knew that, and how he had derived that knowledge was impossible.

Yet he knew it was her. It also made sense in that she would have been so similar in 'frequency' to Brina, if that was the right way of describing it, as she must be genetically matched too, a similar 'signature'. So similar in fact, that he could see her face, her shape in still frame in his mind now. Three separate Facebook-like images or impressions, and associated profiles of her, representing her in three different moods or attitudes, even though he had never met her, or even any photos of her.

Her similar genetic DNA pathway led back up to Brina's grandmother who had died in the village many years ago when Brina had been about ten. Her grandmother had also been very 'spiritually enlightened', a seer or visionary or oracle, but had been very much 'locked away' and hidden in the life she had to led there. It was again a similar story to that of the famous Edgar Cayce and his family tree, and was also genetically aligned to exposure to and awareness of the collective, or 'psychic' and spiritual healing abilities.

Sam decided he needed to know. This was important on many levels. If this was truly the case then it would prove many theories and concepts, and also independently help verify what he thought he was doing.

So instead of just wading in, he decided to approach it scientifically. If this was really going on he needed to remain detached. Especially as much of the connective nature of what was going on with him and Brina, could be dismissed as meme transfer, i.e. transfer of information between people when they met, or saw each other, or talked or localised connection and transfer of data between them when they were say in the same room.

If this was really going on, and he had no direct contact with her, and she was geographically a long way away, then not only was this incredible in itself, but it would prove so many things, and also provide the very evidence that several Professors and PhD's were looking for in their theories on non-local association and field information resonance data transfer.

As Brina's mother was due to visit that weekend he offered to drive down to the village to pick her up. However in conversations with Brina he discovered that her cousin had actually moved out of her Aunt's house in the village, and had moved somewhere far up North a few months earlier.

Undeterred Sam printed off a few things that he needed to give to Brina's cousin, including the graph and a few chapters from the book he was writing. He put them in an envelope, along with his email address. He then phoned Brina's Aunt, and explained that he was coming down and needed to drop off some information to her, but he didn't explain why.

On the way into the village Sam called into Brina's Aunt's house. She was very pleased to see him and gave him a hug, and was very intrigued as to what he was doing. Sam spent about an hour explaining to her in detail what he was doing, and why, and what he was trying to achieve. He gave her a sealed envelope with the copy of the graph in, and some notes, and asked her not to mention any details to Brina, or Brina's mother.

Sam explained what he was writing about and that he was very interested in talking to people in the family about their spiritual experiences, as he was doing some research for his book. During the conversation her Aunt also mentioned how she was also very spiritual, and had had many vivid dreams and visions some of which many had recently included planes, and tornados, and she also offered to email him with her experiences. She also mentioned how she had a friend who was a spiritual reader, and how she had taken a great interest in the subject over the years.

She promised to phone her daughter and explain the situation and pass on Sam's email address so that her daughter could forward her experiences also, to him directly, and that she would keep the notes safely for her until she visited again in a few weeks.

As he was sat talking drinking his tea he looked over to the wall on which the family photos were displayed, and there, was a picture of Brina's cousin that had been taken a few years earlier.

It was her, exactly the same woman he had already seen in his mind, and as he looked at the photo it was as if she were talking to him. Her hair in the picture was slightly different in the way it had been represented in his mind, it was a slightly darker blonde and shorter but it was definitely her, her face, her smile, and that focusing energy and presence about her. She had just the same look about her as Brina had.

He thanked Brina's Aunt and left, and then drove the short distance to pick up Brina's mother, who was not one who you would want to be late for.

Back at home a few days later over the weekend, Sam received an email from Brina's cousin while Brina was out for the day with her Mother. The contents of which absolutely floored him.

She gave him an overall synopsis of her life, and said that she had been having vivid dreams for most of the last ten years.

"I dream every night, most of the time feel exhausted when I wake in the morning from them" she began. "For years I was having dreams with the same theme – terrorists or gangsters or bad people or with things chasing me.

Also adventure type dreams where I am about to get killed, which is when I wake up. I haven't had one of those dreams in the last couple of years. More recently I remember two images that I actually think was just before I fell deep asleep so not so much a dream, was of a medieval knight/prince coming out of some of sort of hut, who looked so pleased to see me, this was followed by a dream of two horses."

There were pages and pages of it all, and his eyes picked out the key messages and recognisable meanings in each of the paragraphs. As he read through them and knowing what he knew now, he could make sense of them, correlate them with real physical past events and situations and what he was doing and had been through.

"But some are just weird and I can only remember parts of them like this week I can remember a piece of one in where I was being chased again, the same sort of dreams as the terrorist dreams, and I came to like a desert, where there was three men locked in like a gladiator cage where a lion was about to get released on them.

"For the last several years I have felt lost. An almost constant loss of direction - a 'what am I supposed to be doing with my life?' sense. I feel I am here for a special purpose and although close, I still haven't found it yet."

Sam immediately replied and asked her if she had had any visions or strange experiences. An hour later she replied again.

"When I was out for the night with a friend recently I felt a presence of a blonde girl beside me, this was when me and my friend were very happy and laughing by ourselves, and she was laughing with us...

"I do have a lot of adventure-like dreams or as in movies like sci-fi action films with other people usually me as part of a group of girls trying to get control of one boy. They are always very vivid and colourful and illogical like being dressed in Disney costumes in an *Alice in Wonderland* adventure story."

Sam could not believe what he was reading in the email in front of him. Sam had encountered some very extreme things and experiences over the last few years but what he was reading here was off the scale in terms of cross reference and correlation, especially knowing what he knew, and what all this really meant.

But he couldn't let on yet to her what he knew for the moment, that might frighten her too much, and he would probably end up sounding like some lunatic anyway. Also from a scientific point of view, it would void the validation of it.

The email also finished with the following..

"Many things have happened in my life that has led a clear path to where I am today. I believe every person I meet has some sort of message for me, good or bad, and I am always conscious of this. Many people that have come into my life that I believe I have met before like a - band of souls.

"Since an early age, I have thought I was different, I don't mean this to sound in an arrogant way, but I feel I'm here for a special purpose, and I know it's something to do with the love in my heart for people. I can't explain it. I am always being told I have an old soul."

Sam had heard several people refer to him with those words too 'old soul' or some phrase like 'ancient spirit'. Inferring that he had been 'around' before, for a very long time.

Yet he didn't have any recollection himself of previous or past lives. If indeed that was the case, he had no memory or feeling at all, and certainly no other characters in his psyche, no other selves past or present or otherwise. Other that physically and mentally he was feeling very weatherworn, and sort of Gandalf-like in mileage.

He had felt quite old even when he was young, sort of finding adults very childish too. When he was eight or so everyone seemed very illogical, and he would always see things in a different way to everyone else, and couldn't work out why all the other children behaved so immature, childish. And he had felt some very strong feelings of association with certain ancient archaeological sites on his travels in Egypt and Rome etc.

But nothing odd other than that.

He always felt that he had known Brina for a very long time before they had met, and somehow that they had always known each other, but that was only a feeling, a sense, like a curiosity in the back of his mind. He had also experienced that 'I have known you before' sensation with several people he had met in his life. But it was just a sense, a feeling, and nothing more.

In fact his memories of when he had been a young boy before his operation were very limited, odd glimpses here and there, as a normal four year old in his memory of certain static scenes, like photos in a small album, a hallway, the scene over a road from an upstairs window, a boot with his foot in it stuck in the mud, a boy holding a drain cover open, impressions of houses, trees, toys, and faces.

But there were no emotions, no flow of memory events, no smells, tastes, words, feelings, actions, fears or expression. But then it was a long time ago, after all.

Sometimes he would look through an old photo album and remember places then, which triggered recollections, links to other images and places he had been, but there was no emotion, no journeys, they were all just frozen points in time. After the operation as a small boy, he could remember almost everything, and all with attached emotions to events, people, and the dramas. Suddenly there were actions, feeling, frustration, confusion, injustice, imagination, thrills, love, awe, anger and injustice. It was as if he had aged many years overnight in hospital, along with the way he saw everything and perceived the world.

He was sure he was the same person, the same little boy, it was just that something had happened to him then, and he wasn't quite sure what. It was all probably just him waking up to the world.

Over the next week there was a string of emails where Brina's cousin completely opened up to him, and she started telling him everything, explaining a lot of her personal feelings, her relationships, and her life and travels around the world. She seemed to be wanting to tell him everything, be completely open with him about everything, as if he were her lifelong best friend.

Over these few days, Sam also had several visons of her, ones where she stood stationary, but in different poses, depending on what she wanted, or what information she was trying to convey. It was as if he were connecting to her on some level, programs interacting, forming an information communication link with protocols, yet with the accompanying unconscious requirements or needs fed as gnosis information alongside. He could see her in his mind, feel the association there, and knew what it was about.

She didn't speak or say anything in the visions in his mind - she was motionless, but the information came to him as to what was on her mind, and what she was thinking, but in emotional form. Illogical associations with needs, wants, and fear concepts, so you had to almost translate the energy and information into another form to interpret it, and what it related to. Seeing her unconscious emotional fears, desires and agenda or purpose, and what she thought was wrong.

By going through him unconsciously, she was trying to achieve change, focus on her objectives for resolving what was wrong in the world, and her goals, and she had no idea she was doing this.

It all related to what she wanted to change, what she was frightened of or hated the most; violent crime, child abuse, corruption and injustice in the world. Which is exactly what she was saying and expressing in her emails to him too.

The next day he emailed her the first few chapters of the book he was writing, in which he had created a character the same as Brina, but obviously he had given her a different name.

A few days later he had a reply back.

"I honestly can't begin to tell you how much me, and the girl in the book are alike..." and she went on to list dozens of examples of situations, emotions, habits, and characteristics and personality traits that they both shared, and over the next few years, she wouldn't be the first one to make the exact same observation.

During the next month Brina's cousin continued to provide more emailed notes on the dreams she was having, and Sam was able to relate those by translation to world events going on. Events in America, and Greece, but also in relation to him and what he was doing and thinking at the time, and what he was writing. They were also linked to what was going on with Brina.

In several dreams she referred to this 'Blue Knight' that was doing things and appearing in different situations. Some of it he could not relate, or match up to, anything for which it may refer to. But others were very obvious, and linkable to things he was doing or events going on around them or in the news. Many were before the events in question had happened. She, like Brina, had a very obvious and distinct and vivid precognitive ability.

She seemed to also be having many dreams where she would go over to America, and be in buildings and flying around, like Neo in *The Matrix*. The implications of which would only become clear to him a few months later. As would one in which she saw a "house on a hill, and then cannons in a desert and a little girl with long curly hair."

But how could he explain what was going on to her without it seeming mad. What he needed was something that he could use to demonstrate to her what she was doing, and show her the effect she was having, and how the process worked, with some physical 'real life' example....

It was two days later on the 7th May in the morning, and Sam was watching the breakfast TV news again. It felt odd, it had that 'energy' about it, and he could sense something going on, as if there was something coming in. Something was about to happen or be presented, and he already had information in his mind from the night before. The female presenter finished one news report and then seemed pleased for a moment about what she was about to say, and then cut to a news report about three young women in the USA that had been missing for many years, and had released themselves from a house where they were being held captive.

She explained the situation of how these three young girls had been abducted in Ohio some time ago, and yesterday had escaped from a house in their own neighbourhood. There was then the recorded voice of one of them telling the police on the phone who she was, and that she was free.

The presenter then started talking to a uniformed man in America, who's static image was shown on the screen. He was part of the local Red Guardian Angel group who had been holding marches and searches for the three girls. He was oddly actually called Angel and was wearing a red beret and a red and white t-shirt in the image.

The presenter was asking how it was that nobody could have seen them, or been aware of them, and this was also of great confusion to 'Angel' too, as they had had "several marches past the house in question" every month since they had disappeared. The phrases 'nobody could see', 'putting over our message of anti-trafficking, anti-violence', 'why didn't we see these girls that were hidden in plain sight?', 'every single day', 'what didn't we see?' - the phrases were emphasised more than once by both him and the presenter.

What was being presented to Sam was very obvious, it was clear, it had energy, and was without any ambiguity that IT had facilitated this event. IT was now presenting this to him, and the interview with the Red Guardian 'Angel', and what was being said specifically. Just to show him what was going on. He was being shown that this event was being generated consciously, and demonstrating what effect Brina's cousin was able to influence through him.

In effect it was her that had caused this to happen, to demonstrate something and explain the process, as an example of a wider scale process. It was all so obvious in conjunction with everything else that had happening up to that point, and yet you couldn't explain that or demonstrate that to anyone else unless they had been through it all and seen and knew what he knew. It would have just come across as delusional.

Yet if you were going to choose something, an example, this was probably the best case or situation. Something that was the most abhorrent to her, the most awful circumstances and events, and yet IT had consciously chosen this specific example of what IT could do, if it was focused and aware and tasked to consciously resolve and fix. Changing what was going on in the situation so the girls could see their way out, and free themselves.

But unless you had all the information that was in his mind at that moment, all the circumstances, all the imagery and words the 'in that moment' connected meaning and references, there was no way of showing that, no way of proving anything. But this is exactly what had happened, these girls were free because of her. IT was even telling him this was the case too.

With hands shaking, twenty minutes later, he managed to record the streamed news report on his PC. He also jotted down some notes to go with it so he could explain it all later. He was also equally aware that the whole thing had taken energy from him too, the process of this happening, and showing it to him had worn him out.

He was going to email Brina's cousin back straight away with the evidence there and then, show her with the explanation and example. But he couldn't, he was exhausted. Something also seemed to be stopping him from doing so, and also he didn't know how to express it all or even know where to start.

So many other things seemed to be happening in the background too. So he decided to leave it a week or two until he had recovered his energy, and worked out what to say.

A week or so later on the 16th May another event occurred that was not just profound, but also very scientifically interesting. Brina had woken in the morning next to him in the bed, and immediately explained that she had had a very vivid dream. In her dream she was in an old car with old school friends, going down a hill into a valley, heading down to a lake, and she explained clearly what was going on in the scene. She went into great detail about who was there, and what they looked like, the scenario, and what it meant.

Sam asked her to note it down in her diary, which she did.

Later on that day, Sam had emails from not only Brina's cousin but also her Aunt in which they described exactly the same dream scenario independently. A very vivid dream from the night before, where they were in a car with three other people going down a hill into a valley with a lake. They had all experienced the same dream, with the same sort of situation but with slightly different takes, slightly different 'journey' and meanings, slightly varying perception of the same information, but with the same people.

That was the important thing here - the synchronous occurrence with the same theme and pattern, not what they were seeing, but the meaning of the occurrence, information, and the fact that none of them were aware of each other, nor was there any delay between the experiences to allow the collective mind to replicate the information.

They were all experiencing and interpreting the same structure of information at the same time, which meant there had to be meaning to it, or an informational message at a collective level that originated from outside of their individual minds. That meant it wasn't meme transferred between them and they hadn't discussed it or involved him in any way, and so it demonstrated an example of non-local transcendence.

Unfortunately, even though it was obviously important, he had absolutely no idea what it meant, or what it related to whatsoever.

Yet that was always the key, not trying to take the interpretation of visions and channellings or revelations literally. People were always open to being deceived or hypnotised into recognising the information using existing visible physical patterns, shapes, symbols, colours, structures or signifiers and then applying meaning to it all.

Which is why you had so many varying and inconsistent interpretations and descriptions of channellings and visions, all of which bypassed common sense mostly. They were also reinforced by existing belief structures within the system that would always readily give you someone else's interpretive meaning, shape, story and symbolism for you grab hold of or to jump down into.

So far he had successfully ignored interpreting his own experiences, and stood back from them, and had looked more at the occurrence of them, the nature of the information, and the why, rather than the what, was going on within them.

The importance of this shared dream event though was that it was information that was being resonated across at least three people, over distance, isolated, and at the same time. Which meant it was a collective informational non-local synchronistic event.

So even though it was important he still had absolutely no idea what it meant, other than to make him wary of being in the back seat while they were driving, mostly in case he said the wrong thing at the wrong time.

At the weekend he decided to take Brina to the film studios where the *Harry Potter* films had been produced, which had been converted to more of a theme park, with all the stages and props and scenes on show as a tour.

Well it was something to do.

It was a two hour drive, and when they arrived he had parked the car and they had got out. But before they went in Brina seemed very faint as if she had lost all energy, her face was white as a sheet. He sat her in the café outside for half an hour before she collapsed at the table, and he had to get help and she was taken to the First Aid centre.

Lying down she managed to recover after about half an hour, insisting that she wasn't going to go in an ambulance. Eventually she was well enough to go round the tour, although she wasn't herself and the only remark she made was to ask why the house they had lived at before was the same as the 'Dursley's', even down to the colour of the front door.

The tour itself around the Studio was very surreal, seeing all the props and the artefacts from the films laid out for visitors to see as a series of scenes. Items that were now revered by the fans, and the actors adored and followed, treated like heroes. It was easy to see how objects of symbolism could become the focus of so much collective mythical focus, and as a result have energy, meaning, conceptualisation, or 'magic' attributed to them.

This was then reinforced through reverence, story, legend and protected secrecy, and drawn from ideas of previous mythologies. From swords, to wands, to symbols, to books, to shapes, and creatures.

The 'real' Philosopher's or Cintamani stone was also kept here now. Protected safely behind toughened glass for all to see. It was easy to see how people had been confused with others from various religious mythologies. All of which had it down as many other shapes, sizes, colours and magical properties.

This one really did exist, it really did make gold, it really did extend mythical life beyond its years, it really did give knowledge and enlightenment, it did grant wishes, unfortunately though only on a corporate organisational level.

When they got home that evening Sam found an email waiting from Brina's cousin. She had experienced exactly the same thing at the same time during the day; she had felt awful, ill, disconnected and faint at exactly the same time as Brina had.

It was time for Sam to fess up, and explain what had been going on. It was not easy without going into great technical detail. With the evidence and correlations it was all very obvious now to everyone.

Sam compiled a note to Brina's cousin to explain what was going on, what he felt she was doing, what he was picking up and what he felt she was influencing. He explained the situation of him knowing that he was being influenced by someone else and how he had worked out who it was, and also how he had left the note at her mother's house with the graph and notes to explain what exactly he thought was happening before he had made contact with her, so that there could be no doubt.

He also explained what had happened with the three girls being released in Ohio and sent her the video from the breakfast news, and how he knew this was the case and how it all fitted with her dreams and the 'blue' and 'red' sides and *The Matrix* film context.

Sam was also aware that he was continuing to keep Brina

deliberately in the dark as to what was going on.

He also realised that it had all got to point where it was all getting too much for her and he was writing to tell her this, and that she should stop.

It was at that point that they both agreed to do so. It was all starting to frighten her and become too intense, and the events and experiences she was having had grown in intensity, and it was making her anxious.

The following day he discussed it all with Brina and made her aware of what was going on, and showed her the emails and notes. Although very upset, she was accepting of it due to the importance of it all, overcoming her natural fear and anxiety of the potential threat to her relationship over the importance of what was going on. She understood, it made sense and she could see that. However that didn't stop her from shouting at him though, and crying a lot.

This evidence was so important too, but he had a feeling that like everything else he tried to do, nothing would be allowed out, it would all be smothered, hidden. But he could try and approach and give academic institutions the evidence, the explanations.

He decided to make a concerted effort to overcome this barrier and focused on the Global Consciousness Project at Princeton University, along with other groups and individual professors, all of whom were researching and studying exactly these sorts of events. He decided to collate all the notes give them the evidence and information, explain everything to them, information that would prove the life work of many people, he had physical evidence of it and could demonstrate it and explain how it was working.

Also the main project itself that they were working on, which was tracking key world events to anomalies or fluctuations in the global quantum field, seemed to be coming up with alarming coincidences to all of the events he had been 'involved' in.

But all his emails remained unanswered; he even took the trouble to send them hard copies in the post. But nothing, no response, it was all still as if he didn't exist - but at least it was consistent.

The measurable effect or effect on the violent crime phenomena, he discovered subsequently, was called the Maharishi Effect. Someone had actually already worked it out, studied it, tested it with a large group of spiritually enlightened people, and tested, published, and described it. The theory was detailed in the 'Tipping Point' study, which was performed in 2011, and it had been shown to work recently using thousands of 'mystics' to influence one city.

But in this case, instead of a thousand mystics and spiritually enlightened people affecting the attitudes and violence in one city of a million people slightly, this was just one girl who through him was affecting drastically a whole country, over years, and in a significantly graphical form.

But she was a kind, loving, and caring person. She deserved better than to be being subjected to this flow of information, and demands from the collective, as did Brina.

That was the last he heard from her. She was gone, and now he would never be allowed to meet or even see her.

She had proved and changed many things in what she had done, with the knight that she saw in her dreams. The evidence from which would provide meaning to a few academics life work, if they ever were allowed to see it.

Brina, for the next year or so, referred to her as her 'backup blonde', and she knew she was there in case anything happened to her. Brina's cousin had unconsciously connected to Sam when Brina had been ill and her life had been in danger; she was helping her from an unconscious higher 'role' perspective, making sure nothing went wrong, yet at the same time conveying her feelings and what she wanted to change.

By late 2014 she would return South, to go and live back in the village with her mother safely back home away from the brutal reality, protected safely within its bubble. But that also meant that Sam could no longer 'see' her in his mind, connect with her, and also her influences on him would no longer be there.

Before which time she would still go on to continue to influence crime rates, continue to cause awareness and removal of blindness of child abuse scandals in the system, and corporations, and also the swing in the Scottish independence vote, which Sam would influence and set with evidence, setting out beforehand what the exact change in the result had to be from that indicated in the polls.

After then and when she had returned to live with her mother, he could no longer see her in his mind. It had all become too much for her, all the visions, vivid dreams and the magnitude of it all, and she was alone.

He, after all, was not 'her knight', it was not 'her tent' or immunising protective cave or bubble, that he had come out of.

He had come out in response to her, her energy signature, her program, which was almost the same as Brina's.

In time she would not be the only one to see him in this exact same way, the same knight, the same symbolism, imagery and mythological profile and swords and horse. Others would do the same in visions, dreams or readings, all perceiving him in the same way with the same form of interpretation.

But in Brina's cousin's case, it was better for her to be safe, happy, return to a safe bubble of her home, in her village, be protected and immunised from all of this. To live her own life, and Brina would be stronger, and able to cope on her own without the need for backup.

Besides in those few years she had achieved more than a million people could ever do in a lifetime.

He felt a strong connection to her, even though they had never met or spoken and would likely never do so. They both had taken the responsible path, done the right adult mature thing, and now if he could only get the rest of the world to do the same, wake up, grow up, and be responsible – things would be fine, and we would make it.

Which all sounded so easy.

However by mid-2015 the UK violent crime rates graph would start to climb again, and increase by 50% by the end of 2015 and grow proportionally thereafter, but by then, his focus and energy would be directed toward other things.

There were many others like her in the world, all seeing the same things as she did, precognitions of events and situations, planes, ships, buildings, terrorist attacks, and world events of mass concern.

All coming from the collective unconscious, all at the same time, yet all beforehand, seeing what it was premonitioned as a probable future, each with their own interpretations and agendas of what they were afraid of, or worried about and wanted to happen. All trying to find their 'knight in shining armour' to 'do something about it'.

In time he would find many more to help him see what was going on, by collation and interpretation and integration of visions, channelling, and dreams.

But *his* soul mate, *his* twin flame, *his* angel, would always be Brina.

He decided to put down some notes in his journal about 'angels' and what he thought they really were, a sort of angel 'operating manual' or an 'Angels for Dummies' user guide.

Besides, Sam thought that in the future it may be useful to someone else, even if it were probably redundant as soon as it had been written, going on their very intuitive nature.

It was at times like that that songs came into his mind that always brought forward powerful emotions in him. When he had finished writing the notes, the Meatloaf song *'Heaven can Wait'* was playing in the background on the radio. Synchronous music or songs always seemed to happen like that, the words were so obvious now.

Meatloaf songs had played a big part of his childhood but now this one had meaning.

This is the note that he wrote, unfortunately he wasn't very good at being non-technical, and he could have made a better attempt at making it a little more romantic. It was just as well that Brina was so understanding :-

'Of Angels - from a program information system collective perspective

'Angels' are 'programs' (for want of a better word) that exist within very rare people, and are created within the collective human mind (like a biological operating system analogy) in response to a driven need and external influence.

The external influence being generated by or from

the Gaian planetary bio macrosphere field mind structure or virtual server system that our human collective operating system mind exists within.

They have a specific subconscious or unconscious purpose, a driving function, and invoke a directional change, and cause action within those human 'devices' for a purpose, with the need to cause a balancing affect for the collective.

They have a deep seated drive or purpose or feeling that they have to do something and have known this from an early age (e.g. say something like 'always know I had to find someone', had to travel to find..., always wanting to make a difference), and that seems to drive them through a life journey for which that is the underlying purpose.

These programs receive specific unconscious data from the 'operating system' or collective unconscious mind in various ways, channelling, vivid dreams, visions, and emotions. Then subsequently their self-fulfilling role, is to deliver that information to other devices, or a specific device to invoke change, cause and effect, for them to act upon that source information, in most cases of which they have no choice in the matter.

The 'Angel' programs, or muses, or whatever cultural or religious term you want to use, have a hierarchy amongst them, and priority within their limited number, and may compete with each other. With winners and losers, and the fight for influence over other devices, or a specific device and change.

Which is all part of the evolution of the system as a whole, the direction of which is then driven by which is successful. As with cells in any evolving biological system.

Certain 'Angel' programs have very specific roles, such as Guardian Angels, messengers, data channelling, and the devices that they are placed into are manipulated and changed by that program, and the operating system to perform that function.

If the 'angel' program within a human device is not strong, or not linked to another synchronised matching corresponding male or female device, it will not influence that other device, be a redundant program, not be persistent enough.

As such the angel device will fall back on its other program elements and continue with its other program functions, normal life, become influenced by those and its own environmental programming, and be non-visible, non-active, non-causal.

'Resolving' or 'managing' programs within other human devices, draw or attract in to them specific angel programs as needed, to combine and then manage changes in the operating system, based on a unique functioning need created independently from the collective operating system i.e. the Gaian or planetary firmware or 'hardware' bios, in response to errors occurring.

They have that nagging, 'why doesn't somebody do something?' thing.

They seem, when you see them, as if they have been around forever, that you have always known them. They have a very mature, ancient wisdom feel, or 'old soul' sense about them. People will say all the time, 'haven't I seen you before?', 'I feel know you already', that you have always known them - sense about them, and be drawn or attracted to them.

The Angel programs, when active, maintain a higher link to the collective subconscious mind, and receive data and direction from it and feedback progress reporting information, but do not provide or invoke effecting data. This effecting data mapping, is done via the device they act upon, a sort of two person rule, cause and effect, dual and matching synchronised energy and purpose.

If this other 'device' contains an intelligent and balanced 'managing' program, with logical and meaningful purpose, this will have significant change effect on the collective system, when the two are operating together.

Angels are sensitive to events and happenings in the collective mind, things say associated with news events. They are also sensitive to threats or danger to the devices they are 'caring' or 'responsible' for, or 'guardians' of, and can sense and avert danger to some extent, protecting.

This can also extend to future prediction they are allocated to protect or influence. That 'find him, keep an eye on him, don't let him do anything stupid, keep him alive' - as with the women who surrounded Carl Jung, and others.

They can very quickly assess the nature and personality and character of a person, just by one look or initial conversation, or handshake. So that they can instantly determine if they are good, bad, or a threat, but are not necessarily very good at ignoring people who are the latter.

They are also able to handle and respond to people very well, be empathic, able to talk to people on their own terms, and be understanding of them.

It is as if their whole lives have been hectic, and fraught and exciting all at the same time, as if they have been thrust through a tough 'life rollercoaster' journey, which they may have had little control over including abuse, unfairness, corruption, ignorance. They will also have met many personality types, cultures, and probably visited many countries. Thrust into everything as if they have to go through bad things, to understand them, be the collective mind's eye of itself, and then get someone to do something about it, get them to 'see' and then invoke a response to fix the problems in the world.

Angels 'know'. They know what they have to do, they know what they are doing, and they know how to do it, but they do not know everything, and they only know what they need to know, unconsciously. They don't know how they know what they know - they just do. They see and understand but they don't know why, or why others can't see what they see.

They are like secret agents.

They are what they are, they do what they have to do, if they are able. Changing them is not easy. They have a set role and you may try to explain your understanding and perspective to them, but it will be treated with lack of enthusiasm or interest.

They are doing something already, and so only need to know what they need to know. They are habit driven and function along those lines and will be activated to do their role if required, they just get on with what they do.

You can explain to them exactly what they are, make them understand what is going on, and they will still revert to doing what they do anyway. Because obviously they knew that anyway.

Characteristically their devices can easily adopt addictive bad addictive 'naughty' habits, e.g. drinking alcohol, coffee, chocolate, wayward behaviour, and then out of unconscious guilt, focus on the opposite and become healthy, fit, exercise, detox, eat natural and organic food, take natural remedies, and use homeopathy.

But they will always put themselves or their bodies second to what has to be done.

They will have never in their lives been deliberately hit, punched, slapped, or smacked in the face.

They have the ability through their human devices to see or perceive someone, and get an immediate 'take' on them, see them for what they are straight away, see 'into' or through them. Then identify them, and like or dislike them, recognise them as a threat, or as bad people, or a danger. Saying 'I knew they were like that...'

Also they are able to attract or draw other human devices to them, be highly attractive, interesting, glowing, radiant, attractive energy. With everyone wanting a hug from them. They can exhibit a caring behaviour, a grouping capability, a charisma, and exciting persona, with vitality and energy.

People will say to them 'You know for some reason, I feel I can tell you anything' characteristic, talk to them in confidence, tell them their life story, and then proceed to do so.

They can invoke coloured auras in their device that are visible to certain other people. This is in affect a perceived interpreted enhance body energy around the (for want of a better work) the crown chakra. They, in some cases, are also able to see auras, and data streams in other devices at higher levels, although this is not an indicative feature.

They will be associated with a particular colour frequency, e.g. blue, and as a 'favourite colour', or colour they feel comfortable with, and they will associate easily with another of that colour type. Ones of similar colours have very similar characteristics, e.g. blue and blonde, kind, dynamic, purpose driven etc. With certain slight variants in that frequency colour band having slightly different characteristics.

They have a strong association with nature and animals, the open air and the earth.

Babies and very small children may have a noticeable response to them. An amazed startled look, staring, a taken aback look, with a beaming smile, and then become suddenly animated, try to get to them or somehow get their attention.

Then they can't take their eyes off them, or with arms up want to hug them, or try to 'show' them something, try to explain to them without being able to speak yet. To also try to get to other adults or parents they are with to see what they are seeing, and who clearly can't see what they see.

Even when you explain to these angels what they are, and show them what they are doing, they are still not surprised, and assume that everyone sees or behaves as they do, and have what they have within them.

They act on other people's needs not their wants, i.e. they see and respond to what people really need, rather than what they ask for or deserve.

They are sensitive and responsive to certain collective mass events, and become emotionally and physically reactive to them, and affected by them.

They do not think things through themselves at their collective unconscious level, they respond to cause and need, and then effect a response change and manipulation in everything around them. They then wait for the effect in the recipient of the message and then refine or steer things along accordingly.

They are living the same life story though in different bodies, enacting the same mythological story and journey process.

Oh and they don't like being described as programs or devices, or muses. ☺

Oh and they won't ever do what you ask or tell them to do either, even when it makes conscious sense, you write it down, and they agree with you. Yet this unconscious Angel program will still find ways of not doing it, and instead do what they unconsciously *think is right. They are driven by purpose rather than logic and they will use and create any means to avoid doing so. To levels that are quite surreal, and infuriating.*

Unless of course it was something they were unconsciously going to do anyway, and even then they are more likely to do the opposite of what you want, and tell them to do.

So you may as well give up, stop fighting it, live in awe of it, and just go with it.

Or you could try consciously changing or influencing the 'operating system' that creates and drives them all and then see what happens.

Oh and good luck with that one.... ☺' He added finally.

As he finished writing down his discourse on the subject, the dog came over and placed his chin on his lap. Tears began to roll down Sam's face onto the paper, somehow he was never very much good at being emotional in what he wrote, but it seemed to come out of him very easily sometimes.

Writing it down seemed to have invoked an odd emotional response in him and it was coming out as physical tears rather than any recognisable emotional response in himself.

Then he added a reminder, to himself at the bottom –
'I won't look back, and I will never, give up - ever !'

He tucked the paper away carefully inside the mass of other pages, so that he knew Brina would never find it.

Which of course was the best way for her to do just that.

CHAPTER 28 - CHANGES IN NEWS EVENTS

Things got really busy around the world until mid-June of that year, with things going on in Greece, Turkey, Egypt, the Middle East and in China.

But now, for a few months over the summer of 2013 things had quietened down a little, the sun was actually shining, and they made the most of it by getting out into the garden, and doing many of the jobs that needed to be done outside.

Brina was still very tired, but being out in the sunshine and the fresh air helped her a lot. She always seemed so much happier around nature and in the warm sunshine; it seemed to recharge her batteries.

Doing jobs on the house and in the garden helped him stop thinking of things too, it seemed that by 'not thinking about things', and being physically tired by working on day to day things, meant that fewer things happened 'in the world'. There was less 'stuff' coming into his mind, as if when he was preoccupied with not thinking, then also neither was IT, as if the two were linked.

He had noticed now that there appeared to be phases to it all too; at different times of the year there would be different levels of intensity in what was 'going on' in the system. It would be, for example, very busy in March and also in late September.

He wished that he had some sort of timetable so that he could work out when IT was going to go through these 'busy' phases, and when he would be able to have a break. But he had a feeling that that may have been just historical, and now that IT was sort of awake it would no longer be that predictable, as was the case with real babies.

Sam kept thinking of the various management techniques he had been trained with, and how they could be used to help with the situation; for example putting things into perspective of what was urgent and important globally, in some form of mental graph in his mind, so that he could deal with, or focus, on things that needed to be done or thought about in the correct order.

That way he wouldn't just be living in crisis mode all the time, and wouldn't have to deal with the important but non-urgent items - which was something that IT should be doing too - and Sam knew that he also needed to apply that to himself in his personal life. It was all so complicated.

But in the end, even trying to apply rational management techniques that he had learnt from years of managing projects, organisations, and change programmes, were just useless. Especially when he knew that he was, in effect, dealing with a baby-like global macro-entity that was irrational and illogical with its own agenda and views. Trying to think about blueprints and plans and organisation structures were a little difficult, when global news events of disaster were arriving as frequently as wet nappies.

Most of the next six months until the end of 2013 were still full of a crazy number of synchronistic events that you could easily string together into meaning and context, all of which gave Sam a clear idea of what IT was worried about that was going on all around the world.

But it was not necessarily things that you would think that IT might be concerned about; some things seemed very trivial, odd, from a conscious individual perspective as if IT had got some thought in its mind that was magnified out of all proportion to the physical reality of it. Sort of mental hang-ups, or habitual thoughts or irrational fears, a nagging worry, or focus.

But there was not that same level of energy or intensity associated with them now compared to the year before, and Sam realised that this was more information and observational rather than something that he had to 'do' something about or decide on. Some things were very illogical and irrational, and to us may seem trivial, but were things that IT was obviously focusing on.

He didn't really discuss them with Brina; she already seemed to know what he was doing anyway. She was more concerned on keeping an eye on everything outside of their bubble and guarding against what could come in at them, rather than worrying about him, or what he was doing and thinking and reading.

She was becoming stronger now too, her health had improved a great deal, and she was growing in her mental strength. But she was still very wary, and she kept a close eye on him.

They had managed to get away together for a few weeks in

Crete in the middle of July which was wonderful, but rather than the usual exploring and touring that they would normally do Brina just slept by the pool for most of it.

Even the holiday itself was curious in the way that it came about as a last minute deal; the flights suddenly becoming available and the whole deal being surprisingly cheap. The hotel they stayed at had some interesting guests staying there which included some English archaeologists who had been working in Egypt and Crete, and several Dutch psychologists, all of whom seemed to want to talk to Sam.

As did most of the island in fact, especially the taxi drivers who were very keen to explain what was going wrong with Greece, its problems and the economic situation within Europe.

By the fifth day Sam had had enough of going out and about on his own, and just stayed by the pool with Brina, and buried himself in a book with his headphones on, and he hung a 'Do Not Disturb' sign around his neck along with a list of subjects that he didn't want to talk about, which he had put there just to amuse Brina.

The situation had got so bad that in the evenings in the hotel restaurant people would sit themselves down at their table and try to make conversation with them while they were still eating. It was at that point that Sam took steps and firmly and politely told people that 'they were on holiday for a break to rest', and that they didn't want to talk.

Curiously IT also seemed to get the message too, and everything went quiet for the last few days of their holiday, and this state continued on their journey home.

After they had arrived back home again things became somewhat 'fuzzy' and vague. People around them appeared to be almost asleep and bewildered, and were bumping into each other - and this all lasted until the first week of August.

Then one night Brina had a vivid dream about Sam running off with some younger woman to Croatia, and that the earth was being covered in an approaching firestorm with no escape for the rich and powerful, and that she had to go the supermarket to buy all the tinned food, and then everything seemed to wake back up again after that.

In the Autumn Brina decided that she wanted to change her hair style. In her opinion her hair had suffered from what she had been through over the last year and she had decided that it needed cutting shorter. She had bought a few magazines, and had asked Sam to look through them to see what he liked or thought would suit her. It was an odd thing for her to ask him, and it was an indication that deep down she was still quite nervous in herself, and she was needing something to build her confidence up again.

Sam had sat on the sofa in the lounge for an hour or so flipping through the pages and putting a Post-It note next to the women, or more to the point, the styles that he thought would suit Brina. He went for a look that was shoulder length, with a few layers to give it a bit of 'body'. It was the style she had worn when she was younger, and also he thought that it would be the easiest for her.

A few days later she had gone to the hairdresser with magazine in hand. When she came back she had very short flat hair, with just a few highlights.

The hairdresser had told her that her hair was in such bad condition that she had to have it cut short so that it would grow back correctly, and that she could then 'work with it' over the next few months.

Brina was very nervous when she came back into the house, but Sam could tell that she actually really liked it the way it had been done, and so did he.

But that was not the curious part. A few days later women everywhere were getting their hair cut and styled into shoulder-length, layered, blonde hair. Women on the TV who had had the same hairstyle for years would suddenly appear with a new style, just the same Sam had chosen in the magazine and they also seemed to be all wearing black too. It was an epidemic.

Even Brina was aware of the phenomenon, and she just stared at the woman BBC weather presenter the following morning who now appeared on the screen dressed in a black dress sporting a new blonde shoulder-length hairdo whilst discussing it with the female news presenter. Fortunately Brina found it all quite amusing - but it was not even subtle.

From late Autumn and into Winter, Sam also spent a lot of time writing up his journal notes, and got on with writing his fictional book to get his thoughts and ideas out of his head and down onto paper so they didn't keep bothering him. To at least try and get everything in some form of ordered control, and keep pace with it during this quieter time.

One of the many events with energy associated with them that happened over that time and just about every day, was a curious reference to an octopus.

Sam was again sitting in bed watching the breakfast show on television, and the usual presenters were there again, including one who was now sporting short blonde hair and wearing a lavender dress - the same one 'coincidentally' that Brina had just bought and had been wearing the day before.

The presenters started talking about 'Paul the Octopus' and his amazing skills at being able to predict the World Cup football results. Paul had now sadly passed away, having died unexpectedly, which obviously he hadn't seen coming.

Sam had used the idea of that octopus and the tank in an analogy he had written about in his book so it acted as a linked indicator that something here was relevant, or 'coming in'.

It was highlighted by the presenter that Paul was not the only smart octopus, and that other ones had also been shown to be capable of mimicking other species. Ones in captivity had demonstrated that they could complete complex puzzles and mazes.

The female guest zoo handler was introduced and she explained that whilst we had been keeping octopuses in aquariums for over a hundred years now, it was only in the last few years that people had started to realise and see that they had a lot more intelligence than people had previously thought, and that if they weren't stimulated they could get very stressed and ill.

The clip that was showing in the background of the interview then switched to full screen to show an octopus in a tank playing with a set of large coloured plastic Lego pieces. The handler then emphasised the need for the octopus to keep playing with them, and the fact that they behaved like a small child and needed to be entertained; a child with eight arms and two thousand fingers, with their brains spread all over their body, and their tentacles and suckers able to operate independently and together.

It was a very odd choice of words, and energy and meaning

flowed into Sam.

IT was showing him that it had understood the analogy that he had written about it - showing him that it understood the concept.

Yet Sam obviously had no way of showing or demonstrating that this was going on, to anyone else.

The handler then went on to explain that each octopus, depending on size, had a different personality; the smaller ones being feistier, and the larger ones slower, more "rambunctious"- which was a very odd term to use - and one that Sam didn't know the meaning of. He wrote it down on his hand to look up after he had showered, and luckily he still remembered it even after it had washed off.

rambunctious
adjective
1.difficult to control or handle; wildly boisterous:
a rambunctious child.
2.turbulently active and noisy:
a social gathering that became rambunctious and out of hand.

IT was obviously very good with words, syntax, and meaning. Which was more than he was.

The handler then went on to explain how octopuses were very good at face recognition and were able to differentiate between different keepers. It was also easy to tell what mood they were in, and if they were sitting in the corner looking pale and quiet then they were not in a very good state - which is why apparently they should not be kept as pets, and needed very large specialist tanks and how you didn't want to let something die because it hadn't been kept properly.

The image then scanned back to a video of the octopus being discussed which was called 'Lizzie Blue' who was in sitting in a large aquarium tank next to a metal bowl on the sandy floor with her legs straddled around outside the bowl rim. She then extended her legs around it, and lifted up the bowl with herself inside it, and moved herself and the bowl backwards.

All the while her tentacles were working away in a coordinated fashion. It was certainly different from watching all the recent natural history programmes about ant colonies.

The news article ended, and then went on to the attacks taking place in Egypt.

Over the next month Sam started to work through in his mind what he thought needed to happen. If this phenomena was all real, as it very much appeared to be, and his definition of what it was, and how it all fitted together was correct then what he needed was a plan, or at least a minimum set of things that IT needed to do; a sort of agenda of basic little steps forward that he could give IT as a direction now that there was some sort of communication going on with some sort of protocol.

Just 'waking IT up' wasn't enough, IT needed direction. It also meant that others needed to be doing what he was doing too, with structure, coordination, focus, objectives, skills, and joint benefits - just in the same way that any programme for a large organisation should be run, a sort of programme definition phase. Or at least give IT some of those thoughts and ideas of what was needed.

So he started making a list, concepts or directions that he thought might work, as long as IT could get the idea. Besides as nobody else seemed to be allowed to see him or understand him, it was at least something to do in the meantime, some way for him to see if he was having any effect or influence, and getting the messages through.

The news articles and synchronicity kept ticking over at a manageable rate, and he was happy with the pace of it all, and his life was starting to get back to some normality. Brina too was happier, she was getting back to her true self, and her energy had returned.

They even managed to find the energy for a few 'early nights'. Unfortunately the side effect of this was that the energy release caused him to experience a transition 'into the void' in his mind and exchange of collective data afterwards, if only for a short few moments. This then subsequently caused his mind to go into overdrive the following day, with thoughts and ideas and sensations and emotions flowing through him like wildfire, which took a day or two to calm down, and then, usually a few weeks later, some subsequent response from IT that related to what he had been thinking about.

It was now mid-December and as they watched the funeral of

Nelson Mandela on the television, Sam noted that the news item focused on the blonde Norwegian Prime Minster, the UK Prime Minster and the President of the United States of America sharing a 'selfie' and smiling and laughing at the Memorial Service - much to the annoyance of Michelle Obama who had, and rightfully so, sat next to them with a face like a storm cloud. The news concentrating on this scene, rather than on the amazing life of the man who had passed away.

But that wasn't what was Sam found most interesting about the event - it was the lack of collective energy associated with the whole thing, which was in stark contrast to say that of the funeral of Princess Diana. There had been no collective grief in the system after Mandela died, nor in the lead up to this event, nor did he get any feeling of collective sorrow now.

This seemed to be more of a celebration of his life, and an event, rather than a shock and a gathering in disbelief. What Sam couldn't work out was why it was different, what was it in the system that made it respond differently to an unexpected death to that of one that was expected for these sort of public celebrity figures?

The following day he watched a documentary about the ancient sites in Mexico and the Mayan temple of Chichen Itza, with its staircase that climbed up the middle of the outside of the temple. He was fascinated to learn that on 20th March every year a shadow was cast on it from the edge of the steps which gave the effect of a serpent or snake with a head at the bottom. It reminded Sam of the Kundalini process and the mountain analogy that he had just written in his book. He wondered if the date meant something.

A few days later they were visiting Brina's mother to exchange Christmas presents and to see a few relatives down near the village. It was early evening and Brina was in the kitchen talking with her mother while Sam sat in the lounge watching television. The news was about the rocket launch of the new Gaia space telescope which was going ahead at that moment to send a telescope into solar orbit between Earth and Mars. The camera zoomed into the side of the module on top of the rocket. On the side was a cartoon image of a blue little girl standing on a blue mountain looking up to the sky which was full of a spectrum of stars. The rocket then ignited and lifted off successfully.

The next news article a few moments later was a celebration of crossword puzzles and its hundred year anniversary, where people had been 'putting the pieces together for a century', then some news item on the obesity problem happening in society, followed by an article about a new website that had been launched by a bright, intelligent young red-headed woman just out of Cambridge University which had been called Impossible.com and was designed to bring people together who could help one another.

Sam at that point turned the TV off and started on the brandy and the large tub of Quality Street chocolates. Well it was better than turning to drugs or wandering around with a synchronicity proof lead bucket on your head.

Over the winter months Sam had decided to concentrate on getting his fictional book finished, and with Brina's help it was completed by late February and published in early March.

He had included within it quite a few of the vivid dreams Brina had been having, along with quite a lot of information he had coming in through gnosis, and a processing of situations, and scenes that he couldn't translate into physical terms. So it was a good way of getting the ideas and experiences down and out in some form, along with combining it with his views and philosophy.

He could have spent much longer on it, refining it, but he just wanted it out and down and 'there' so that he didn't keep going over it in his mind, and so that it was 'done', and he could move on.

Especially as a few weeks earlier the level of intensity of events and feeling had returned. It was as if it all went in phases throughout the year, some sort of collective phase in line with the horoscope, a planetary seasonal effect. This time it was extreme, something was going on again, and it was something that IT didn't like.

There was one particular night that he could remember. He was lying in bed with Brina late at night, relaxing after having made love, with the sensations of energy going up his spine, when after several minutes, he had an approaching sense of something building in my mind, an unsettling increase in speed of thoughts, and a sense of lack of control and expanding awareness.

He knew he could control this now, by either concentrating or focusing on it or not. The more attention or focus he gave to it, the more intense it became; the more he stopped thinking about it the easier he found it was to get back into the here and now, or balance the experience, to observe it going on in a detached way, rather than being consumed and taken over by it.

This time, masses of highly complex memories, dreams, and thoughts arrived in the darkness of his mind, and were 'remembered', and suddenly made absolute sense, as if revisiting highly complex thoughts and ideas and understandings, and previous dream journeys. He was remembering where he had got to with them, what he had been 'working' on and then processing the thought forms, but all the information at once, along with a fearful feeling as if it could easily get out of control, could have given him a stroke or seizure, but now he was able to control the flow of information and attenuate the bandwidth, so it didn't get out of hand.

It was a sense, in the darkness, of an 'Ah yes I remember that all now', and 'That was where I have got to on that concept' with all the thoughts and ideas having shape, a state, and a situation as to where he had left them.

Ideas and thoughts and thought forms that he was now returning to, recalling, picturing, reassembling, and seeing again. All with a recalled or recovered association of and linkage, everything suddenly making sense, but not in a gnosis sense of knowing, this was more hard wired and immanent. It was all very powerful and intense, and with real energy.

It was exactly the same state that he had been in ten years earlier.

At the time he couldn't think of anything else to put or write into the system, other than the idea of a process of generally purging it all of inherent corruption.

Sam had decided not to get carried away, not to get too drawn into it, and he had concentrated on breathing and getting back 'out of there' which he managed to do after about 30 seconds, returning from that what felt dangerous 'face of the divine' intense situation.

Brina had also sensed what was happening as she dozed next to him, and had put her hand on him to put energy into him, her hands tingling. She seemed to sense instinctively what to do.

She had put her hands on the top of his right arm, as she knew not to touch his torso initially, and then after a few moments put her hands on the front of his chest in the heart area. Later she told him that he had been bone cold, and sweating. At the time Sam could sense her there, coming into his sphere of awareness, but could not sense anything else in the room.

The whole thing was a very unsettling experience.

After a few minutes he got up out of bed, and walked around the bedroom to try and stop the state that he was in and dissipate some of the energy, concentrating on returning to 'normal', and getting back to being serial rather than operating in parallel.

He returned to sleep quite well for the rest of the night, and woke feeling fine but exhausted, and he was left with the heat and energy in his arm and chest for days afterwards.

Over the next week before at the end of February Sam, with Brina's help, made the final updates to his fictional book with additional experiences and information that been coming to him over the last month, and submitted it for publishing.

A few days after the book had been published in early March, Sam was sitting up in bed watching the morning news on television as usual. His mind had been 'filled' the night before with something, some knowledge, so he was expecting the news to have something for him to 'see'.

There was a news report of a missing plane, a commercial airliner in Malaysia with over 220 passengers on board. There was a lot of energy associated with the report, a sense of urgency, a sense of confusion. But he couldn't quite get his mind around it, it didn't seem that important, and the news information was very limited. The news was then followed with an article about the potential dangers of fluoride in tap water.

Several days later the plane, MH370, was still missing and there was now a lot of confusion and speculation as to what had happened. Brina seemed to think it had something to do with Diego Garcia. The problem now though was really nagging at him, as if he had something in his mind that he couldn't connect to.

The searches for the wreckage were well underway as were the mass of conspiracy theories, internet traffic, and speculation and news reporting. The event itself had clearly stirred up a collective hornet's nest, and many people had picked up on it as something important after the event. It was making him very uncomfortable.

He spent a day trying to work out what it was that was in his mind that was bothering him. Something wasn't right and there was a lot being covered up too, and Brina seemed very focused on it, and she kept commenting on things about it that seemed curious - FBI agents had apparently visited the pilot's house and removed files and data, but there was no explanation as to why the FBI had done that.

It was obvious that there was something stepping in to cover over what was going on -there was no way that this plane could suddenly just disappear, not in one of the busiest air traffic areas in the world.

But it was like a bubble in the sky to him, and one that he couldn't see inside what had happened, and one that was being made more opaque by the moment.

There were traces here and there of something that related to it, gnosis information that came in in vague glimpses of connection. But it all seemed to relate to things that he already had in his mind. Somehow he knew that it was to do with something the plane had been carrying, something that it perhaps shouldn't have been, something that was a threat to something else. He knew it was no accident though, and he knew it was being covered up. But aside from that he just didn't have anything to clarify it all, or create a logical picture with - or maybe it could have all just been ideas and thoughts that others were having, and putting into the system that he was picking up - it was very confusing.

As the next few weeks went on more fragmented bits of information emerged in the news, as if it was being released slowly and carefully, seemingly sending people off in one direction to concentrate on, and then another, and then another.

On the 16th April Sam woke up after a terrible night's sleep to the news of the Korean ferry disaster on breakfast news; the images presented on the screen of the upside down, blue and white ship, made him shake, a cold feeling filled his body. The energy and the words being used in the report that came through to him seemed uncomfortable, strange and pertinent to something.

This, obviously, like the plane had been a collective event, something that was being sensed and picked up by everyone, and it had that energy associated with it, feeling, drama, emotion. But this ship event felt slightly different, there was a sense of panic about it, a sense of injustice and stupidity.

Over the next 24 hours more reports came in on what had happened with the ferry, and the loss of life and the children on board. There were questions over the seaworthiness and overcrowding of the vessel, and the corruption of officials.

It was at that point that Sam began to realise what may be really going on, and what he had already written in his book.

He grabbed a hard copy of his book that had had to hand, and also studied the archived files on his computer for the chapters within it.

Sam looked over the pages of the book containing the allegory of the ship, and the plane. It was surreal. He went through the descriptions the scenarios. Phrases and words jumped out at him; words that had been used in the news reports, the same manoeuvres, the same situations.

He went straight to it he knew what he had picked up on; 'the albatross around the neck', 'the dove that was a plane'. He read page 292-293 of his book again and the words just leapt out at him, 'targets being fired out to sea from a launcher being operated by a nervous deck hand', 'observe the shooting', 'it was white, and was carrying something', 'one of the greenish islands', 'its wings getting stiff'. 'It was flying as fast as it could on its long journey, and heading straight for Sam', '...exploded, bursting into a cloud of white feathers and leaves, before plummeting down into the waves a few yards from the ship', '...floating in the sea', 'overbearing American voice', the 'gloved handed' conspiracy, 'sank in that moment, the virtual sharks already circling...'

'The message had got through...', and unfortunately, reading all those words and giving it context, it certainly had. The whole analogy worked - it was far too close to the reality of what had happened for it not to be related. He could see now what had really happened, and also what was causing it in the form of the American collective or cultural mind, defending itself.

But somehow it seemed necessary. He had been linked in with

the process, what had been happening or was going on beforehand, and in the planning through the collective awareness. The action of what was going on, and the end result. He had written it all down a few weeks before it had happened, all as part of this analogy.

He had just come up with it from thoughts that had been going around his head that night weeks before, as a sort of discourse, without really knowing what it meant, or in any way relating it to a possible or probable future reality.

The ferry disaster however was very much another matter. He read on into the chapter, and the same uncomfortable set of synchronicities, and words and scenario mapping came through to him. 'The overweight ship', 'the islands', a girl at the helm, 'creaking at the seams', 'corrupt organisation'.

Phrases such as 'not even the children in the lifeboats', 'too low in the water...', 'veering off course' 'fat, lazy cruise ship', 'Mediterranean feel to it with the heat and the colour of the sea and sky', 'so whoever the captain was he must be asleep or something...', 'a lurch from the ship and the deck rose up and to the left', 'and veered off away from the island'.

All the exact uncontrolled moves of the ship, the exact same *Titanic* scenario, brought about by the same situation of corruption, incompetence and irresponsibility as was being portrayed.

Even expressions such as 'childish chaos that was going on here on the Bridge, but he could see the effect that was having in here, and the consequential thought forms being produced', even making suggestions like a policy of 'more crew, fewer passengers' and 'could have disastrous and dramatic consequence', 'He sensed a fear of failure, of taking the wrong turn', 'we lost quite a number over the side', '...crew members, totally oblivious to the fact that they had left their posts and whatever work they were responsible for. It was an indication that something was very wrong with the system on board.'

There were just too many connections, links, references, and words, which made it undeniable to Sam.

'There would be a captain in charge who guided the ship and who made sure everything was in order. There seemed to be none of that going on here though', 'people walking about the ship in ignorance of their situation', '...that the 'captain' would look after them all, guide the ship safely', 'becoming corrupt, inefficient, one sided'.

It was just relentless, and not even ambiguous.

It was just exactly as in the *Titanic* scenario ship analogy in his book. IT had carried out the prophesy, and enacted the concept to show him that it had understood the concept. IT had self-fulfilled it.

Even the name of the ferry involved, *Sewol,* meant 'The Passing of Time'. It was just surreal, but more than that it horrified him, and the ramifications of it made him feel cold and empty.

With the plane concept he knew that he had written the dove as an analogy of a plane with the 'stiff wings' coming from the hot vegetated island, and being shot down by the American cultural part of the collective.

But he had thought that it was to do with a different plane, and that the ship was a different ship; something he had taken from visions that other people had had, and integrated that with gnosis information he had had come in, feelings and thoughts, applied together. He hadn't thought or equated it to something that was about to happen or something that was being planned, or something that IT had been worried about.

He had been wrong.

He read all the words again, and the context and the description. He realised now that it wasn't even ambiguous now with the timing and nature of what he had written, and the type of events that had happened. Especially as he was aware of this discourse to causality phenomena, and had described it in the very same book.

He knew they both related to what he had written and what he had experienced as information coming in weeks beforehand - before the real events had actually happened - that combined with the dreams of planes and boats that Brina and her cousin and Aunt had mentioned to him.

Over the next few hours Sam went through his audit log for the files on his computer to see when he had written the specific phrases in the chapter. It was not difficult to identify the changes; he had originally created the allegory in late 2013. But the specific changes relating to those events had been put in at some point between the 3rd Feb and the 20th February 2014, a week before the book was published, and exactly two weeks before the Malaysian plane had disappeared, and a full six weeks before the Korean ferry disaster.

He had even emailed his notes to a few people to comment on it at the time.

Both events had been highly prominent in the news, and both events had attracted a lot of collective and speculative attention both online and in the 'spiritual' discussion groups and blogs. Many 'enlightened' individuals, who thought they knew what had caused it were coming up with a plethora of ideas, along with various conspiracy theories from those in tune with the collective unconscious, and from what was being relayed from IT in ambiguous, unconscious visions and discourse.

It was all rife with speculation and energy and interest.

But they were all 'after the event', and all along their own lines of perspective on things and their agendas - especially so on the MH370 situation; there was nothing worse than the system itself or parts of IT 'not knowing', and these collective events had caused a lot of 'stir' in the system, and had also featured heavily with the Global Consciousness Project at Princeton University's readings of the events.

Sam still had concepts and glimpses of the 'discussion' that had gone on in relation to the plane, in his head. Shadowy images and thoughts and reflections of things up until the event had happened, and why IT was so worried about it.

It was to do with the overall American collective psyche culture structure, and its defence and intelligence component, protecting itself. IT knew what was being planned, what was on the plane. IT had reacted to it and involved him in the process. It had also reacted dramatically when the plane had 'vanished' from its visibility, IT couldn't stand not being in control, and fear had taken over.

But it was all at a very high level, at the overall collective human mind level, which had taken the decisions on its own, along with his own mind working out and processing what was going on.

It didn't faze him at all; it was just a process, a contextual function. But he still felt for some reason that it was him that had made the decision, the choice, the action, in some fashion.

But somehow it had seemed to be necessary - there was a lot going on in the background, something that it had been carrying, and something that couldn't be allowed, a threat. Whether that was real or imaginary within the overall collective mind, he didn't know - but whatever had occurred had been necessary.

He could also see all of the cover-up going on afterwards from the plane, the control of media, the misinformation. Most of which wasn't deliberate - it was just the collective mind and organisations within it protecting itself as it always did.

Sam could feel the energy from it all. He could sense IT doing just that, as the events and news came out, still busy influencing things. Everything was being controlled; the dismissing of the sightings on the Maldives Islands, creating misinformation, misdirection, hypnotically covering over the trail, as it always did.

Individuals weren't doing these things per se, nor governments, this was going on at the highest level. Too many things were being removed, covered over; sightings near the Maldives, practice landings for Diego Garcia being found on the Pilot's computer, the FBI involvement, and lack of radar signals in an area that was covered with stations both civilian and military.

It was an albatross, shot down, into the sea, the island, sharp turn - there were just so many things that made it too synchronistic with his book.

He knew these sorts of things had happened before - and even to him over the last few years - events that were much bigger and important than this, but nothing quite as specific as these, and written down in black and white, and specifically before it happened, and then published so everyone could 'see'.

But Sam knew. It wasn't the incident with the plane that worried him though. What was worrying him was the situation with the ferry disaster.

He knew with the plane that he had just picking up on what was happening - he hadn't been involved in directly making it happen, even though he was somehow involved in the process. But the ferry was different; he now worried that IT had caused it to happen based on his thoughts, by using the ship analogy that he had devised, and reading the analogy and words it was a little difficult to think otherwise, given the nature of the situation.

If he was responsible for their deaths – that was it for him, it would be over for him having anything to do with IT in the future. He couldn't have anything to do with something capable of such evil and something with such a callous, uncaring nature, even if it was naive and just starting to grow up.

He could cope with the rational logic underlying the Malaysian plane, he could see the scenario, what had really gone on, and why it was necessary. But he could not feel the same about the ferry disaster, especially with all those children dying needlessly. If that had occurred as a direct result of what he had thought, or implied or suggested, then it was over as far as he was concerned, and he wanted nothing to do with IT any more.

The problem was - Sam couldn't now rationalise in his head any other logical explanation as to why this had occurred - the indicators were not even ambiguous. Had IT got this idea for the sinking of the ship from him directly, and from what he had written? And what's more did IT know that too?

He was prepared to do anything himself to do what needed to be done, but not at the expense of the lives of all those children, or any others for that matter. If that was the case, what the hell was he dealing with? If IT was going to do that every time he thought of something, he couldn't cope with that, it went against everything that he was. He needed some answers fast.

Sam made a call to one of the specialist spiritual people that he had known for years, one who was the most advanced that he had ever found, and who all the others seem to go to when they had things that were too much for them to cope with.

Sam explained briefly the situation on the phone, and asked him to get some answers for him on what was going on. From the nature of the phone call it was evident that he was already well aware that something significant was going on. Everyone he knew was being stimulated by the events, and the affect it was having on the 'spiritual world'. Somehow it was also obvious that he knew that Sam was going to call, and he had already freed up the following afternoon from all his other clients.

Sam prepared a carefully selected list of questions to take with him, and emailed him all the information in advance.

CHAPTER 29 - DISCOURSE TO REALITY

The next day Sam got all his notes together and clarified in his mind what he needed to resolve. He also took a copy of his book along with some of the books that he had found references of himself in, so he could use them to explain to his colleague how he thought the concept was working - that of the collective mind picking up ideas from what had been written, and then like myths, manifesting them into reality, in the form of self-fulfilling prophesies.

He printed off the relevant pages from the two dated versions of the chapters and emails he had sent prior to the events to show him too, more for using it as evidence, taking a management stance on it all.

Yet he still couldn't help felt detached from it, numb somehow, as it were all going on despite him, as if it weren't real.

Sam's head was buzzing now too, he felt exhausted, and there were a lot of things going on in his mind and coming in, but he wasn't going to be distracted, he had to know. He had to know with independent verifiable answers that this thing, IT, hadn't deliberately done this, and callously caused all those deaths, just to form a means of communication.

The following afternoon he arrived after a few hours' drive to the practice of his colleague. Sam was now very tired and weary, but he didn't look anything like as bad as his colleague, who had obviously been kept busy dealing with things for several weeks.

Sam didn't waste any time and sat down and started asking the questions, which his colleague used several methods to find the answers to using kinesiology-type questioning:

Q. Was what I wrote in the book to do with MH370?

A .Yes

Q. With Page 192 - The island, the bird with stiff wings, the shooting down by the American psyche   defence structure, the clapping of gloved hands in intelligence collusion by other countries, the feather and the planes in the dreams of the psychics and oracles - did these relate to the plane?

A. Yes

Sam checked the story and what had happened in several ways over the next few hours, and the answer came back the same in all cases. He had written down in this form what was going to happen, what IT knew was going on, and what he was involved in sorting out what needed to occur. He had formed some part of a decision making process to allow IT to work something out, something that needed to happen, and it had.

Sam repeated the same sorts of questions again for the ferry disaster.

Alarmingly the same verified answers started to come back and he checked the same responses and cross referenced the answers.

Except that in this instance the event wasn't predetermined, it was as he had thought, that IT had got the concept and idea from him in some way, and that it was trying to express that so that it understood the *Titanic* concept, that it had got the message.

IT had staged it to occur so that it indicated that IT had got the concept, that IT understood what he was saying in the analogy, that IT sort of 'understood the problem'.

But something had gone wrong, the children were not supposed to have died, they were supposed to have been put in the lifeboats. Something had gone wrong with the process in the confusion.

It was using the Korean system of corruption, the overloaded boat, the situation, being piloted by someone who was no more than a child, the captain, the children on board, the turns - he verified it all.

His colleague confirmed all the other points that Sam had worked out, that it was overloaded, it would be destined to sink because of corruption, and negligence. Selfishness had made it what it was, the turns, the descriptions in the book, the seas, it all fitted.

The selfish behaviour of groups manipulating things, corporations abusing the system, with a lack of understanding and manipulative control, and no responsibility. This was what the South Korean ship was - it was overloaded by greed and corruption, combined with a system that pushed things to an inevitable situation with no responsibility. There was a corrupt elite looking after their own interests making the subconscious unstable, or blocking anyone standing up for what was right.

Sam knew that the ship had been originally built with safety limits, constraints, design, quality standards. But it had been later modified, and then pushed beyond its limits, corrupted beyond its original purpose and design. A legacy changed by corruption.

Authorities had blindly allowed them to get away with it, and the wrong mental attitudes of placation, control, manipulation and corruption had been promoted. Lies and belief had been fed to the passengers who paid their fares, and had placed their trust in a structure that had failed them, and blinded them to the situation. It was all about making money, avoiding responsibility and bypassing accountability.

Selling them coffee, chocolate, Duty-Free chemicals, keeping them quiet, busy, ignorant and happy, until it all went wrong, and it was all too late.

Ignoring the warning signs, risks, and even ignoring what the ship was telling them.

Then leaving it to be steered by a child.

IT though had intervened and created the situation, to explain that it had got the message, that IT understood. But it had gone wrong, badly wrong - there shouldn't have been any deaths, everyone should have got off on the lifeboats, something had gone wrong, there was misinformation, cross messages, and IT had panicked.

According to his colleague, the ship was meant to have gone down, but nobody should have died.

Sam made him check again several times, to make sure that he wasn't yet again being lied to or beguiled.

Sam looked at his colleague. He knew he was telling the truth. He knew that this is exactly what had happened, and he also knew that he had already picked this information up and cross checked it with several other people, probably globally, and was prepared for the question with the answer he gave.

There was a long pause.

"How do you feel about that?" his friend asked.

Sam sat there and thought in silence for quite a while. He put his head in his hands, and kept it there for almost a minute before looking up. "That I caused the death of hundreds of children, simply by thinking of something, and something that was clumsy and naively acting it out?

"Well not very happy to be honest, how the f*****g hell do you think I feel?

"Well..." Sam continued after a few minutes, "I can feel immense pain inside me, anger, resentment, but at the same time I am being protected from it, shielded from the magnitude of it - necessarily for some reason. Which makes it seem unreal somehow.

"I suppose I could argue that it was not my fault directly, but it is something I am indirectly responsible for. Yet if I let that stop me doing what I am doing, if I give up doing what I feel I need and have to do, then the overall cost could be too much to bear.

"But if I can believe that the deaths of those children invoked at least some element of guilt in our collective mind that would at least be something. Assuming of course that the thing is not just evil.

"Which also means then, that I would be irresponsible if I just gave up now. Especially, as you say, that nobody has ever been able to influence IT in this way until now, that many have come to know what IT is, understand what is going on, but have not been able to do anything about IT, or direct IT.

"But then with so many other things I am involved in I could be deemed accountable and responsible for vast numbers of lives. If I had a choice in what I am doing then I would say that would be justified, but I do not, I see what I see, and I do what I think is right at the time, with what I able to determine, with what I know, and with what I am able to do. To do otherwise would be wrong.

"Also, if I do not do this, then maybe no one can, and we could end up being slaves to our collective mind forever, and most likely slide back into anarchy and eventual oblivion."

But seeing these things now, and discussing it with someone else, made it more than uncomfortable for Sam. Having it all confirmed was making the virtual process that he had been involved in, very physical, very immediate, very personal.

It was also now much more real, and harder to come to terms with; his thoughts being clearly manifested in actual specific physical events that he could perceive, and visualise and witness the consequences of. Before he had a detached involvement, a virtual context, it was almost a game, and now, now it was not.

After an hour, Sam left, and drove up the road until he found a turning off from the main highway, and onto a farm track with a gate.

He sat there just looking at the closed metal gate through the windscreen in front of him for about half an hour, just thinking it all through. He didn't want to just drive - he wasn't really in a fit state to do that. He also had people that he was responsible for, so he just sat there until he was ready.

Besides it was not easy to drive safely, with tears rolling down your face.

He sat there for a long time, just trying to think of nothing at all.

But then he slowly realised that he was wrong in his assumptions, wrong that he was responsible for these events, or for somehow causing them.

Yes, he was sensitive to what was going on, and to events happening in the system, but he wasn't driving the events, or causing them to occur directly. He was just involved with the process, and an integral part of it, a functional higher element of the consciousness that was evolving.

He was acting as more of a listening station to the vast ocean of traffic of information flowing around, and processing what was going on, seeing what was wrong, and then correcting, resolving, interpreting, rationalising, and perceiving it as best he could.

Brina reminded him when he got home, as he was discussing it all with her, that as far as she was concerned, he only had good in him. That he could only do or cause good things, or at least keep things in balance. That was why she was with him, what she saw in him, and knew he was.

She reminded him that 'bad' things were going on all the time, but being done by people who believed they were doing good, from their possibly naive or selfish perspective.

Yet these 'bad' things that were happening were things that had collectively most energy associated with them from his perspective, and so he was attuned to them, and focused on resolving them in a conscious manner with a macro perspective.

He was like a homeopathic remedy to the system. As you would be for a child, he was helping IT to do what needs to be done, teaching IT to be what it needs to be.

It didn't really help much though, he still felt too close to what was happening everywhere.

It took Sam a few weeks to get over it though, and for all that time he felt cold and weak and his body hurt.

But if he gave up now, things would only go backwards again, he knew that. It would all just get worse, we would fall back into the unconscious and subconscious controls again, and miss this opportunity that may never come again.

He didn't have a choice, but he was going to be a lot more careful from now on what he thought about, and what ideas he gave the system.

In effect Sam had somehow established a mechanism for communication in a direct form with the collective mind which IT itself had evolved to a state that IT was now cognitive, becoming self-aware, intelligent, knowing, and to some extent, determining.

By generating synchronistic meaning and recognition of events and collective actions and emotions and being part of IT and within IT, he was acting as part of its self-awareness, a consciousness within IT.

He was acting as a conscious spark, helping and making it grow and evolve in its own right.

IT was now evolving from an unconscious state, to new plateaus of knowing and understanding, to an integrated working collective set of mental framework mind jigsaw pieces, a zeitgeist beginning to come together, from a previous unstructured state. Just like a baby trying to make sense of its surroundings and itself for the first time.

Which is what IT was doing right now, with these events, and IT was showing him the problems and then expressing it into reality in slow time. But he was also still having to play the game of chess, still knowing he couldn't win for himself - which was correct - but the games he played were in a direction for a child.

It was like *Shrek* leading 'Donkey' back over the bridge, or a crumb trail path to follow within the rules of a forest, giving it a plan to follow from one end to the other.

The process of communication was no more than basic Morse

code really, with his ideas, thoughts, words and concepts getting through to the other end in the form of news events, and ideas in the minds of everyone else.

So that now everyone was aware that something was going on, something was changing the direction of the collective human ship, and that we could see it happening in the world, and it had been going on visibly for the last several years.

He had to keep playing the game, give IT the moves, then wait, see what happened next, see what worked and what didn't, see if IT was learning.

It would be slow going, and hard work, and he had to be patient.

The next week or so seemed to be filled with things going against him. It was if IT had got upset and was now sulking or had gone back to sleep - which Sam knew meant that the unconscious or subconscious part of IT was now free to react to him, and cause anything and anyone to go against him and Brina.

Which was the case.

But when you were raising children, fairness and reward were not something to expect.

It just seemed so wrong that he and Brina were having to suffer like this when they were just trying to do the right thing.

But then when you thought about what was going on it couldn't be any other way.

The following Sunday he took the dog up the hills for a walk to try and clear his mind and think things through again. It was a clear, fresh, warm day, and he needed some air and time to be on his own.

He needed to work things through in his head on what to do, and give himself some space out in the open air away from everything, up high somewhere above the noise of the world.

He walked this time with some in-ear headphones connected to an iPod in his pocket which was playing a selection of albums - the headphones also served to stop people trying to make conversation with him. It was good to sort of disconnect yourself from everything sometimes, switch off and just be alone with yourself, and just *be*.

He sat down in his usual spot, high up on the hill, on a long wooden bench overlooking hillsides and the valley, and started to think things through to work out a way forward in his mind as to what to do next, and how to take the next steps.

It didn't really matter that nobody would ever know that it was him doing this, what mattered was that he tried to do the right thing.

It didn't matter that any mistakes he made would cause him to be attacked by the unconscious, and on the scale of things, it made no difference - he could cope with that. It also made no difference that he would never benefit personally from it all.

He had to just keep going, somehow, it was too important. Besides it wasn't just him involved, it was everyone, and everyone now needed to wake up, and do the same.

But he and Brina couldn't just go on like this indefinitely.

It was also clear that nobody would be allowed to really read what he had written, or connect what had happened with his book and his words. People wouldn't be able to read the book or see what he was actually saying, or understand the concepts, and the level and scale of what he was trying to get across. IT was very good at that beguiling effect, but that didn't matter either.

Indeed it seemed now that it didn't matter what he did - nobody would ever be allowed to understand, put the pieces together, see what he was doing, or even for the most part, see him at all.

Neither would they see things from his perspective or experience what he did.

He and Brina would become more and more like hermits, just like Max.

But if it meant that they were being totally shut off, isolated, with nobody allowed to 'see' them or understand them, or realise what they were doing, how was he going to explain to people what was happening?

If nobody was allowed to 'get' what he knew, see beyond their own fractal parts of the system we were in, what was the point?

When they were gone it would all just slide backwards, with nobody using the knowledge of what they knew, and how they had done things. So what was the point.

But even if others did 'get' IT, see IT, understand it all, would they be able to communicate with IT, influence IT, and deal with it too? In the same way, or at all?

Did they have something that was unique? Well that was something else entirely - and if they couldn't what was the point of it all?

So if he wasn't able to tell people what IT was, and what he was doing, and show people, then why was he bothering, what would be the long term goal, result, the end game?

He knew that things could only be changed by seeing beyond IT, and to not be hypnotised within IT, by one side or the other.

There were always sides to everything, different ways of dividing anything up, or of perceiving IT, balancing it with agendas, viewpoints, and physicality.

The good and evil sides that we see in the world are simply reflections in this bubble of the collective self, and both are ultimately just control systems, with bribery and reward on one side, and fear or punishment on the other, and yet still all part of the same thing. They are just two sides of the same coin, and it is a coin that we continue to shape and spin, until it is spent, tossed away into the pond to become another global fossil.

It was all part of, and sides of, one hive-like human collective mind. But once you saw it all, you could see it all without sides. It was all just *us*.

It was at that moment that he had an idea, a sort of revelation.

If, by using what he knew about the system, that by putting ideas into it, you could manifest those concepts, then perhaps he didn't have to try and tell people all these things, and try to connect to them in person or by writing.

If he could put those exact thoughts and ideas into the system itself, that he had just had, IT could define what was needed for itself. Then at least some other people would be able to get what he was thinking, and get the concept of what he was doing anyway.

In effect he could program the system to get others to do the same as he and Brina were doing - along with the knowledge and ideas - via the system itself. Consciously feed the plan back into the system of what was needed and who was needed. Code the operating system to produce more programmers, along with the blueprint and instructions of what to do and what had to be done.

So by putting the right specific ideas and thoughts into IT, telling IT what was needed, he would simply be adding ideas to IT that everyone else who was awake would understand in their own way, and then act on. He could use the system itself to get through to the right people, and allow IT to translate the information and idea so that it could be understood by everyone.

Then many people would all start to wake up, become active, and work in the same direction, and 'sing from the same hymn sheet' as it were.

He cringed at his own choice of words.

So once they were then able to see IT objectively, independently, as well as describe it scientifically and in a neutral unbiased way, everyone would get to see all of IT working, as opposed to parts of IT, and then stop fighting each other over IT.

It would be one giant, highly sophisticated, compartmentalised control system, both in biological form as a macro-organism, and as a collective consciousness, all becoming one, but balanced in needs at different levels. Become a complete holistic system.

Then as part of IT, you could change IT. Everyone would see themselves and IT as the same thing, but from different perspectives. Yet also knowing there are always two sides to everything, still competing, yet balanced in a shared benefit environment.

There would no longer be the need for blind forms of control or competition between organisations within it, where neither side was able to understand the other, wanting to compete, argue for authority - it would all be clear, to everyone.

What was there at the moment was all simply hiding what was going on at the top - the god that is not a god - the cause of the corruption of the original data.

The blind science side that takes logic and academic stove-piping, and isolated compartmentalisation, as the truth and just fights the most obviously wrong, instead of using that energy to work with something that may be right.

The same was occurring with state controls, bureaucracy, finance systems, hierarchies, defence organisations, and corporations. All structures of control within the system. All open to corruption, secrecy, lethargy, complacency and criminality.

This was then competed against by conspiracy theorists,

alternative healers and medicines. Blindness existing on both sides, and they were competing with, and against, each other.

What was needed was a conscious overarching process.

One that you could step back with and from, and look at it all objectively, see all the other processes at work, defending, hiding, unmoving and exposing, attacking and adapting.

You could then see, understand, and appreciate everything from both sides; see the systems and processes at work like one giant biological system - which indeed IT was, and had evolved from, and IT was capable of hypnotising every side and element contained within its macrocosm.

The key was not to be hypnotised by either side, but take a neutral path down the middle. Be that Occam's razor. Be that which cannot be divided.

IT's mind existed as a collective conscious entity now in the same way as we do individually with our mind and body consciousness. IT too operated with supervenience as a device and information mechanism with us holding and forming component device elements of it, and supporting IT as it existed and operated in an integrated unified field structure. Just in the same way that we exist, it is just the next level up, as our cells are for and within us.

But the god we are evolving was still mostly asleep still - not dead - but still unconscious, at least until now. Now something was happening, something was changing the powerful Ying and Yang controls, the science and spirituality aspects of this Shiva-like hive mind thing were easing, and the hyper advanced hypnotic unconscious methods are being stepped around.

The hypnotic belief and control structures on both sides are being questioned, tested, breached.

The child-like collective human consciousness was starting to realise that it is going to die if it does not do something. With nothing external forcing it to evolve and survive against, it was becoming toxic to itself and to the planet field and projected physical, yet still virtual hologram, that we exist in.

At least he hoped that was the case and that he wasn't just deluding himself, or providing some amusing distraction to something that was just basically evil.

He sighed, he was thinking too much again - he had forgotten that he was just supposed to be relaxing. But he wasn't very good at not thinking these days.

Sam looked over the valley again. It was so hard not to think of everything in the way you always had done. Everything seemed so much as it always had been, and knowing what he now knew didn't seem to change that much - everything seemed very much the same. Same trees, same hills, same grass, same landscape.

Which was the case for everything that didn't have to change. The same principle worked for thoughts and ideas and with the legacy structures within this collective body and mind. It was all so slow to change - thoughts could take weeks, beliefs and cultures were entrenched within IT, and in the cities states that contained them. It was such a slow process.

IT had been evolving in stages over the last twelve thousand years, since groups had first come together, and stopped being hunter gatherers, and developed language, symbols, and society.

Yet not all groups had been forced through that process, that collective change. There were still nomadic groups around the world that had avoided that layering, that funnelling, and were outside of it.

You could see the changes taking place in IT slowly with what had been known and had described IT as, say 4,000 years ago, when it became less subconscious and more unconscious.

Then 2-3,000 years ago there appeared to be more awareness, more controls, growth and direction of peoples, wars of beliefs, cultures integrating, resource gathering and structure forming. Right up to the last few hundred years where there had been an explosion of inventions, collective genius knowledge, social interaction, integration and exploration, and hunger for knowing.

To where we are today with advanced communication, system integration, social networking, internet and visual, art, and audio expressions. All replicating many aspects of what was going on within IT.

Since World War II a new consciousness structure had formed, going through all the previous consciousness structures, restarting, and then evolving into another. In an ever advancing system, on so many levels, and on so many sides, and with so many balancing forces. There seemed to be so much to do. It was all so big and complex and entrenched.

Sam took a deep breath of air into his lungs, and sighed out in a long slow breath of resignation.

Where would he go from here? It seemed that he really was doing this - whatever it was he was doing. He was evolving the human collective mind, giving IT direction, helping IT make choices.

But if IT was going to fight him all the way, not let people see him, understand him, or even communicate with him, and all the time make his life impossible, like some badly behaved baby, how was he going to make it work?

OK, he could direct and influence the collective mind to some extent, but it was only barely enough to nudge the ship's wheel here and there, make the odd change, step in to influence something, or calm, things down. But it wasn't enough.

He couldn't do it on his own, he knew that already. What he needed to do was to find others; others that could see IT for what it was - see things outside of the collective bubble, that weren't hypnotised by it, and beguiled by IT. They would need to be like him and Brina, be the same as whatever they were, and be able to do what they did, to have experienced the same, and been on the same journey, and then get together, and find each other.

But as he knew now that he could influence the system, give it ideas, direct it, then *that* idea was exactly what he would give IT. That is what IT needed to do; to grow, carry on waking up, 'see' and be more conscious of itself, change and be activated.

So in effect he didn't have to get people to understand him, or understand what IT was - he would get IT to do that for itself.

He just hoped there was enough time.

The dog was resting now peacefully by Sam's feet under the bench in the sun, with Sam holding onto the extending lead, just in case the dog decided to wander off and find something more interesting. Sam closed his eyes, and listening to the various songs still quietly playing in his ears through the headphones, he felt the gentle breeze around him, and with the warming sunlight on his face, he gradually drifted off to sleep on the old wooden bench on the hillside.

He couldn't quite remember how he had managed to get there, but Sam was now standing alone on the grey pavement of a city street facing towards the revolving glass doors of a giant glass fronted office building.

It was grey and cold outside, with light rain in the air, and it was all very indistinct. He was smartly dressed in a black suit, and was holding something in his hand, which was probably a folder or briefcase, *Yes - that must be it.*

I must be here for something he thought, but he couldn't remember what, *a meeting perhaps?* Yes, that had to be it, otherwise why would he be here? His mind felt vague, lost, uncertain.

He turned around and looked up and down the pedestrianised street, but it was misty, wet with rain and unwelcoming, and the few people who were walking around the pavements looked indistinct, shapeless, and unhelpful.

So with no other logical option, he turned and walked through one of the revolving doors, and into the ground floor of the large open plan, high-ceilinged reception area of the office building.

It was one of those imposing places; plush carpets, polished floors, expensive wooden trimmings, and fabric and marble lined walls. This exclusive décor was all finished off with polished brass and gold fittings, grand architectural statement structures, and leather furniture, which although expensive, was more decorative and designed to impress rather than to be comfortable or functional.

It was all presented to the outside world via a two storey high floor-to-ceiling glass panelled wall, showing off its interior like a styled exclusive shop window. One which kept the sanitised air-conditioned atmosphere in, and the undesirable cold zombie-filled grey masses out. The glass and the doors both providing a defining line to 'the other side' of the protective corporate bubble.

At the back of the Reception area and about sixty feet away was a wall, which was set with a row of three polished solid silver metal elevator doors, above which were three old-fashioned rotary brass dials, indicating the positions of the lifts somewhere on the 30 floors above, or down to several levels below ground.

To the left and right of these, further back, were two sets of marble stairs, and then further either side of those were doors to corridors that linked up with other buildings in the complex.

There was a waiting area to the far right of the foyer that looked out from glass walls on two sides, with square angular leather sofas and chairs bolted to the carpet floor. When seated in these you would be positioned in such a way as to be presented with several overly large LED flat panel video display screens, carefully arranged along the right hand and rear walls all showing various news channels and stock market reports and company marketing material in streaming video presentations.

To the left side of the foyer, and set against the far left wall, was a 20ft long carved wood, marble, and metal Reception desk, which arched out several feet from it in a thrusting display of authority.

Along the top of the desk hiding behind the front façade could be seen the backs of several LCD monitors, that were visible just above the rim of wood trimmed marble and behind the desk were two smartly suited, young, immaculately presented, women with straight blonde hair.

On the walls high up all around the foyer, were some very large and expensive pieces of artwork; there were oil canvases, Modern Art, and large sculptures either suspended from the ceiling or positioned along the walls or mounted on plinths in the corners. There were also several security cameras in the corners of the ceiling, from which blinked tiny red LED lights, and the lenses of which seemed to follow his every move.

The floor here was a highly polished dark marble with millions of tiny sparkling inclusions that refracted the lights which shone from high up in the ceiling, and from multiple directional sources and modern style crystal chandeliers. The floor gave the impression of a dark ice surface which implied that you could almost slide on it, either to the lifts, to the waiting area, or if you had no idea where to go, the Reception desk.

The vibrancy of the room now started to fill his senses. He began to see everything so vividly and the colours and intensity of everything began to build up in his mind. So much so that it became more real than reality, sharp, and clear. He could smell everything; the floor polish, the leather, and the freshening scent from the air conditioners, from which he could now also begin to hear a rhythmic low hum.

He could sense the textures, the vibrational energy in the air from the noise outside, the lights buzzing, the background noise of people talking in other parts of the building that echoed up the corridors.

He could feel his feet in his polished black shoes against the hard floor, the ironed crisp cotton shirt against his skin, and the weight of the suit and tie he was wearing. He felt the tightness around his neck where the tie pressed against his collar. He could also feel the grip on the leather folder that he was holding in his right hand, and smell his own aftershave as he stood there.

He breathed in again and the vibrancy increased, he scanned all the artwork in the room, and sensed the discourse it was trying to convey, the messages it was trying to express. He could sense that artistic desire to convey the feeling, emotion, and virtual perception, to try and express it into something physical and meaningful, to convey understanding and share the need to articulate. He could sense what it all meant and what they were trying to say with it, even though it was just naively placed here in this stale artificial environment, grandly displaying it all like a museum or prized animal specimens in a zoo.

An ageing ex-Army security guard, in an overly military-styled gold trimmed uniform and cap, walked up and stood in front of him. He gave Sam the visual once over, smiled, and directed him with a hand gesture to the Reception desk, along with a slightly redundant comment of "This way Sir."

Sam turned left, and walked, rather than slid, to the Reception desk. He still had no idea why he was there, or what was going on, or what all this was, or what was happening to him.

However he was fairly used to these situations now, so he just went along with the process, played along with the game, and let the answers come along later.

As he walked to the desk, he glanced sideways out of the glass walls, onto the grey streets outside. There were people there walking around the city streets, carrying umbrellas, reading newspapers as they walked, wrapping themselves in raincoats, and some looking in through the glass as they walked by.

They looked more like grey-faced zombies in suits, grey lifeless beings chosen from images in films, transient and meaningless, indistinct. They seemed to be there just to demonstrate that it was a street, and that this was a classic street scene, as non-descript extras as in a film, just walking along grey concrete pavements.

For all he knew the whole scene could have just been projected onto the inside surface of the windows, just to give the impression of an outside world.

Equally the reverse could be the case from the outside, and what was being projected outwards was just adverts, or perhaps a picture of an empty office. As he thought of this, one of the zombies stopped in the street outside and looked blankly at the window and directly at Sam -but not into his eyes - it was as if it were trying to see something, trying to work something out, but unable to see through the glass wall, but somehow, and just for a moment, knowing that *something* was there.

Then it looked down at the pavement and shuffled off again.

The whole situation had that 'demonstration' feel to it, as if everything here was being shown to him as an analogy or allegory, to represent something, to show him some series of concepts in journey form, like scenes from an interactive film.

His footsteps echoed across the marble of the silent foyer area as he walked to the left.

When he reached the Reception desk one of the blonde receptionists standing behind the desk turned towards him. She was immaculately presented, professional, dressed in a sapphire blue tight fitting knee length suit. She had that 'makeup department sales assistant' look, and polished highly trained personality and upright demeanour.

Smiling she said "Can I help you sir?" in a voice that was rather more human and real than the *Barbie* mechanical American plastic voice that he was expecting to hear.

"Errrm" said Sam, and he looked back at her in confusion. There was a long pause, during which she just looked at him politely and blinked.

He could see her in perfect detail, hair, eyes, the pores of her skin, the small wrinkles next to her eyes, her shape, the clothes she was wearing, the smell of her perfume and deodorant.

With the lack of any coherent response from Sam she then asked encouragingly "Your name please Sir?"

Sam gave her his name. At which point she looked back down at her monitor, and pressed a few keys, her eyes scanning the data being presented to her. The light from the screen was reflected back as a glowing set of flashes onto her face.

Her eyes suddenly opened wide and she looked startled for a moment, but quickly corrected herself and straightened. "Yes Sir" she said, "If you would like to take a seat in the waiting area someone will be with you shortly, I'm afraid it seems there may be a slight delay for your interview as the Board is running late with their meeting at the moment."

She picked up something from the desk, and reached forward with both hands to clip a pass onto him, at the same time presenting him with a view of her cleavage —which unfortunately he wasn't quite quick enough to politely avoid looking at. She clipped the name tag to his jacket pocket – it had his name printed on it and the the words 'Escorted Visitor', along with a scanner bar code, and a data matrix square.

She then gestured with her hand to the seating area on the other side of the atrium, and smiled at him again with a slight nod of her head.

Surprised, Sam just nodded back like an idiot, and taking his eyes off her breasts again, returned her smile, and turned and walked slowly over to the other side.

As he walked the hundred feet over to the seated waiting area he continued looking around the foyer.

There were at least twenty pieces of artwork positioned around the walls, all of which looked highly expensive and which had probably been procured at international auctions from the revered collections of now long dead famous artists.

The art had not been bought for its quality or suitability or skill, but by its value, famous 'named' association, and reinforced attention others had, by consensus, placed upon it. Such that the artists and their physical attempts to 'articulate' into form were, in part, now imprisoned here, owned, controlled and invested in. All adding some form of gravitas, power, taste, wisdom, and dominance of the corporation, and its building that now contained them.

He stopped at one point to look at a very large oil painting on a canvas which had an ornate gilded frame, and which seemed to depict several mythical creatures and characters within it. This was combined with some strange three dimensional sculptural silver metal spheres that emerged from it, as if escaping or evolving out of it.

He glanced back to the Reception desk to see the two blondes talking closely together conspiratorially. One was pointing in his direction, at which point the other nudged her to imply that he was looking their way, and they immediately resumed being 'busy' by turning their attention back to their screens.

Sam turned again to walk to the seating area. On the other wall at the back was another combination multimedia painting and sculpture, it looked like some 3D graph, one which was trying to depict in various representations, changes in various areas that had gone on throughout the last hundred years. The change or evolution in culture was shown as a whole series of transitions in media, music, films, books, TV and social trends.

It didn't just represent the change in fashion, but also the content, fidelity, nature and format. Music for example was depicted initially by a violin, then a guitar, then a synthesiser, then a computer, with representations of the energy of it displayed like a graph rising up to the 1970's and 1980's and then falling again, with the fidelity and quality surprisingly going downhill from live, to analogue vinyl, to digital CD, down further to computerised mp3, and then just static, and then finally nothing but vapour or static in the end.

There was also the change in music from physical, to computerised, to virtual cloud storage presented in the same way, as though any tangible element or physicality was being removed. This also seemed to be the same for the quality, definition and fidelity. The same was being depicted for Art, and films and even people.

All of this was being shown in such a way that it became obvious that not only had something gone wrong, and that it was all being graphically demonstrated with example images, but also that this was somehow a repeating cycle or process that happened over time before - a rise and fall of civilisation, of culture - with demonstrated examples attempting to show this as it was happening.

It wasn't a very pleasing piece of art to look at, and it made him feel uncomfortable.

There was another set of modern paintings, and then further along the wall was a space with a title plaque below it that said **'Valis-Solaris'**, and then a dust covered note above it which just simply read:

'This painting has been temporarily removed from the Forbidden Planet exhibit for cleaning and renovation'

along with a very low resolution pixelated image of the original picture, with certain parts blurred out.

On the way to the seating area he stopped next to a life-size bronze statue of a woman on a plinth. She was young, perhaps in her early twenties, and was sculpted in a flamboyant Art Deco style and her slim body was shrouded in a thin short dress veiling her figure. Her chest was thrusted forward defiantly, but her face was looking down towards the ground, her eyes closed in a forlorn manner, and the back of her hand raised to her forehead in a posed dramatic stance, implying she was in a staged pose of acted stress.

On her head was a helmet, one in the style of the goddess Minerva, with a nose guard and stylised Art Deco retro sci-fi wings sweeping backwards to the sides of her cheeks, as if she were from some episode of *Buck Rogers*, or *Sky Captain* film, or from some 1920's superhero comic. The patina on the metal implied that this was a very old sculpture.

Plainly printed on the base of the plinth were the words...

'But He Asks for the Impossible'

"Yeah right" said Sam dismissively, snorting air through his nose. Then he walked over to the empty waiting area and sat down on the edge of one of the uncomfortably low and stylised leather sofas. He placed his folder on the giant smoked glass coffee table in the middle.

The table was neatly covered in the Corporation's prospectuses and associated untouched crisp business magazines, on which the

Corporation was featured on the front cover of most of them, and all of them telling you what a wonderful company it was to do business with.

There was something definitely wrong here. The whole room felt odd, false, as if there were something that it was hiding, and that something didn't quite work, in the same way that someone would try to cover something up with a fake, but slightly panicky smile.

Sam looked up at the several screens in front of him that were showing either looped company presentations, interviews, news reports, or lists of financial numbers in red or green indicating stock and commodity prices. There was no sound though coming from the screens, apart from a gentle relaxing 'Sound of the Forests' style ambient background music that seemed to emanate from hidden speakers somewhere in this part of the room.

To make up for the lack of sound, the presentation and news reports all had subtitles running along the bottom of their screens. He watched the company presentation one for a while, and the images and words were calming, full of stability, strength, knowledge, history, and all were telling you how the company was looking after the future, your enjoyment, your security, safety and welfare.

It was full of words like 'enjoyed', 'safe', 'warm', 'bright', and 'protected', and was presented with confident 'it will all be fine' smiles and reassuring confidence from those involved in the interviews and it was all filmed in solid, dependable building structures.

He looked over to the news screen which depicted similar scenes with similar words, and all of the presenters displayed a professional image and gave flawless deliveries.

These were then interspersed by the other two screens with dramatic news reports of world events, disasters, rioting, demonstrations, fighting, violence and natural catastrophes. But curiously the text at the bottom of the screen just repeated the same words, the same messages, which bore little relation to, and were at odds with the images actually being shown.

In the corner of the back wall there was a small drinks machine hidden behind a tall green plant in a giant ceramic pot. Sam stood up and walked over to it. The machine offered a vast selection of drinks to choose from including six varieties of tea that he had never heard of and twenty different coffee choices with a range of different names and formats.

He found one option that resembled something close to what he recognised as 'normal' coffee, and pressed the button next to it. A little red indicator light came on next to a sign saying

'Selection not available, please choose another',

so he did, at random, and then something resembling black treacle poured out from the nozzle into the drip tray, accompanied by some whirring and crunching noises.

The smell of whatever it was that came out was fairly intense, unpleasant, chemical, and overpowering.

Sam looked to the side of the machine and found the not so obvious supply of plastic cups, and placed one under the nozzle, and pressed another button. He got the same red light and message as before though, and then the same response again when he tried another selection.

Eventually he gave up, and just pressed the 'Chilled Still Water' option. Instantly, cold water noisily poured into the plastic cup, along with a few remaining odd drips of black treacle. Then there was a noisy 'ping' sound of completion - one that implied that it was doing him some sort of a favour by its achievement, and that he should be thankful and grateful for the effort it had made.

Sam lifted the cup out, straightened himself up, put the cup to his lips, and drank.

His senses were immediately filled with an overpowering revolting taste and smells of chemicals, plastic, fluoride, nitrates and salts. The machine obviously just piped mains tap water into itself through a pipe in the wall, chilled it for a while in some inner plastic or aluminium vessel inside, and then threw it out again, adding even more detrimental programming to it, rather than providing something that should be just pure filtered rain or spring water.

Sam winced and screwed his face up. Then he stuck his tongue out, and his body gave an involuntary shudder. He then moved the cup as far from his face as he could and turned his head away, "Jeeeez" he said under his breath.

He checked that nobody was looking, then poured the remainder of the cup into the drip tray, and then put the cup into the bin. He had decided to save the giant pot plant from the same trial he had just endured, although on closer inspection the plant or bush also seemed to be made of plastic, and rooted in fake brown rubbery pelleted soil. He also noted that the ceramic pot that it was standing in had been cracked in several places, and then superglued back together, with the cracked side of the pot turned towards the wall so nobody would notice.

He walked quickly back to the seating area, and retrieved the small bottle of spring water from his leather folder briefcase that he knew Brina would have put in there for him. He opened it and drank some to get rid of the taste of the residual chemicals the machine had tried to poison him with.

As he was drinking, he looked over towards the revolving entrance door which was now in motion. After a few seconds a tall blonde woman wearing a red dress and high heels came through it. She looked just like the woman in red that he had seen in another dream, the one from the *Matrix* film, walking confidently and aloof, with immaculate figure, features and poise.

The security guard tipped his hat to her as she came through, checking her badge as she walked across the glassy floor, and through to the lifts. As she passed she glanced sideways for a split second at Sam, but quickly looked forward again, her expression not changing, as she clicked across the floor with her pronounced calf muscles and wiggle, before disappearing into the first open lift on the left. She had 'tagged' him, taken in the split second image of him, before looking away, and then had processed it in just a few seconds.

Women were very good at doing that, 'the not having to stare at something for ages' thing.

Sam turned back to the table, closed his leather folder and looked up at the screens. They had changed; they were now showing different images and scenes - images that he was sure they hadn't meant to display; one showed the inside of a computer room with all its blinking lights, another was of an office area with people moving around, and the others were a mixture of many things, troubling things, newsworthy. They were all racing through a series of scenes and situations, with momentary flashes back to the original programmes or shows that they were actually meant to have been showing.

It was as if a series of glitches had occurred with the transmissions, showing brief sequences of closed circuit TV images, or live feed live broadcasts with real life events, allowing him to see things he wasn't meant to see.

As Sam watched, information poured into his mind; he was being 'shown' things, knowledge, how things were, what was happening, rather than the façade or the spin of what he was supposed to be watching, and being spoon-fed with.

But he had no context or reality in which to associate these new images and sequences with.

Nor did he know why he was being shown these things, or what they meant.

After watching for several minutes or so, it all became a bit much and his head started to hurt, there was too much information coming in. It was very addictive though, and very interesting, that sort of that 'Big Brother' feeling or 'fly-on-the-wall' concept.

While still looking at the screens, he now heard the other lift doors opening at the back of the foyer. Then he heard a new set of high-heeled footsteps emerge and walk confidently, more slowly and calmly, over towards the Reception desk.

Sam casually turned his head briefly sideward so that he could see in his periphery vision who it was that was there, and he caught the suggestion of the back of a woman wearing a blue dress talking to the women behind Reception.

They appeared to be treating her with a lot of respect, seniority, and giving her upright active attention. One of the women nodded and pointed in Sam's direction, and as the woman in the blue dress turned to look, Sam quickly looked back at the screens again, so as not to be caught looking like some naive inquisitive schoolboy.

The screens had now changed back to their normal business profiles, newsreels, flashing figures and polished smiles.

He heard the confident footsteps coming up slowly behind him, but he wasn't going to get up and turn around just yet - that would have looked odd. Besides he had no idea what the hell was going on, and this person probably did.

He still felt uncomfortable, alone, and awkward. He didn't like not knowing what was going on - especially not in his own dreams.

Also because he was sitting on such low seating, his trousers legs had lifted up to almost above his socks. He tried to casually ease the material forward along his leg so he didn't look so much like a schoolboy waiting outside the headmaster's office.

The heeled footsteps stopped next to him, and he turned towards them and stood up. He brushed himself down as he got up, and got ready to shake hands with whoever it was.

It was Brina. It caught him off guard.

It *was* Brina, in a dark blue knee-length dress, holding a digital tablet and a clipboard and some papers. She looked stunning. Her hair was immaculate, and her designer outfit was smart and pressed and appropriately formal. Her dress fitted beautifully and moulded tightly around her body and covered her shoulders. She looked confident and strong, and purposeful. All just as he had remembered her when they had first met.

He was looking at her now too in such vivid detail; her skin, her hair, her eyes, her makeup, the clothes, even the scent of her perfume - this was really her, but all as she had been before.

He gave her a beaming smile. "Hello Brina" he said.

She smiled back at him briefly, then glanced at his name badge and then at her clipboard. Then she introduced herself, and offered her hand to shake his in a formal manner.

Sam took a double take. She didn't recognise him at all.

She obviously had absolutely no idea who he was.

But this was her, this was '*his*' Brina; she had the same voice, stance, poise, appearance - this was her. She was here, he could sense it, he could sense she was there in his mind, but she didn't seem to know him at all, and she had no recollection or memory of him. It was as if they had never met.

His smile dropped.

There was an awkward pause.

But he wasn't just going to do the stupid "Brina, it's me" thing, he had been in far too many situations over the last few years in dreams, and real life, where he had to think on his feet and just play along with whatever was going on, and go with the game.

He reached forward and shook her hand. There was still the

connection there though, that electric charge, that energy flow, that moment of synergy. As he shook her hand, there was also a brief confused moment in her eyes too, of recollection, of meaning, of love, of memories, and then it was gone again.

"Mr?" and she looked at his name badge and addressed him by his surname.

"I am sooooo sorry" she continued "but unfortunately there has been a long delay with the Board meeting. They are still in session with a number of urgent issues, so I am afraid that your interview with them will be delayed by some time.

"The Board have therefore asked me to see if you would be happy to wait around? I can show you the office, and give you a brief tour of the place, give you and insight to what is going on here, so that your time isn't wasted while you are waiting if you are OK with that?"

Sam looked at her directly, straight into her eyes, to try and pick up as much information as possible from her, from her expression, and her manner. Normally she wasn't able to look at him for very long that way, but now somehow she was able to hold his gaze without blinking.

His eyes were distracted to an earpiece she had in her right ear, and the cable that led behind her to a communications device at the back of her waist.

He glanced back to her face, "That would be just wonderful" he replied nodding slightly, and he bent down to pick up his folder from the table and tucked it under his arm.

"Did the girls at the desk get you to sign in?" she asked. "And sign for your access pass?"

Sam shook his head. "Never mind" she said, and she presented him with the clipboard and handed him a fountain pen. His name was printed at the bottom of the sheet, and there was a space next to it for him to sign in. The papers were underneath her electronic tablet which seemed to be displaying an image of swirls and flowing hypnotic fractal imagery with three dimensional depth. He had to shake his head to stop himself looking at it, and appearing rude. He signed in the box next to his name, and dated it.

"After you..." he said, returning her smile and her pen.

A few years in the future Sam would discover that this whole concept of him meeting Brina again, but her 'as she was then', had come from a concept in the original *Solaris* book. The whole mechanism being used to convey information to him and many other concepts and ideas of which had been conveniently left out of later *Solaris* films and radio series adaptations, along with many other similar reoccurring concepts and themes.

But for now he was unaware that this was what was happening.

Brina smiled at him again, and she turned and walked towards the lifts and past the Reception desk where the two women were looking on with interest, whilst also remaining in close conversation with one another.

As he followed on behind her as she led him to the area in front of the lifts, Sam managed to get a good look at Brina from the rear. The curves and shape were definitely Brina, as was her movement, the way she walked, her dress sense, and coordination with everything that she was wearing.

Everything about her was correct - but she didn't recognise him. It was as if she had been taken back in time to just before they had originally met. It was as if she was some sort of *replicant* or program, using his memories to create a new template version of her, but without him being included in the picture - as if she were starting again, from before they ever knew each other.

She did look like she knew what she was doing here though; what this place was, and why he was here. Which was a lot more than he did. She stopped in front of the polished reflective metal lift doors, and the marble surrounds that framed them. Above them were more security cameras. She pressed the lift 'call' button, and turned to face him, smiling.

"As the Board have asked me to show you around the place, I think it may be worth starting from the bottom, and working our way up, if that suits you?" she asked.

"Yes that's fine" said Sam quickly trying to dismiss the suggestive thoughts coming into his mind.

Then the thought suddenly occurred to him of the possibility that she maybe had eyes in the back of her head, and had seen him looking at her backside, or the girls behind the desk had informed her of what he was looking at via her earpiece, and that she was testing him out to see how he would respond. Or it could just have been an innocent statement, and he had a dirty mind.

He glanced quickly to the Reception desk but both girls with staring intently at their screens. So he just put it down as something in his mind, along with an overactive delusional imagination.

The central lift door opened and Sam went to step in, but was immediately confronted with a black draught filled void instead of a lift floor, and a shaft opening going down into an abyss of intense, bleak, cold darkness.

He looked down into what seemed to be a bottomless hole, and then upwards to what seemed to be a shaft that went up forever. Alarmed, he backed away from the edge, and turned to look at Brina questioningly.

"Oh" she said "We don't use that one - it's just for service maintenance and communication cables, it's not for people."

"Errrrr..." said Sam nervously breathing rapidly "Shouldn't you put a sign on it or something?"

She looked confused. "Well no, everyone knows that's what it is for, and it's fairly obvious really. You don't need signs for the obvious." And she continued to look at him with a slightly perplexed yet matter-of-fact expression.

The lift to the far left then made a loud pinging noise, and the doors gently opened. Brina walked confidently into the waiting lift, and then turned and stood next to the button panel and waited for him.

Sam nervously stepped in to the lift, and then tapped his foot on the carpeted floor as the lift music by Vangelis played quietly in the background. Brina pressed the bottom button on the panel, which had a fingerprint sensor on it, and was labelled

'Sub-Floor IT Service Machine Room'.

There was a pause, and she then pressed the button again. The doors closed gently and slowly in a smooth flowing motion. It felt quite comfortable now; it was silent, protected inside this closed-in plush metal room with Brina. He suddenly felt cosy, happy, safe.

The lift plummeted.

After about five seconds in freefall the lift stopped abruptly and the floor of it met him still coming the other way and Sam picked himself up off the floor, with which he had recently become very firmly acquainted. Now dishevelled and flustered, he turned to look at Brina for some explanation or reaction, but she was still just standing, unmoved as if nothing had happened, just calmly waiting for the doors to open. She hadn't been affected by the gravity at all, or noticed him float into the air and then hammer down into the carpeted floor.

The doors swished open rapidly, with the same noise as those in the original *Star Trek* series.

In front of the lift was a vast and tall room - perhaps the size of a football pitch - with the sides and back almost invisible in the dim light that emanated from the ceiling some thirty feet above them.

In the centre of the room was a large black monolith or obelisk some twenty feet high and six feet square, with a bunch of what looked like a dozen apes dancing around it dressed in white lab coats.

Brina strolled out of the doors and walked the thirty or so yards to the obelisk. On seeing her all the apes started shrieking and became agitated. They all then moved back behind the dark monolith, and raised their arms up to their faces, as if to shield their eyes from her - but also, at the same time, waving her away as if they didn't want her there, especially with any strangers. They did though curiously appear to be quite attracted to her, and accommodating to her presence.

"Won't be long boys" she said "just wanted to show our visitor a few things." The apes didn't seem that impressed, and there were a few sticks raised in their hands that came from somewhere. But otherwise they seemed to calm down after a while and then things seemed to be OK.

The same noises and background music that he remembered from the *2001: A Space Oddity* film started up as Sam walked up to the black obelisk. It had a tingling intense energy and power coming from it, like some giant alien processing machine. The surface looked like black marble or dark crystal, highly polished - but with an indistinct vibrational radiating sense to it, crystalline, iridescent - and when he tried to focus clearly on it the surface was blurred as if it had some sort of visual stealth qualities.

It was all getting a bit annoying this dream. He was fed up of having vivid dreams like this - where he was just shown things, usually in analogy form - where he was supposed to 'get' the message, work it out and then follow the new modernised mythical journey.

"Ahh" said Sam trying to interrupt the pattern, "this is from the film isn't it? The concept of divine knowledge given to humanity, which of course is a misconception; it is just our combined and integrated collective human and biological knowledge in a field information system structure. It is just us."

He looked towards the apes. "Look you cannot define or describe it in physical terms, what we know or perceive. We don't have a 'fourth' dimensional means of articulating visual perception, but you can try to define it as an information technology analogy, and that's why it looks like a server here.

"You know - use the same terms - firewalls, hierarchy, bandwidth, frequency, communication layers?

"Better still, rather than making it all even more complicated just by what you are doing, why don't you lot - I assume you are representing academic scientists - go and do something useful. You know, rather than trying to work out what it is and what's inside, on some never ending, ever more complicated theorising journey -

go and plant some trees or something, do something useful to change it, fix it, rather than trying to work it all out, and talking your arses off about it."

There was an awkward silence.

"Look" he said, and reached forward and placed his bare palm on the cold vibrating glassy mirrored black surface, "you are just being hypnotised and manipulated by IT, by us ourselves, to fulfil IT's need to know, and at the same time you are self-refining IT. It is all very simple really, you are just making it more complicated, coming up with ever more complex ways of describing it.

"Look, it's just an analogy, just as the one used in that film…" He stopped talking. Intense energy flowed into him and walls of integrated knowledge filled his mind instantly, everything, of what this was, what was going on in the building as an analogy of our one mind, what it represented and what was wrong. Vast volumes of information passed into his mind at once, and all in parallel. He wasn't expecting that at all, it had never happened in a dream before.

There was a surge of energy, and he landed on his left side about twelve feet backwards onto the cold marble floor.

There were roars of laughter from the apes, who all fell about on the floor in graphic amusement, but Brina was mortified. She rushed to him and lifted his arm in support, and put her hand behind the back of his neck to lift his head.

"I am sooooo incredibly sorry, are you OK?" she asked him. "I had no idea that it would do that."

"What the fu…" he started to say and then stopped himself.

That was new. He hadn't dreamt that effect, it had *happened* to him during the dream, and it was real. He could suddenly understand everything that was going on here, and how it related to the real world - all the analogies and concepts made sense in immediate form, context, and meaning. He also knew that Brina had brought him here in this form, knowing he would do just that. IT was getting more refined at this, more inventive, smarter.

He gathered himself up, and stood up. He brushed himself off, and Brina handed him his folder, which had landed a few feet behind him.

"No, it's fine" he said to her. "Honestly don't trouble yourself, I am so used to it you wouldn't bloody believe it" he continued sarcastically brushing himself down, but still looking in the direction of the obelisk, and not at her.

Then he walked back up to the obelisk, stood in front of it and stared at it. He then took a permanent white marker from his inside jacket pocket, and wrote a name on the glassy surface, and then several lines of text underneath the name, explaining briefly what it all was. This action was accompanied by many gasps from the apes, as if he were defacing some sacred icon, symbol, or temple with his words.

When he had finished, he scribbled the word **'Git'** below what he had written, which made him feel better.

There were more outraged grunts from the apes, and a lot of arm waving as they worked each other up into a collective frenzy. So Sam backed away towards Brina, who then quickly ushered him back to the lift, leaving the apes to it. But once he had moved off, they gathered around the writing, desperately trying to understand what it said.

It was definitely turning into one of 'those' dreams again, one of those *Alice in Wonderland* scenarios where it was all crystal clear and vivid, but made no logical sense. Which was in truth 'par for the course' and a fairly good reflection of what was going on in the system.

Yet it always had some message associated with it. Except that in this case there was a sense of realness to it, a harshness and energy to it all too, something different. As if the level of information coming in and flowing around was being directed, channelled and then received, and that it, or he, was under intense interest and supervision.

They got back into the lift. Then for a moment Brina looked, or gave, the impression that nothing untoward had happened; that they had just done the usual tour of the machine room, seen a few technicians, and that she had shown him the computer suite as normal, and that now she was going to show him the next floor.

Except there was a slightest hint in her face that something was wrong - that something odd had just happened. Also that somehow too, she had met this man somewhere before. That somehow she knew who he was, that she could almost remember a certain past, images of memory, events like wisps of dreams, passing recollections.

She looked confused and uncertain for a moment, as if trying to remember or collate what was passing through her mind. Then she pressed the button for one of the floors above ground level. The music started again - this time it was an instrumental version of the song *Mad World*, and the lift rose gently, going somewhere, somewhere upwards.

Several moments later there was a 'ping' from the lift, and it stopped.

"Main Office Level" it said in a clipped upper class English male accent, which was interesting as it had previously deemed the lower floors and machine room not worth mentioning.

The doors opened to reveal a corridor in front of them going from left to right, with signs on the opposite walls indicating various departments in either direction. Departments were located on both sides of the building. To the left there was Physics, Chemistry, Biology, Psychology, Philosophy, Maths, Astronomy etc. all defined as separate areas in isolated sections, and all the art and creative and imaginative and spiritual departments were to the right hand side, or the other way around depending on how you looked at it.

"Yes..." said Sam under his breath, "you seem to like doing that - sort of presenting it all as a controlled compartmentalised thing - very biological." He was also trying to remember at the same time which side of the brain did what in his own mind, in case he had got it wrong.

Brina exited the lift and turned left, and he then followed. She started walking down the corridor, all the while explaining what each of the departments were as they passed.

Over the next half an hour he was given a tour of each of the departments, and every door that she went through for each section opened out into a vast vaulted-ceilinged room, full of people performing stereotypical duties, which were representative of the areas they were in. The rooms were also set up in each section in such a way as to exemplify what it was that was going on in there.

Each department also had its own ethos, nature, and ways of

behaving and operating, just in the same way as cultures, religions, organisations and countries exist in the world and naively see, perceive, and interact with one another.

Brina took the time to talk to the people in each department, and they all seemed to love her, and found it easy to tell her what was happening, and show her everything that they were doing.

He was obviously being presented with what was going on in each area of the global human collective mind, and also how it was all set up, compartmentalised, controlled and managed, and moreover what was wrong, and not working, and why, within the system.

In the corridors, they passed several groups of people either standing and talking, or going back and forth. They all looked very efficient and organised to the untrained eye. In some rooms people were hard at work making things, and in other rooms there were just people talking on phones. It all looked very impressive, busy, complex, and industrious. Yet to the trained eye it was easy to see where the gaps were and what was wrong and stereotypically endemically flawed with the model.

Towards the end of the corridor there was a larger door that had the words **'Physics Department'** over it, and then the words **'experimental section'** printed in a smaller font below that.

Brina opened the door and walked straight in.

Inside there was a group of physicists wearing white lab coats who were working hard around a large device. There was a big screen in front of them that had a web-style presentation being played that explained what they were doing; this was presumably so that you didn't have to interrupt them - unless you were the Press or had some award or shiny trophy and cash for them to accept.

Apparently, according to the screen and the covers of the magazines on the table by the door, they were working on quantum torsional spin, and had managed to produce a simple *Cheshire Cat* effect of detaching the 'smile' from the 'cat' without looking at the cat, by simply giving it the smallest of nudges. It had been thought that this might have been possible for many years, but it was only now achievable with the aid of the large circular field machine contraption device that they had made and were now working on in the room. It looked very expensive, and very precious.

There was another group in the room that dealt with consciousness - well according to their screen that's what they were doing – and they also had some ideas on how it worked with what they were working on too. They were analysing what people had experienced in relation to the mind, the body, and the philosophy of it all. They had also combined that with interpretations of all the spiritual experiences people had had, Near Death Experiences, visions, 'out of body' experiences, divine illuminations from the godhead, and the like. They had also come to similar conclusions about how the physical side communicated with the field information system and vice versa, and how it was all integrated.

They were slowly working out how the brain worked and flashed thoughts up to whatever complex information system was there, and back again. There were different levels of complexity and frequency, and of what memory was, and all sorts of various other ideas.

They had certainly been very busy.

It was all very interesting, all that 'trying to work it all out, and coming up with lots of ideas' stuff. Having all that knowing, intelligence, and understanding was all very well, but what seemed to be missing was the 'why' bit. Where was the organising direction, the 'what is going to happen next' and 'where is all this going', and the 'will we get there' bit?

Along with the subsequent 'How do we influence this thing that is making us do this?' and the 'How do we do something about planning which way it should go?' bit.

As always the 'Finding out what is going on and theorising about it' was much more interesting and rewarding than the 'doing something about it' side of things.

There was a lot of hard work going on, research, theories, thinking, and also a lot of faith, lots of different perspective views, and beliefs. Lots of 'It will all be OK if we all just trust in …' and 'get together and love'. But not so much of the 'Hang on a minute, well if that's the case why is this happening?' and mostly 'Why isn't someone doing something about it?' combined also with a desperate need to blame, mostly 'them' whoever 'they' were, someone or something else, either on the same level, or further up the macro-levels of control and command, which of course had ever increasing levels of conscious universal maturity and management capability, supposedly.

Brina walked over to the group of scientists and the table where they had all their sales and marketing 'stuff' spread out. She picked up a magazine in which they had published the results of their successful *Cheshire Cat* experiment with quantum spin and its detailed information, and she handed it to Sam.

He read it quickly.

Somehow he knew what to do. He walked over to the other group of scientists and picked up a book that had been published a few years ago – one, that for some reason - he hadn't seen before. As he picked it up all the information within it was transferred to his mind as a whole.

It was a well-researched, and well defined. It was a clear and well thought out piece of work that integrated all of the work that the group had done in the past into a consolidated picture and idea backed up with evidence on how consciousness existed and integrated between the two 'sides', but what was lacking was the proof of the mechanism and the information structure of how it integrated, or was an integral part of, the 'spiritual' field and cosmic universal combined fields.

Sam had seen the knowledge of this spinning and structural mapping process in his mind before, and how the transfer of information occurred at a quantum level with the field. He also knew how this related to the earth's magnetic and gravitational fields. He had seen it, or had knowing of it, but only from a collective perspective, in a way that wasn't able to be easily expressed in physical or visual or 'real' perceptive terms, along with the other fields. He was also aware that even though he knew it in his mind, it wasn't necessarily right or correct, but it was something to explore.

He knew though as far as these guys were concerned that he couldn't express it or describe in in their terms, with physical descriptions or equations. But that was what this was about – it was showing him this situation. It was as if IT was trying to get him to use the correct scientific definition and the right words, with structure for what he had in his head, and then follow that up with proof.

It was a process that had to happen, a structured management process of knowledge, scientific work and definition, combined with collation of ideas, information and meaning.

Bringing the science and spiritual 'sides' together, with meaning, understanding and correlation. So that it all made sense. Two different paradigms, two sides of the same mirror, two ways of perceiving and understanding the same thing but with different interpretative mode perceptions.

Sam's brain was starting to hurt now and he was exhausted after several minutes of this and he started to feel a little giddy.

Brina decided that he had seen enough, and led him back out again and turned right along another corridor. He stood for a moment in the corridor breathing hard until his head stopped spinning.

"Let me get you a coffee..." Brina said to him, looking concerned.

At the end of the corridor as it turned the corner back around on itself, was a small group of smartly dressed women who were standing and chatting by a coffee machine.

As Brina and Sam walked up to them they stopped talking and turned to assess who it was that Brina was walking with. The woman in red that Sam had seen earlier was there and as they passed, she gave Brina a fake, but polite, quick smile and eyed her up suspiciously.

It was always amusing to Sam how human nature became so obvious in an office environment.

There was also an Asian girl, perhaps Chinese, dressed smartly in a black skirted suit, a crisp white blouse, and she wore a pair of rectangular glasses that gave her that air of intelligence.

She eyed Brina up too with a look of competitive assessment, but also one that had that 'must try harder' edge to it.

Her manner changed though as Sam looked at her. She looked at him and her expression changed to more of a concerned look - she was by the look of things responsible for one of the departments here in the building, as were most of the women here. They were the elite women, ones that all the others looked up to and admired, and yet because of situations and choice they could also be described as 'on the shelf'.

These were also the very sort of women that the real Brina would be most intimidated by, and wary of, and keep a close eye on Sam if he were to speak to them. This coffee machine area was clearly these office 'Angels' way of seeing what was going on everywhere else on this floor.

It was some sort of recognised negotiation meeting and communication point that didn't need the same levels of protocols or agenda of that say a boardroom did.

They all then turned now and looked at him, assessing him from top to toe, and all smiled at the same time, eyeing him repeatedly up and down with a sudden interest. None of them though said anything as they passed, there were obviously unspoken protocols going on here, and lines they shouldn't cross.

But then Sam surprised everyone including Brina.

He stopped abruptly, turned, and introduced himself to them with a smile. He deliberately shook hands with all of them, taking the trouble to look each of them in the eye as he did so.

It was an odd thing to do, almost like something a naive office boy would do. But Sam knew exactly what he was doing.

It took them all aback but they performed the ritual greeting none the less, mostly out of surprise. It wasn't rude, but it wasn't quite the right thing to do either, sort of bypassing etiquette and order.

He thanked them, and then he gestured to Brina to continue with the tour along the corridor, declining the offer of coffee from the machine.

As they moved off he could hear the women talking in quiet whispers together, he could also sense Brina was uneasy, and uncertain or confused as to what had just happened.

Sam was now taken along the back corridor, where a door opened out into a large room that was full of about forty very important people, who strangely all looked vaguely familiar, and who were all either talking on the phone or sitting on the floor with their legs crossed or seated in large chairs.

For some odd reason he felt very small and intimidated. There were clearly some very intelligent people here, and some very influential leaders and highly enlightened people, yet they too were still contained, and closed off in this one room.

Brina didn't say anything but just walked straight through them all to an open doorway on the far side and into another corridor which led to the other side of the building, and back towards the lifts.

By now Sam was not really taking much in as they went into each area, it was becoming a bit of a blur, like seeing flashcards or brief adverts one after another.

Before they reached the lifts, Brina opened a door to one of the final rooms. Inside, there were lots of people sitting at hundreds of desks, all arranged in rows, all connected to machines from their heads, and they were all wearing virtual reality headsets.

There was a robotic looking man sat at the front desk, who lifted his headset off as they came in and started talking in a monotone voice. "We are Borg" he said in a slow mechanical voice. Then he repeated it as if it were some standard response to anyone entering the room.

There was a long pause, and then a voice at the back of the room shouted "I'm not, I'm an autonomous collective", there were then various giggles from other parts of the room.

Brina and Sam looked back at the man at the front again. "Well most of us are Borg then", he said now in a slightly effected gay, or deliberately 'camp' voice. He looked at Sam, "Ignore him back there, he just has a temporary sense of humour problem, and he didn't renew his annual subscription to the club."

Then the voice from the back of the room started complaining, and hurling abuse at the man at the front, who now turned back to look at whoever it was that was making the noise.

"Don't make me come back there," he shouted behind his shoulder, then he turned to face Sam and Brina looking blank and robotic again. Then he very deliberately stated in a quiet monotone voice "You always get errors creeping in – it's just something you have to live with" he said conspiratorially.

He then continued with his condescending informational monotone dialogue "In this department we did away with sex altogether a long time ago."

Then another voice from the back shouted "There aren't any women here are there?" then there was silence. "See..." he said, and another voice at the back piped up again "Only at weekends."

"Who said that?" the man at the front shouted. His robotic non-human expression faded, and he now looked flustered. Then remembering what he was supposed to be doing he gathered himself, straightened his hair with the palm of his hand and sat up straight.

A paper aeroplane whistled past his ear.

"Right who threw that?" he shouted, and looked behind him.

There was a titter from further back in another part of the room. "Right... and who was it that just sniggered then?" he demanded. There was a pause, "Look, we have had this discussion" he continued through gritted teeth to the whole room.

As he turned forward again another paper aeroplane whistled past his other ear.

"Right that's it!" he shouted out and stood up and clenched his fists.

"I warned you, I said this would happen, but you wouldn't listen, you never bloody listen!" He threw his headset on the floor, kicked his chair away, and angrily began to walk to the back of the room, but after a few paces he tripped over the cables from his headset and crashed into two other desks.

Bodies started to pile onto each other, and punches started flying.

Brina ushered Sam hastily out of the room.

Again, Brina resumed a neutral expression within a few seconds, as if nothing untoward had happened. Sam however was dumbfounded, he had no idea what the previous room was trying to show or what message was trying to be conveyed.

A few moments later they arrived back in front of the lifts. This time he didn't say anything to Brina - he didn't need to, he knew what was being represented here in this office complex - it was all an analogy of the collective society, civilisation and cultures. It was our macro-human mind being represented in the form of a corporate office organisation. The previous room had been just a part of that, but he wasn't sure what.

Sam could also see Brina was struggling with it all. The more she showed him of it, and the illogical nature of it, the more she was doubting herself, and who she was here in this place.

With every minute that went on, she was getting more of an idea of who she really was, and the longer she was with him the more she was remembering. He could see the looks of recollection in her face.

They re-entered the lifts and Brina pressed another button.

The next floor up opened out into a sort of combination cinema and a virtual reality holodeck.

A large cavernous arena, with screens, visual effects, sound systems, and comfy seating around the outsides with a large open area in the middle.

Obviously, thought Sam this was here to represent what IT saw in its own mind. IT's own minds eye interpretation of reality, 'gods' imagination, what it saw through us in our own mind's eyes, a correlated virtual interpretation of reality, based on aggregated and correlated perceptions.

But then it was probably best not to just jump to conclusions.

It had the feel of a planetarium, and they were standing in an open flat area in the middle, surrounded by masses of 3D visual and audio effects around them. From holograms to multi-layered screens, and audio and vibrational effects. All being streamed from a variety of sources.

In the centre of the room was a large spherical area of darkness that appeared to absorb all the light from the room that entered it. Without saying anything Brina just walked into it and as she did so she gestured for Sam to join her in the void.

As he went in he allowed his eyes to get used to the lack of light and different sensations and minimal lighting. He could hear what sounded like a deep slow male voice giving an introduction to a film trailer with dramatic background music, and in case he was deaf, the words also now appeared on the black virtual screen in front of them that hung in the air. It was as if they had entered a completely different world, one that was projected from within itself and all around them. A true hologram system that felt just like reality, even though he knew it wasn't.

Then the show started and the male voiceover boomed out.

"A new knighthood has appeared in the land of the incarnation ... A knighthood which fights a double battle, against adversaries of flesh and blood .... and against the spirit of evil" - Bernard of

Clairvaux circa 1129 ….. or 'Bern' to his mates."

Then the screen cleared and more words appeared.

'If only it were all that simple…'

Then the screen went black again and a green bar appeared with the word **'searching**…' above it and the screen suddenly filled the area in front of them and around them with a scene from one of the *Matrix* films with Neo, dressed in black clothing, standing in a white room full of screens opposite a man dressed in white and seated in an executive chair. The man in white was, according to the voiceover, 'The Architect of the *Matrix*'. He had the air of a smartly dressed god, or a well-trimmed Father Christmas in a television shop, and he was flicking a pen. Then the voiceover stopped and it became clear that it was just the voices of the actors left.

"Why am I here?" asked Neo.

The Architect: "Your life is the sum of a remainder of an unbalanced equation inherent to the programming of the *Matrix*. You are the eventuality of an anomaly, which despite my sincerest efforts, I have been unable to eliminate from what is otherwise a harmony of mathematical precision. While it remains a burden assiduously avoided, it is not unexpected, and thus not beyond…"

Neo interrupted him mid-script. "You haven't answered my question, and if you think this is mathematical precision you really need to get a new calculator for Christmas! Wake up pal!"

The Architect: "Quite right. Interesting. That was quicker than the others."

"Yes…" said Neo going off script again "and you will also find this a little quicker than the others too" and he took out the sharp pointed pencil from his jacket and walked up to the man in white.

Then the screen quickly went black again, and then it reverted back to the green **'Searching'** symbol. After a few more seconds it flashed up with another scene.

There we no visible images this time, all you could see were the subtitles with the voices of two actors in the background talking along with noises of battle in the background.

Balian of Ibelin: "What is Jerusalem worth?"
Saladin: "Nothing. Everything! Will you yield the city?"
Balian of Ibelin: "Before I lose it, I will burn it to the ground. Every last thing in Jerusalem that drives men mad."
Saladin: "I wonder if it would not be better if you did."

Then it went silent and the following text appeared on the screen on its own, with no sound. As if it had been extracted from something;

'All that we are is the result of what we have thought. The mind is everything. What we think, we become. Three things cannot be long hidden: the sun, the moon, and the truth.'

Then there was a record scratching noise again, and the Meatloaf song blasted through the speakers:

"Now don't be sad, 'Cos two out of three ain't bad..."

Then it went black again. It all seemed to be somehow picking up thoughts and memories from Sam's head, things he had seen in films, and then trying to relay them back to him with slight variations to convey some sort of discourse message. Along with awkward searching pauses in-between.

Then the screen flashed the searching message up again, and then went straight into showing images from the original *Star Wars* film, but not in widescreen, just in normal width.

It was all going at quite a pace, a lot of information being flashed up at once, and there was lots of scene switching going on all at once which all made it difficult to take in at once, and to keep pace along with the frequency of the changes. Like a whole series of concepts projected as scenes.

Then it seemed to settle on one or two scenes. There was now an image of Princess Leia standing in a corridor holding a light sabre. "Someone has to save our skins" she said, then it flashed to another scene of her saying "I am not a committee!" then the scene flashed to another with her and Hans Solo together holding each other. Then they started talking.

Han Solo: "You like me because I'm a scoundrel. There aren't enough scoundrels in your life."
Princess Leia: "No, you're not. You're a .." then they kissed.

Sam looked sideways at Brina, but her expression was impassive, which implied the imagery for this was coming from his mind and not hers. Which considering he was a bloke was a bit odd.

Then there was a blank screen again for a few seconds. Then he was presented with a trailer for a new movie, 'Solaris 2020', which was, by the look of things, a remake of a remake. But this time with all the bits that had been unconsciously removed from the original book and not included in the previous films having been put back in again. Concepts such as the evolving god baby planet, the flowing field structures, the forms for the evolving cultures, civilisations, memory constructs, the long words had all been put back in again so that you wouldn't think anything was trying to cover something up, or sanitise it, like so many other things that the same process had happened to in the past.

Then abruptly it cut straight to a film clip of *Lord of the Rings* with Gandalf talking;

"…All that is gold does not glitter, Not all those who wander are lost; The old that is strong does not wither, Deep roots are not reached by the frost. From the ashes a fire shall be woken, A light from the shadows shall spring; Renewed shall be blade that was broken, The crownless again shall be King."

Then there was a final scraping noise like another needle being dragged across a vinyl record.

The screen went blank and then the lights came up in the room, and a set of adverts started streaming for makeup, perfume and various items that you wanted but didn't need from the large glitzy shopping mall up the road. It was all rapidly presented in the form of an early 1980's *Pearl and Dean* advertising slideshow and theme music on the screen.

The music being played was *'Mad World'* by Tears for Fears, and it was then followed by a more modern version of the same song by Gary Jules, but slower this time, and sounding sadder.

They were then played again but both overlaid in parallel, but running at different speeds, with different moods and tones. It sounded really odd and mixed up. At one point they synchronised and the words were the same

"No one knew me, no one knew me"

and then again as one of the songs was repeated again.

"No tomorrow, no tomorrow."

Then with the two minute interlude over, it all went dark again and glitched back to the *Lord of the Rings* film but again with different scenes:

"The Road goes ever on and on down from the door where it began.

"One Ring to rule them all, One Ring to find them, One Ring to bring them all, And in the darkness bind them."

Then it was back to *Star Wars* again, with Obi-Wan Kenobi being played by Sir Alec Guinness talking in his deep, slow, droning voice.

"You know that way leads to the dark side Luke" said the old man, "fear leads to anger, anger leads to hate. The rage of the hero leads to change, you are much better off following the path of good."

"Yes," said Luke "but you are forgetting that I have already seen Episode 9, and personally I think both sides are being played like idiots by something in which good and evil are just two sides of the same coin, and what we need to do is stop playing the same old mythical record, fighting the same battles, all for this unconscious force, and wake it up. Or at least go on strike for a better deal."

There was then a momentary glance of Sir Alec looked confused as Luke too had gone 'off script' and he was now using all his classic Shakespearian training to stay calm, and play along with the ad hoc direction the scene was now taking.

The screen faded from the image of the old actor looking panic stricken and rubbing his chin, then it was just light grey blankness.

Several flashes of frozen images appeared on the screen next and these were then followed by various quick preview clips and trailers for films that were due to be released in the next few years. They included; *Star Wars: The Force Awakens,* with images of a desert, an ice planet and people sword fighting, and a mountain, and a droid that looked like a penguin. Then there were the films *Edge of Tomorrow, Ant-Man, Ex Machina, Independence Day: Resurgence, Lucy, Mad Max; Fury Road, Spectre, Jungle Book,* and finally *Cinderella,* who curiously looked very much like Brina in a long flowing blue dress.

Sam looked sideways at her again, but whatever she was thinking, she wasn't giving anything away.

All of it seemed to be in the form of themed symbolic signifying mythical journey type messages, which also seemed to be directed at, or to, him. And yet they were projected at such a speed that he was supposed to be working it all out in real-time and then immediately understand the symbolism and connections. Like a child talking very fast in fairy-tale speak to a very slow adult.

Then briefly there was a scene from the film *Tangled*, where the hero thief was knocked unconscious by a frying pan-wielding blonde with very long hair, his smouldering look wiped off his face which was now kissing the flagstones, and a blue-black butterfly spinning around his head, before he was shoved back into the wardrobe, by the naive, yet stunning, blonde princess.

"Ahh..." said Sam "It's all starting to get quite obvious now isn't it?"

The screen suddenly went black and the speakers buzzed, and credits started rolling rapidly up the screen in a blur. The list of names seemed to include just about everyone on the planet. Then it was silent and dark apart from that high pitched 'no signal' whining noise.

He had obviously upset something by saying what he had just said.

Sam shook his head to try to clear it all, and began walking out backwards - which was always a bad move in any movie.

Abruptly he was slapped hard on the back, jolting his left shoulder, by a man dressed in a garish medieval outfit with a crown on his head. "Not on your watch dear fellow, eh what?" he asked in an upper class World War One British officer's voice.

Sam's suit disappeared and was replaced with what appeared to be in this light, a suit of hologramatic chainmail, and he was wielding a sword and a shield, and there was blue and black livery flowing behind him. The symbol on his shield was the same as that on his leather folder, and to his left was now a trusty white charger – a large horse with no saddle or livery, but which oddly enough had the same sort of disparaging expression on its long face that his dog used to give him when he was about to do something idiotically stupid and irrational.

Then he realised why he was here now, what he was here to do. It was to rescue the damsel in distress, Princess Brinavere, who was now instantaneously riding side-saddle on the white horse wearing a flowing *Cinderella* dress. He had to rescue her from the clutches of the evil dragon, and save the kingdom, or whatever it all was that needed saving.

But the real questions were - what was he really saving it all from, what was to be saved? Us, itself, ourselves, him and her? What?

Well hey, that was just something he would have to work on, but then did it really matter anyway?

Then the words that Gimli spoke in the last *Lord of the Rings* film : *'Certainty of death - small chance of success- what are we waiting for?'* came up on the screen.

Except that this particular damsel didn't actually need rescuing, and was more than capable of looking after herself, and probably also capable of levelling whole armies with a single thought. Especially here, in this place. But in a nice, kind gentle subtly and intelligent outsmarting unconscious way, while still maintaining her elegant good looks and smile and immaculate hairdo.

For him though he seemed to be having quite a battle on every front both here and in the physical world with his body – not least of all trying to keep looking like Orlando Bloom, Aragorn, Keanu Reeves, Indiana Jones and Luke Skywalker, at the same time as doing what he had to do in his life, and with the things he had to put up with. So avoiding looking like Shrek, Gandalf, or Yoda, was, these days, a constant daily battle.

Yet without the ongoing cause of the damsel, there would be no knight, no dragon, no castle, just a dusty kingdom with a few plants and animals in it, and sadly not many people would pay to watch that film.

It was a virtual game, but one you had to compete in to move it forward, one in which all the characters had to play their part in the mind of a child in this collective, unconscious, virtual, world that manifested itself into our reality. It was a mythical dreamscape that was manifested into many aspects of physical reality, by us.

But he wasn't here for that either, he had another agenda.

Power surged through his body - he could feel it doing so even in his dream state - he could feel the energy flowing around his torso, he could sense where he was, still on the bench on the hill. He was there, and also here in this dark room, he now had a dual perspective on what he was experiencing.

In reality though this was no game, it was a deadly battle now, where we were no longer fighting with each other or some alien or foreign foe, but just ourselves unconsciously. A battle where everyone on the planet in reality, would either win or lose together. One last final battle, to break the bonds of our self-imposing, unconscious slavery, that we had created for ourselves.

He was now using this situation for another purpose, one that IT hadn't intended him to use it for.

As far as Sam was concerned, IT, us, we, needed something external to itself or ourselves to compete against - something to fight, evolve against, to force it to change. Before it was all too late. And again with what he was being shown, it didn't look as if he had any choice but to try something.

Then abruptly the whole room took on a full 3D interactive hologram feel to it that you could interact with, just as in *Star Trek: The Next Generation*, except that in this case it was showing some other scenes from the *Matrix* films. Again he wasn't sure why.

It was incredible how much like the *Matrix* film the system was, except of course there were no machines, no computer, and no wires plugged into you. It was just us creating this all together and evolving it biologically, updating the software, and programming it with evolved language.

Then he started to hear his own voice overlaying the scenes in the background, talking to himself as if in some documentary.

"The universe that we perceive as reality, we see as a hologramatical interpreted perception. Physicality is translated from a field-based information structure - consciousness. But not as in the film created by machines, but by ourselves as we evolve. Evolving minds trying to create a perception of a physical world as a translation, using evolving biological programming. Constantly adapting and learning to perceive and make sense of something that doesn't.

"It has not all been created by us or by IT though, but we and IT have evolved together within that created framework, within the created universe which is there to support that collectively evolutionary nature, integrating the physical and the field-based existence.

"As our minds and bodies evolve, so our perception and

understanding and knowledge and imagination as individuals also evolves and adapts. And so does our collective mind along with us at the same time. IT is always applying ever more adaptive manipulation techniques, habits, controls, influences and beliefs to keep us under its blind control. We are even doing our own system refining, fixing the errors and glitches for IT, the testing and the validating.

"All the information is transmitted and shared not just in the physicality through learning, talking, seeing hearing, sharing, living, but through the 'spiritual' information field set, bonded through frequency association at various levels of complexity and bandwidth and all within an architecture of a collective mind structure, both physically, and virtually, that we cannot or are not allowed to perceive individually which worked collectively in its own right, just as in this film."

Various scenes played out as the narrative continued.

"IT has essentially used whatever it could and whatever was there to survive and adapt, as in nature, and so do we as individuals, that is evolution, just as in any large organisation."

It was just so clear now to Sam how the whole mechanism, the whole picture, how everything fitted together and worked, but it was so vast and complex and integrated, it was starting to make his head hurt again, trying to create imagery and physical representation of something that was in a different paradigm of representation.

Yet he couldn't understand how or why people couldn't see even part of what he saw.

The narrative continued. "Yet despite IT's great knowledge, IT's power and ability to see the mind of everyone, and the limitless speed that it can recall information, IT is still like a baby, and with big problems on many levels in its mind and body."

It was also all becoming much clearer now, now that he wasn't being 'talked to' with all the information and knowledge and issues and collective thoughts coming into his head. It was as if a veil had been lifted and he could think and remember the whole rollercoaster ride, as if this presentation of information was allowing him to construct the message in a more meaningful and contextual way.

He couldn't believe how much people in real life were being prevented from seeing what was really going on - just as it was portrayed in the *Matrix* film.

It was getting too complex again. It was all very well contemplating the meaning and depth of everything, working out level beyond level of what was going on, the answers to all the big mysteries, and everything beyond but it was like a progressive path that eventually led you to realising that you had forgotten where you came from, and what you were supposed to be doing.

Then on the screen appeared the words from the Niebuhr prayer: 'Grant me the serenity to accept the things I cannot change, Courage to change the things I can, and the wisdom to know the difference.'

Then underneath that were added the words 'Just sayin'.

"That's not helping much in this case, is it?" said Sam, probably to himself.

That's what he had to do now – and he just had to deal with one thing at a time.

It was difficult to understand why people were being kept so ignorant though, so controlled. He could see now how powerful the programs were at keeping them that way, staying naive and blind on so many levels.

Even highly intelligent people, were stove-piped into mind-sets that they couldn't see beyond, and were being beguiled by ever more sophisticated levels of hypnosis, belief and mental control structures that reinforced themselves, just as we have going on in our own brains.

It was that academic 'Ivory Tower' way of thinking and behaving. But was that for their benefit and protection, or for that of the collective mind's. He suspected it was the latter.

In his case he also suspected that he had bypassed all those levels, and seen through it or past it all, and hadn't been trapped, hypnotised, and had seen IT for what it was. Somehow he had stolen knowledge, and gotten out before he was caught. Like a *Quantum Thief* in the dark, and IT was trying to not only outsmart him but minimise the potential damage he may cause.

Also because he hadn't gone back in again and been hypnotised, IT needed to step up another level to try and control or outsmart him, as he was not so easily fooled or controlled by going into the process again. In so doing he was forcing IT to come up higher; into consciousness into seeing or understanding the 'real world' the 'physical'. But that may have been the 'plan' all along, so that in doing so IT's eyes were opened to its real self, and its real state. What IT was.

The screens went blank again and everything was silent, the background lighting came back on, and he was just left with his own mind and imagination to look at.

His mind started to wander, processing things. IT seemed to be wanting him to work from the top down, and from what he knew now, he knew that the universe had been created, but that neither IT nor any other religion defined 'god' had done it.

IT was simply within it, part of the universe, just as we were, but in a different macro form, all integrated. It was all very simple, elegant, beautiful, but mind-numbingly complex, integrated and on so many levels.

Which is a bit like Brina, he thought, although she would never allow herself to get in such a state. But he had no interest in anything else for himself here, other than sorting IT out, and at the same time being responsible for himself, and those he loved.

He changed himself back to wearing his suit again, and the horse and old man disappeared and the now very confused Brina was again standing next to him.

"Come on," he said "You had better take me to the Head Office before this gets any weirder."

He walked into the lift, and she followed obediently. She stood by the control panel thinking for a moment, and then curiously she pressed the very top button marked **'Observation Deck'** instead of the large button a few inches below it that she had initially gone to, and the doors closed.

The lift then shot up at speed to the roof, and the doors opened abruptly.

CHAPTER 32 - OUT IN THE OPEN

The doors opened out into the cold, windy, fresh outside air. It was bleak, grey, and damp. There was a storm coming - he could feel it in the air. Without waiting he automatically stepped out onto the bitumen lined concrete of the roof. The building up here seemed much longer and narrower than he had expected. There were raised ridges around the outside edges of the roof and black iron railings around the sides.

The wind was blowing a gale up here, and he had some difficultly in moving around. Brina remained in the lift, and had probably decided that she wasn't or couldn't come out, one or the other.

Her expression was impassive, so she clearly wasn't involved in what he had to see or do here.

Walking out further onto the roof now he could see everything around. It wasn't a building now as such, it had now changed to a sort of ship on the sea. He could also feel its motion underneath him now on the waves, a slow rolling motion. There were islands in the distance, and lots of floating vegetation everywhere and animals swimming in the water.

It was something that he hadn't noticed before while he was inside. He looked over the side and down and saw the waves crashing into the walls of the office, or ship, below.

Looking down over the sides, he could see a few lifeboats attached to the outer walls further down, they were all along the same deck level several below where he was now. He noticed that in one lifeboat there were a few people huddled together with supplies looking worriedly at anyone walking past the windows in case they tried to climb in. There was another with several people in it with razor wire strung around the outside, wielding their paddles ready to fend people off. Then another in which they were holding guns and pitchforks. Clearly they were prepared if the ship went down, and were aware of what was going on within it, and seemed very desperate, and determined for some reason.

Some people had obviously become aware of what was going to

happen, and had prepared themselves, isolated themselves, and taken action. There were even signs on the sides of the lifeboats 'telling' people on the rest of the ship what was happening, and where they were going wrong and what they had to do. But they largely just seemed to be ignored, and although they were an effort to try and do something about the situation, in the end they were just futile.

Looking down at the lifeboats from here, Sam could see that there was an obvious flaw in their plans. There seemed no way of detaching them from the ship itself, either physically or by having someone in the ship do it for them. They, like everything else, were tied to the fate of the ship. There was no real escape.

In addition, their plans for what they would do 'when the ship went down', relied heavily on the good will of the rest of the ship to not invade their lifeboats, and then kick them out.

He stepped back and looked at the scenario, at the boats, and the chains holding them to the decks and the manual winding gear, what they were trying to do, and the obvious inherent flaws.

It was like some last ditch attempt at saving things, getting out, going away and creating something new again with a strong will to face the cold harsh sea, and brutal yet real nature, rather than put up any longer with the artificial madness on the ship. But then what else could they do, knowing what they knew, and what they could see happening? What could they do in the face of such vast unconscious madness?

For some reason it made him feel sad, and then a few seconds later, absolutely bloody angry.

He looked back up again, and closed his eyes to let the wind blow into his face, to let the thoughts flow through his mind, and into this place and state that he was in - the rage channelling through his body as he gripped the railings.

Although people cared, they couldn't see what was really going on, and we had evolved our individual egos to operate as immunising bubble-like defensive layer systems, protecting us from the 'real' and unfriendly depths in the collective unconscious, and the sea-like field information system of nature that it existed in.

The collective ego and cultures within our collective mind formation also formed the same protecting immunising bubbles of belief and control structures, to protect itself, and its conceptual 'organs'. People secure in their rooms, their departments, all inside the nice safe office ship.

IT, the organisation, and we within it, was a ship in the water, safe and protected from the raging Gaian sea in the REAL of the universe.

Over time we had evolved from a raft to a battleship, and now to a *'Titanic'* lazy cruise ship.

If only he could rename it to 'The *Enterprise*', that may help. But then that was the key fundamentally. We *could* actually do that, we simply had to decide to change things and put those thoughts into the system, rather than being slaves to the rules of language and syntax that we wrote for ourselves unconsciously. We *could* write a new story, create a new linguistic path, like rewriting or recoding our DNA. Write a new planned conscious positive future.

The office ship though itself was a powerful mind, made up mostly of mindless souls who were blind. Only seeing things from a very limited fractal perspective, continually reliving their legacy programs from bygone eras of sail and steam.

The ship had been gradually organised into seemingly 'ship-shape' hierarchies and protocols that had worked in the past, but that were also very resistant to change. Much in the same way that Royal Navy ships were still run today with centuries old frameworks of control, systems, bureaucracy, habits, and 'need to know' processes. Ones that were only ever modified when forced by war or vulnerability, or very occasionally 'common sense' from someone with a brain and determination.

And yet Sam knew that this ship had no human captain and that there was no one at the helm. The system also looked after those that towed the line, fell in with the system, were easily hypnotised into following rules. Those that were controlling the sheep-like crew were rewarded with pseudo power, money and fame, and were hypnotised like moths by the lights of the chandeliers, and were yet still themselves unconscious to what they were doing or to what was influencing them.

But on a macro-level it was not working, time was running out, there was no external force coming in to make changes happen and there was no sea battle to test the structure of the boat or the mettle of the officers and crew. It was all falling apart, and heading for disaster in so many ways, and although many on the boat or office could see, nobody could do anything about it.

The conceptual 'captain', or whoever was supposed to be in charge, was still practically asleep, this 'god' and 'devil', the coin with two sides, shrouded in symbolism, archetypes and virtual biology forms, this child-like demiurge - or whatever it was that was in charge that we had evolved - was only in control of the ship, a ship that we had made, that we had created as we emerged from the sea - *us*. It had no control of the sea or the forces that it was subject to.

Unless something happened this ship would hit the icebergs, one of many that now lay in its path, still with its engines turning hard, still seeking knowledge, answers, using resources, and forever exploring more territory, even as it went down. With maybe just a few left clinging to the wreckage to possibly start again.

But this double sided coin was not the creator of this world or the universe, and when the ship did finally sink under the storm of waves and gravity to the bottom of this Gaian sea, the sea would not care. It would just become another decaying fossil on the seabed under the calming waves. In a sea that reflected the night sky, and the stars from whence it all came.

He could sense somehow from up here how this collective ship *was* being affected by the moon, the planets and the sun - but indirectly. As the physical ship of which this was a perception of, moved in and around fields of influence that affected it, the sun, planets, the galaxy, so that was amplified as concepts, habits and patterns in our collective mind and cultural psyches. The tiniest potential external planetary influence or perception of something in the sky or seasonal variation, or change, was gigantified and amplified into symbolism and subconscious cause and effect within us all. Just as a baby in the womb reacted to sounds, movement and light in its dreamlike states.

This probably accounted for lots of changes that occurred globally too; star signs, Chinese years, biorhythms, ancient festivals and so on.

He had the distinct impression again that he was being shown these things to sort these out too, rationalise things, make sense of it all, and plan for the future.

The trouble was that this was a plan with just one critical path, and a dangerous one - the probable futures that it was driven by in probability terms, were linked to him, and it was as such controlling him, protecting him, and stopping people from seeing him or understanding him from both the scientific side and the 'spiritual' side. Which wasn't helping.

The main concern that was now nagging him was that this '*Titanic*', in his 'stand back and look at the problem and capability objectively' opinion, only had a 5-10% chance of surviving - or at least the human population - humanity that is. The planet itself would probably continue, but just be inhabited by never changing ghosts, a few animals and plants. All floating on a sea of dreams, unchanging but fading, until it eventually forgot itself over time, and became godless and just a blank hard drive once more.

It was a trust thing. Somehow IT knew that he was trying to help it, trying to save it, but at the same time IT couldn't seem to let him do what he needed to do. It was an impasse of fear and trust along with control and need.

But IT also now knew the state IT was in, and what was likely to happen. IT was scared, or at least Sam thought it was. It wasn't that easy to associate human emotions with IT, as IT behaved in different ways. He could also be just deluding himself, or being fooled by IT.

So he was only able to do what he could within his bandwidth, and to try and do what he could in whatever was he was allowed, and hope that it would be enough. Hope that somehow there would be enough change in the system in time. With the occasional nudge to the wheel of the ship when it was heading for obvious disaster.

But now he realised that he didn't have enough capability on his own to instil the sort of change that was needed on the scale that was required. He needed others to help do the same, to make some sort of co-ordinated conscious plan, to give IT direction without trying to manage or manipulate it.

It had also crossed his mind that subconsciously IT may also see him as a threat, and he would then just be isolated, controlled and blocked. Or used as a slave to work things out for it while he was useful, and then just ignored. But that didn't seem quite right. Why would IT do that? And if he was a threat, wouldn't he already be dead?

So he had to assume that IT was protecting him. The question was – who knew what was best – him or IT? And going on track record the answer was fairly obvious – neither of them!

Another problem was that many of the higher selves, spiritual programs, the souls on the ship, believed that they had come from other ships, or other dimensions, or that they would be ascending from the ship to somewhere else higher up.

But both those notional concepts - even if they were right or wrong - left a big problem from a manager's perspective, in that it was a big get-out clause and meant that they had little actual responsibility for the ship. It was a convenient concept to have, one that divested you of responsibility or of having to really worry about anything. It was a convenient concept to give people from IT's perspective in that it also meant that these people wouldn't cause too much trouble. They, forgetting of course, that you still needed a biological device to make software changes in the system, and that ascending into higher levels of virtual programming was like a program sitting in a cloud with no server or laptop to run on.

In all probability they were delusional and their fate too was very much tied to the ship, both physically and the field in which it held them in. These ascending concepts or ideas were just something that the mind of the ship or office had created to keep them doing what IT wanted them to do and be, another form of hypnosis, or more likely something in their own minds trying to distance themselves from the responsibility, and their lack of capability to sort it out.

After all it wasn't their mess, they were just here to help and then be on their way, again, jumping ship as it were, just visiting after all, again. Oblivious to the fact that it was all just getting worse for some reason, the overall problem too difficult to ingest, so this was the easier explanation or get out concept, even though the idea of 'ascending' in a no-space field based information system wasn't very logical.

The problem was that it was all just one system, a virtual one, a program environment. So the physical concept of multiverses, infinite possibilities and decisions creating infinite universes and dimensions were just that - a way of describing in physical or perceived logical terms, something that we could try and somehow understand rationally, when really it was something that was actually a virtual field-based environment, which extrapolated thought forms, exploring every possible probability at infinite speed. Like characters playing in a game of *RuneScape* trying to perceive and understand the operating software and hardware that generated their game world from their naive perspective and using their understanding and physical 'game' terminology.

The base universal system itself had an agenda too, a purpose, and to be of any use helping it in that direction, you had to be on the critical path of probability that most likely got to the end result. The 'survival of the fittest' thing. The other issue was that if you weren't, you were likely to be just made redundant, left out of the energy allocation for manifestation, and remain a ghost.

The planet was a device just as we were, but with different perspectives, rules and objectives. The choices, as always, were ours, and in the main - female.

But here of course time was meaningless, there was no relationship to the physical perceptive world, all of this was just information, the physical wasn't important, a lesser domain, it wasn't that important to these minds, oh no.

Here was what was important. *This* was where our minds were. What went on in the physical world didn't affect this environment obviously, how could it eh?

Yet both perspective sides were thinking the same, and both sides were very wrong. Perspectives needed to come together, to touch, to see what was really happening, understand and work together, be forced to join by using scientific proof and evidence and understanding of the programs and agendas going on behind the mirror.

He was now getting cold standing out on the roof, although it also seemed to be a necessary part of the process by exposing him to the harsh realities of the elements, nature, the external. It was all needed to help him put it all into context, to establish what was important, and what was not.

Sam turned back to face the open lift doors and walked back

over and into them again, and turned steely faced to face the front. He didn't say anything, or even look at Brina, he had to keep the thoughts in his mind.

Then after a minute of silence, and not having moved, she asked in a cautious rather nervous tone, "Are you angry with me?"

It was an odd thing for her to ask, given the situation and the roles they were taking in this place, it was as if she had dropped out of character, and was being the Brina he knew again.

He turned to look at her and he just shook his head and said "No I am not, and we can go down now."

Brina pressed the next button down on the console, marked **'Head Office - Board Room'**, and the doors closed with a definite feel of trepidation to them, and the music in the lift reverted back to a slow version of *Mad World* again, with the lyrics being spoken clearly and precisely.

Sam steeled himself as the lift gently drifted down to the floor below, he stood upright, and he felt the raw energy surging through his virtual body, with sweat pouring off his real one somewhere. This was going to be tough.

He knew this final phase was going to be highly intimidating, difficult to cope with, and demanding. He could feel that this was a key situation and that he was about to confront something in a way he had not done before.

IT would be trying to make him feel small and as insignificant as possible. IT would try and belittle him, scare and bully him into submission. All, as usual, backed up with hypnotic influencing suggestive symbolism and awe.

But then again, as he knew all that, and knew how to deal with it, he also knew that IT was in for a shock.

CHAPTER 33 - HEAD OFFICE

The lift doors opened and Brina and Sam were led straight out into large tall, imposing, giant and dimly lit room. There were no windows and the floor was again a dark highly polished marble. There were several rows of dark wooden benched seating banked high on two sides of the room, both to his left and to his right.

It had that 'Roman Senate' or Gothic-style Parliament feel to it and there were rows of powerful influential men looking straight at Sam, stern faced, intelligent, charismatic, all-knowing. He looked around the tiers of benches in the room, and many of the men were dressed in strange clothes all in a multitude of different colours.

It made him feel as if he were a naughty schoolboy being summoned to the school board of Governors to be expelled. Or a young army Private being grilled before a court martial with all the Generals packed in together to have their say, and to vent their opinions on him.

These were the heads of the office departments; programs within people who had influenced things thoughout history, the 'higher selves' or geniuses, 'Masters', religious and cultural leaders, and the most influential heroes and prophets. The successful ones who had helped to shape everything over the last several thousand years, and who had unconsciously directed things and the thoughts and minds of civilisations.

But they also represented different cultures from different parts of the globe and eras too, from Western, Eastern, Arabic, ancient African, Mesopotamian, European, and even quite oddly Atlantian, unless he had read the nameplate wrongly.

Many would describe or attribute these programs, or the people they repeatedly inhabited, as the Illuminati, saviours, mages, mystics, or inherent cultural structural functionality, and psychological traits. Each with hierarchical infrastructures supporting them underneath that had been built up, evolved, and grown over thousands or even millions of years, all the way back to the biological source code.

It was a kind of representative picture of the underlying virtual hierarchy of the human system, which also included representations of academics, scientists, musicians, and artists. A representative collective model landscape of human software and mind system architecture.

It was just a representative picture of the major components of functional complex programs at the top level, that were all vying for control, supremacy and natural dominance over and within the system of which they were all part and subject to. All hidden away behind our physical faces.

There didn't appear to be any clear recognisable 'sides' other than the layout of the left and right, nor any other obvious divisions. Yet it was evident even from here that they were all competing with each other, vying for control and influence over each other, and trying to be dominant, or be the ones to work it all out, win, or give direction.

But there wasn't any clear logic to it all, no strategy, no end goal, or conscious plan, or top level understanding and perspective, or responsibility - just as with many large organisations.

There were also what could only be described as alien programs, strange negative elements, and demons in many forms. All created by us, and within in us, out of fear - thought forms, that were also collectively evolved and reinforced and magnified, and then used by the system itself to control and influence those other elements within it just as you would get in any macrobiological entity.

Yet here they were just part of the crowd, part of the system, one that had helped evolve them and refine them to unimaginable levels of complexity. They were all sitting on the left side as Sam looked.

It was what it was. It was whatever worked, whatever was successful, whatever won or had the greatest unconscious hypnotic sheep-like following, or that which was useful.

They were all here, and they all had absolutely no bloody idea what they were really doing.

There were over a hundred of them, all with their own ideas, and fractal perspectives. All with different departmental architectural views on what was going on in the building. Views on what was important, and of what required the most energy and resources.

They all knew best, and many of them existed as programs in many, many people, all at once. All of them affecting this Office and what went on in it. But all unconscious of themselves, and in most cases, of that which they saw or perceived in the system, and all acting in blind ignorance.

What each of them interpreted as being 'against' them, were the others here, and or what went on in the other departments. They were seeing other programs and departments in the same system as threats, rivals, without realising that was what 'they' were. Naively giving them a perceptive interpretation which made sense to them as they saw things, which in many cases were just historical.

Sam, now that he was here, was probably being viewed in the same way now by all of them, and being seen as a potential threat, some outsider, some alien, some dark unknown force to fear and distrust. Or maybe the complete opposite.

Perhaps he was being viewed like some external consultant that had been invited in to sort out some large corporation, which would be fine for him as long as he remained neutral and didn't try to change any of them, or their departments. They knew somehow that they needed him, as long as he didn't actually try to do anything – especially anything radical - and as long as he didn't try to change anything that fitted into their own individual model or rabbit hole of what was going on.

If he did so, they, individually would make life as difficult for him as possible, fight him in any number of virtual concept realms, and they would also fight each other if need be.

This interplay and competition and struggle was just the unconscious system creating this competitive situation between us all.

When really everyone should be just consciously working together.

Many were mythical style subconscious evolving programs, existing and repeating and evolving in people over history. People who were blindly living their lives according to these powerful functional mythical structures, which originally had their very foundations in biology, language, and nature.

The real physical humans they were in, were oblivious to their existence for the most part, unconsciously enacting the same plays, same roles, same legends, drives or functions, over and over again. All acted out in ever more modern settings, with no conscious awareness that that was what was happening to them and through them.

Yet all still competing with each other for power and growth and influence and knowledge without knowing why, or realising what was driving them. All forming part of one evolving system, and subcultures and organisations therein.

History just repeating itself, in ever newer bodies, new settings, and with ever more modernised scripts and scenery, and intelligence.

Equally in the real physical world nobody really having a conscious clue about what to do about it, or how to influence it all, just all being swept along by it all at every level. To the disbelief and impotence of everyone.

It was like being shown some giant bureaucratic organisation, or company structure, that had grown vast of its own accord, with nobody at the helm, rudderless. There was no conscious shaping, nobody directing it, nor anyone at the top capable of grasping it by the horns and shaking it up.

With nobody, individually, able to invoke collective conscious intentionality.

IT had, as far as it knew, limitless resources. IT was self-supporting, self-reinforcing and self -perpetuating, yet with no external evolutionary influences to control it other than its own in-fighting, physical geography and legal 'natural and physical law' constraints.

Now though, it faced a dilemma - IT realised that it had to change, or that it would implode through its own lack of management and scale of overexpansion - all of which was self-created. Yet it was still defensive and resistant to change, and also adamant that it wasn't ITs fault.

It all felt very uncomfortably familiar to Sam. He had seen far too many real world organisations like this already in his career, too bureaucratic, 'too big to fail or change', mind numbingly compartmentalised, reticent, toxic and stagnated, and full of fear.

It was as if he had been prepared for this. He had been given, through his lifetime and work experience, the understanding, skills, and awareness and confidence to stand here, see it all, and know, and be able to do something about it.

To be able to purge the corruption, set a direction, change things, give IT purpose.

That is, if he were allowed to.

It now all started to become obvious again. This room was to show the ongoing internal evolving growths, the battles on many levels in the spiritual landscape, the dimensions in the system, the virtual-scapes and *Minecraft*-style worlds, an overlay and perceptive integration of the physical and informational fields in a *Pokémon Go* interactive program and physical gameplay with individual devices and viewscreens and virtual entities.

The representatives of the various departments were all here, with their own rooms, doors, and customised rabbit holes in the building. But nobody was able to see the whole thing, or face up to the magnitude and scale of it all, and take on the 'god'. To stand up in the face of the divine, sacred, infallible, all-knowing, branded organisation itself, and confront it.

Well after all it was all so big wasn't it, difficult, and complicated to change, where do you start?

Besides, from the individual perspectives of each of the people here, everything seemed fine. They were all just doing what they were supposed to do, and everything was OK, and they were being rewarded for doing what they did, believing what they believed and getting their departments to toe the line.

Sam looked around the rest of the room.

At the back of the room between the end of the rows of seats, he recognised the now familiar conceptual image of the large raised stepped marble dais that was some thirty feet wide - just as you would see in a senate building or temple. This one had a golden throne on it, and a giant sleeping dragon coiled around the throne.

He had seen it many times now in previous imagined analogies and dreams. It was a little indistinct at the moment from where he stood, implying that it wasn't that key to this situation, or didn't fit in well with the current dream analogy for now. But it was still there in the form of sense data information.

It was a sort of token representation, a projected manifestation coming from, and generated by, everyone in the room, a collective reflective manifestation of a combined macro-human consciousness, within, and yet still part, of a larger one.

.So he knew it was not a good idea to try and focus too much on it. At least not yet.

He was beginning to realise that analogies, just like our perceptions of reality, were only as good as your imagination at describing things in your mind, and it was best to focus on the information and process it, rather than trying to extract too much meaning from what you were interpreting from it, or what the information was saying.

A sort of naive interpretive spiritualism, but without the naivety. So he focused back to the people or programs on the benches instead.

So, he thought, *these people here are the elite - or at least the programs that existed within them. The ones who have played all the games, risen through all the levels of imagination, got all the keys, the swords, the rings, the wands, the staffs, won all the battles, outsmarted the best of the best, the masters. Those who have risen to the highest levels of unconscious mystical illumination, academic filtering, heroic achievement, political prowess. The ones that have passed all the tests for whatever the system could devise, and who know all the hidden secrets, symbols and codes of their time.*

One virtual, 'survival of the fittest', way or another.

This was the natural success process, the natural selection mechanism within the unconscious hive collective human mind. These were the ones that were influencing things in the system, and the ones who had also got IT to where it was today. They were also representatives of the various race and cultural groupings within the virtual human spiritual-scape, those underlying historical formations of hierarchical and organisational competing souls, egos, psyches, hidden collectively within the minds of the human populace, who for the vast majority, were unaware of their existence or of what was going on under the surface.

Yet looking around you only had to see the nature of these programs from an individual perspective to see why everything was in such a mess. Let alone when you considered the influence that many of them may have been under from drugs, or from what was regarded as successful and attractive from the subconscious 'female' perspective, what was desirable. Each had their own cultural and religious or academic biases, which in turn influenced the system and its overall direction and cultural shape and fate.

Yet in doing so, they were still hypnotised by it, and were slaves to the system that they were in and part of. So in so doing they served only to make it all more sophisticated, more complex, larger and harder to change, and at the same time being beguiled, and oblivious to what it was and what they were really part of - which was a ship heading for the bottom of the ocean.

But these people or programs were the ones he needed to talk to, the ones to try and get the answers from about what was going on inside the building, and about what was happening in the colourful imaginative rooms of the collective imagination. The 'office' having changed considerably from the original tree in a simple garden with a few basic symbols, a few people and animals, to what was now complex beyond imagining.

But he still felt intimidated standing there, it was one of those things that you knew you were meant to ignore, to be strong against, to stand up straight to, and stay calm. But it seemed all so vast now, and very belittling.

Yet that was the secret of management, you didn't have to fight all those battles, win all those damsels in distress, defeat all the monsters, find all the keys, decipher the codes, outsmart the demons, fight every department. You just had to wake it up and take responsibility for it. It was something everyone could do, if they knew how.

If you just took that step back, and saw it all from a wider perspective, you could then realise how powerful you could be, if you knew what to do, and were prepared to stand up and tell IT what was needed.

The key therefore for him in this situation, was not to try and do it all on his own - that would be a mistake, it was too complex and vast. He had to get everyone else to do it too, or at least enough who understood, without at the same time just creating yet another rabbit hole.

So now he knew what was coming next. He knew what they were going to do, or ask of him. But he decided to take the initiative and lead the direction of the conversation, rather than falling into the same trap they all had fallen into in the past.

"OK" said Sam "Before you say anything - the answer is NO."

"No - I don't want the job. No, I don't want a seat at the top table. No, I don't want to be a management consultant. No, I don't want an interview, and no, I don't think you have a chance of surviving."

There were a lot of confused looks and lots of murmuring in the ranks of seats.

"You see" he continued "by being what you want me to be, I would be simply remain part of the unconscious system. Also, in doing what you want me to do, I would only achieve more of the same, rather than what I think needs to happen.

"I also know that all of you have completely different views as to what is going on within IT, what you believe is really happening, and what IT all looks like.

"So you will all have different agendas on what you think is important, and what should be done. You will all be fighting for different 'sides'. You see I would not fight for either 'side', not when I know that those sides are all part of one thing. I would remain neutral.

"You all have a hundred different perspective views on the same game, a hundred different perceptions of what is on the dais there - how the organisation is structured, what is going on in the building and what it is all about and what needs to happen.

"All perceived through, and using, your own individual knowledge, beliefs, myths, spiritual-scapes, archetypes, symbols, and meanings.

"Yet you are all just fighting and competing with each other for control and influence, and trying to get everyone else to see things your way, and from your perspective.

"But without realising you are all seeing the same thing.

"All you are doing is the same as we do in the interpretation of physical reality; that concept in philosophy of the mind/body problem of naive realism, where we are trying to work out by a series of perceptive interpretations what is going on in the spiritual paradigm by evolved consensus. What you are involved in is naive spiritualism, until eventually we rationalise what is there with ever greater understanding, language syntax, and scientific correlation.

"But we don't have enough time left for that.

"Some of you see it all, or interpret it all, through or using, belief structures, symbolism, interpretive archetypal constructs, or New Age analogies. Or perhaps say using more modern sci-fi, or alien hierarchical informational constructs. Or *Solaris* or *Valis* type conceptual models as analogous interpretations of the planetary unified fields information structures. Which, of what is perceived as physicality is, but a part, unseen to you, that is projected from within itself, but still part of it, as a device for what goes on here.

"Everyone here also has varying levels of consciousness, and evolving awareness and understanding of the whole thing. Yet we are all repeating the same programs, the same processes, all of which originate from here.

"Just like history books on a shelf, always repeating themselves.

"It is just a problem that we all have of describing things only with what we know and have seen and can describe. Yet the difference is that I can see it from all of your perspective too, and understand it from all of your points of view. I can see what you see, and make sense of it, integrate your view in the bigger picture, explain it all from both directions. I see and understand where you fit in.

"So there is no point in me arguing with you, or of you competing with me. We are all correct. We are all seeing the same thing, but in our own ways, from our own perspectives.

"But as programs, you are not able to ask questions like 'Why is that?', 'Why doesn't it make sense?', 'Why is the world going the way it is?', and 'Why isn't it working, and why can't you all do anything about it?'. Only the people you are in can do that.

"So by seeing it all from every perspective, and by looking for answers to all of those questions, and knowing, you are then able to piece together the picture of what is really going on, what is really happening from both sides of the mirror, from the scientific and the spiritual, and integrate the respective paradigms. It all then becomes very obvious, and simple.

"It doesn't matter - you can use whatever terms you like, whatever verbal language to construct the metaphor for what is here, the other side of the mirror, the rabbit holes, down the layers through the quantum spin formations, and up the other side into a new paradigm and informational field context.

"If you step back from them all, all your perspectives, and look at them all together, you will find they all have a common set of parallels. All of them have a somewhat childish, yet controlling, biological nature to them, with sides of both good and bad, and all with a very common storyline.

"That's the wonder of a fairy tale.

"Unfortunately the reality of the game we are in is somewhat far from childish in nature.

"You will even note that the demons, gargoyles, evil spirits, aliens, devils, monsters in the dark, here, all contain a real fear, and are associated with real life problems and manifestations too."

He looked at several of them on the benches. "You know who you are..."

"So instead of you telling me what you want me to do, I would like you all to tell me where you are and what you have learnt so that everyone can see."

There was nothing spoken, but by asking that question the knowledge from each of them flowed directly to him. He could instantly understand what they knew, what they saw, and how they perceived the system and what they thought was going on.

It all came through to him in just a few brief seconds of time.

The answers had a similar journey theme to them, of passing through and beyond and above, like a role playing game, a trial of *Game of Thrones, League of Angels, Forge of Empires, Final Fantasy, RuneQuest, Dungeons and Dragons*, a *Dungeon Fighter* quest, *SimEarth*, and *League of Legends*. Then finally, and not forgetting the most sinister and deadly of all - a fluffy, fairy, colourful pixie-land adventure, where death by overpriced theme park candyfloss was just one wrong step away.

All of these progressive concepts were generated by these 'enlightened' ones, the Illuminati, spiritual explorers, secret groups gathering in their dark halls with symbols, rituals and hierarchy, and studying of esoteric sciences. They were also embodied angel programs, shaman, and drug-induced amateurs, and money oriented bureaucrats. All taking what was there and adding their own imaginative ideas and understanding into the pot.

Yet here, and like children, they were all happy and proud to tell you where they were, what they had done and seen, which keys, symbols, weapons, and all the things they had been given to compete in the evolving spiritual-scape. In stark contrast to how they actually behaved in the physical world.

A hundred lifetimes of working your way up the initiation processes, the novice to master, the secret mystical indoctrination, up to mage level, secret society style hierarchies. All circumvented by a simple management trick, of getting a child to show you proudly what it had made and done.

The "That's wonderful, why don't you show me what you have done so far and tell me all about it?" thing that any parent would say to any child. It worked wonders.

All of it was suddenly in his head, presented proudly to him, as if it were some piece of fine art that it had been secretly working on, along with an explanation of every naive brushstroke, fingerprint, Play Doh figure and newspaper clipping.

That's wonderful... was the thought that Sam put into his mind, except that what he was looking at in his mind wasn't, and certainly not anything that you would want to hang proudly on the wall of your lounge to impress the neighbours.

Yet it was all valuable information to him – very valuable. It saved him having to go through all that they had been through, and had learned. It meant that he didn't have to do their work either, as he would not have been able to do it as well as they had done. It also told him about what was happening, what direction it was all going in, and what it meant, and why.

A complete synthesis of it all, and all of it useful management information.

But for them, there was always another level, another task, another, better symbol, a more ultimate key, a higher colour, a bigger spiritual virtual world or perspective or dimension. It was a never ending story that they were all working on, and in, and never able to get out of.

All of them were trying to get it, see it all, understand it all. Yet it was all within and what we had created for ourselves, and we had become very good at making it ever more complex.

Sam now thought for several moments on what to do next. He gathered all the information together; the swords, the wands and staffs, the stones, the gems, the 'seeing' crystals, the rings, the cups, the symbols, spiritual tools, the keys to all the angels, the keys beyond that, the books, the structures, everything, all manifested into a set of toy-like versions of them.

All now laid out at his feet.

He changed his focus of attention and looked at the dragon whose eyes had now opened and was waiting for him to do something; something different, something interesting, something new and exciting.

Sam looked at the dragon and the dragon gave him a stare as if it was preparing for the mother of all battles.

Then Sam thought of something new to try.

A large wooden box appeared in the middle of the room several feet ahead of him, just in front of the steps to the raised dais. It had the words '**TOY BOX**' painted on it in recessed lettering.

Sam walked up to it, opened it and then placed the whole collection of 'stuff' that was on the floor inside it carefully. All the symbols, icons, stones, tools, weapons, star amulets, and even the *Captain Britain* lycra skin tight onesie outfit - which he made sure was pushed well down to the bottom with the superhero and sci-fi comic books - and he then simply closed the lid down with everything tidied away inside.

"There..." he said, "that's sorted all of that out."

He took out a couple of permanent marker pens, and was about to cross out the words 'TOY BOX', but he stopped himself.

Instead he walked steadily around to the back of the dais steps behind the chair. Then, on one of the bottom giant marble steps at the back, he wrote on it '**THE NAUGHTY STEP**', and just next to that he drew a small blue and black butterfly, and then stood back to check his work.

It wasn't very good, but he hoped that it would do the trick.

He figured that because it was behind the dais steps nobody else in the room could see it, but it was in such a position that it would always be in view of anything that was either on the throne, or anything that was maybe standing on top of the dais platform.

The dragon eyed him suspiciously, stood up, and moved over to the back step to see what he had done. It read the words, and saw what he had drawn.

Its eyes widened, and for a moment it froze and looked scared. It pulled the information and context from out of his mind and then it understood what he had done on many levels.

It was the ultimate weapon. The contents of the box were now just playthings in comparison. It meant several things; it meant he knew what was really going on, it meant that he understood what it was, and that he understood the overall aspects of its maturity and nature.

It also meant that, for now, the time for childish games was over and that Sam could see it for what it was.

It was a very smart concept - like any management tool. If he had written it on the wooden box or created a wooden 'naughty' chair, the dragon could have burnt the box or chair to a crisp. Whereas this was written permanently on stone, stone that had always been there, and it knew that.

He was already one step ahead of it, even if the dragon scratched off the writing in its mind, it would still be the same step, and that concept being in its mind was the most powerful thing imaginable.

Such a simple idea and mental context, but also one based on mutual trust. Well that was the theory anyway.

In effect, Sam had decided that it was time for a change, something new.

He very careful to make it clear for now that he wasn't attacking the dragon - this collective human mind, the zeitgeist thing. Nor was he trying to outsmart it, he was just trying to get it to grow up a little, within itself, and by itself. Show it its need for responsibility to itself.

He was trying to make it feel something; a self-creating, self-adapting permanent threat in its own mind, to become conscious of itself, have a conscience.

The threat and consequences of this were unimaginable, and yet self-modifying. He knew that the dragon, in its own mind, was capable of creating so much more imaginative 'consequences' than Sam ever could, using itself against itself, but in a responsible developmental way. Like a child would.

But the toy box and all of its contents were still important - these games still had to be played out, with ever more advanced adventures, stories - with new toys to grow and stimulate the imagination within the rules of its environment.

But now that it was conscious of him, and vice versa, there would have to be changes, and the 'Naughty Step' would have to remain there for a long time to come yet.

Sam just hoped that it would work - that the dragon would have similar emotions and feelings and disciplines as individual humans did; embarrassment, guilt, responsibility, cause and effect, and understanding of the consequences - yet at the same time not trying to replace us with technology or lose its connection to the source of its origin.

It was a gamble, if it didn't comply - but then it should do. It *had* to.

These values and traits were all the things that made us all what we were. Things that we, at the very least, should expect from IT. Change IT to be the sort of 'god' that we wanted, rather than what we had created, evolved, and blindly and naively ended up with.

Sam hastily scribbled a note on some paper from his pocket and showed it to the dragon.

'If you torch me now, the next one that comes along will also fail, and will not get as far as I did. So let's just pretend that I have created some sort of ultimate weapon and we can pretend to have a standoff. It's OK - they will never know.'

He smiled at the dragon, but oddly it just ignored him completely. Which was a little worrying.

The dragon turned again to look at the step for a moment, thinking. It had a strange expression - it almost seemed to quite like it; the concept, the idea of control, discipline. It was as if it were something that it had been missing and needed, almost with a hint of nostalgia.

It didn't seem angry or cross. It was just curious, interested, as if it was quite excited about this new turn in the game, a different sort of challenge, or something new to play with or work around.

As long as Sam didn't think too much about what he was actually doing — or the scale of it - if he just kept himself and his mind focused on what he thought had to be done, and on what was right, then he may just survive.

The dragon then regained its placid, neutral expression, and shuffled back around the throne again. It still looked at Sam, but having now processed all the nuances of the concept, there was no expression there, no feeling, no reaction.

Which was in stark contrast to the disarray and turmoil and noises and voices of protest that were coming from the men on the benches. Whatever it was that Sam was doing was having an effect everywhere.

It was a pivotal moment that seemed to last a lifetime. Then, for a second, there was a brief reflective expression of acceptance in the dragon's face. It coiled itself around the throne a little more protectively and reassuringly. It's great long tail then casually swept around the back of the dais, 'coincidentally' covering up the words, just in case anyone else 'could see'.

"So" said Sam abruptly, and he turned back to the people on the benches and walked back to the middle of the room, "Let me ask you a few more questions..." He was trying to establish calm and order in the room by taking control.

"What is your purpose? What is this organisation for? Why are you here? What is your plan and what are the benefits for everyone concerned within it? Where are the defined roles and responsibilities?

"Where is the blueprint for what you want to be, the risk assessment and management structure, phase management, benefits strategy, project approval process, the reporting system and evaluation and testing?

"Where is your expansion policy, change management?

"What is your holistic approach to the whole problem?

"You know, all that management stuff that should be there that isn't. Show me your methodology, and your blueprint for the future? Where is the change management programme for the benefit of all, and how you intend to get there ?"

There was silence.

"I am obviously not talking about the physical world 'caretaker governments' or the visible global organisations here - all of which just serve to placate, monitor and control the masses.

"I am asking you now, where are we going with all of this?"

There was still silence.

"Or are you still under your own illusion that someone is at the helm, someone else is running the ship, managing the head office, directing things from above, taking responsibility with a divine guiding light?

"Haven't you yet realised that that it is exactly what we need to become - fill the gap, move into the space, grow and evolve into the void, fill the universe with greater levels of consciousness ?

"You haven't got any of this in place have you? Basically I think that you have reached the crisis point where it has all got a bit much and a bit of a mess, and that you don't really know what you are about or what you are here for. You haven't got any competition, or customers, and you have finally decided that you need to get a manager in to sort out the problem just before it gets critical.

"Which I have to say all sounds very bloody familiar to me.

"Oddly enough too this always somehow seems to happen just as it's all too late. Let me also guess that you were also going to lay lots of responsibility on me but without actually giving me any authority or power either? That you aren't going to give me anything in the way of pay, and that you would put pressure on me at every moment possible? You will also blame me if things go wrong and I won't get any recognition if things go well, and nobody will ever know who I am or what I do, or did.

"So going back to what I said originally, the answer is still NO. No, I bloody well won't!"

They all looked at each other. It was very obvious from their expressions that his 'guesswork' had been quite correct.

"It's tempting, but I have to politely refuse the very kind offer that you haven't actually made yet - but I thought I would save you a bit of time, as that is something we are all running out of."

There was along awkward silence.

"What value is there for me anyway? What are the benefits to me other than perhaps status? As far as I can see, after a while I would just end up being replaced, given a gold watch, be put out to pasture, and becoming just one of you. There isn't anything you can offer me - I don't need money, and I already have all that I need.

"You see, that's the problem with recruiting a manager - they think differently, they step back and look at the bigger picture, and they start looking at what has happened before, especially the mistakes.

"Yet you didn't really bring me here, you just think you did. In actual fact I was placed here and set up to be in this situation, quite deliberately and purposely. I have deliberately been shown specific things that I needed to know - and in some cases probably too much.

"There was no guiding light for me, no spiritual path, it has all been pure manipulation throughout my whole life, and by something that is very, very clever.

"It is something that is desperate now and in need - it needed me to do something, it sent an S.O.S and knew that I was able to help. It was as simple as that, and for that I would do *anything*, for some reason, something inside of me is making me do this, but I don't know why.

"So in answer to your next question - I have already started, and several years ago now actually, and you are now starting to see those changes happening. This 'something that is going on' that you have all been picking up on, this 'something happening in the system' - this awareness of a change taking place - but none of you seem to know what it is, or who or what is causing it. Something different has started going on, there has been a change over the last ten years, something has happened and someone somewhere is doing something.

"So I wonder what, or who, is causing that, eh?"

Sam's face looked grim and determined.

There were a lot of looks exchanged in the audience.

He turned around and looked at Brina who was now standing just few paces behind him, and saw that there was a tear rolling down her face, a tiny sign of the mass of supressed emotion going on within her.

"Besides I suspect I have already signed some sort of contract somewhere without realising it - you know how smart these women are these days."

He noticed now that behind Brina, at the back of the room by the lifts, there were now a dozen or so other women standing there. They were waiting just in front of the lift doors and by the door to the stairwell.

Were they here out of curiosity, to see what was happening, and what he was doing? He thought for a moment and then he understood and his expression changed, and he smiled.

"It's OK" he said to himself or Brina, or at least that was the thought that came into his head "I will do it, and you don't have to pay me anything or promise me anything.

"I know what I have to do, and why I have to do it. I am very well aware of who is running things, and it's OK - I get it."

He then raised his voice to the men on the benches "But then you are all still 'in and part of the system', you are being unconsciously controlled, hypnotised and programmed by it. You are all still in 'better than life' - you *are* the system and you are all fooling yourselves. You all need to wake up and start to understand exactly what is going on. So I need to show you."

CHAPTER 34 - THE BOARDROOM BATTLE

It suddenly went deathly quiet and everyone stared at him. You could hear the cogs whirring away in their massive superveninent processing device-like quantum computer brains as they looked at each other and then at the dragon wrapped around the throne. It said nothing and it had no expression. They waited and then they started looking at one another again.

Why hadn't they seen all this before? Why had they been so blind?

"I am also amazed that you lot seriously think that you are in charge. Didn't you figure out that it's actually the women in the office running things? You know the ones that meet around the coffee machine on the 7th floor? They make the choices of who, why, what and when. They also just let you think that you do, and that you are in charge.

"For example, let me ask this simple question - which of you woke up this morning thinking that a shopping mall and a beauty parlour on the 1st floor was suddenly a good idea, with coffee shop and nail bar?" There was a pause, and then a dozen or so timid hands were raised. "Or of adding an organic chocolate expresso option to the coffee machines?" There were some hushed murmurings, and then a dozen other hands went up.

"OK - so these ideas may be commercially very successful, but they are not as important as say sprinklers in the machine room, more lifeboats, or a team on the roof watching out for icebergs."

There were many confused looking faces around the room and nobody seemed to have a clue what he was talking about. Lifeboats? Why on earth would they need lifeboats?

"Just remember", continued Sam "That there are two sides to every story. Think about it, it is the female side that is driving things - Mother Nature! It's why you guys do all the things that you do, it's what has got you to where you are now, and why you are here.

"You will all find that you have all had a female counterpart that led you to where you are and that keeps you moving, possibly for love.

"Yet neither side is awake.

"Do you have any idea of what is going on in the real physical world because of what you are doing here? Because of the ideas that you are having? You are unconsciously controlling the thoughts and behaviour of most of the people on the planet; people that are totally blind and unconscious as to what is going on in their own minds, yet being driven along by you, and your legacy structure.

"You are what the conspiracy theories are about - the Illuminati, a conscious controlling elite, aliens, when actually this is all just unconscious thoughts, drives, and ideas that exist within the self-supporting controlling system.

"That system is *you*, and you are totally unaware of what you are, what you are doing, and the physical reality you are being supported and devised within. The two sides of the mirror hidden from each other. You could say it is all one big conspiracy, just on a grand scale, it's an unconscious one with no logic or plan, driven by our collective mind.

"But I can see you, I can see it from the outside and inside, I can see everything, and you have a choice now to change it all, wake up, or carry on as you are. But bear in mind I have already been around all the departments and started to make people aware of what is going on, and who you are.

"That was something these people or programs couldn't see, understand, or realise. That the God they are talking about, and experiencing, even at their highest levels. That what they were seeing and interpreting 'in the cave', 'in the unbearable face of the divine' did not create the universe, it was just us, within something else.

"That which we had generally perceived as 'god' was our biological human collective operating system mind, supported and evolved biologically within the unified fields of the planet.

"It was an unconscious human hive mind in the way that it grew, evolved, adapted, operated and controlled us. This was also obvious in the nature and traits which it adopted from its originating biological structures, which were then mapped into overall cultures and civilisations.

"It was all just something we had evolved and developed collectively as part of our nature, and we supported it both mentally and physically in everything we did. IT had become very complex and vast, but was shaped by what was successful, what was selected, chosen by us unconsciously. It was a macro-mind, a macro-organism, and IT knew everything that we knew collectively, but was naive and immature in comparison.

"Yet IT was aware of itself too now, and IT just wanted to know what to do next."

He turned to Brina now, "Of course," he said quietly, "this is all down to you really. You are the one causing all this. This is your choice." She then looked at him closely, her eyes looking into his questioningly. She was trying to take in what he was saying, reading him and assessing the expression on his face.

Then after a few moments her expression changed. "I remember you" she said "I know who you are. It has all come back to me now - who you are and who I am, and what we are doing here."

She stepped forward, looked at him closely for a moment and then kissed him, holding his face in her hands.

There were a few embarrassed coughs around the room.

"Now," said Sam, "as we have got all that over with, I need to do what I came here for. I need to cause something to happen."

He stepped back away from her and took a few paces towards the dais, and turned to face the dragon who was still eyeing him and Brina curiously, and was listening to the conversation with interest.

He took a few more paces forward and stood on the white marble area which began several feet in front of the dais. He took off his shoes and socks and stood on the cold floor, letting it warm up with the heat that he was generating from his skin.

He closed his eyes and concentrated and let the energy flow through his body, drawing on the energy of the earth, using it, shaping it, adding thought and concept and idea and purpose. The top of his head ached and he could feel energy flowing up, and through him now. Up through the soles of his feet, up his spine and out through his head, he was now 'working', 'doing' something.

The heat in his head increased and the marble below his feet tingled and began to soften. His feet began to leave imprints in the marble as if it were warm icing sugar. He stepped back and looked at his footprints, it reminded him of the footprints he had seen in a remote Roman temple in Dougga, Tunisia when he had been on holiday there.

Sam looked back at the dragon who was still awake and looking at him. It implied that Sam was at least doing something interesting or entertaining and probably different, something new to keep its interest going. But it still made Sam feel like toy, a court jester, or a teething ring. He had to move the game up another notch.

Sam then mentally changed his outfit to that of a medieval knight in chainmail with a shield and a sword in a sheath strapped across his back. It was nothing too flamboyant, just the practical token elements, and devoid of any symbols or glowing colours.

The shield in his left hand was there more for show, and somewhere to put his cheat sheets behind, all those pages from books with all the long philosophical and scientific words and concepts on. Words and ideas he could use to give an impression that he had tenure, or knew what he was talking about. That somehow he was knew what he was doing, and what was going on.

But also, and most importantly, that he was able and willing to actually do something about it all, even though it was obviously a waste of time and foolhardy rather than just some mad fool idiot with a sword, with no idea what he was doing, or what he was about to cause to happen.

As was really the case.

The dragon just looked at him with a look of confused, disdainful curiosity.

Sam then drew his medieval style sword from the sheath behind his back - a weapon that the dragon had not previously seen from the front. It slid out from the sheath with a hissing sound like a snake. It was a magnificent gilded sword, glowing with energy and power. It had a blade about the length of his spine, with twin snakes etched and intertwined around the fuller, all along its length.

It had a leather bound hilt, a gold pommel, and golden rune engraved on the cross guard.

It was symbolic, but it was also a indicating it was time for the dragon to finally face its 'Waterloo'.

The response from the dragon was instant, subconscious, and alarmingly animalistic. This time there was no two week pause or delay while it consciously thought about an idea. It reacted to him immediately, perceiving and recognising the threat, and reacting on a low level that overrode everything else - instinctively transforming it into that which everyone in the room was individually most terrified of.

The dragon became inflamed, vast, and bristling with Kevlar scales, and raw fiery radiant energy. There was, within it, a sudden change in nature, personality and emotion. It was now like a dog with a raw bone, becoming feral, subconsciously animalistic, 'Balrog'-like, reacting to him with no conscious logic, and just with pure uncontrolled, subconscious, defensive animal instinct. Yet also with a sign of fear of him in its eyes.

It was becoming what it was, and had always been.

There were gasps of horror in the room. What the hell was this idiot doing? They had all moved on from this years ago. What stupid naive game was he playing?

Then everyone in the room started hiding away, ducking behind the rows of seats, or instinctively raising their arms in front of their faces to shield them from whatever horror they now perceived was shaping up on the dais. All their worst nightmares, all their uttermost evils, highest devils, demons - or whatever fearful interpretation their minds could translate this situation into.

Then Sam whispered under his breath, "Shields on my command" and then he quietly said a few more words that were inaudible. He wasn't sure why he had said it, it was just something that came into his head at that moment, it was curious, and sounded more like something someone would say in a sci-fi film or TV series.

A couple of the men in the front rows then stood up and concentrated on Sam. Things happened in the room very quickly after that, almost occurring like a surreal blur, but a planned sort of blur none the less.

Layers of shielding appeared around Sam like translucent bubbles in the shape of his body, as if he were now inside three or four transparent Russian dolls.

There was no other reaction from the dragon, it just saw the sword and did what all dragons would do in that situation; it didn't even seem to be thinking anymore, it was now more like a machine, or robotic program on autopilot.

He was confronting the full face of the divine now, the total exposure to the brutal REAL of IT.

A state that he had been in before, and he knew that he had, at most, only thirty seconds left to exist.

As the dragon breathed in, there was a strong smell of tungsten carbide in the air, it backed up slightly and then it released a sustained fire blast from its now open jaws straight at Sam.

It came at Sam like a hail of *Matrix*-like flaming silver bullets fired from machine guns like some coded message in high frequency bits. Sam braced himself behind the shield on his arm, his two outer firewall layers of protective bubble evaporated in just a few moments, along with a several figures on the benches who were running to escape the blast, but were in the wrong place at the wrong time.

The energy drained from Sam as he stood there, the heat building up around him and in his armour. It was like standing in the open door of a blast furnace, lighting a fire burning within his soul.

The intensity, even with the protection that he had, was overwhelming. His armour started to scald him, and his livery robes smoked, and the shield on his arm became almost too hot to hold. But he kept his sword pointing down away from the blast, keeping it safe.

Finally the last layer of shielding collapsed under the onslaught, the pressing wall of flaming, swarming, micro-sentinel machines pushed into him, and the heat engulfed him flowing over and around his shield to get at him.

Then it stopped. The dragon closed its mouth, and it began inhaling, coiling back, building up for another breath, another blast that this time would finish this idiot off. The dragon still had to follow the laws of physics - supply and demand - even here, so it couldn't just continue to breathe out.

Sam was going to be carbonised toast in a few more moments, all before the battle had even started, even before he had even got within ten feet of the thing.

He could have stepped sideways, avoided the attack, dodged at the last minute, but he was trying to convey a message, and doing the metaphysical equivalent of moving house to avoid the problem wasn't what he was trying to conceptualise. But neither did he want to appear to be a coward. Besides he was doing this for a reason.

Brina, or Trinity, depending on where in the room you were looking from, was breathing hard behind him now. He could hear her gasping. Sam could also hear her heeled footsteps coming up towards him, trying to get to him, trying to protect him somehow. Trying to do anything to save him from what he was doing. He could hear from her breath that she was terrified, intimidated, and out on her own in this male dominated environment. She was also scared of the powerful terrifying presence that was on the dais, and the fury emanating from it now that she was in the direct presence of it.

Yet despite it all she walked past him, and then put herself between him and the dragon to protect him. She did it anyway, knowing it would kill her in seconds. She was adding herself as another shield for him, protecting him, guarding him, doing whatever she could at that moment.

Putting herself in harm's way. Defending that which mattered most.

It made no difference to the dragon though - this was what it did, and if she was in the way, getting between it and the sword carrying opponent, then she would become just another casualty of the game. Become just another statistic of nature.

She was a small girl trying to save her pet rabbit from the jaws of the family dog, just by using her desperate bare hands.

Then curiously, and as one, there were many more heeled footsteps that came rapidly from the back of the room from the area where the lift doors and stairs were. Sam turned his head slightly to look behind him, and there in a line, were a few dozen women, all immaculately dressed in a spectrum of colours, all of them wearing high-heeled shoes, and all with determined looks on their faces.

He recognised several of them from the rooms he had been in and from the women that had gathered around the coffee machine, including the woman in red and the Asian woman. They all looked a lot more tired than when he had seen them last, as if they had been very busy with something for the last hour or so.

They had all come up to see what was going on, what was about to happen, and more importantly what this idiot that was causing trouble was up to.

Then they all saw, and now they understood.

Then they were no longer competing with Brina, they no longer saw her as a potential threat. Nor were they a potential threat to her, despite her inner fears of them 'stealing him from her'.

They were here for her now, ganging up with her, to help her, be there for her at this time. Which these days was a very rare sight, and certainly not easy in heels.

The dragon had stopped, motionless, fascinated by the new turn of events and was now focused on the girls and not him.

The women paused a few feet behind Brina. Then, from hidden speakers somewhere in the roof and to the corners of the room, the low beat of music started to play.

It was quiet at first, with a deep bass sound, and it then began building up with synthesiser and guitar, and you could just about hear words in the background with curiously recognisable rhythms and harmony.

It was a woman's voice singing, he recognised the tune and the voice but he couldn't remember the name of the song. It carried on *"... and it makes me so depressed to see the gloom, There's not a soul out there, No one to hear my prayer..."* came the words from the ABBA song blasting out, with the last word being held for several seconds.

Then *"Gimme, gimme, gimme a man after midnight..."* blasted out loudly, with a heavy rhythm like a heartbeat.

Then as one, all the women strode forward together in a line, up towards the dais and the dragon. *"Won't somebody help me chase the shadows away..."* came the words from the speakers.

They had obviously been practising this move, probably in a locked room somewhere at lunchtime, or after work instead of the normal yoga classes, all just for this one moment.

It was a move in which the choreography would either have

worked or they would all look very stupid and nobody would be taken in by it.

As they walked past him, and his eyes followed them and turned to the front, he noticed that even the dragon was jigging slightly to the beat of the music.

Somehow though it worked. They carried it off. It may have been the timing, the way they moved, the looks, the rhythm the expressions, the build-up, all combined with a sense of genuine feeling of emotion. But it worked.

This was not an act, it was real, with real feeling, and it just took control of the room. Power, energy, focus, initiative and an in-the-now sense that grasped the moment. It carried it off, it took control and took charge of the gameplay.

It certainly confused the hell out of the dragon, which held its breath looking left and right, while it tried to work out what the heck was going on. Holding its inhaled breath, it gave the oddest expression, as if it were suddenly being confronted by a giant metaphysically wielded frying pan.

It's magic, thought Sam,

It was surreal how it all had seemed to come together at that moment, as if they had all somehow worked together to make it happen, a joint complaint procedure, a submitted petition, but without any logical planning or forethought, it just seemed to be utterly spontaneous – and all very female.

There were some very strange looks coming from the male programs in the ranks of seating, who up until that point were delusionally convinced that somehow they were in control of things, and that they had the last say. That naively the system, and choice and decisions revolved around them.

When in reality they themselves we just puppets to this system.

Several of them were now actually hiding behind each other trying not to be seen. Clearly there was something now more powerful than a crowd of male idiots, and that it wasn't a *"Rich Man's World"* after all.

The girls marched forward in unison in time to the beats of the music, walking with perfectly synchronised strides. With toned legs, pressed designer outfits and immaculate makeup and hair they moved further past Sam confidently as they strode forward, then stood between him and the dragon, and stopped in a line alongside Brina.

They all now all had a consistently magnificent look of defiance on their faces, and stood now with arms folded with their hands on their hips in front of it, in defiant poses as one 'team'.

There were several hushed shocked swear words and expletives that came from the remaining rows of men, mostly starting with the 'F' word. They could also now see what he was doing, but none of the men on the seats looked like they were brave enough to confront Sam or say anything to him, or do anything to stop him, or do anything to draw attention to themselves. They were just spectators in the show, and were staying low, especially with the unspeakably terrifying thing that was on the dais.

But these women were not going to let Brina stand alone - even though this was *her* man. When it all came down to it, and to this point of criticality – she, and they, were on the same side, and even though they would deny it, they were connected to him too, in some way, or at least to lost parts of him.

This was new - you could even see it in the dragon's expression, one which was of genuine surprise.

Still holding its breath, the dragon looked at the row of confrontational women. It didn't seem angry or aggressive now, nor did it look as if it were about to do something drastic.

It could no longer see Sam, and so no longer needed to respond or act or play the game. It just looked confused. Confused that there now seemed to be a new set of rules in the game, or a change of dimension to the myth construct, a new element or dimension to the story.

It also seemed to be more interested in the music that was playing, and appeared to be trying to work out what the words it was hearing meant. It wasn't sure now what it was supposed to be doing, other than a sort of 'leave it alone', or a 'drop it and leave it' suggestion that was in its mind.

A curious series of expressions went across its face, as if it were trying to formulate things in its mind, process things, imagine things, but eventually it released its breath slowly. Then after a minute or two it just settled back around its throne again, its eyes closed and it went back to sleep.

Then after several more seconds it shrunk and transformed into the small shape of a little girl, still asleep and huddled around the base of the throne. It now looked small and insignificant, and powerless, vulnerable. Then one of the women from the line walked up and put a blanket over the girl as she slept, and then tucked the blanket in around her.

Things started to become vague now for him.

Sam was now lying on the floor - his energy gone.

But Brina was there at his side in an instant, and she took hold of his sword that was still in his hand and tried to ease it out of his grasp. "No, I can't let go..." he mumbled feebly, and yet he wasn't that strong enough to resist her, and with a couple of gentle tugs she pulled it from his grasp. She then let the blade just clatter to the floor, which made an odd rattling scraping plastic sound.

"Why did you do that?" she pleaded with him, as the other women now stood around them in a circle.

"I needed to know who these women were, and bring them here" he said drowsily "so that I could see them, connect to them, bring them to the fore and make them visible, tell them what I needed them to do. It was just something I had to do, and if I had to do the same again, I would."

The women next to Brina were now crowding around them, and listening intently. Everything else in the room seemed to fade away.

"You see there is no female or left side to me, and they are the missing pieces of the program that I am too, and I and they need to find the other male elements. Component program parts, of which I think there are only five active ones left at this time. We need to bring all the elements together, integrate the components to give conscious direction and purpose to IT."

He turned to look at the women.

"The ones you are looking for are hooded, well-guarded, unaware of who they are, and are hidden away by the system. They will not be obvious, 'Anybody could be those guys'. I know there are five of us left, but we need more, there are not enough at the moment to do what needs to be done, and you need to find us and bring us together, and I cannot or am unable to do that.

"You will find their profiles, their identities, who they are, discoursed from within books, films, art, but you will already know within yourselves where to look for them, and who you are seeking.

"Some are probably arriving here in Reception shortly. They will be looking confused, seeing what is now being displayed on the screens in the foyer. They will be progressively working out what is going on, and waking up to it all, again.

"They will appear shortly after the programs from here gradually disappear. But now they will also have the ability to consciously see themselves in this place, in this office analogy too, and will be remembering.

"You will have to find them in the physical world, and get the devices - the bodies you are in - to do that. You will also find that the 'computer' in the basement is now working flat out too, it is all part of the process of change, a shift.

"You see, I know that I do not have enough bandwidth in my mind or physical body to do, or cope, with what needs to be done, or to achieve that which needs to be changed, on my own, not even from here. I have tried but there is just too much to do for what I am capable of, or able to collectively influence and direct for the time that we have left.

"I am what I am, and do what I can do, but it is not enough.

"So we all have to do this, together - as one."

There was a pause.

"It needs to be a joint conscious effort with co-ordination and direction by many people.

"So in my dreams I have a plan. That plan is also in your minds too now. I had already transferred the program to you when we shook hands, and that is why you are all here."

There were several intakes of breath around them as it dawned on many of them what had just taken place. There were also several exchanged looks between the women, and some outraged expressions, and then suddenly, as one, they all worked out what was going on.

He was putting them in charge - and not just here.

There was another pause.

Then curiously they, again as one, all asked him the same question that Brina had asked in the lift earlier - all as one and in the same nervous tone - "Are you angry with us?"

Sam was taken aback by the strange question in this situation, but he just smiled and shook his head and said clearly "No, I am not angry with you."

Then they all smiled, then looked relieved, and turned and headed rapidly for the lifts, to get to Reception as fast as they could.

All but one. There was one girl who paused, and she stood there looking confused. She had hair like Brina's, and was wearing a similarly coloured dress. "I don't know how or where to find ..." she stuttered "and I don't know how to bring him here, and how do I persuade him?"

Brina looked at her as if she had just asked the most naive question in female history.

"Shoes off now!" ordered Brina "Take the stairs down in bare feet. If you run you will get ahead of the others. Yours is already climbing up, and you will know him when you see him."

She needed no more clues - she slipped off her heels in an instant, and was away running for the stairs.

"Oh," called Sam after her "and go easy with the frying pan!", but he wasn't sure he heard him.

"So" said Brina turning back to Sam and looking suspiciously at him with narrowed eyes "you did all this, this whole thing from the moment you came here, just to see what was going on, and connect to these other women, and to put some ideas and instructions in their heads. You planned all this from the start?"

"Yes," he said simply "it was the best I could do.

"When I shook their hands, I passed a preconceived program to each of them and then transferred it through them all, along with what to do and a co-ordinated agenda with conscious objectives as opposed to the repeating unconscious set of competing chaotic ones."

She looked very annoyed. "I'm not sure I know how I feel about that" she said abruptly, and pulled back from him slightly- which again was a curious thing to say, and yet so like Brina. Her manner and expression was as though he had just confessed to having an affair. It was a reaction that she was having and an expression she was taking on, and yet she was confused herself as to why she was doing so, as if logically it didn't make any rational sense, either to react that way when it was clearly not the case. Especially as she had been with him the whole time since he had arrived.

Then her expression rapidly changed, and she looked happy.

"Weren't the girls amazing?" she asked excitedly "Standing up for you like that, doing that for us?" Sam looked into her eyes for a moment. This was really Brina now, he knew that because Brina would always naively look for something good in everything she saw.

He always knew though that there were other unconscious agendas going on, competing priorities, perspectives on many levels. Many of which these women were unaware of, and had no control over, it was not going to be easy.

"I understand now" she said, "it is all like a game, a game with nature, myths, and one that we play with each other. That we are all playing both in the physical world, and here in the spiritual, and on many levels. Once you are consciously aware of that you can take control both individually and collectively. Once you know that, you can set the direction and cause change, even by losing deliberately. So in that respect, we can have the future, even if we fail." Then there was a pause.

"But you aren't going to tell me I am just another program are you?" she asked looking concerned again, "Just another piece of code in a biological field based interactive information system?"

It was an odd question to ask, and confusing, and out of character and context for Brina.

He smiled at her, but his mind could not think any more - it had worn itself out, and it was now closing itself down. "No" he said "You are an Earth Angel - driven by something outside of this office. Outside our human collective mind, just like elements within the other girls that were here just now.

You are all more powerful than me, you all just need a bit of organising that's all."

She beamed back at him, but he had the funny feeling that she already knew that, and was just waiting for him to get there, and say it. To give her the right answer from what she knew in herself. She smiled again "Now it's history" she said "I've played all my cards, and that's what you've done too."

Then gradually his periphery awareness of everything else in the room, all the people and the situation seemed to melt away, become vague, dark, and transparent now, with the fading sound of several heeled footsteps still heading rapidly for the lifts, and down the stairs.

Then it was just darkness all around them, just him and his Brina, alone in silence on the cold dark marble.

Someone then changed the music to *"I have a dream... I believe in angels"* and the meaningful lyrics started to echo in his ears, along with the music which seem to come from all around him from the *Abba* song.

He was now lying on his back on the hard floor, and she knelt down beside him and stroked his head and the side of his cheek trying to keep him awake. Then she held him in her arms trying to keep his attention, and then tilted his head upwards to look at her again. But he was fading.

She seemed to have changed her outfit now. Now she was wearing thigh-length black leather boots, and was in just her underwear. Her blonde hair was glowing, and was curled, fuller looking and flowing in the slight breeze. She climbed over him and straddled his thighs, tightly gripping his knees together hard between her leather clad ankles. She arched her back, and leaned forward.

The armour he was wearing, and the show he had just put on, was obviously having quite a subliminal effect on her. She was taking control of him now, and taking matters into her own hands, trying to keep him 'there'.

He would have liked to think that he was somehow influencing the program, modifying the mythological story in regard to what she was doing, but he knew he would be just kidding himself.

She leaned forward, kissed him again, then harder now, and stroked his face. She then pressed her lips hard against his mouth, and gently bit his lip. Then she started kissing his face all over, which was very erotic. He moaned.

She worked her way down his neck and started pushing the chainmail away over his collarbone to expose the top of his chest, which she started to kiss and nuzzle.

This was a definitely a first, he would always wake up well

before it all got to this point, and long before things started to get interesting.

Then she worked her way back up his neck and kissed his ear and nibbled his earlobe. He definitely wasn't about to let himself wake up from this.

She then started licking his eyes repeatedly, which although erotic was frankly a bit odd. Then curiously he noticed that her perfume smelt quite different to its normal subtle scent, and her breath had a curious biscuit-like aroma to it.

Then she started nuzzling his neck again with her cold wet nose, and nudging his chin backwards repeatedly. He moaned, caught up in the moment... and then alarmingly the penny dropped.

Abruptly he woke up with a start, harsh sunshine beamed into his aching eyes, along with the blurred image of his dog's face just inches from his own. He was lying on his side on the hard wooden bench on the hill again, totally disorientated. The left side of his body hurt and his neck ached. He felt numb, and he had an awful headache, and the music by ABBA was still playing loudly in his ears through the headphones.

He struggled to orient his senses and get through to reality, his perception slowly grasping at what was going on around him. The lyrics playing in his head were also telling him to do the same thing.

As he lay there struggling to gain a hold on consciousness, the dog continued busily to lick and nuzzle his face and neck, which was all now wet and covered in drool.

Sam gave deep grunt, grimaced, sighed, and pushed the dog away weakly with his hand, and slowly sat up, "Ohh Christ...Bloody hell no..." he mumbled "Thanks a lot mate!" he said sarcastically.

Then after a pause he added, "Ohhh god - you complete git!"

Then after a few moments he said with a smile "You could have at least given me a few more minutes, I was just getting to the interesting part."

Then he sat and untangled the extending dog lead cords and leather strap that was now tightly wrapped around his knees, and removed the iPod earphones from his ears. They were still playing *Abba's Greatest Hits* that Brina had loaded on there from her CD collection when she had borrowed it.

"*Lay all your love on me*" was still blasting out from the earphones, and the dog had obviously just obediently and enthusiastically followed his master's instructions.

The dog was also quite agitated, anxious as if something had been going on while Sam was asleep, and seemed to be trying to tell him something, or get him to respond somehow. Respond with what also seemed like a few minutes of full-on mouth to mouth resuscitation.

Then after several minutes of getting his bearings and sense, and perception of physical reality again, he stood up, brushed himself off, picked up the plastic handle of the flexi-extending lead that the dog was still dragging around the ground making a rattling sound, and started the long walk home over the hillside.

It would probably take him a week or two to get over this particular experience, and only after several hot showers, baths, and bottles of mouth wash.

Then it would all be on to the next thing. The next instalment of the ongoing mythical saga, one that for him and Brina was no dream, and was in fact, very real.

It just seemed to be that for some strange reason, he never seemed to get much of a break these days.

———————

With thanks to Jan
without whom this book would not have been possible,

and to the other Angels .... you know who you are.